Asking for Trouble

Books by Rosalind James

The Kincaids **series**

Welcome to Paradise: Mira and Gabe's story

Nothing Personal: Desiree and Alec's story

Asking for Trouble: Alyssa and Joe's story

The *Escape to New Zealand* **series**

Just for You: Reka and Hemi's story (Novella)

Just This Once: Hannah and Drew's story

Just Good Friends: Kate and Koti's story

Just for Now: Jenna and Finn's story

Just for Fun: Emma and Nic's story

Just My Luck: Ally and Nate's/Kristen and Liam's stories

Just Not Mine: Josie and Hugh's story

The Kincaids: Book Three

Asking for Trouble

Rosalind James

Killer Tuesday

Alyssa Kincaid's Tuesday started out badly. And then it got worse.

She'd begun to hate Tuesdays anyway, the last year or so. When the past weekend was a memory, the next one four long days away. When her Sunday-evening pep talk, about how this week was going to be different, had proven fruitless yet again in the face of another meeting with her sales manager.

"I'm seeing the calls," Tim was saying now. "But I'm not seeing the orders for Mylexa."

"I'll meet my quota," Alyssa insisted, trying not to get rattled at the sight of the graph behind his desk showing all his reps' numbers. Hers weren't bad, she reminded herself. Not the best, but still right there in the middle. A solid performer. So she didn't have the killer instinct. So what?

"Your quota includes Mylexa. You're supposed to be pushing it." Tim bent his head over the contact report, giving her a great view of his new hair plugs. One hateful, pudgy, micromanaging forefinger stopped at an offending line. "Olsen's office. Where's his order?"

"His order's right there."

"For Mylexa. Where's that?"

The recklessness came over her like a rising tide. "Not there. Because I told him to stick with Zylase."

"*What?*"

"It's a better drug. You know it is, I know it is. And Dr. Olsen knows it too."

"And manufactured by the competition," Tim said, his heavy face mottling red. For a pharmaceutical company

1

employee, he didn't exactly walk the walk. "Did somebody neglect to tell you that you're supposed to be pushing *our* drugs?"

"My way's working pretty well so far, isn't it? I have credibility. Ask any of my doctors. They know I'll tell them the truth, and if I say it's good, it's because it's *good.*"

"I don't care about *credibility,*" Tim snapped. "I care about numbers. Yours are down this month."

"Most people's are down. It's December."

"Electra's aren't." His lips were drawn thin with displeasure, his face seeming to swell above the tight collar that squeezed his fat neck.

Because Electra makes every doctor she calls on think he's about to get lucky, Alyssa didn't say. *And half of them probably do.*

She'd been so excited when she'd been hired by Moreau Industries, into what was by far her best-paying, most prestigious job ever. But it hadn't taken her long to realize that most pharma reps were young, female, and good-looking. Just like her. And now she knew exactly why that was.

"I'm not going to prostitute myself for sales," she said. "I'm not going to mislead anybody, I mean," she added hastily. Too much honesty was not necessarily good policy, even for her.

She didn't fool Tim, though. "This job isn't about saving humanity. It's about getting sales any way you can. I don't care if you have to give the guy a blow job in his office. Do what you have to do, just get the sale. That's what it's about. That's what you're paid for."

And that was it. That was what turned another bad Tuesday into the last Tuesday.

She shoved her visitor's chair back and stood abruptly, reaching for her wheeled sample case. She could feel her cheeks flaming, the wave of anger heart-high now and rising fast, about to push her past the point of no return. "Find somebody else for that," she got out. "I quit."

Tim looked startled. He didn't want her to leave, she realized with a mixture of astonishment and satisfaction.

2

These were just his normal bully tactics, what he thought of as motivation. Well, they sure didn't motivate her. Except to motivate her right out the door.

"You'd better rethink that right now," he said. "You're not going to get another job that pays like this. You don't get an attitude adjustment, you're not going to make it anywhere, doing anything. You're sure as hell not going to make it in sales."

"I'll take that chance." She turned, started to wheel her case out, then stopped in realization, hitched her shoulder bag up and left the case where it was, laptop, samples, and all. "Have a nice life."

Her indignation carried her through the long drive in the usual creep of traffic on the 10 to Santa Monica, but then the doubts started closing in. They were raging in full force by the time she pulled into the smoothly paved parking lot of the white-stuccoed garden apartments set in the midst of towering palms and landscaped grounds, grabbed her purse, and stepped out into another gorgeous Southern California day. She walked up the curving white sidewalk and through the glossy green front door of an apartment she wasn't going to be able to afford much longer. Not unless she got a new job right away, one that paid as well as the one she'd just walked out of. Which, right now, didn't look too likely.

She picked up the phone to call Dennis, because she needed to tell somebody, needed somebody to tell her that she hadn't been an idiot, and that was your boyfriend's job, right?

Which was when her Tuesday went from bad to worse.

"So you just quit?" he asked her incredulously. "What the hell, Alyssa! You don't quit a job until you have another job, didn't anybody ever tell you that? That was just unprofessional. You never, *ever* do that, walk off like that."

"What else could I do, though, after he said that?"

"I don't know, let it roll off you, like every other rep does with their sales manager? And started scouting other jobs?"

Dennis repped for a software company, had been in the industry for years, moving smoothly from one position to another when he got restless or something wasn't working out, always seeming to land in a better spot. He'd been more than a boyfriend, he'd been a mentor, too. She'd met him on a Sierra Club outing, and over the past few months, the relationship had changed from casual to something more.

He was still talking. "What were you thinking? Why didn't you stop and consider before you burned your bridges?"

"I was supposed to overlook what he said? Are you serious?"

"I've heard worse. Sales managers are all assholes. It's part of the job description. Quitting was bad enough, but it's December. Who hires in December? You aren't even going to be able to start looking for a month."

She was getting mad now. He wasn't even going to be outraged for her? "I don't want to do the job any more anyway," she said, and recognized the truth of it. "I can't sell things I don't believe in. It feels like ... pimping."

"No." She heard the frustrated exhalation of breath, the *Alyssa screwing up again* sound that she'd heard so many times in her life, and felt her temper ratcheting up higher. "It feels like sales."

"Helping the customer make the best decision is sales," she insisted. She was walking up and down the black-and-white tiled floor of her little kitchen now, pacing in her agitation. "This is pimping."

She had to calm down, she told herself. She got too hasty when she lost her temper, the events of today being a sterling example. "Anyway, I can't do the Utah trip, that's for sure. I'll have to eat the plane ticket, but you should be able to get the hotel room refunded, right, almost three weeks out?"

They'd planned a ski vacation for before Christmas, a trip that had loomed large and promising on her horizon. Their first real vacation together, doing one of her favorite things.

4

"Oh, come on," he said. "Don't bail on me now. It's not that pricey, just your half of the room and some meals, lift tickets for a few days. And all right, maybe I overstated. You'll have a job within a few weeks, I'm sure."

She waited for him to suggest that he could help out. He could afford it, and then some. But he didn't.

"I need to save my money," she said when no offer was forthcoming. "I'm sorry to spoil your vacation too, but maybe we can do something local instead." He was bound to be disappointed, she reminded herself. And he wasn't obligated, after all.

He hesitated so long that she thought she'd lost the connection. "Dennis?"

"Well, I'm sorry too. I'll miss you, of course, but I think I'll still go," he said. "I've been looking forward to it, and the snow's great this year. Who knows when I'll get the chance again?"

She actually held the phone away from her ear and stared at it for a minute. "You're going to go without me," she was finally able to say.

"I said I was sorry. But I'm not the one who quit my job in a huff because my boss was mean to me. It isn't really fair of you to expect me to cancel my plans because of your—somewhat naïve, I have to say, idealism."

"I thought we were building a relationship here," she said. "I guess I was wrong. I guess we're not."

"What, I'm supposed to say, 'Alyssa, right or wrong? I'll take care of my woman?' I respect you too much for that. We're two independent people."

"I see. Not a couple. Well, all right, fine." The temper was right back again. "That pretty much tells me everything I need to know."

"What, you're going to break up with me because I won't cancel my hard-earned vacation for you, because you had a snit fit? That's just childish."

"No. I'm going to break up with you because you're selfish. Because you don't care that my boss insulted me so

5

badly I had to walk out. Because you don't support me. And that's not my idea of how a relationship works."

"You're just setting yourself up to be disappointed, then," he said, and she could hear the anger in his voice now too. "Over and over. The world doesn't revolve around you and what you want and how you think things ought to be."

"No. But my world has rules. And when you break the rules, you're gone." And with that, she hung up.

Minus one boyfriend. Minus one job.

Rolling on the Ball

"Any luck on the job search yet, Liss?" Alec Kincaid asked his little sister.

It was late in the evening, two days before Christmas, and Joe Hartman was sprawled in an easy chair in the living room of the Chico home belonging to Alec Kincaid's parents, listening to two of the three Kincaid siblings catching up. Alec and his wife Rae were on the couch across from him, Alec with his stockinged feet on the coffee table, Rae with hers tucked beneath her.

Alyssa, of course, wasn't doing anything nearly so decorous. No, she was sitting on a big, bright green exercise ball, rocking in circles, her hands behind her head, which made the front view a whole lot too interesting. And twisting her pelvis in ways that Joe was having a hard time not watching, although he was doing his best not to. As usual.

"No," she sighed mid-rock. "Because I think my heart isn't in it. I got the unemployment, though," she added. "Thanks for coaching me on that, Rae."

"What unemployment?" Joe asked. "What job search?" This was the first he'd heard of it.

Alyssa swiveled her hips again, a grimace on her pretty face, her shiny dark hair swinging around her shoulders. "I quit my job a few weeks ago. A little unexpectedly."

"Because her boss made some comments that were beyond the pale," Rae explained. "Alec didn't tell you about this? What do guys *talk* about?"

"Hey," Alec objected. "We talk about work. Which is important. And sports, and … cars. Lots of things. Joe's not exactly the best conversationalist either. Not my fault."

Rae ignored that, turned back to Alyssa again. "But the unemployment came through?"

"Yeah," Alyssa said. "Because I was able to show a pattern, like you said. Like how he started off telling me to wear my skirts short. That I should show some cleavage, lean forward when I talked to my doctors. All that. And then that thing he said at the end."

"What thing?" Joe asked, already feeling his blood pressure rising.

Alyssa didn't look at him. Instead, she swung around so her stomach was on the ball and rolled forward, walking on her hands all the way until her slim brown toes were the last thing balancing, then walking back again. In her tight jeans, which stretched over her curvy body. Which Joe really didn't need to be looking at right now, with her brother looking at *him.*

"He said," she said through the curtain of hair swinging over her face as she made it back onto her stomach again and prepared to take off once more, "that I should give the guys a blow job if I had to, to get the sale. Which turned out to be for the best, because it was bad enough to get me unemployment."

"Though it would have been a whole lot better," Alec said, while Joe was fighting the urge to hunt the bastard down and strangle him, "if you'd taken that up the chain at the time instead of quitting on the spot like that. Who knows, you might have even got him fired, got a better manager. It's a good thing the company decided just to take the unemployment hit and make it go away, because you really didn't have a case."

"You think I don't know that?" Alyssa sat up again, her face red, whether from embarrassment or her exertions, Joe couldn't tell. "I know that. I got mad. What would you have done if he'd said that to you? Or if he'd said it to Rae?"

"Yeah, well," Alec admitted. "Punched his teeth in, probably."

"Don't think that didn't occur to me too. And I didn't. I think I was quite restrained, all in all."

"But seriously. You need to learn to handle things that come up," Alec pressed. "That's a big company. All right, walk out of the meeting, fine. But then you should have written it up, given Moreau the chance to make it right. You'd have had documentation too, then, even if they hadn't come through. Maybe a settlement as well as the unemployment, who knows?"

Joe could see Alyssa getting mad, and Rae could obviously see it too, because she jumped in. "Well, live and learn. Glad the unemployment worked out. Any leads? I can probably connect you with some tech outfits, if you want to stay in sales."

Alyssa shrugged and started the stomach thing again. "I don't want to sell software, or drugs either," she said from her face-down position. "I want to do something that matters, that's going to make a real difference in people's lives."

"Hey," Alec objected. "We're making a difference. That's the whole point, that the software we create makes people's lives easier. If it didn't, we wouldn't have anything to sell."

"You know what I mean," she said as she made it back to her ball again. "A real difference."

"Maybe you should have majored in social work, then, instead of business."

"Wait, now," Rae said. "That's not fair. Every kind of organization needs people who can think in a businesslike way, and who can persuade. Alyssa doesn't have to be a social worker to contribute."

"I hope not," Alyssa said, "because I don't have the patience. But, yeah. Something that matters. I thought this was it, but it's clearly not. But I don't know what would be."

"Something that matters isn't going to pay much," Alec pointed out.

"So?" She balanced with her knees on the ball, her palms on the floor, looked up at him with a frown.

Joe was listening, honestly he was, but he was also noticing that her position, and the scoop-necked, stretchy top, gave him a view of some major cleavage.

"So you don't exactly have a track record," Alec answered with the bluntness that could only come from a big brother. "You like to play too much. And you never stay and work it out when things don't go your way. Never. You just quit."

She rolled off, got to her feet in one neat motion, picked up her ball and cradled it in her arms. "Well, yeah. I quit. I admit it. You heard why. And that was *this* time. I was doing well, before. Pretty well, for almost two years. Two *long* years. And maybe I'm changing. I'm thirty, or did you forget? And I want to do something. I want to get somewhere. That's what I'm telling you."

"And now you're going to stomp off," Alec sighed. "This is exactly what I mean."

She didn't answer. She just stalked out of the room, and then spoiled her big exit completely when she hit the doorway hard, jolted to a stop against her big green ball and bounced off it. She gave it another huge shove that did the trick, popping through the door after it like a cork shot out of a champagne bottle.

The three of them sat silent for a moment, listening to her feet on the stairs, the soft thud of her bedroom door shutting.

"Alec ..." Rae said. "She's trying. That wasn't too helpful."

"She needs to grow up," he said in frustration.

"It sounds to me," Rae said, "like that's exactly what she's trying to do."

"Now I've got both of you mad at me," Alec said. "Double trouble. Come on." He stood and held out a hand to help her up. "Time to head back to your grandma's. You can yell at me in the car all the way home."

"I should get a room." Joe tried once more. "You should stay here. This isn't right."

"Nah," Alec said. "Rae would be the one in trouble then. And me too, for stealing her away from her grandma. Can't have that. Besides, I have a special fondness for that mobile home. It has a definite spot in my heart. Enjoy that twin bed, though."

Joe could see the elbow heading right into Alec's ribs as Rae laughed reluctantly. She said her goodnights and the two of them headed out the front door, leaving Joe in sole possession of the Kincaid living room. Even though he was not even close to being a Kincaid.

Family Ties

His fifteenth Kincaid Christmas. Fifteen. It was a big number. A significant number.

That first time, he'd been more than reluctant. Because he'd known what to expect, and it was the one thing he couldn't handle. Rejection he could take. He knew all about rejection. But he couldn't stand to be pitied.

"No, thanks. I've got lots to do, already made my plans, and it's your family, not mine," he'd said without looking up from his Multivariable Calculus textbook or lifting his mechanical pencil from the notebook where he was working through a final problem at the desk on his side of their Stanford dorm room. His other books lined up on the shelf above, his bed neatly made, the aged blue cotton sleeping bag with its plaid lining stretched over the white sheet and flat pillow, because he felt more comfortable when things were neat. And Alec's side looking like a hurricane had struck.

"My mom about killed me when she found out you'd stayed here alone at Thanksgiving," Alec argued, lying on his bed and tossing a bright yellow hacky sack lazily into the air, grabbing it with a sure brown hand before flicking it up again. "Come home with me, or my life isn't going to be worth living. You don't know my mother. She'd probably haul ass down here herself and pull you up to Chico by your ear. And anyway, it's just too damn depressing to contemplate. Microwaved frozen turkey dinner in the dorm room. Merry Christmas to you."

"It's just a day," Joe said. "Doesn't mean anything to me."

Alec paused with the squishy ball in his hand, gave his roommate a quick, searching glance. "Do me a favor," he said at last. "Come with me. I want you to meet them."

And he got his way, because Alec always got his way. What would it be like, Joe wondered as he gave in, as he'd wondered so many times since the day they'd met, to be born under that lucky star? To be that good-looking, that magnetic? To have everything come so easy, always? To have it all?

Joe had assumed at first, seeing the look of him, that Alec was rich, like so many of their classmates. He *looked* rich. And Joe knew that he himself had looked anything but, the first time he'd knocked at the door of the room.

He'd arrived late, had had to make his way through sidewalks crowded with little knots of parents saying tearful farewells to their beloved progeny before getting back into their shiny late-model sedans and SUVs and driving off to their leafy suburbs, or maybe their townhouses. Wherever people like that lived.

Whereas he … Fourteen hours on Greyhound, riding the dog through the dark, silent hours, watching the merciless summer sunrise glow into morning, brighten towards afternoon while he was carried ever farther north and west across a flat brown landscape, across passes that had turned to suburban green, then to urban sprawl, until the pneumatic doors hissed open and the big silver bus spat him out in San Jose. Then the walking and waiting for the city bus that would get him closer, until, finally, he'd swung up the steps into one of Stanford's own personal shuttles, looked out the wide window as it rolled onto a campus of perfectly groomed squares of perfectly green grass, tall, neat palms, white stucco buildings roofed with red tile. Nothing striking a false note, nothing out of place. Except him.

Joe Hartman, owner of nothing. Dressed in old Wranglers and a faded gray T-shirt that he'd outgrown but couldn't afford to replace, a little grimy and a lot sweaty from the long, hot journey across the Mojave Desert, the pack containing his precious, aged laptop on his back. Carrying the green Hefty bag that held the rest of his worldly possessions over his shoulder like a scruffy, low-rent Santa Claus, walking into a dorm room that was nicer than anyplace he'd ever lived, and meeting a roommate who looked like he'd just stepped out of *GQ*.

He hadn't had high hopes. But it hadn't been a disaster after all, because Alec was all right. A full-ride scholarship student, just like Joe. And just as broke, no more able to get a Coke from the machine or go along for a late-night pizza run than Joe was, which had formed a bond all the stronger for being unspoken.

And just as good at programming. That was the main thing. Every bit as good, speaking the language of computers, the language Joe knew. Alec didn't work as hard as Joe did, maybe, but that was because he didn't have to. Alec was smarter, no doubt about it, better prepared, too. And he didn't have as much riding on this.

So not a bad roommate, all in all. But Christmas, that was something else. Christmas was families, and traditions, and knowing you had a place to go, a place where they were counting on you to be there. All the things Joe didn't have. So he didn't want to go. He didn't need reminding.

But he did go. Of course he went, because he'd never met anyone more persuasive than Alec in his life. He rode home with Alec, with a girl Alec knew from Chico who had a car, because Alec knew everybody. With Joe's same green Hefty bag tossed in the trunk.

"Taking your laundry home to get washed?" she'd laughed. "Me too."

He hadn't corrected her, had just climbed into the back and let Alec get in front for the four-hour drive, had let Alec fill the car with easy chat, laughing and joking and looking forward to his Christmas with nothing but happy anticipation, while Joe relapsed into his customary silence. When in doubt, shut up.

The girl, Kathleen, slowed to 35, then 25 as the rural highway gradually changed to city outskirts and then to a city

14

proper. A neat, tidy city, if a sleepy one, the streets all but deserted in the winter dark.

"Winter break," Alec said over his shoulder to Joe. "Usually, it'd be getting rowdy by this time of night, but the students are gone."

Not many people, but lots of trees, the ones in the town square strung with tiny white lights. Kathleen kept driving at Alec's direction, through the town center and a couple miles beyond, pulled to the curb on a block of small houses mostly decorated for Christmas, colored lights or dripping icicles outlining rooflines and windows, reindeer made of lights nodding in front yards, Santa Claus driving his sleigh across rooftops. Like some kind of documentary on Christmas in America, lacking only the snow.

"The ancestral pile, old boy," Alec said. "Someday she'll be mine, don't you know." He laughed, full of the ebullient spirit of coming home. "If I'm the next minister at Bidwell Presbyterian, that is. And unfortunately, we can rule that right out."

Joe picked up his backpack, opened the door and swung out, grimacing at the stiffness of long legs stuffed into the back seat of a compact for too many hours, shivered in the sudden cold. He slid his pack onto his back and shoved his hands under his armpits, stamped a couple times as he waited for Kathleen to open the trunk.

"Supposed to get down below freezing at night, the next few days," Alec said as he pulled his duffel bag from the trunk and Joe picked up his Hefty bag.

Joe shrugged. He'd been cold before.

"Thanks for the ride, Kathleen," Alec went on, slamming the trunk shut again. "We still on to go back on the thirtieth? I could drive, if you want."

"I did *not* drive that badly," she protested. "And it's my car."

"But just think of the nice rest you could have," Alec coaxed. "Sit back, relax, and get delivered to your destination. How upscale would that be?"

"Not too upscale sitting by the side of the freeway with some cop shining his flashlight in the window to write you a ticket," she tossed back. "I know you. You can talk and keep me awake, and I'll drive."

"Slowly," Alec pointed out.

"Safely. Legally."

Alec laughed, reached out, and gave her a hug. Alec always hugged girls, and he always got away with it. "Thanks again. It was awesome. Talk to you soon. Merry Christmas."

"Yeah, thanks," Joe added. He didn't hug her. Joe didn't hug. And she didn't look disappointed.

He watched her taillights recede down the quiet street, the decorous blink of her turn signal before she hung a left and disappeared from sight. Then he forced his feet to move, followed Alec up a long driveway to the back of the house, into an unlocked rear door that led into a spacious linoleum-floored laundry room.

Alec toed his black rubber-soled sneakers off, still holding his bag. "Mom likes shoes off," he instructed.

Joe set his Hefty bag down on top of a white washing machine and bent to unlace the yellow laces of his scuffed brown work boots as Alec waited. He pulled the boots off and set them at the end of a long, untidy line of footwear, tried to find an unobtrusive way to pull his left sock around to hide the hole that had formed over the second toe, then gave it up.

Alec swung the inner door open, calling out as he entered a big, warm kitchen. Nothing fancy, nothing new, white tile countertops and worn pine cabinets.

"I'm home!" he called out, and now a middle-aged woman was hurrying in. Middle height, still pretty and slim in jeans and a red sweater, brown hair in a tousled cut that curled into the nape of her neck, laugh lines around eyes that were the same vibrant blue as Alec's. Laugh lines because she was laughing in delight, throwing her arms around her son, who had dropped his bag to lift her into a hug, whirl her around.

"Miss me?" he asked her, setting her down at last.

16

"You know I did, you wretch." She pulled his face down to give his cheek a kiss. "Alyssa doesn't give me quite enough trouble to make up for you being gone. And this must be Joe." She held out a slim hand after a moment when Joe had feared that he was going to be hugged as well, and he shook it in relief.

"Ma'am," he said. "Thanks for having me."

Her eyebrows rose a little, but she didn't comment, just smiled at him. "You're more than welcome. Your dad's at the hospital, making a couple visits," she told Alec. "He'll be home soon. Have you two had dinner?"

And it was like that. Joe dumped his bag and pack onto a trundle bed that Alec pulled out from underneath the twin bed in his small bedroom, which made it so there was just about no room at all in there, and ate hamburger-noodle casserole and green beans at a big oval table in a comfortable living-dining room, and listened to Alec's mom—Mrs. Kincaid—catching her son up on the news, and asking him questions about his classes, about Stanford. Tossing the occasional question Joe's way, but not pressing him, not like he'd feared.

Alec's dad came in in the middle of it, gave his wife a kiss, his son another big hug—they were the huggingest family Joe had ever seen—and shook Joe's hand, echoed his wife's welcome.

He was a bear of a man, as tall as Joe, and even broader across the shoulders. Barrel-chested, thick-thighed, with massive hands, more like a construction worker than a Presbyterian minister. Black hair, a strong nose and cheekbones, a face to reckon with, kindness in its lines, but firmness, too. His dad was a quarter Cherokee, Alec had told Joe with some pride, and it showed.

Mr. Kincaid was eating his own casserole, catching up with Alec, and Joe was having seconds that Mrs. Kincaid had urged on him and seeing that even the huge roasting pan of noodles, meat, and cheese wasn't going to last long, when the back door slammed again, the kitchen door burst open a moment later, and a girl whirled through it like a sudden gust

17

of wind, talking as she came, and the room was charged with electricity. And Joe was staring, his fork in midair, all the air sucked out of his lungs.

"Alec!" She was on him, her pretty mouth stretched in a smile, and he was standing up, and, yes, hugging her, laughing in his turn.

"I'm *so tired!*" she said, flopping into a dining chair next to her brother, picking up the spatula sticking out of the casserole pan and dishing up a healthy serving, grabbing the milk carton and pouring herself a glass. "Practice was *brutal.* Coach Saller thinks just because it's Christmas, we're going to get all fat and lazy, so she has to work us *three times* as hard now, or we're going to lose in disgrace or something."

Everything she said seemed to be in italics, or have an exclamation point at the end. Darting glances flicked between Alec and Joe out of sparkling dark blue eyes extravagantly fringed with black lashes, the delicately curved, nearly black brows quirking as she smiled, lowering into a brief frown, her pretty face with its finely carved features in constant, vibrant motion, her energy more effective than any makeup could possibly have been, and Joe was a lost man.

"Alyssa," her mother said. "Slow down. Say hello to Joe, and then wash your hands before you eat."

"Hello, Joe," she said, and popped up again, danced into the kitchen before Joe could even answer.

He watched her go, because he couldn't help it. Red sweats over long legs, a red-and-gold Chico High Basketball t-shirt that clung to her slim torso. Which had plenty of girl curves to it. Which he shouldn't be noticing. But he couldn't help it.

"And that," Alec said with a grin as they heard water start to run, "in case you had any doubts, is my little sister. That's Alyssa."

She was in the room again, and the words were tumbling out again. "Do you remember Heather Monroe, Alec? She's our point guard. You wouldn't *believe* how fast she is! I wish you were going to be here to come to the game, so you could see. She's gotten really pretty, too. You should see. Really."

18

That was the first night. The next morning, it got worse.

He was sitting at the table again, eating pancakes and eggs served up by Alec's mom and thinking he'd be happy to stay in this house forever, because she'd given him three eggs to start, and then just kept sliding more pancakes onto his plate and urging him to eat them. Butter and syrup, orange juice and black coffee, and the hole inside him that had so rarely been filled since he'd started to grow was filling, and he thought that if she kept this up, he wasn't even going to be hungry until lunchtime.

And then Alyssa walked through the door from the hallway into the living room. Wearing her pajamas. Which would have been bad enough, but her pajamas were a skimpy red T-shirt and low-slung flannel pants printed with candy canes.

"Morning," she said. She raised slim, strong arms over her head and stretched, her lithe body curving, her young girl's breasts rising with the movement, proving to Joe beyond any shadow of a doubt that she wasn't wearing a bra. The little shirt rode up and showed a couple inches of flat stomach, the devastating curve of her waist, the elongated oval of her belly button, the dangling tapes of the untied pajama pants. Her hair was in a messy ponytail, and when she straightened up, reached back to pull off the elastic, and shook out the shiny hair that reached to her shoulder blades, he thought his head would actually explode.

"Good morning," Mrs. Kincaid said, coming to stand behind her husband at the head of the table and sliding three more pancakes from her spatula onto his plate, and Joe tore his gaze away fast, looked down at his breakfast. He could feel his face getting hot, and he didn't dare look up.

"Go put a robe on, Alyssa, please," he heard Mrs. Kincaid say.

"I hate wearing a robe," she complained. "I'm always hot."

Joe shoved himself closer to the table, reached for his orange juice in desperation.

"Go," her mother said firmly, and Joe looked up for just a moment to see her walking away, a sassy little flounce in her step, and then he could breathe again. For a while.

There was yet more hugging later that morning when Alec's twin Gabe arrived home from the University of Washington, where, Joe knew, he was attending on a football scholarship. At least Alec and Gabe didn't hug, not beyond a grab at each others' shoulders. Instead, Joe was amused to see, they had a special handshake. Well, they were twins. He guessed a secret handshake was part of the deal.

It got rowdy and noisy after that, Alec and Alyssa both talking at the same time, Gabe interjecting, responding, and their mother laughing and enjoying it all, clearly so delighted to have her family together. It was exactly like some kind of sitcom family on TV, the kind Joe had always thought was made up.

Alec's hacky sack eventually made its appearance, and, inevitably, a challenge was laid down. Alec acquitted himself pretty well, but Gabe did better. And then Alyssa blew them both out of the water. She was quick, and she was fluid, and if she played basketball like that, Joe thought, she was probably pretty good.

"Here, Joe," she said. "See if you can do better." She tossed the little crocheted ball to him, high, so he had to reach for it.

He grabbed it out of the air, popped it back to her. "I'll pass. Let's see if you can beat your record."

She stared at where his gray T-shirt sleeve had ridden up at the movement. "You have a tattoo."

"Yeah." He smoothed his sleeve back down over the ink.

The blue eyes sparkled at him just a little bit more, her mouth curving in a teasing smile. "Wow. Did all the guys on the football team get drunk and do it together, or what? What did your parents say?"

He didn't really have an answer for that one, so he didn't answer.

"Can I see?" She'd come closer, and he couldn't exactly say "no," so he lifted the edge of his sleeve. And then it got worse, because she put out her hand and traced the blue-inked pattern where it curved over his triceps, the target superimposed on the shield, the missile streaking toward the bulls-eye, the scroll beneath, on which you couldn't really read the writing, because the artist hadn't exactly been the best.

"What is it?" she asked, bent close, and he could smell a flowery scent that was probably her shampoo wafting up to him from the dark hair, so shiny it gleamed, could see her scalp showing along her center part, because he had a good eight inches on her, even though she was tall. "It's not a team."

The light touch of her fingers was like a brand. "It's the 57th Wing," he said, wishing his voice didn't sound so strangled. "Of the Air Force."

"Did you want to join?"

"No. It was my dad's unit."

"Oh, I get it. That's why you're here for Christmas," she said. "Your dad's in the Air Force?"

"No," he said again. "He died." He knew it sounded too bald, but he didn't know how else to say it.

"Oh. I'm sorry." She took a step back, confusion in her eyes, and he felt like he'd kicked a puppy. Girls like this weren't supposed to know about the bad things, the hard things.

"You hassling Joe, Liss?" Alec said from the couch. He got up, started to grab for the hacky sack, trying to wrestle it from her, and she was turning, twisting, and laughing again. "You are such a brat."

They fell on the couch together, and Alyssa tossed the little ball to Gabe, who caught it with an elbow, kicked it with the side of his foot back to her, and the game was on. Soon all four of them were involved, Joe drawn in despite himself, because when it came his way, he couldn't spoil the party, could he? And they were irresistible.

Their mother came through the room as the little ball sailed through the air, whipped her white plastic laundry basket around and caught it inside in a deft movement. "You guys. Four short months away and you're savages. The work of a lifetime undone. No playing ball in the house."

"Hacky sack isn't playing ball," Alec objected. *"Football's* playing ball. Hacky sack's like—playing yo-yo in the house."

"All right," she said. "No playing yo-yo in the house. Honestly. You need to get *out*. Come on, now. A little peace and quiet here."

"Oh, nice," Alec said, making a sad face. "We're home a couple hours and you already want to get rid of us."

"I don't want to get *rid* of you. I just want you to run around a while, run some of that energy off."

Alec and Gabe looked at each other and laughed. "It's like we're three, Mom," Gabe said.

"Well, really," she said tartly, "it's like you *are* three sometimes. And people wonder why I already have to dye my hair."

"Do you want some help?" That was Gabe. "Sorry. I should have asked."

She took one hand off the heavy basket where it was balanced on her hip, rubbed a palm over his broad shoulder. "Thanks, sweetie. Later I would. But for now, just go outside for a while, OK?"

"We'll take Joe for a walk, show him the town," Alec decided. "That'll be a fun-filled time."

"And then basketball," Alyssa said. "I've got some new moves to show you, Gabe. And Joe's here, so we can have teams. Can you play?" she asked Joe.

"Of course he can play," Alec said. "Every guy can play basketball."

"Well, *I* don't know," she flared back. "He can't play hacky sack."

"Hey," Joe protested. He had to smile a little. "I did it."

22

"Huh." She tossed her head so her ponytail did a flip. "You kinda stunk." And he had to smile a little more.

"I play basketball better than that," he promised. "A little better." Actually, a lot better. Thank goodness.

There was a fairly organized scramble for shoes and coats, and Joe went back to Alec's bedroom, pulled his jacket out of his bag, went into the laundry room for his boots, leaned against the doorjamb between laundry room and kitchen to pull them on and tie the laces.

Mrs. Kincaid stood back from the fridge, where she was taking vegetables out of the bin and piling them onto the counter, and looked him over. "Hold on," she said. "You can't go out like that. It's cold out there. Don't you have something warmer? And what about a hat? And gloves?"

He straightened up, stuffed his hands into the pockets of the worn black leather bomber jacket. "I'm good."

"It's supposed to drop into the thirties today," she said. "It's probably there already." She shoved the refrigerator door shut and hustled into the laundry room, taking Joe by the upper arms and moving him out of the way as if he were one of her own boys. She shooed her children out the back door and onto the porch before opening a worn pine dresser in one corner of the room, dug inside for a while and came out with a black watch cap and a pair of brown gloves, handed them to him, then flipped quickly through pegs of coats and sweaters, pulled a brown plaid woolen jacket out from underneath a couple rain jackets, and shoved it into his arms as well. "There. All set. You can keep the hat and gloves. I wish you could keep that ratty old jacket too, but that's Dave's leaf-raking jacket. I've been trying to get rid of it for years, but he won't let me."

He pulled the jacket on over the black leather, because she clearly wasn't taking no for an answer, and under her watchful eye, put the hat on as well. "Thanks. I'll borrow them, then. But I don't need a hat. Or gloves."

"Don't be ridiculous," she said impatiently. "I don't even know whose those were. Some friend of the boys', probably, leaving his belongings behind and driving his mother crazy.

You're doing me a favor, saving me donating them like I should have already."

He was outmatched, so he mumbled his thanks and went out to join the others as the proud new owner of a hat and gloves. And it was probably just as well, because the air *had* turned colder, must have been down into the thirties already, like she'd said. Low clouds had turned the sky to a leaden gray, and a dampness in the air spoke of rain to come.

They set off, Joe behind Alec and Gabe on the shoulder of the quiet street. More of that 1950s sitcom stuff. No sidewalks, just the big trees lining the street on both sides as far as he could see, a final few leaves still clinging that would fall in the coming storm. And Alyssa next to him, of course, a blue knitted hat with a perky pompom covering the dark hair, a puffy blue jacket zipped against the cold, seeming to bounce on her toes as she walked.

"They're in Twin World," she said, nodding ahead at her brothers. "Bonding time. It's what they do. No outsiders allowed, back to the womb."

Joe shrugged. "That's OK."

"Do you have brothers and sisters?"

"A sister. Half-sister."

"Older or younger?"

"Older. Four years."

"So ..." She hesitated, then went on. "Is your mom far away, then? And your sister? Is that why you aren't home for Christmas?"

Here they were, the questions, and even though he'd been expecting them, he tensed all the same. "Yeah. My sister's in Alaska."

It diverted her, as he'd hoped. "You mean she lives there? I never think about people actually living in Alaska. Did you live there too?"

"No. She's in the Air Force. On a base outside of Fairbanks."

"Have you been there? To visit her?"

"No."

24

"So do you get to see her? I can't imagine not seeing my brothers. Not at *Christmas.*"

"Not for a while." Not for a few years, and then it had been quick, a couple hours at the airport during a layover on Cheryl's way to a new duty station. But he didn't tell Alyssa that. "You're on the basketball team, huh?" he asked, trying to think of something new to talk about. Conversation had never been his strong suit. "Varsity?"

She laughed up at him. "I wish. JV, but I really hope I can make Varsity before I'm a sophomore. There's this girl, Colleen Fitzhugh? She's a sophomore this year, but I know she made Varsity in her freshman season, so I think I can do it. Wouldn't that be cool?"

He was barely listening. "You're a freshman?"

"Well, yeah. Halfway through freshman year," she hurried to add, as if that would make a difference.

A freshman in high school. Alec had probably told him that, but Alec had told him a lot of things. "How old are you?" he asked. Alec had told him that, too, he was sure, but at the time, it hadn't mattered.

"Fifteen. But I'll be sixteen in March," she hastened to add. "How old are you?"

"Nineteen."

"This is my old school, up here." She gestured with a mittened hand. "I played basketball there, too. That seems like such a long time ago, you know?"

From the standpoint of six months, or whatever it was. *Chico Junior High School,* he read in two-foot-high letters stenciled onto concrete block. He was hot for a girl who had just graduated from junior high school. What kind of a pervert was he?

"This is my favorite tree in the world," she was saying now, reaching out for a trunk and swinging herself around it with a laugh. "Aren't the leaves gorgeous?"

Joe looked dubiously up into the mostly-bare branches. "Well, I can't really tell."

She was scooping a few up from the concrete. "Gingko. See, they're fans."

25

The graceful leaves, a rich golden yellow, were indeed shaped like delicate fans, and she was arranging them like a deck of cards, fanning herself with one hand, then holding the whole arrangement close to her face, peeping over them, her eyes flirtatious. "Why, Rhett. Sir, how dare you." She fluttered those black lashes, and he could see her smile behind the blue mitten, and he was struck dumb.

"Liss." Alec and Gabe had wheeled around, and Alec was calling out to her. "Are you teasing Joe? He's thanking God right now that he doesn't have a little sister."

No, Joe was wishing that Alec didn't have one. Or wishing that she wasn't quite so little. Or something.

She was fifteen, he was still telling himself desperately an hour later as he played basketball with the three of them, watched her dribbling, showing off her jump shot, laughing at him, bumping him, killing him. *Fifteen.* She was a *child.* And he was nineteen going on fifty, and if her brothers, if her parents could read his mind, he'd be right out of that house and out of their lives. Out of the warmth, the light, the laughter, hell, minus some teeth, probably, and on the Greyhound bus straight back to Stanford. He would just have to ignore her, and the way she moved, and the way she laughed, and the fierce, insistent craving she stirred in his body. He could do that. He'd done tougher things. Although, at this moment, he couldn't remember exactly what.

Everybody Except Alyssa

Alyssa's unemployment blues eased a little with the arrival of her brother Gabe on Christmas Eve. Alec had always been her exciting brother, equal parts glamorous, demanding, and exasperating, but Gabe had been her protector and confidante ever since she could remember. Although, she sadly admitted to herself, he'd had less time for her A.M.— After Mira. She liked her sister-in-law, but she missed being alone with Gabe. And with both of her brothers newly married ... the phrase "fifth wheel" came pretty forcibly to mind.

"You need to tell us all about the honeymoon, Rae. I want to see pictures," Mira said when they had sat down to dinner, nine of them including Rae's grandmother Dixie, all squeezed around the dining room table eating spaghetti with meat sauce, their traditional Christmas Eve dinner.

Alec and Rae had been married on the day after Thanksgiving. A short engagement, a small, simple wedding, but Alyssa knew that Dixie's health was fragile, and they hadn't wanted to wait. And, Rae had said practically, they wouldn't have to take as much time off work if they did it over the holiday weekend. Which had made Alec groan, and everyone else laugh.

"It was ... " Rae smiled. "Great. It was great. As honeymoons go, I'd rate it right up there. I'll show you my pictures later, if you want to see. Other people's vacation pictures are never that fascinating."

"They are to me," Mira protested. "I've never been to Paris. So romantic."

"Thanks, bro," Gabe told his twin. "Raising the bar again."

He got a shrug in return. "Got to do it right. I'm only going to get one bride. Sadly." Alec heaved a martyred sigh. "I tried to sell her on the merits of plural marriage, the whole sister-wife deal, but she's not going for it."

"Nope," Rae said. "Afraid you're stuck with one. But yes, you did it right. Although it was strange, too," she told Mira. "That was the first time it really sank in how much money Alec has. Flying first class, staying in a suite at the Georges Cinq, it was all like a movie, some movie that would never be starring me."

"What a nightmare," Alyssa deadpanned.

"Well, yeah," Rae said with a laugh. "I'm not complaining. But he didn't even check with me, he just set it all up, and it was … way beyond my pay grade. We'd go out to dinner, and I'd look at the prices on the menu, do the currency conversion, get this—" She put her hand on her heart. "Whoa, major shock, and have to remind myself that he could afford it."

"That *we* could afford it," Alec said. "And here I thought you married me for my money."

"Nope," she said. "I married you for your good looks."

"Oh, that's right. I forgot. And it's true," he told the others, "I could see that calculator brain working every single time we went anywhere. They need to make those date menus without the prices again, like they used to."

"Always order from the middle of the menu," Alyssa's mother pronounced. "That's what we were told when I was a girl. You didn't order the chicken salad, because that was an insult, like you thought he couldn't afford anything more. But you didn't order the lobster, either, because that would make him feel taken advantage of."

"Until you started dating me," Dave Kincaid put in. "Then you *knew* you had to order the chicken salad."

"Good thing you were worth it," Susie said. "Lots of picnics, too."

"I was hoping you'd think they were romantic," her husband complained.

"They were." She smiled back at him, and Alyssa felt about her fifth pang of envy since they'd sat down. Great. Now she was jealous of her *parents*.

"Sometimes I think it's better just to split the check," she said, trying to lift her mood, join the fun. "What do you guys think?" she asked her brothers. "Better, or no? It always seems like it should be, but then, when I've been out with a guy the first time and he lets the check lie there in the middle of the table, and I can tell he's thinking I should offer to split it ... ugh. It turns me off."

"For sure, he pays the first time," Gabe said.

"That's right," Alec agreed. "Big red flag, Liss."

"But then," she mused, "why should he, really?"

"Because he asked you," Gabe said. "He doesn't have to take you someplace he can't afford. If he can only take you out for a hamburger, or a picnic," he said with a smile for his mother, "that's fine. I've been that broke plenty of times. But if he asks you out, he should pay the first time. You can offer to split the check the second time, if you want."

"Of course," Alec said, "if you ask him out, all bets are off. Though most guys I know probably wouldn't be comfortable with the woman paying even then, not the first time."

"I still don't ask guys out," Alyssa admitted. "I should, but the kind of guy I like, I just can't imagine asking out. I don't like New Age men. I mean, I *like* them, I'm just not attracted to them. I should be, I know I should be, but I'm not."

"So nobody special right now?" Gabe asked her.

"No," she said, the fun and laughter wiped away. "Nope. Single again."

"Broke up?" he asked with the sympathetic understanding he always showed, and she wondered why she could never meet a guy like her brother.

"Yeah. Broke, broke up, and home for the holidays." She lifted her water glass in a toast. "Merry Christmas."

29

"Never mind," Rae said. "You have to kiss a lot of frogs, huh, Mira?"

"That's right," Mira said. "You'll find the right one soon, Alyssa, I know it. He's out there waiting for you."

"What about you, Joe?" Susie asked. "You know, if you ever have somebody special that you want to bring home with you, we'd love to meet her."

He shrugged. "Nobody special. Nobody to bring."

"Seems to me you'd be a real catch," Dixie said. "A big, handsome man like you, with that real good job? Lots of girls must be interested."

"Not so handsome," Joe said with a rueful smile, running a big hand over his shaved head.

Alyssa watched him do it, the sheer size of his shoulder, the bulge of bicep that the dress shirt he was wearing in honor of the occasion couldn't conceal, the crooked grin twisting his mouth amidst the closely trimmed stubble he'd begun wearing when he'd started shaving his head.

No, not so handsome. But so tough, with his rough edges barely concealed, leaving you wondering what sorts of banked fires might be burning underneath.

Dixie snorted. "More important things than hair. Any woman worth having knows that. Maybe you're just not giving them a chance."

"I don't think that's it," he said. "It's something else. I don't know. It starts out OK. They start out thinking I'm mysterious, I guess. I'm a challenge. That's what they say, later." He stopped, reached for his glass. No wonder. That was practically baring his soul, for Joe.

"And then what?" Susie prompted. "Come on, Joe. Tell us."

"Guess they think there's something there that turns out not to be," he said. "They want me to share my feelings. They say I don't." He shrugged. "They want a different guy."

"Don't know where women got started with that notion," Dixie said. "Share your feelings? Men don't have that many feelings."

"Oh, now," Alec protested as all the men at the table laughed. "We have feelings."

"What?" Dixie challenged. "A man thinks, why's the truck making that funny noise, should I take it into the shop. Glad to be home for the day. What's for dinner. And I hope it's bedtime soon. That's a man's feelings."

That got a good laugh out of everyone. "I won't say you're wrong," Alec said. "But hey, those are some powerful feelings. You can't really blame us for that."

"And who wants a man to yap at them all the time?" Dixie went on. "She's got girlfriends for that. Can you listen?" she asked Joe.

"I can do that," he said. "I can listen."

"There you go, then," she pronounced triumphantly. "If you can listen when she talks, that's plenty. A woman with any sense at all wants a good, strong, reliable man, one who's going to be there to hold her when she's had a bad day, fix things when they break, solve problems. That's what a man's good for."

"Well," Joe said, "that's good for me, then, because that's about what I can do."

"Then you just need to find yourself a quality woman," Dixie insisted. "Maybe you're looking in the wrong places. You tried church?"

"No, ma'am. No, I haven't." Joe was struggling not to smile now, Alyssa could tell.

"There you go, then. Find a good church, and you'll find a quality woman."

"There are more places than that, though," Rae said. "I've met most of the guys I've dated at work, or through friends. Both of those are good. I'd never have gone out with Alec if I hadn't known him through work. *Never.*"

"Wow. Thanks," he said, laughing. "How immensely flattering."

"Me too. I mean, I got to know Gabe by us working together too," Mira said, as always a little flustered when everybody looked at her. "Sort of."

31

Dixie waved a liver-spotted hand. "Same difference, or maybe even better. You met him where you could see him day in and day out, see how he treated other people, how he acted when things didn't go right. It's easy to act all nice and lovey-dovey taking a girl out on a date, trying to impress her. It's a whole different thing to do it every day."

"You're right there, not that I'd ever argue against church as the best dating service," Dave said. "But if you want a marriage to work, you have to be able to work things out when the going gets rough. That's where I'd disagree with you, Dixie. Joe doesn't have to talk much, but he has to talk some. You can't fix things if you can't talk them over."

"So true," Alec sighed. "I can attest to that. Rae tells me I'm wrong, and I tell her she's right, and there you go, we've talked it over. Problem solved."

"I do not," Rae laughed. "We don't argue much because I'm so good at knowing what you want, I've already made it happen."

"Also true," he said. "And in Mira and Gabe's case, Mira thinks Gabe's perfect, so they've got no differences to work out at all. That's the other approach."

"That is not true," Mira protested. "We have differences. I know he isn't perfect."

"All right," Alec challenged. "Name my brother's imperfections."

"Well ..." She hesitated. "He doesn't like to use his turn signal," she finally produced with triumph.

"Uh-huh. He doesn't like to. But he does?"

"Well, yes," she admitted. "If he's driving me. Because I don't like him not to." Even Mira had to laugh at that one, which put her in company with the rest of the room.

"Oh, yeah. He's an outlaw," Alec said. "And let's hear Mira's flaws, Gabe. Since we're sharing."

"Not critical enough," Gabe said with a smile. "Come on. I'm not answering that. I may only have been married six months, but I've already got the cardinal rule down. Girlfriend: sometimes right. Wife: usually right. Pregnant wife: always right. And wife pregnant with twins: infallible."

32

That caused an outburst that didn't die down for a full minute, during which Mira was laughing, pink with pleasure, and Susie had come around to hug her, and Gabe had put his arm around her, looking, Alyssa thought, like he'd personally done something incredibly clever and talented, because he was obviously pleased as punch and twice as proud of himself.

"You've got that one right," Dave said at last, wiping his eyes on his napkin. "Twins. The fun is just beginning."

"Let's see, Mira," Alyssa said, pulling her sister-in-law up from her chair and taking both her hands, standing back to check out her waistline. "I *thought* you were looking pudgy." Which caused everyone to howl even more.

"What's your due date, Mira?" Susie asked when the laughter had died down.

"July twentieth," she said, sitting down again, still looking flushed and flustered, but so happy.

"Oh, perfect," Susie exclaimed. "Halfway through my summer break from school. Though twins will probably come early. Even better." Her mother still worked at the elementary school secretary job she'd held for years, seemingly happy to stay. "I do get to come and help, don't I?" she asked in sudden alarm. "Before the babies, and afterwards? I could stay in the trailer," she began to plan, "so I'd be out of your way, and Dave could come down from time to time."

"And just like that, I've lost my wife of thirty-six years," her husband said in resignation. "I can see I'm going to be spending the next six months saying, 'Repeat after me. These are *Mira's* babies. Not your babies. *Mira's* babies.'"

"Of course I want you to come," Mira said hastily. "Of course I do. I'd be so happy. I'd be so *grateful.*" She was actually crying, Alyssa saw with some shock. "Sorry," she said, gulping a little, laughing, but still crying. "Hormonal. I'm crying at phone company commercials. But I want you. I do."

"You'll want her more when you see how much work twins are," Dave said. "You have no idea. And people say God doesn't have a sense of humor."

33

Susie looked at him and laughed. "Oh, dear. It's so true. But oh, my goodness, Mira, you're already so far along!"

"Ten weeks," she said, brushing at her eyes with an apologetic laugh of her own. "But we didn't want to steal Desiree and Alec's thunder from the wedding, so we thought it would be better to wait to tell everyone."

"Pretty fast work there, bro," Alec said.

"Thanks. I do my best," Gabe said modestly. "But," he added seriously, "it's because we knew we wanted to have more than one. Of course, we didn't realize we'd be having more than one right out of the gate."

"And I'm thirty," Mira added. "I'll be thirty-one by the time the babies are born. We figured if we wanted to space them a few years apart, it was time to start. And we thought it might take a while, once we started trying. But it turned out that it happened the first month." She smiled at Gabe, her color mounting a bit higher, and he smiled right back at her.

"Just another example of Mira's efficiency," he said with a grin for his brother. "And don't tell me Desiree doesn't have a full time line mapped out for the two of you, because I won't believe you. Or that Dad agreed to marry you without some major premarital counseling, including who's cleaning the bathroom and how many kids you both want and whether you keep your money in a joint account, because I know he didn't. I'll bet you got it from Rev. Wilder, too, just like we did."

Alec laughed. "Could be. On both counts."

"But wait a minute," Alyssa protested, still stuck on Topic A. "I thought twins only ran in families on the female side. I thought I was the only one more likely to have them."

"Fraternal twins, that's true," Gabe said.

"Oh." Susie's hands were clasped in front of her chest, and she looked like she'd just got the best Christmas present ever. "Are you saying ..."

"One placenta," Gabe said. "Identical twins."

"Identical twins," she breathed. "Oh, that's ... Girls or boys?"

"They think boys," Gabe said. "We won't know for sure for another month or so, but it's looking like they've got the equipment." And he looked even more smug.

That made her parents laugh at each other again. "I am *definitely* coming to help," Susie said. "You just try to keep me away."

And that was all very lovely. All very heartwarming. And depressing as hell. Everybody so wonderfully successful, everybody so happily partnered. Everybody except Alyssa, unemployed and single, sleeping alone in her childhood bedroom on Christmas Eve with not a single good prospect on the horizon, boyfriend-wise, job-wise, *anything*-wise. And this year, she was thirty.

It was time to start. Pretty hard to start all by yourself. Well, she thought as she scraped plates and loaded the dishwasher, at least she'd get to be an aunt. She tried to feel good about that. It wasn't that she wasn't happy for Mira and Gabe, because she was. But it was so hard not to be jealous.

"Don't save that," she told Joe as he began to put the leftover spaghetti noodles into a plastic container, working deliberately, the way he always did. Which made her want to grab the container from him and show him how to do it *fast*, like a normal person.

"Why not?"

"They don't taste good warmed up. The texture's all wrong. It's better to use fresh ones."

"But if you save them, you don't have to cook fresh ones. And they'll have sauce on them. You won't really be able to tell," he said, sounding perfectly calm, perfectly reasonable.

Mira had a husband who used his turn signal just so she'd feel safe. And Alyssa couldn't even get her way about the *noodles*, because Joe didn't think her opinion counted for anything, and he didn't care if she was happy. The tears came to her eyes even as she recognized the childishness of the thought, and she shoved the last plates into the dishwasher,

35

then threw the dish brush with a little extra force into the sudsy water she'd been running into the left-hand side of the divided sink, hard enough so foam and water splashed out and splattered onto her sweater, soaking it to the skin over her stomach.

She jumped, pulled at the wet fabric and swore in helpless frustration, the worst word she ever said, which was pretty bad, and saw his head jerk up at it. Because she didn't usually swear in front of him, but why shouldn't she? Why the hell not?

He didn't say anything, just handed her the plastic container. "Toss them, if you want. Makes no difference to me."

She snatched it from his hand and stuffed the noodles savagely down the disposal, feeling like she was going to either scream or cry. "Why won't you ever *fight* with me?"

"Do you want to fight?" He looked startled again.

She realized how stupid she sounded. She blew out a breath, flipped the switch for the disposal, and gave the noodles a couple pushes to help them down.

Joe grabbed her wrist hard, pulled her hand out of the sink. "Get your hand out of there!" He reached around her, turned the motor off. "You *never* put your fingers that close to something that sharp. Use a spoon! Use the brush!"

"I wasn't going to cut them!" she flared back. "I was being careful. I'm not going to stick my hand down the hole. Do you think I'm an idiot?"

"No. I think that was careless," he said, back under control again. Of course he was. "I think you need to think before you act, so you don't get hurt."

She opened her mouth to defend herself, but couldn't think of anything good to say. She'd said she wanted him to fight with her, and he'd yelled at her. She'd got her wish. She picked up the dishcloth and turned away from him, began to wipe down the stove. Saw him, out of the corner of her eye, starting to scrub serving dishes with her abused dish brush.

"I'm grouchy," she admitted after a minute. "Too much family time. I did a run this morning, but it wasn't enough, I guess. Want to go for a walk with me when we're done with this? Look at the Christmas lights?"

He kept washing, and she wondered mutinously why Joe always took so long to *answer*. How long did it take to answer a simple question like that?

"I brought some work," he said at last.

"On Christmas Eve?" She felt the lump forming in her throat, the prick of tears. He couldn't even stand to take a walk with her?

Luckily, Rae came through the swinging door into the kitchen then. "Hey, Alyssa. You guys need any help?"

Alyssa began wiping off counters. "About done," she said. Then added impulsively, "Want to go for a walk with me?"

"Sure," Rae said. "OK if Alec comes too?"

"Fine," Alyssa muttered. Couples again.

"I'll come too," Joe said.

She stared at him. "I thought you didn't want to go."

"I didn't say that," he said. "I said I brought work. I'll do the work after the walk."

You just didn't want to go with me, she didn't say, and swallowed against the sudden desolation of it. Tomorrow morning, in church, she'd count her blessings. But not tonight. Tonight she was going to feel sorry for herself. Because Joe still didn't like her, not really. He just put up with her, as part of the family. Alec's silly, careless, troublesome little sister.

He'd been so hot, that first Christmas. When she'd first seen him looking at her, his face set and still, rough-hewn even then, seeming to have been carved, not too expertly, out of slabs of rock. Cheekbones, brow ridges, jawline, chin, all so strongly drawn, so uncompromising. His light brown hair cut short, the pale blue eyes intense, so compelling that she'd found it hard to look away.

He had eyes like an animal, she'd thought in a flight of fancy, lying in bed that night and remembering the way he'd looked at her, savoring the image of him. Not a lion or a tiger. A wolf, maybe. A blue-eyed wolf, intent, watching. She shivered at the thought of it, not even quite sure how to put a name to the feelings that were making her hot enough to kick off the covers, shift restlessly in bed, shove the pillow between her legs.

And it got worse the next day. When she saw him in his boots and black leather jacket, it turned her insides to liquid, started delicious tingles down low in her belly. He was taller than her father, six-three at least, even taller with the boots on. As broad across the shoulders as her dad, too, as broad as Gabe, though there was a rawboned look to him. He was all thick muscle and heavy bone, nothing soft about him, not one bit a boy. So much a man. So much older than her brothers, especially when he turned that level gaze on her.

She'd done her best that week to make him like her as much as she liked him, to penetrate his wall of reserve. She'd teased him, the way that usually made boys smile, made them laugh, made them hang around her locker to talk to her. And when she'd got Joe to smile, a quirk of the lips, a warming of the eyes, she'd felt a rush of triumph that had proved short-lived, because after that, she could feel him drawing back as if he didn't want to be close to her, didn't even want to look at her. And the more she tried, the more she seemed to drive him away. She'd concluded at last, a little hurt, a little angry, that he just didn't like her. Or, worse, that he could tell she had a crush on him, and it embarrassed him, and he was trying to discourage her.

There had been one bright spot, the morning of the day when he and Alec had left to go back to school. She'd been lying on her stomach on the couch, watching cartoons on TV, because she was bored and there was nothing to do, and he came into the room with something bunched in his hand, then stopped halfway in, seeming to hesitate.

She sat up, grabbed for the remote and hastily turned the TV off so she wouldn't look immature. She wished she'd been watching something educational, or reading a book, or doing homework, even though school was out. Studying.

Wearing glasses, maybe. Looking serious, like him. He probably liked serious girls.

He was still standing there, so she shoved her hair back behind her ear and smiled at him, hoping she still had some lip gloss on. She'd put it on along with some mascara this morning, as she had every morning during this vacation, but that had been before breakfast. She should have checked again.

"I have this," he said, frowning at her the way he always did and hefting the thing in one big hand. "An Eielson T-shirt. The Air Force base," he explained. "In Alaska. And I thought ..." He cleared his throat. "It seemed like you like T-shirts."

"I do," she said, still smiling encouragingly. "I love them." She was wearing her Huskies Football T-shirt right now, the one Gabe had brought her from Washington.

"My sister sent this to me," he said. "For Christmas. But she didn't know I'd grown, I guess, and it's too small. So I thought ... I mean, just if you want it. I don't want to throw it away."

He held it out, and she jumped up from the couch and took it from him, held it up in front of her. A simple dark-blue T-shirt, the base's name emblazoned on the front.

"It'll be too big, I know," he said hastily. "And it's a man's. So maybe not."

"No," she said. "It's perfect. I'll wear it to bed. I love it."

He looked even more stone-faced, not even pleased, just gave her a little nod. "OK, then." And then he turned around and left the room, and an hour later, left with Alec.

She'd worn his shirt to bed every night for months, and thought about him, and dreamed about him. Her first tentative sexual fantasies had been about Joe. Vague and romantic, with kissing heavily featured, and him telling her how crazy he was about her, how he couldn't get her out of his head.

But when she'd seen him next, almost a year later, when Alec had brought him home for Thanksgiving, he'd been more grown up, more remote than ever. And nothing had changed. Fifteen years later, and he was still spending his Christmas vacations gazing unsmilingly at her as if he were measuring her, and she wasn't measuring up.

Well, she was tired of it. Fifteen years was long enough to want a man who'd never want her back. She was going to get over Joe Hartman. This was the last Christmas she was going to spend fantasizing about him. She was done.

Nothing Like a Necklace

Joe opened his eyes the next morning and looked up at the old-fashioned, popcorn-textured white ceiling. Alec's room, Christmas morning.

Which started with church, because it always started with church.

That first year, he'd tried to decline. "I'll stay here, if that's OK," he said when the subject came up over Christmas Eve dinner. "I could do the breakfast dishes, any other kind of chores you have." He knew how to make himself useful. That tended to make you more welcome, too.

"If you stay in this house," Mrs. Kincaid said, "you're coming to church. You don't have to believe. You don't have to participate. But you have to come."

"I don't ..." he began, then stopped. "I didn't bring church clothes." He didn't *have* church clothes. He had jeans, and he had T-shirts. He had his boots, and he had a pair of well-used tennis shoes. None of which would be right. He hadn't been in too many churches, but he knew that much.

Mrs. Kincaid paused in the act of dishing more meat sauce onto Gabe's plate to look Joe over, a speculative gleam in her eye.

"Oh, no," Alec groaned. "Now you've given her a project."

She handed Gabe his plate, flapped the back of her hand at her elder son. "Hush up. And it doesn't matter what you wear, Joe. That's the point of church. It's what's on the inside that counts, isn't it, Dave?"

41

"More honored in the breach than the observance," her husband said, "but that's meant to be the idea."

"But if you'd be more comfortable," Mrs. Kincaid said, "we'll find one of Dave's shirts for you to wear, because you're about his height. That's the only way we'll get sleeves that'll fit you." She pushed her chair back and started to get up.

"Hang on, now, honey," Mr. Kincaid said, putting a hand on her arm. They sat together at one end of the table, not opposite each other like you'd expect in a TV sitcom family. "You can get Joe set up after dinner, but don't you think you should finish eating first?"

She laughed, sat down again, and picked up her fork. "I get impulsive," she told Joe. "But as soon as we're done here, we'll find you a shirt. And don't worry about the jeans," she went on, forestalling his next, clearly futile objection. "Jeans are fine. You'll be sitting down anyway. Nobody will see."

And that had been that. He'd done the breakfast dishes, all right, but after that, he'd gone to church, and he'd been going ever since, when he stayed with them. And doing the dishes, too. With Alyssa, which he could have done without. Being alone with her made him nervous, but Mrs. Kincaid had been clear on that, too.

"I'd be some kind of hostess if I invited you and then made you do all my housework for me, wouldn't I?" she'd said with a laugh the first time he'd offered. "But you can help Alyssa."

So that had become Joe's chore on Kincaid holidays, which had given him the idea for the present he'd thought up for Susie this year, which he was pretty proud of. When it was his turn to distribute his gifts on this fifteenth Christmas afternoon, he handed her a long white envelope, then sat back and watched a little nervously while she opened it.

"I know you've always said you didn't need it," he said as she unfolded a certificate for a year's worth of weekly housekeeping service, "but I needed to give it, to both of you. To say—" He shrugged. "To say thanks."

42

It had occurred to him over that busy wedding weekend a month earlier, watching her move from one set of endless tasks to another, that the reason she'd always declined Alec's offers of a housekeeper wasn't that she enjoyed housework, because who did? In a flash of insight that had left him astonished that he hadn't figured it out sooner, he'd realized that she hadn't wanted to embarrass Dave by accepting something from her son that her husband couldn't provide, that she didn't want him to think that the life he'd given her wasn't good enough. But if it came from Joe instead, he thought—he hoped—that it would be different.

"It's not even that much work anymore," Susie said. "Not with just Dave and me."

"Seems to me that everybody should get to retire sometime," Joe said. "And the lady I found to do it, she's a single mom. She needs the work."

That did the trick, just as he'd planned. "Well," she said, putting the certificate carefully back into her envelope, "I'd better not say no, then, had I?" She got up, came over and bent to give him a kiss on the cheek. "I think I should just say thank you, sweetheart. That was very thoughtful of you. Very sweet."

He could feel a lump forming in his throat, to his horror. Luckily, Dixie came to his rescue.

"I said you'd be a catch," she pronounced, "and dang if I wasn't right, wouldn't you say, Desiree? Don't you think some girl's going to get mighty lucky one of these days?"

"Rae's not going to agree with you," Joe said, the vulnerable moment past. "She doesn't think I'm good with women."

"Hmm. Maybe slow to warm up," Rae said. "You're all right once you get there." She smiled at her business partner. "I've got no complaints these days."

"And I think you're just fine," Susie said. She reached to adjust the shoulder of the gray sweater she'd knitted him, along with the ones she'd made for her sons. "I messed up on this seam. You need to give it back to me later today, and I'll redo it."

43

She'd always given him clothes, ever since that first year. He hadn't expected anything, had felt awkward enough sitting around the Christmas tree with the family, still in his borrowed shirt. But when Susie had handed out her presents, two squashy packages had landed in his lap.

"Because you need a Tall size. Those things you have are too short," Susie had explained when he'd ripped the tissue paper open to reveal a pair of new Hanes T-shirts, one each in navy blue and gray. He'd have felt embarrassed about that, like a charity case, especially when he'd opened his other package and found three pairs of socks, except that she'd just given her sons the same things.

"Just be glad she didn't give you underwear," Alec said with a grin. "It's been known to happen. Nothing like wearing boxers picked out by your mother."

"If women didn't buy underwear for men," Susie retorted, "half the men in America would wear them until they couldn't tell which ones were the leg holes. I have to sneak in and throw out Dave's old things while he's not looking."

"Because they're not comfortable until they're broken in," Dave protested. "And who's going to see them? A little hole or two never hurt anything."

"I see them," Susie answered. "I'm not having my husband walk around with holes in his socks, looking like he has a wife who doesn't care enough about him to notice. And you can just live with it."

She was still giving Joe shirts. This year, she'd upgraded to sweaters, though Susie wasn't a very good knitter, he thought privately. The shoulders *were* pretty funky. But he'd put on his new gray sweater with pleasure all the same, because she'd made it for him.

Alec and Rae's presents were the last, at Alec's insistence. He'd started with gifts for his father, his brother, and Joe. Joe got an atomic clock with a weather station, which he appreciated. You always needed to know the weather. Alec gave regular things, practical things, the same kinds of things Joe gave him.

Christmas presents for men seemed kind of stupid to him anyway. If he or Alec needed something, why not just go ahead and buy it, and know they were getting exactly what they wanted? What was the point of buying the other guy something, having to guess what he might like—because there wasn't anything Alec actually needed that Joe could buy him, or vice versa—and wrapping it up in pretty paper?

But the Kincaids always gave presents, so Joe did it too. He'd done a wool stadium blanket in the green-and-red Kincaid tartan for both Alec and Gabe this year, which he'd thought had been all right. A blanket was useful, at least. That was his idea of a present.

He'd veered a bit from the norm with Dave's gift, though: Sacramento Kings season tickets. They had a lousy record, but Dave was loyal, and he'd been pleased, Joe could tell. So Joe had been happy he'd had the thought.

Women were different, of course. Women liked presents, and it had always seemed to Joe that the more useless the present was, the better they liked it. Well, they liked to feel special, and he had no problem with that.

Sure enough, it was the women's turn for Alec's gifts now, and Alyssa and Mira were exclaiming as they opened their gifts, lifted the lids of identical flat black velvet boxes, and each drew out a pendant hung from a gold chain. They weren't identical, but they were the same basic idea: one single, large, lustrous pearl, nestled in a curving disc of gold that looked like some sort of shell, or a leaf. Something delicate and pretty, anyway.

"Thank you," Mira breathed. "It's so beautiful." She held it up for Gabe to see, and he turned a rueful gaze on his brother.

"Rae said it would be all right to give your wife jewelry," Alec said, clearly reading his twin's mind. "Don't blame me. I asked her. I checked."

"Are you kidding?" Mira said happily. "I'm not giving this back. Oh, he means it might hurt your feelings." She turned

45

to Gabe with a bit of a stricken look, but Joe noticed that she was clutching her necklace pretty tightly all the same.

"Never mind." Gabe was already taking it from her, fastening the clasp behind her neck, and her hand went up to stroke the smooth surfaces as if she couldn't help herself. "You just consider it a fringe benefit of being married to me. We'll leave it at that."

"Oh, guys. Wow." Alyssa had her own necklace on. She jumped up and went to the big mirror over the cabinet next to the front door to check out her reflection. "It's gorgeous, and I can wear it with anything. Where did you find them, Rae?"

"It wasn't me," she said. "I had nothing to do with it. That was your brother all the way. That's from Tahiti, via Paris. He didn't even show me until after he'd done it, after he'd come back from his mysterious errand. I thought maybe he was buying me a pony, but," she sighed, "turns out not."

"Mmm," Alec said, smiling at her. "I may have got you something too. We'll get to that. But meanwhile … I've got a couple more things under here." He crouched beside the tree, fished out two slightly larger flat packages wrapped in shimmering paper that had an opalescent quality all its own. He handed one to his mother, one to Rae's grandmother. "A variation on the theme."

Both women made a fuss, of course, the same fuss they'd made over everything they'd received that day. Women couldn't just open a present and look at it and say thanks. They had to make a whole production out of it.

"What beautiful paper, isn't it, Dixie?" Susie slid a fingernail under the tape, folded the wrapping paper and set it aside carefully.

"It sure is," Dixie agreed. "That's fancy."

"If I'd known you were going to be so easily pleased," Alec complained, "I'd just have given you the box. Come on, open them."

They were already there. "Oh, my," Susie said helplessly. "Oh, my. Alec."

46

Two simple, perfect strands of pearls, their luster core-deep, were held up by two sets of hands, turned in the light.

"Honey," Dixie said to Rae, fumbling with the clasp until Alec came over and opened it, settled the strand around her wrinkled neck, and fastened it for her, "I think you caught yourself a live one."

"I think I did," Rae laughed.

"The ladies at church aren't going to know what hit them," Dixie said happily, reaching for her reading glasses in her purse, then lifting the necklace to take a better look. "These are real pearls, aren't they?"

"That's what the man said," Alec told her with a smile. "Got to decorate my favorite ladies."

"Sibling wars won yet again, by a mile," Alyssa sighed. "I'd complain that you cheated, Alec, but you might take my necklace away."

"Oh, honey," her mother hastened to assure her, "I loved your present too. I don't need anything more at all to be happy today. You all know that. I have everything a woman could want."

"And now your mother's crying," Dave said in resignation. He put an arm around his wife, but he was looking misty-eyed too, Joe noticed. It wasn't the first time he'd seen Dave Kincaid cry, either. He didn't actually sob, not that Joe had seen, but he definitely teared up from time to time, and it didn't even seem to bother him.

"Got one more here. You want your present now?" Alec asked his wife. "Or later, when we're alone?"

"You've got to be kidding," Alyssa said. "After all this, you think we're going to miss out on the chance to watch her open it? I can only imagine what it is. Probably Queen Elizabeth's spare tiara or something."

"She wouldn't sell it to me. I had to go for something else." Alec handed the package to Rae, and this one wasn't small at all.

"Alec," she complained. "I gave you a *scarf*."

"And I love my scarf," he assured her. "It's a great scarf."

47

"I have a really bad feeling," she said, her fingers poised to open the package, "that this isn't a scarf."

"*Open* it," Alyssa said.

"Save that pretty paper," Susie urged, and Alec dropped his head into his hands and groaned.

"Mom," he said. "I'll buy you a package of special paper. I'll buy you *two* packages of special paper. Desiree does not have to save the paper."

But Rae hadn't even heard, it was clear. She had the box open, and was sitting staring at what was inside.

"Let's see," Dixie urged.

Still wordless, she turned the deep blue velvet case around and held it up. And Joe could see why she hadn't said anything.

It was a necklace. More pearls. Two rows of smaller spheres at the top fastened with a diamond clasp, gathered by three triangular panels at each side, their surface made up of more diamonds and each panel larger than the one above, finally falling into three graduated rows of pearls below. And by the time it got to the largest, the ones at the bottom, they were pretty damn spectacular.

"Oh," Susie breathed, and that was about all there was to say about that.

"I'd say you did good," Gabe told his brother, and Joe had to agree.

"Alec," Desiree said. "You didn't buy this at a store."

"Let's just say I called ahead." He took the thing carefully out of its case and put it around her neck. "Merry Christmas." He gave her a kiss. "You're beautiful. Thanks for marrying me."

And that made Susie cry again, joining Mira, but then, Mira had cried about five times already that day. Joe guessed that pregnancy really did make women emotional, because he didn't remember her crying this much the year before. She'd cried at Alec and Rae's wedding, but everybody'd done that, everybody except him.

Of course, Rae had to stand up and take her turn looking in the mirror. "I am seriously overdressed for this event," she

48

said. She was wearing camel-colored slacks and a brown sweater, and the pearls stood out against the knit fabric as if they were lit from within. "We're going to have to get opera tickets or something, Alec."

"No, we're not," he said. "I hate opera. I'll take you out to dinner someplace really nice, how's that?"

"It had better be someplace *really* nice," she said, fingering the rows of pearls.

"I can probably manage that. How about coming over and giving me another kiss? Don't I get a thank-you?"

"You get a thank-you," she assured him. "You just needed to let me look first." And he did get it.

And, Joe thought, he'd got it wrong again, or rather, he hadn't dared to get it right. He'd thought hard, as he thought every year, about what to get Alyssa. He'd wanted to give her jewelry, because he knew as well as Alec did that that was what you bought a beautiful woman. He wasn't the most romantic guy, but even he knew that. Jewelry was the best, when it was appropriate. Which it wasn't.

But seeing the look on Alyssa's face as she admired Rae's necklace, he wished he'd forgotten about what was appropriate and done it. He hadn't made quite as much from their partnership as Alec had—the CEO always got the most, that was the way it worked—but he wasn't too far off. So, yeah, he could have bought Alyssa just about any necklace in the world. If it had been right. Which it wasn't.

So he'd given her a box instead. Well, not just a box. A carefully prepared case of emergency supplies for her car, because he'd seen her car, and at some point, she was going to need emergency supplies. He knew she wouldn't have the right things in there, so he'd given them to her. A complete tool kit, flares, a red signal flag for her antenna, a big Maglite flashlight and a smaller one, extra batteries, a wind-up flashlight/radio combination in case the batteries didn't work, a first aid kit, a compact sleeping bag in case she broke down someplace cold. Everything he could think of, and he'd had the case specially made to hold it all, with dividers, so she could find things fast in an emergency.

It had been too big to put under the tree. He'd had to go back into Alec's bedroom for it, when it was time.

"You're clearly thinking I'm going to break down at any moment," she'd protested when she'd gone through it all.

"Anyone can have an accident," he'd said. "Anyone can have an emergency. I just thought it was better if you were prepared. Because do you have that stuff?"

"Well, no," she'd admitted. "I have a flashlight. Not sure if the batteries work, though. I haven't checked in a while."

Which had made everyone laugh, and which had given Joe a little glow of satisfaction, because he'd been right, she'd needed it all, and having it would make her safer. It might not be the most romantic present, but it was what she needed, and didn't that count?

So, yeah. He'd felt pretty proud of it, but it wasn't a pearl necklace.

Moving On Up

"I have an announcement to make."

That was Alec, and Alyssa looked up from her heaping plate of Christmas dinner. She was *definitely* going to have to take a walk tonight. "Don't tell me," she said. "You guys are pregnant too."

"No," Alec said with a laugh. "No, Desiree says it's not time yet. And as you all know, she's the boss."

"I am not the boss," she protested. "You're the boss."

"Maybe at work. *Maybe*. Huh, Joe?"

"Maybe," Joe said, his little smile crooking the corner of his mouth. "Technically."

"Announcement?" Dave reminded his son.

"Yes. Announcement. This one will make you happy, Dad," Alec said. "This one's just for you, your real Christmas present. You know that foundation we set up?"

"The one Desiree set up, you mean?" Dave asked, a decided twinkle in his eyes now.

"Go on, rub it in. Yes. That one. We figured out—all right, *she* figured out that for now, we shouldn't try to hire a whole staff and all that, eat it up with expenses. She says we should wait till we've built up the capital. But we've made our first big donation, to Project Second Chance."

"What's that?" Mira asked.

"Foster kids," Dave said. "Right?"

"Right," Alec said. "They do mentoring and college scholarships and support and all sorts of good things. And they're based right there in San Francisco, so Rae could do her due diligence without leaving me lonely."

51

"Desiree's idea, I assume," Dave said.

"No," Rae put in. "No, Joe's, actually. I knew I wanted to do something along those lines, but I didn't even know they existed. Turns out Joe's a donor."

"Good for you, Joe," Susie said. "I didn't know that."

"Rae's doing more than I am," he said, his expression even more wooden than usual. "She's the one getting involved."

"They've asked me to join the board starting in July," Rae explained. "And since I'd looked over all their statements pretty thoroughly …" She shrugged and laughed. "You know me. I'm going to want to tell them how to do things anyway, I might as well put myself in a position to do it. Although it's really Joe who should be on the board. He's the one with the history."

"I'm not good at being on boards," Joe said. "Not too good in meetings."

"No, that's true," Alec agreed. "You're not. Give the money and go away, that was my idea too. But of course Desiree had to get involved. Such a managing woman." He sighed.

"Oh, you love it," she said.

"Mmm. Could be."

"But," she said, serious again, "they do really good work. And oh!" She jumped in her chair. "I just had a thought. About you, Alyssa. Oh, this could be perfect."

"Me? Me what?"

"You want to do something different, right? You said, something that mattered. I don't know what that is, but there's a job there, at Second Chance, that I think would be just right for you." She was getting really animated now. "They've got an opening for an Assistant Director of Development. They're planning to hire in the New Year. What do you think?"

"Uh …" Alyssa was taken aback. "In San Francisco?"

"Well, yes. You said you were looking for a change. Maybe not that much of a change, though?"

"No," Alyssa said. "No, actually, it sounds good." When she'd graduated from high school, she'd wanted nothing more than to move away from her family, get the chance to be her own person. Live a little, not be the preacher's daughter anymore, not be expected to set an example. San Diego State had been the answer to a very unholy prayer, and she'd never got farther north than LA in all the years since.

But now, the idea of being closer to her brothers, her parents was … good. She had no real ties in southern California to hold her, nothing but friends she didn't see enough. Too much sprawl, too much traffic, too much time at work, lives that were full of jobs and partners and, increasingly, kids.

"Why not?" she decided. "Why not move? Except, well, I don't have any background with nonprofits. All I have is sales. What does an … an Assistant Director of Development do?"

Rae waved a neatly manicured hand. "This is what I mean by perfect. It's sales. It's fundraising. You could do it with your eyes closed. All that Kincaid charm and looks and brains—you were *born* to do this job." She laughed with obvious excitement, then grew serious again. "If you're all right with the money, that is. It probably wouldn't pay half of what you were earning. That could be a real roadblock. But down the road, you can do all right in development. Don't get me wrong, you wouldn't get rich, but you could do all right."

"Call it an investment in a career change, you think?" Alyssa asked, beginning to get excited herself. "Maybe so. Maybe. I have some money saved."

Rae smiled with satisfaction, and Alyssa's parents were following right along and smiling, too. Right up their alley, and Alyssa realized that the idea of doing a job that would please them didn't make her uncomfortable. She seemed to have lost the need to rebel for rebellion's sake, which meant she must be maturing after all. Who knew?

"I can make a call right away," Rae said. "If you want me to. Just let me know."

That caused Alyssa's first moment of hesitation. "I'm not sure. I know it's all about who you know, but having them know I'm Alec's sister—wouldn't that put both of you into an awkward position if it didn't work out? Especially with you on the board? Nepotism, and all that."

"Hmm," Rae considered. "Probably true, but without experience in the field," she added with her usual frankness, "you won't have much of a shot unless you get a push from somebody."

"I'll do it," Joe put in. "I'll call, if you want to go for it. I know the Development Director a bit. Just let me know, and I'll make the call. Rae's right, they do good work."

Which was why they got his money every year. Not because Project Second Chance had helped him, but because they hadn't. Because he could have used the help, and he wanted to give it to some other kid. Something they could count on, something that wouldn't get their hopes up only to dash them again.

He'd thought he'd had that something once or twice. One time, for a little while, he'd really thought so. On that day towards the end of his sophomore year, especially, when Mr. Wilson, his Computer Science teacher, had asked him to come by after school to meet with him.

Joe had hesitated. "If I miss the bus," he said, reluctant as always to reveal any details about his life, "I don't have a way to get back." He didn't say "home," because the foster home wasn't home. Not this one, and not the one before that, or the one before that either.

"Right. I should have thought of that," Mr. Wilson said. "Come by at lunch, then."

Joe wanted to ask him if there was something wrong, but he didn't. His heart sank, though, because his Programming class—well, going to A-Tech at all—was the best thing in his life, and if he'd messed that up ...

He tried to forget it. *Focus on now.* Pre-Calculus, AP Chemistry. He did the work, he paid attention—well, he did the best he could, with the long list of things that could have got him kicked out running through his mind. But wouldn't it have been the dean or the assistant principal talking to him, not a teacher? He shoved the thought away again. *Focus.*

Lunch period came at last, and he was hesitating at the door of Mr. Wilson's classroom.

"Come in." His teacher waved him to a chair next to his desk, pointed to his own sandwich, neatly encased in wax paper and sitting on the neatly arranged desktop. "Hope you brought your lunch, because I hate to eat alone."

Joe pulled out his first peanut butter on white bread and took a bite, barely sparing a thought for the embarrassing meagerness of his lunch, because as always, he was hungry.

Mr. Wilson worked on his own turkey on whole wheat for a minute before he began.

"First of all," he said, "I want to assure you that this is just an idea. And if you aren't interested, if it doesn't sound good to you, that's fine. It'll make no difference to how you do in my class. You're the best student I've ever had, and if that's it, that's plenty."

Joe stopped chewing.

"How long have you been in foster care?" Mr. Wilson asked now.

Joe swallowed. "Two years." This was either very good, or it was very bad. "Almost."

"And how many foster homes?"

"Five. Counting the short ones."

"And how many days have you been absent this semester?"

Joe could feel himself turning red, but he looked back and answered. "Six."

"Because?"

"Things happened."

"Joe." Mr. Wilson put his sandwich down. "I've got a reason for asking. I won't be passing along anything you say here. Because?"

"Fights, mostly," Joe said reluctantly. "Getting kicked out."

Mr. Wilson nodded. "Did you start them? The fights?"

"Well, yeah. If I had to. I mean, if something was happening." Like when he'd heard Lenny crying and pleading from the next room, the last time, and had ended up breaking the door down. He'd been kicked out, but so had Craig and Ronnie, Lenny's tormentors. And Craig had left with a broken nose, Ronnie with a black eye. And a few other problems, too.

"Do you have to fight?" Mr. Wilson asked. "Do you need to?"

"No." He knew what Mr. Wilson meant. He'd known plenty of people who enjoyed hurting other people. Starting with Dean, his mother's boyfriend, and going right on from there.

Another nod. "What about alcohol? Marijuana?"

The heat was rising again. "Yeah. Some."

"Willing to stop? Need help to stop?"

"Uh ... I don't know. Yeah, willing to stop." He'd like to stop. But it helped. It took the edge off, and he had a lot of edge.

"Need help to stop. Got it."

"Uh, sir? Is the school kicking me out? I mean, thinking about it? Because I can stop. I can do better." He clamped his mouth shut so he couldn't say any more. So he couldn't beg. The Advanced Technologies Academy didn't just have the best test scores in Las Vegas. It had the best test scores in the entire state, and it was his only ticket. If the day Joe had found out that his dad was dead had been the worst day of his life, the day he'd got the letter from A-Tech had been the best. It was all he had, and he'd screwed it up. How could he have been so *stupid*?

Mr. Wilson was holding up a hand now. "No. Wait. I'm asking if you'd like another place to stay." He laughed a little, looked down at his sandwich. "Go figure, I'm nervous. I'm asking if you'd like a guardian until you graduate from high school. We'd have to petition the court for it," he warned as Joe continued to stare, "and your mother could fight it. It is your mother, isn't it?"

Joe swallowed. "Yeah. But she probably won't. She probably wouldn't."

"Does she have an addiction?"

How did he know so much? "Yeah," Joe said desperately. *Please don't ask any more.*

"So what do you think? You've got a fine mind. You know what they say, it's a terrible thing to waste, and I don't want to see you waste it. It won't be forever," Mr. Wilson warned. "But we can get you through high school. You stay on the right track, no reason you can't get a great scholarship, go on from there."

"You mean, with you?" Joe asked slowly, hardly daring to believe. "At your house?"

"Yes. And I should tell you," Mr. Wilson said, stolid himself now, "I'm gay. And that has nothing to do with this, but you should know, in case it makes a difference."

"But this isn't about ..." Joe went ahead, because the only way to deal with things was head-on. "It's not about sex?" That was what it had been about with Lenny, and it was one reason he knew how to fight. Because when you were fourteen and skinny and in foster care, you learned how to fight.

"No." His teacher looked straight at him. "It's not about sex. And I can promise you that it'll never be about sex. I have sexual partners, yes, but they're adults. I'm not interested in children, and I'm not interested in you, not like that. But I need to know that you'll go to counseling, and that you'll stay clean. I'm not having anyone in my house who's doing anything illegal. That's a deal-breaker."

A man always keeps his word. Joe could see his dad as if he were standing there, frowning down at him when Joe had asked if he could skip the Boy Scout service project he'd promised to help out with. And about a hundred other times, too. *A man always keeps his word.*

He straightened up in his chair, looked Mr. Wilson in the eye, and answered. "I can stay clean."

New City, Same Old Me

Alyssa stood shivering in a piercing mid-January wind, looking across a broad stretch of asphalt at the unlovely sight of Burlingame's Auto Row, where she and Joe were spending a winter Sunday on what had to rank high on the list of life's least-fun experiences: used-car shopping. They were standing outside, instead of in the nice toasty dealership, because Joe had just made her walk out.

She hadn't planned on buying a car, that was for sure. That had been no part of her new frugal life plan. But once again, life—and her bossy brother—had forced her hand.

Alec had frowned when he'd felt the jerk and shudder her little car had given as she'd reversed out of her parking spot in her Santa Monica apartment complex for the last time, exactly one week earlier.

"What the hell *is* that?" he complained when it happened again as she turned out of the lot.

"Oh," she said, tensing a bit through the next stoplight, then relaxing as they got through the moment, "it does that. It'll be fine once we get to cruising speed on the freeway. It's just when it starts out, cold or something."

"Cars do not just 'do' that. It's not cold. It has to be in the sixties out there."

"You know." She took a hand off the wheel and waved it airily. "When the engine's cold. When it's starting up."

"Did you take it to the shop?" he persisted. "What did they say?"

"Not yet." She merged onto the freeway, thankfully moving much faster than usual at all of seven-thirty on a

58

Sunday morning. Alec—and Joe—had flown down the previous morning. The two most overpriced movers in America, but when Alec had heard about her plans to tow a U-Haul trailer up I-5, he'd barely bothered to insist, he'd just told her he'd be showing up. And even though it galled Alyssa that her brother still thought she was that helpless, she'd been grateful for his help, and Joe's, too. Because, she'd thought privately, she really *had* been nervous about the trailer thing, and moving vans were expensive.

"Not yet?" Alec reminded her when she didn't go on. "What do you mean, not yet?"

"I mean not yet. Because it's fine now, see?" Which it was, now that they were doing 65. And besides, she hadn't wanted to hear what the mechanic would say. Anyway, all cars got quirks when they got old, didn't they? Just like people.

Two hours later, though, after a delay for some road construction that had had the car jerking again, Alec told her, "Pull into the rest stop up there."

"Men," she sighed, putting on her blinker so Joe, following in the truck, could see. "You should have gone before we left the house."

Alec wasn't listening. As soon as she'd pulled into a spot in front of the restrooms, he was out of the car and motioning to Joe, just jumping down from the cab of the truck.

"You know cars a lot better than I do," Alec told him. "Come drive this, tell me what you think."

Joe raised an eyebrow, but didn't comment, just held out a broad palm for the keys, which Alyssa surrendered reluctantly. He squeezed himself into the driver's seat, looking much too big for her tiny subcompact, backed out with another jerk that had Alyssa wincing, and did a circuit of the lot before pulling back into the same spot.

He got out and slammed the door, handed the keys back to Alyssa. "It's your transmission. Pretty obvious. Didn't the shop tell you that?"

She sighed. "I didn't take it in yet. It's just got a couple hiccups. You guys need to *relax.*"

"It's not a hiccup when you're merging onto the freeway, and then all of a sudden you're not," Joe said. "It's an accident. How long has that been happening, that rough shift?"

"I don't know," she said reluctantly. "Before Christmas, anyway. Maybe a month?"

"A *month?*"

"I had a lot going on," she defended herself. Like losing her job, and looking for a new one, and interviewing in San Francisco, and getting ready to move to a brand-new city, which had involved a drastic downsizing in her life. You could call that a lot going on.

"Think we can make it?" Alec asked Joe. "Or buy a car right here, do you think?"

"I can't buy a car right here," Alyssa protested. "I can't afford a new car. OK, maybe there's something wrong. If there is, I'll get it fixed. Happy?"

"A new transmission's going to run you a couple thousand," Joe said. "More than it's worth." He eyed her little yellow car with a cynical eye that made Alyssa want to give it a reassuring pat.

"We don't even know that it needs one," she said.

"True," Joe said. "Not until they run the codes. We could try having them flush the fluids, see if that helps. When was the last time you had them checked? Your fluids?"

"*I* don't know. How would I know that?"

"You don't keep a record in your owner's manual?"

"Does anybody really do that? Anybody but the seriously anally retentive?"

He smiled a little. "I do."

"Annnddd ... my point's made. Bet Alec doesn't."

"Well, no, but I have a Mercedes mechanic making some pretty good boat payments on my dime," Alec said. "I let him keep a record."

"Sure you do. You've got people for that."

Joe focused on the matter at hand. "We'll take it to a shop." He pulled his phone out of his pocket, did a quick search. "Another hour, looks like. Should be all right that far on the freeway, keep the speed even. No hard braking if you can help it, no hard accelerating, keep it in the same gear. We'll get the codes run, get the fluid changed, see where we are."

They'd made it to San Francisco a bit later than they'd intended, but they'd made it. And after that, Alyssa really started getting bossed around, because Rae came over to help with the move-in.

Well, "help" might be the wrong word. She actually just plain took over. Starting with going out to buy new shelf paper to line Alyssa's dresser drawers, and moving on to unpacking all her boxes.

"I can do it tomorrow," Alyssa had said in a futile bid for independence. "If you'll just help me get the sheets on the bed and my bathroom stuff unpacked, I've got plenty of time for the rest. I don't start work for another week."

"You don't want to spend days stumbling over boxes," Rae said. "We'll do it now. It's just one room." She looked around the large but otherwise completely unimpressive bedroom, the off-white walls with a scuff here and there, the uninspiring gray carpeting, clearly chosen to hide wear but losing the battle, the stiff, ugly beige drapes across an aluminum-framed window with a view of the apartment house across the street. "It'll look a lot better when we have it all set up," she said, which made Alec, humping two boxes of books through the door, give a dubious snort. "We'll get you unpacked, and the guys can take the empty boxes back with the truck, get them out of here. And I'll bet Joe can hang those for you, too," she added as he came in with an armload of framed pictures, the only ones Alyssa had kept, wrapped in a moving blanket, and set them on the bare mattress.

"Joe doesn't have to hang my pictures," Alyssa tried to protest, but it was like arguing with the tide.

"Sure I do," Joe said. "If Rae says I have to." He bowed his head in mock servitude. "Just have to go home and grab my tools."

"Need any help?" Alyssa's new roommate Sherry had come to lean against the doorway, which made the room

61

seriously crowded. A curly-haired, petite brunette, Sherry had a personality that belied her small stature, and Alyssa had known almost as soon as Sherry had opened the door to her on the fourth day of her so-far-disastrous housing hunt that they were Meant to Be. Although the way Sherry was looking at Joe right now was giving her some second thoughts.

"Want a ride?" Sherry asked Joe. "I'm free."

"Sure," he said, and Alyssa scowled. "Soon as we finish unloading."

"What's this?" Rae asked, holding up a threadbare item from the box she was emptying into Alyssa's second dresser drawer. "You can't mean to keep it. It's a rag."

Alyssa whipped it out of her hand, stuffed it in the drawer. "Just something I like."

She dared a quick look at Joe's face, saw him looking back. If Joe ever looked startled, he was looking startled now, and she knew he'd recognized it, even with the white lettering peeled away in spots. *Eielson AFB.* The shirt she'd worn until she'd worn holes in it. The shirt she had never been able to throw away, because it would have felt like throwing away Joe.

"Maybe you wouldn't mind looking at the dripping faucet in my bathtub, too," Sherry suggested to Joe, oblivious to the moment. "If you're handy, and if it wouldn't be too much trouble. I'd really appreciate it. I've told the management company twice, but they don't seem too eager to hop on it. And it's so annoying when you're lying there in the tub, you know?" She gave him a smile that had Alyssa seriously reconsidering her housing decision. "Listening to that drip-drip-drip, just when you're getting all warm and relaxed."

"I should be able to fix that for you," Joe said, and he looked, Alyssa thought irritably, like he was all set to help Sherry relax, too. He wasn't offering to help *her* relax. He was just nagging her about her car, exactly like Alec.

"Next weekend, Liss," Alec had said when they'd gone out for well-deserved pizza and beer after the move, including Sherry, because Alyssa hadn't exactly been able to get out of inviting her, "I'm taking you to buy a new car. I'd do it this week, but I've got too much going on. And if you can't afford it," he went on over her protest, "I'll buy it. You heard what the man said. A new transmission, or a new car. And that car isn't worth putting a new transmission into, would you say, Joe?"

"No," Joe said. "You need a new car."

"All right," Alyssa agreed, her heart sinking at the thought of the hit to her already-stretched budget. "But I'll buy my own car, thank you very much."

"Call it a Christmas present," Alec coaxed. "From Desiree and me."

"Wow," Sherry said. "Want to buy me a new car too?"

Alyssa ignored her. "No. Thank you, I guess, but no. You're bad enough now, Alec. If you buy my new car, you'll think you can tell me how to drive it. You'll be asking me if I got the oil changed. You *already* ask me if I've had the oil changed. But if you buy my car, you'll think you have the *right* to ask, and what's worse, *I'll* feel like you have the right to ask. Forget that. If I wanted a guy to boss me around, I'd get married."

"Ha," Alec said. "Trust me, that's not what happens when you get married."

"She's right," Rae said. "It's better for her to buy her own car. As long as you're not destitute, it's better to be independent. But somebody should go with you, Alyssa. Car shopping works a whole lot better with two people. Not Alec, because he's not a good enough negotiator. You're not," she went on as he opened his mouth to object. "You either get impatient and pay the money, or you get impatient and fire the person, or you walk out. I should go."

"Or me," Joe put in.

"Hmm." Rae eyed him speculatively. "Yeah. Even better. Because I *am* a good negotiator, but you know cars, and the car-dealership business has to be the last bastion of 1950sstyle male chauvinism in America. I could probably get the same deal you could, but it would take me a whole lot longer."

"I'll bet you *are* pretty handy to have along," Sherry said to Joe. "I'll bet they take one look at you and drop the price."

"Joe doesn't want to take me car shopping," Alyssa said, having some more second thoughts about her choice of roommates. The apartment was cheap, but the price was looking way too high. She'd always known Joe dated other women, and it had always hurt. She didn't need it shoved in her face. "He already spent his whole weekend moving me. He's supposed to spend next weekend used-car shopping with me? Maybe Joe's got a life."

"You got a life, Joe?" Alec asked him.

"Nope."

So here they were, one week later, at their fourth dealership of the day, having just done their third walk-out, and Alyssa was getting more than grouchy.

"Is this about which car?" she asked Joe, wrapping her arms around herself for warmth. "I could have told you which one I wanted without coming all the way out here. The dark-blue one."

"We can get a better deal on the other one," he said. "Only got ten thousand more miles on the clock, a year older, and it's sat on the lot for three months, which means they want to get rid of it that much more."

"It's *beige,*" she complained. "Inside and outside."

"I think if you look at the sheet," he said, a smile threatening, "you'll find that it's gold, with cloth upholstery in—" He looked down at the printed list of specifications he held in his hand. "Winter wheat."

"Winter wheat my—foot. I know beige when I see it. And I am not driving a beige car. I'm not poor enough yet to have to drive a beige car."

"All right. But I'm warning you, we'll be walking out another time."

And they did, but Joe ended up with a deal that the salesman complained his manager had barely approved.

64

"Good thing Ford's paying you to keep the doors open, then," Joe said calmly, which made the salesman's relentless good humor slip for a moment. And then Joe negotiated her trade-in, and refused to allow the finance guy to even go into his spiel for undercoating and "stain protection," which Alyssa appreciated even more, because she was hungry and tired and ready to be done.

And at the end of it, she had a new car, and it wasn't even beige.

Not a Date

"I've got a new car," Alyssa said, standing next to the dark-blue compact, reaching a hand out to stroke the hood as if she couldn't help herself. She laughed, and the happiness in it rang out loud and clear. "I honestly wasn't sure it was going to happen. You had *me* convinced we were walking out without it."

"It was always going to happen." He had to smile back, she was so excited over this boring little sedan. Well, it was a major improvement, although if he'd had his way, he'd have put her into something a whole lot better. Well, if he'd had his way, he'd have put her into his own car, and he'd have kept her there.

He'd showed up as agreed at ten that morning to take her car shopping, had rung the bell down at the street, waited a while, then rung it again. At last, he heard her voice on the intercom. "Joe?"

He spoke into the brass-plated grille. "Yeah."

"Shoot," he heard. "Come up. Sorry." The door buzzed, and he shoved it open, climbed the three flights to her place, already resigned to a wait.

It wasn't Alyssa who opened the apartment door. It was a guy. A barefoot guy, tall and thin and with serious bedhead, wearing skinny hipster jeans and a slim-cut black button-down shirt. A guy who'd got out of bed not very long ago, wearing the clothes from the night before.

"Hey," he said. "Come on in."

Alyssa came out of her bedroom looking flustered and ... strange. "Sorry," she said. "I haven't got in the bathroom yet. I need a minute."

Joe looked between her and the guy. He had no right to be jealous, and he knew it. He *knew* it. Her sex life was no business of his. But he wanted to shove the guy right out the door and keep on shoving. At a minimum. He pushed his hands into his jacket pockets and reminded himself to breathe.

The bathroom door opened on a cloud of steam and Sherry came out, tightening the sash on a very thin blue bathrobe.

"Oh. Joe," she said, faltering to a stop. "I didn't know you'd be here today."

"Hi," he said, carefully not checking out the bathrobe.

Sherry recovered her balance pretty fast. "Bathroom's all yours," she told Alyssa, then looked at her more closely and laughed. "Great hat."

Alyssa stared at her blankly for a moment, then put her hand to her head. Her mouth opened and shut again, and she snatched the thing off her head, went to her bedroom door and chucked the hat inside.

"Five minutes," she told Joe, ducking into the bathroom and shutting the door behind her.

"Oh, did you meet Jonathan?" Sherry asked Joe. "Joe, Jonathan. Jonathan, Joe. Want some coffee?" she asked the guy—Jonathan.

"Yeah," he said. "Or we could go out to breakfast, if you want."

She perked up. "Breakfast would be good. I'll get changed."

Ah. Sherry's … guest. Joe felt the tension leaving his body like air from a balloon.

Jonathan flopped onto the couch and picked up a magazine from the coffee table. "Could be a while," he told Joe. "In my experience."

Joe was pretty sure he was right, so he took a seat in an armchair. It wasn't too long, though, before Alyssa was back out of the bathroom door again, and he rose to his feet.

"Ready," she said. "I just have to get my boots."

"And a coat," Joe said. "It's cold out there."

She came out of her room a minute later carrying a pair of low red boots with pointed toes and Western tooling, perched on the arm of the chair Joe had just vacated to pull them on and zip them up. She was wearing a dusty red quilted coat that hung open over a ribbed dark-blue sweater that matched her eyes and clung to her figure fairly convincingly. And a skirt, a flimsy little gray thing that didn't come close to reaching her knees, and swooped up at the sides quite a few inches too, which hiked up a whole lot more during the boot-fastening exercise.

"Ah …" Joe said, "do you think a skirt is right? I mean, you might want to look more serious."

She looked at him in surprise. "I'm wearing tights," she pointed out. "Almost like pants."

No. A short skirt and sexy little boots weren't like pants. He didn't know what tights had to do with it.

"Besides," she said, "aren't most car salesmen guys?"

"Yeah," Jonathan said. He'd looked up from his magazine to check her out, Joe saw, some of his tension returning despite his best efforts. "They're guys."

"And guys like skirts better, right?"

Joe didn't know about other guys, but he knew he did. And Jonathan apparently did too, because he was nodding agreement.

"Then," she said. "I'll distract them, get them off-balance, and you can look all serious and scary, Joe, and intimidate them. Don't you think?"

"Could work," he said. "Though if you really want to distract them, you should put the bear hat back on."

She burst out laughing, and Jonathan joined in. "Yeah, that was a surprise," he agreed.

"You weren't supposed to see that," Alyssa complained. "It's cold in my room. There's no heat in there. I was waiting for the bathroom, to do my hair and makeup, but Sherry was in there, so I was keeping warm, and I … I forgot."

"Never mind," Joe said. "I might need to see it again, though. The ears were pretty special. Where'd you get that?"

68

"Gabe. He gave it to me for my birthday. He thought it was funny. I found it when I unpacked, and like I said," she shrugged, smiling again, "it's cold in my room. Anyway, you ready to go?"

"Yeah. Good to meet you," Joe told Jonathan. He got a raised hand in return and was thankfully able to leave the guy behind.

"Sounds like the first thing is breakfast," he said when they were descending the flights of dingy stairs. "Because I have a feeling you didn't manage that this morning either."

"I overslept," she admitted. "Well, sort of. I haven't had a roommate for a while, and I forgot how ... awkward it could get at times. They didn't have the door shut, so it seemed like a good idea to wait, but it was kind of a long wait, and then I fell asleep."

"Sherry's got a boyfriend, huh? I wouldn't have guessed that."

She shot him a quick look as he held the front door for her. "Ha. I bet you wouldn't have. And I didn't even tell her how rich you are. She figured that one out later, all by herself, with a little online research. If she'd known you were coming over today, believe me, she would have made sure she didn't have company."

Was she jealous, or was that just wishful thinking on his part? "You're saying I've got a shot there?" he asked, following her to the little yellow compact and holding the door for her once she'd unlocked it.

"You know you do." She scowled at him, then tossed her head so her shiny dark hair bounced before climbing in, and if a person could be said to flounce getting into a car, she flounced. "But she's not your type."

"Oh, I don't know," he mused before he slammed her door shut. He walked around the car and squeezed himself in on his side feeling a whole lot better than he had been a few minutes earlier. "I have a weakness for sassy girls with smart mouths."

"Only because you probably think they need a big strong man to straighten them out," she muttered.

69

"Mmm," he agreed. "That's about it."

No, that was exactly it. Because he wanted to do everything wonderful there was to do with Alec's little sister, and everything nasty there was to do, too. Absolutely everything. There was nothing he hadn't thought of, nothing so dirty that he hadn't done it to her, again and again, in his wild, undisciplined, out-of-control mind. He just hoped she didn't know. Sometimes, when she looked at him, he thought she did. And that thought made him sweat at night as much as the rest of his thoughts did. Well, almost as much.

But he hadn't done any of it. Of course he hadn't done any of it. He'd taken her car shopping. And afterwards, out for a hamburger, because that was what she'd wanted.

"You sure?" he'd asked when they were making plans over the hood of her new car in the dealership's lot. "I know I don't seem like a very classy guy." He ran a hand over his stubbled cheek, cast a glance down at his leather jacket and jeans. "But I could go home and change. And I do occasionally eat piled-up food."

"Piled-up food?"

"You know." He measured serving portions with his hands. "Three sprigs of asparagus on a big white plate, covered up with a tiny piece of meat, a leaf of some bitter thing you wouldn't even eat in a salad on top of that. And then... figs, or organ meat, some lumpy thing, and a sauce with a French name, poured around into patterns that some guy thought looked interesting. Piled-up food. Date food."

She laughed. "I know exactly what you mean. You know what my best date is?"

"No, what?" He smiled down at her. He knew what *his* best date with her would be.

"A sports bar, a beer, and a hamburger," she admitted. "So if it turns out you don't like the guy, at least you get to watch the game."

He laughed. "You just put yourself on every guy's wish list." Like she wasn't there already.

"But I'm freezing," she pointed out. "And I'm starving, and I want a hamburger. You going to take me to get it, or what?"

"I'm going to take you to get it. We'll drop your car off at your place, how's that, and I'll take you in mine. That way you can have as much beer as you want with your hamburger. Unless you want to drive your new car some more," he realized he should add.

"No," she said. "I want you to drive. I want my beer. I think I deserve *two* beers, after all that car shopping."

"I have to say thank you," she said when they were sitting in Chez Maman—hamburgers, but bistro hamburgers, because he did have *some* standards. And she looked so pretty, he hadn't wanted to take her to some dive. "Moving me was bad enough, but taking me used-car shopping on your Sunday? You'd probably have paid money *not* to spend your weekend like that. And I'm not even your sister."

"No," he said. "You're not my sister."

"And another thing," she went on. "This is what I really want to say thanks for." She picked up a french fry, dipped it in mustard, then held it in midair and wrinkled her brow a little. Alyssa could get more expressions out of one face than anyone he knew. "That you didn't do it *for* me," she finally said. "Thank you for that. I assumed that I'd be trailing along while you chose my car for me and told me to like it. That's what I'd have done if Alec had gone with me. Rae would have been more tactful, but same difference."

"It was your car, not mine," he said, gratified that he'd got it right. She'd clearly been surprised when he'd suggested that she search ads for cars she might be interested in, contact the lots and let them know she'd be coming by, and he'd worried that she'd thought it was because he didn't care enough to do it for her. "You know what you like, and I don't. And

71

anyway, things you get for yourself are better. Besides," he said, and he had to smile at her now, "the look on their faces when I got out of the car, after they'd heard your sweet voice on the phone, when they'd been in there rubbing their hands thinking how easy it was going to be ... that was worth the price of admission."

"You think I have a sweet voice?"

He was lousy at compliments, he knew it, but he had to get better, because look at what had just happened. He'd said all that, and her takeaway had been that she had a sweet voice. He had to get better.

"You know you do," he said. "You have a great voice. All lively and ..." He shrugged. "Female," he finished lamely, which wasn't any progress at all.

"As opposed to a male voice," she teased.

"Mmm." He took a bite of burger.

"This was the first time I've ever ridden in your car, do you realize that?" she asked after taking her own bite. "You have a different car than I was thinking."

"What did you think it would be?"

"Hmm." She put her head on one side and considered. "A pickup truck," she admitted, and laughed. "An old, battered one. Not one of those shiny new ones with the crew cab. Which is making me rethink your one-bedroom apartment with the white walls and the board-and-brick bookcases, too. I realize I have no idea at all where you live. Do you have hidden depths, Joe?"

"Maybe." She was making him nervous now, so he shifted back to her. "How about you? What's your dream car?"

"I don't know. I never thought about it."

"Really?"

"I don't think women necessarily spend a lot of time dreaming about cars," she explained. "At least I don't. I might think about the house I want someday ... All right, scratch that, I *definitely* think about the house I want someday, but cars? No."

"Really. I always had a dream car, though it changed a lot over the years. And I can imagine yours pretty easily."

72

"So what's my dream car?" she asked, holding her messy burger in both hands, her head on one side again like a perky little robin, smiling happily at him.

He worked on his fries for a minute while he thought. "Porsche Boxster," he decided at last. "Absolutely. That's your car."

"Is that a convertible?"

"Yeah. Red. A red Boxster." He got an image of her coming downstairs with him today, out the door of that scruffy apartment building, expecting to get into that piece of junk with the shot transmission. Seeing a red Boxster with a big red bow around it waiting for her instead, just like in the TV commercials. A car to match her, just as hot, just as sleek, just as sexy, the curving lines of it asking you to run a hand over them, the dangerous promise of being able to go just as fast as you wanted, of taking every corner too sharply, of taking it all the way to the limit.

Yeah. That car. And then putting a hand in his pocket and handing her the keys, seeing the look on her face. He'd love to have done that. He'd love to have had the right to do that.

"Tomorrow's the big day, huh?" he asked, deciding that he should probably change the subject. "Nervous?"

"Yes." She took a sip of her beer. "Especially since you recommended me. I don't want to let you down, or make you look bad to the board."

"You won't let me down. And besides," he added practically, "nobody but Suzanne knows I recommended you. I asked her to keep it quiet. So no pressure."

"Well, except from her, of course. But I like her, and I think I can learn a lot too. I'm sure going to try. I'm going to try *hard*."

He was reminded once again that it couldn't be easy to be Alyssa, to be the baby, never to be able to catch up.

"First days are never fun, though," she admitted, setting down the burger and wiping her hands. "Are they?"

"Hmm. It's been a while," he admitted.

73

"That's true," she said. "Because you've been working with Alec for so long. You haven't even had a boss, have you? Since ... when?"

"Not really, not since Alec and I got that first idea, senior year. That was it. We never looked back. I don't even know how we graduated." He laughed a little, remembering. "We were breathing and eating DataQuest."

"Can I ask—" She played with her fries, then abandoned them, looked up at him again. "Was it that you really liked it so much, what you were doing? Or was it more about being successful? I've always wondered what was wrong with me, that I've never worked as hard as Alec," she said in a burst of confidence. "Or Gabe either, for that matter. I'm just not ... I'm not driven like that. Or maybe I'm just lazy, I don't know. What makes a person do that? What am I missing?"

He thought it over. He usually hated answering questions about himself, but Alyssa was different. If it would help her, he wanted to tell her. "I don't think you're missing anything," he finally said. "I think some people just get lucky, find something they care about early, and keep caring. I wanted that diploma. I needed it. And I had no idea at the time that DataQuest would do so well, that it'd do anything at all, really. As far as I knew, it was just a cool idea, and we were making it happen, but it just ..." He gestured helplessly. "Sucked me in. Took me over. I had to hold myself in my chair to get through the rest of what I was supposed to be doing. Especially this class on Ethics in Computer Science. I had to write three papers for that class, and that was a killer. I didn't want to write about it, I wanted to do it. And I still do. I get into it, and I think it's been a few minutes, and it's been an hour. People say I work hard, but I don't feel like I work hard. I feel like I work ... easy."

"So it wasn't just trying to be successful? Wanting to make it?"

"Well, that too. That was part of it. I needed to get enough so I knew that whatever happened, I'd be all right." That he'd always have a place to sleep, a place of his own. That he'd never be hungry.

"But you give away a lot, too," she said. "I'm guessing."

"Believing that I'd be all right, that happened quite a few years ago. Time to, I don't know." He shrugged. "Give back."

He could see the questions hovering on the tip of her tongue, see her searching his face. And he could see the moment when she decided not to ask them, because Alyssa's own face was an open book. "I'd like to enjoy what I do as much as you do," she said instead. "I've had jobs that were OK, but I've never had a job I loved."

"It'll happen. You just have to find something that matters enough. You've got the passion, you just have to ... match it," he finished lamely, wishing he were better at talking.

"Well, you know what they say," she said more cheerfully. "Every wrong job is one more thing that you know you weren't meant to do. I have a whole list of things I know I wasn't meant to do, starting with McDonald's and moving right along."

"That's right. I remember that that was your first job." His second Kincaid Christmas, and Alyssa bicycling in to work almost every day, because she'd turned sixteen. She was about the only person he'd ever seen who looked good in that uniform. Especially the baseball cap. She'd sure looked cute in that baseball cap.

"Yep. Not the worst one, but sure not the best. The worst, actually," she decided, twirling another French fry that Joe was pretty sure she wasn't going to eat, "was the latest one, even though it paid the best. That was the only one where I'd wake up and *dread* going to work. How about you? What was your first job?"

"Stocking shelves at the Nellis Commissary."

"What's that? Some kind of store?"

"Yeah. Grocery store."

"Did you get that through your dad? He was in the Air Force, right?"

"Sort of. Through a friend of his."

It had been the year he'd turned sixteen, at the start of the summer after his sophomore year. He'd been living with Mr. Wilson for a few months, and his life had already got so much better, it was like a dream. No more bunk beds in rooms shared with budding psychopaths. Packing a lunch every day, a lunch that was *enough,* because he was allowed to get in the cupboards and the fridge, even to do his own food shopping. Having a ride to and from school instead of an hour-long trip on the bus, doing his homework at a desk in the quiet, secure space of his own room instead of trying to solve math equations on a jolting bus before he got back to the house and there was no way. Being able to put his few possessions into the drawers and start to believe that maybe, this time, they'd stay there a while.

And then it got even better, because Conrad came back.

Conrad had been his dad's buddy, but Joe hadn't seen him for a couple years, not since all the trouble had started. Conrad had been posted to Kadena in Okinawa, about as far away as you could get, and Joe had only found out he was back at Nellis when he'd run into him at the Commissary with Mr. Wilson, when they were doing the grocery shopping on Joe's military dependent ID.

Catching up had taken more time than that, because it wasn't something you could explain easily, not in the ice cream aisle. Not anytime, not if you were Joe.

Conrad had come by that evening and picked him up, taken him for pizza. Had watched him eat a whole pie, and then had looked steadily at him, not giving up until Joe had told him the truth. Just like his dad. Exactly like his dad.

"Why didn't you get in touch?" Conrad demanded. "Why didn't you let me know?"

Joe shrugged. "I didn't know how."

"Bullshit. You knew where I was. I told you to let me know if you needed anything. You knew I'd be there for you."

"It was just that ..." Joe looked down, not sure how to explain. "People say that." Nobody else had meant it. Not his mom. Not any of the social workers. Not even his sister, though he didn't blame her. She'd had to survive herself. She didn't have anything left for him.

"Well, I'm here now," Conrad said. "So let's figure out what you need. You've got a place to live. That working out?"

Another shrug. "Yeah."

"Say again?"

Joe heard the warning tone, straightened up fast. "Yes, sir." He'd forgotten, and the shame of it was almost the worst.

"Look me in the eye and tell me," Conrad said. "Tell me if that's working out. If it isn't, I'll fix it. I promise you that."

"Yes, sir," Joe said. "It's working out."

"OK, then." The older man nodded his short-cropped head in satisfaction. "Next things. Transportation, job. You don't have either of those, right?"

"No, sir. I just turned sixteen, but it's hard, without a way to get anywhere. I tried with the bus, but it was late, and I was late to the interview, and ..." He trailed off again. Excuses. "No excuse," he muttered, because that was the answer.

"What about your dad's bike?" Conrad asked. "What happened to that? He told me in Kuwait that when he got home, he was going to teach you to ride it."

Joe swallowed. "My mom has a boyfriend." He'd managed to avoid mentioning Dean so far, because even saying his name was like drinking something corrosive.

Conrad's face hardened. "He took your dad's bike?"

"He wrecked it." Joe felt his fists clenching, forced the emotion down. "He totaled it." When it had happened, he'd wished so hard that Dean had died. He'd been young enough then to think that life worked that way. Now he knew better. Only good people died. Bad people lived, and the things they did never seemed to catch up with them.

Conrad nodded. He didn't get all sympathetic, but Joe knew he understood how it had felt to see his dad's Yamaha 800 that had been sitting in the garage, a memory and a promise, under Dean's skinny butt, then gone entirely, and the knot loosened a little.

"OK, then," Conrad said. "First step is, teach you to ride my bike, get you your license. Second step is find a bike for you. Third step is get you a job. You got anything going on the next few weeks, evenings and weekends?"

"No, sir." He could hardly believe it. The past couple weeks, since summer vacation had started, all he'd had to do was help out Mr. Wilson with the house and the yard, study for the PSAT, and play basketball at the North Las Vegas Boys' and Girls' Club. It was all fine, but it wasn't getting him anywhere. And he needed to get somewhere. "But I don't—" He stopped.

"Don't what?" Conrad prompted.

"I don't have any money for a bike," Joe admitted, feeling the flush rise. "I don't even have any money for gas." He had his dad's leather jacket, because that had been in his closet, and Dean hadn't been able to take it. But that was about all he had. A jacket, a military ID, and some memories. None of that would make the first payment on a bike.

"It's going to be a loan," Conrad said. "Believe me, you'll be paying me back." He smiled, the first time that evening. "I know where you live."

And Conrad had come through. A month later, Joe had a bike, a Honda 400cc bought cheap from an airman being posted overseas, fixed up in the shop under Conrad's guidance. And he had a job to ride to on it.

"Get your hair cut," Conrad had instructed. "Short. Military-short. Wear a clean shirt, one with a collar. Clean jeans. Not clean enough. *Clean.* Take a shower. Be on time. Get there half an hour early if you have to, to make sure. Talk like you'd talk to me, like you'd have talked to your dad. Do all that and you'll get the job, because I know Gary Roswell, and I've told him about you, and he's ready to give you a chance. But keeping the job," he warned, "that's up to you."

"Yes, sir," Joe said, his feet itching to get out the door right then. He'd have a *job*. He'd have *money*.

But Conrad wasn't done. "I knew your dad a long time," he said. "He was a good man. I never knew him to do a cheap thing. I never saw him give less than his best. He's gone, but you're still here. You've got his name, and you can still know that you'd have made him proud. That's something nobody can take away from you. But you make the wrong choices, you can throw that away. Don't do it. Don't let him down."

"No, sir," Joe said over the lump in his throat. "I won't."

"Was that the worst job you had?" Alyssa asked now, bringing him back. She was making circles around the rim of her empty glass with a finger. "Stocking shelves? That doesn't sound too fun."

"No, that one was OK. I did that for a couple years, till I went to college. That was fine. I never minded the physical ones that much, washing dishes or whatever, as long as the boss wasn't too bad. Just happy to have the work."

"Washing dishes? That was at more than our house, huh?"

"Yeah. I did lots of stuff, summers, during the school year too. High school, first few years of college. Washing dishes, busing tables at those Palo Alto restaurants. Working at 7-11. They like a big guy behind the counter, just in case."

"Mmm," she said, looking sleepy, or maybe just like a woman who'd had a couple beers after a tough day of used-car shopping. "They liked that you looked so tough."

"Well, you know the good thing about looking tough. You know the secret of it."

"No," she said, and the sleepy look had changed to a dreamy smile that was kicking his pulse rate up a notch, "what's the secret of it?"

"You look tough enough, you know you got the stuff to back it up, you almost never have to prove it." He raised his beer in salute, then drained it.

"Can I ask you a question?" she asked.

"Sure."

"Why do you shave your head? I can tell you're not bald. So why?"

"How can you tell I'm not bald?"

79

"Bald guys have …" She gestured with a finger at her own head. "That line, where they're losing their hair. You don't have it."

"You're right, I'm not bald. It was always short, but you know that. Military-short. I started cutting it that way when I started working on the base. I got one of those electric clipper deals," he said, running the imaginary shaver over his head. "Cheaper than haircuts, you know? I got used to doing it that way. And I was busy."

"Too busy to get your hair cut?"

"Well …" He smiled. "Haircuts take time. I was busy. And then one day, I thought, why not just shave it? Why not see if I had—" He shrugged, looked at her, and laughed. "Any weird bumps on my head, or anything. And I kind of liked how it looked."

"Tough," she said again.

"Yeah. I guess. So what do you think? Tough? Or just bald? Better with hair?"

"Tough," she said, "definitely. But maybe … You really want to know what I think?"

"I definitely want to know what you think."

"Then, yes. Some hair. I remember military-short, and I thought it looked good. If you want my opinion."

The server stopped by their table again. "You guys good?" she asked. "Anything else?"

Joe looked at Alyssa. "Another beer?"

"No, thanks. I'd better stop."

"We're good," Joe told the woman, and she nodded and put the check down, exactly in the center of the table, and Alyssa put a hand on it.

"Let me get this," she protested when Joe's hand came down on top of hers. "Let me say thank you for taking me car shopping."

"Nope." He was pulling it out from under her palm. "No way."

"Joe …" She sighed. "You bought me breakfast. You've spent the whole day helping me. You've done so much for me."

"You're welcome, but that doesn't matter. Don't you remember what your brothers said at Christmas?"

"What?"

"The guy pays the first time." And every time. He'd been called a throwback, and he didn't care. He could afford it, and he couldn't sit back and watch a woman pull out her wallet. He just couldn't.

"That was for a *date,*" she argued. "This isn't a date."

It had felt like a date to him. Too bad he'd been wrong. What was it she'd said? *I'm not even your sister.* But close enough, still. Too close. "Maybe it isn't," he said, "but it's the first time the two of us have been out together, so it counts."

"It does? Are those the rules?" she asked, all sweet and sassy again. "Another part of the Man Code that I'm unaware of?"

"That's it," he said, barely knowing what they were talking about, but sure of this. "Those are the rules. This is my job. I pay."

She was smiling. "You seem pretty sure of that. So what's my job, then?"

He smiled back at her. "To be here."

Another Second Chance

When the doorbell buzzed the next evening, Alyssa groaned, kept her eyes firmly shut, and decided not to get up.

Sherry came in from the kitchen. "Was that the door?"

"Yeah. Probably selling something," Alyssa said, opening her eyes with reluctance. "Don't answer."

A second insistent buzz, and Sherry went over to the intercom, pushed the button. "Hello?"

"It's Joe." Not even the tinny distortion of the cheap intercom system could disguise those low tones. Alyssa swung her feet off the coffee table and sat up.

"Hi, Joe." Sherry said, her own voice perking right up. "Want to come up?"

"Please."

Sherry pushed the button even as Alyssa hissed, "Wait!"

"Makeup time," Sherry said, and headed for the bathroom.

Alyssa swore, shoved the heavy quilt off her, stood up, tripped herself, and finally got loose. She folded the quilt hastily, finished hanging it over the arm of the couch just as she heard the knock. She swore again. Why wasn't Sherry answering it? What kind of a friend *was* she?

A second knock, and she gave it up, went and twisted the locks, pulled the lightweight hollow-core door open.

Joe stood there holding a box. A bulky, shiny white rectangular carton printed with a picture of something she didn't instantly recognize, two and a half feet high and a couple wide.

"Hi," he said. "I won't stay long, just wanted to drop this off."

"Uh ... what?"

She stepped aside to let him in, and he turned with the thing in his arms, indicated her bedroom with a jerk of his head. "Heater," he said economically. "For your room."

"You brought me a *heater?*"

"Yeah," he said, looking surprised. "You said it was cold, because you didn't have heat. So I stopped by the hardware store after work and picked one up."

"Uh ... OK. Thank you," she added hastily. She was painfully aware that her eyeliner was probably smudged into raccoon eyes, and that she didn't have any lipstick on at all. And worst of all, she could tell she was breaking out on her chin. She wanted desperately to touch the spot, convinced that it had somehow grown into something huge, red, and disgusting since she'd got home. She kept her hand off it with a serious effort, did her best to turn the unblemished side of her face towards him.

"Maybe we should set it up," Joe said patiently, and she realized that he was still standing there holding the box, and that it looked heavy. She darted to her bedroom door, opened it for him, shivered because, yeah, it was freezing in there, the reason she'd been in the living room. The reason she hadn't even changed out of her work clothes yet, because she'd been too tired and it had been too *cold.*

He followed her inside, set the box down in the middle of the floor space, and pulled a metal gadget out of his pocket, squatted beside the box and opened a blade, because of course Joe carried around some sort of multipurpose survival tool. Naturally. She watched as he cut the box neatly along the front edge, down the two front sides, rolled the radiator-style electric heater out and removed the Styrofoam, then took a moment to cut the box all the way flat and fold it up, stacking the Styrofoam packing pieces on top.

Sherry came in halfway through the process, leaned against the doorway—made up, Alyssa noticed sourly, her curly hair perfectly, messily casual, her sweatshirt replaced by a snug green sweater that matched her eyes.

"Hi, Joe," she said. "You being all capable and manly again?"

Joe gave her his crooked smile and stood up. "Hey, Sherry. Nah, just brought this over. How's that bathtub faucet working for you?"

"Great," she said. "I took a bubble bath last night, Sunday night luxury, you know, and it was so nice to lie there and relax without the drip. Thank you for fixing it for me. I really appreciate it." Laying it on thick, Alyssa thought with another stab of irritation.

"No problem," Joe said, then turned back to Alyssa. "I think it'll work best to put it over here," he said, rolling the big cream-colored appliance over next to the dresser and plugging in the cord. "You don't want it right in front of the bookcase. Keep a good foot of clearance from the wall when it's on, OK? And not right next to the bed, either."

Alyssa glanced at the bed, wished she'd made it a little more neatly this morning, that it wasn't covered with hastily discarded clothes, and that her closet door wasn't open. And that her birth control pill case wasn't sitting on the bedside table, she realized with horror. She edged her way around Joe and half-backed her way to the head of the bed, opened the drawer of the nightstand behind her, and shoved the case inside.

"OK," she said, then remembered her chin again and tried to angle herself, which was impossible in the narrow space between the wall and her bed. "Thanks."

"It's filled with oil," he said, positioning the heater to his satisfaction. "Pretty energy-efficient, so you shouldn't see a big change in your electric bill. It's got some different settings. Two switches, see, besides the dial? So if you just want a little heat, you turn this one, the left one. And if you want medium heat, just the right one. Put both on, and it'll be full heat. And this up here," he continued, "that's more of a thermostat. Here." He squatted down again. "I'll show you."

She glanced at it. "Two switches. OK. Turn one on, turn both on, turn the dial up. I've got it."

"It's not quite that simple," he said. "It actually works better in the midrange."

She edged her way out from beside the bed, picked up the owner's manual he'd set on her desk, set it down again. "I'm sure they tell you in here. I'll look later."

"I can just show you now."

"I don't want to *look* now. It was really nice of you. I know it was. Thank you. But I don't want to look. I'm too cold right now." She looked at the pile of debris instead, and her blotchy chin was quivering, because now she either had to go down and put it in the trash or look at it lying there, and her room was already messy.

He glanced up at her, startled, made an adjustment to the heater, then stood. "Bad first day?" he asked, his voice gentler. "Hard?"

"It's just ..." Despite her best efforts, her arm began to go up and down like an oil derrick, and the words were tumbling out. "My room's a mess, and I'm cold, and it's too *hard.* Moving, and the job, and ... now it's all *messy,*" she repeated, and turned away from him, wiping her eyes. "I'm sorry. I'm just ... I'm sorry. Thank you for bringing the heater." And *go away,* she thought miserably. She shouldn't have opened the door. She hadn't wanted to see anybody tonight.

"Do you have a bathrobe?" he asked.

"Huh?"

"A bathrobe. Or a sweater."

She gestured at the closet, her arm flapping again, and he took a quick look inside, pulled her fuzzy sweater off the hook, and helped her on with it. "How about going and getting something to eat?" he asked. "Did you have dinner?"

She shook her head. "No. I don't want to go anywhere. I mean," she gulped, "thanks. No."

He stood a moment, obviously thinking. "Tell you what. You go take a shower, get warmed up, put on some ... " He gestured at her blouse, skirt, and tights, her first-day clothes. "Some sweats or something. I'll go get some Chinese food. What do you want?"

"I don't know," she said, and she could hear that it was more like a wail. She was acting like a baby, she knew, but she was at the end of her rope, and the rope was fraying fast.

"OK," he said. "I'll get some stuff. How about you?" he asked Sherry, still watching interestedly from the doorway. "What would you like?"

"Kung Pao Chicken," she said brightly. "I know a great place, right around the corner. I'll go with you to get it. We might as well sit there and wait for it. They give you tea."

Joe hesitated a second. "All right. We'll be back in half an hour or so," he told Alyssa. "Take a shower. I'll take this stuff down with me." He gathered up the packing debris. "By the time you get out of the shower, your room will be warm, and you can change, and we'll be back with dinner."

Alyssa nodded, because she was too close to crying. And she did cry a little in the shower, because she was miserable, and she was making Joe feel like a big brother again, which was exactly what she didn't want to do.

She did feel better when she got out, though. Her chin didn't look nearly as bad as she'd feared, especially once she covered the spot with concealer, and her bedroom *was* warm now, and changing to yoga pants, a long sweater, and cozy socks helped, too.

Joe and Sherry came back with the food, set the white cartons on the coffee table, and Sherry stuck spoons in, brought over plates and napkins. Joe didn't ask Alyssa what she wanted, just put a pile of rice on her plate and added some meat and vegetables, and she ate, and didn't talk, and realized how hungry she'd been.

"Well," Sherry said when they'd finished, "guess I'll do the dishes."

"I'll only stay a couple more minutes," Joe said. "I really just wanted to check in with Alyssa."

Sherry looked at him. "All right, then." She stood up, began to gather containers, and Joe stacked plates and forks for her.

"So." He shifted on the couch to face Alyssa when Sherry had left the room. "Hard first day? Not as good as you thought? Not going to work out?"

"I don't know," she said, wrapping her sweater around herself a little more tightly. "I hope so. But it's different from what I thought, because Suzanne's leaving."

"Leaving?"

"Yeah." She laughed, though it really wasn't funny. "Ain't that a thing? She told me she knew when she interviewed me, but she couldn't say yet, because she hadn't given notice. She was really *sorry,"* she added bitterly, "but that doesn't help much."

"So what does that mean?" he asked. "For you?"

She shrugged helplessly. "They've hired a replacement. Some woman who's been at the Carolyn G. Haskill Cancer Foundation, and Suzanne went on about how good she is, how she's sure it'll still be a wonderful opportunity for me. I just wish I'd *met* her."

"When does she start?"

"Two weeks. Suzanne leaves in a week, then a week in between with nobody, just me, and then this new person—Helene—comes."

"That means you'll have two weeks to get familiar, though, right? So you won't be brand-new, and you can be the one showing her around. Could even be better."

"Yeah. I know, I told myself that. It was just a shock," she tried to explain. "I was nervous already, and I've gone out on such a limb here. Moved, and the car, and using so much of my savings, and ..." She took a breath, close to tears again, and admitted the truth. "What if it doesn't work? What if she wants to hire her own person? What if she fires me right away, before I even have a chance?"

He didn't tell her she was being silly, to her relief, or not to "borrow trouble." She hated that phrase. She didn't need to borrow it. Trouble *happened.* "Then you'll find something else," he said. "Then you'll try again."

"But this was supposed to be my big chance. This was my change."

"It was *a* chance. Nothing's the last chance. There's always another chance. And the change was in you. You already made it."

She looked at him, trying not to cry. She didn't want him to talk. She wanted him to give her a hug, tell her everything would work out. She wanted him to *hold* her, but he didn't, and she didn't want to ask him and have it be awkward, so she didn't.

"I'm being a baby," she said. "I know it. I'm sorry. Thanks for coming over, but ... I'm sorry." Which made the tears come even closer.

"You're not being a baby," he said, getting up off the couch. "You're tired, and you've had a hard day. Go to bed, and it'll be better in the morning. Things are almost always better in the morning. But I'll get out of here so you can do it. Say goodbye to Sherry for me, OK?"

She nodded miserably, got up and tried to smile, to thank him. And then she shut the door, went into her room, lay down on her messy bed, and cried.

But at least it was warm.

Yes, a Date

Three weeks later, on her way home from her second "first week" that month, she thought back on how she'd behaved that night and cringed yet again. Why did she always have to see Joe at her least competent, most vulnerable times? At her parents' house at Christmas, while she was moving, the first day of a new job? Those were nobody's shining moments, were they? Why couldn't she see him when she was getting some professional award or something? Closing some deal? Not that she ever *had* got a professional award or closed a big deal, but she'd had a lot better moments than the ones she'd shared with him recently, that was for sure.

The next time she saw him, she resolved, she'd be all calm and self-assured, and she'd have good news to report. Because he'd been right, that had been a low point, and things had got a lot better.

She'd soaked up everything she could from Suzanne during the one week she'd had with her, had put all her efforts during her in-between week into learning the fundraising software and familiarizing herself with Second Chance's past campaigns, all the major donors and their backgrounds.

All that effort looked like it was going to pay off, because this was the end of her first week with Helene, the new Director of Development, and her new boss had invited her to lunch today, had listened to her ideas and even complimented her on them.

"I have a feeling we'll make a good team," Helene had said. "I realize you don't have any development experience,

89

but as long as you're here to learn and here to work, I'll be happy. Two heads are better than one, right? So if you have any bright ideas, please, go ahead and share. We need to shake this place up. There's so much untapped potential here."

"That's exactly how I feel," Alyssa said eagerly. "Especially in tech. We have hardly any tech companies contributing. Here they all are, getting more and more prominent, in the City and in Silicon Valley, too. They're the only ones with money to burn, and they *want* to be good community citizens. And here we are, offering such a media-friendly opportunity. Individual children, right here in the United States. What could be more appealing than that? And yet we aren't reaching them. I was thinking," she said, taking a breath, because this was her chance, "maybe a campaign aimed specifically at them. Something that would grab them."

"Great idea," Helene said. "Too bad you're not related to Alec Kincaid. That would really be perfect. You're not, are you? Not a cousin, or anything?"

Her blue eyes held Alyssa's, and Alyssa willed herself not to blush. "No, alas." She laughed. She hated to lie, but she wanted to do this on her own. She'd come to think that Suzanne's departure might have been a blessing in disguise after all. Now nobody knew who she was. She was free to make her own mark.

"No," Helene said with a laugh of her own, "I guess that would be too good to be true. But when you get that killer idea worked out, who knows, your name might just get us a little further."

Us. Alyssa hugged the word to her. "I wanted to tell you, too," she said, "I have a couple of meetings lined up with smaller potential donors. Suzanne told me that the Assistant Director handled those calls in the past," she added hastily as the other woman's gaze sharpened, and tried to project confidence.

"Really." Helene raised a sculpted eyebrow. She was one of the best-groomed women Alyssa had ever met. "Well, then, if you've got meetings set up, you'd better go ahead and handle them, don't you think?" She smiled at Alyssa. "I'll come along too, if you don't mind. It'll give me my own chance to get my feet wet."

"I don't mind," Alyssa said, though she'd been looking forward to the opportunity to go out on her own. She'd sat in on several calls with Suzanne, and she *did* know how to present, and to sell. But what else could she say? "Of course not."

"Wonderful," Helene said. "I have a feeling we're going to get along just fine."

Alyssa hoped so, too. She'd been right, this was a job that mattered, and she thought it was a job she could do. It was a job where she could make a difference. It was what she'd wanted.

Everything was looking up, she thought, jumping off the N-Judah streetcar at her stop, And tonight, she even had a date.

"Doing the check-in," she said a good five hours later, leaning against the wall next to the hand dryer in the ladies' room of 111 Minna, the heavy thump of the bass through the thin walls rocking her body like a beating pulse.

"How's it going?" Sherry asked at the other end of the phone. Her roommate had taken Alyssa to the party last week where she'd met Greg, who'd turned out to be a friend of Sherry's cousin.

Alyssa shrugged as if her roommate could see her. "All right. About to leave, though, so wanted to let you know. Home in a half hour or so." Dating Safety 101.

"Sparks?" Sherry asked. "Should I go to bed, give you some space?"

"Not enough to light a teeny little campfire," Alyssa admitted. And she wanted to burn down the house. She couldn't help it. She *wanted* it, and nothing less was going to do. "I know he's a friend of yours, but ..."

"Nah, I don't know him that well. What?"

"Well, you know those first-date conversations? The job interview kind?"

"Oh, yeah. One of those, huh?"

"And I flunked. Not a Worthy Girlfriend, not now that I'm, you know, poor."

"You are not poor. You're normal."

"He spent half of dinner telling me how materialistic most women are, how they see him as a meal ticket because he's got money. Practically had the message blinking in bright red letters across his forehead. And the other half talking about all the stuff he has."

"Ooh. Fail."

"Yeah."

"So why didn't you ditch him?"

"Well, you know. Dancing." Alyssa laughed. "I figured, after putting up with that, I deserved some dancing time. And he deserved to have to pay for it."

She heard Sherry's answering laugh. "Serves him right. Sounds like Greg isn't getting lucky."

"Greg isn't even getting mildly fortunate. Greg is getting a hearty handshake and a cordial thank-you. Oh, well. Another one bites the dust. Where are the great guys? I know they must be out there somewhere. My dad's a great guy. My brothers are great guys."

"Mmm," Sherry said. "I've only met one in person, but you're right, Alec is a great guy and then some. And Gabe ..." The gusty sigh came right through the line. "Haven't seen him, but on TV, yeah, he's a winner too. No fair that I meet you when they're both married. But they can't be the only ones. Why can't we meet nice guys?"

"Well," Alyssa had to admit, "that wouldn't help me, because I don't like nice guys. They're always boring, or I can push them around too much."

"Mmm," Sherry said again. "Bad boys."

"Yeah. I want a bad boy who's a good man. Is that so much to ask?"

"Probably. I'm still surprised you never hit it with Joe. I mean, come on. Helped you move, took you car shopping ...

92

And I know he's one of those old-friend types, so maybe you don't see it, but he's *hot*. So big and tough, and that quiet deal he does, how you can't tell what's going on underneath. Love that. Did you ever give him my number? I know that was awkward, that one time, but hey, we can't just sit around and pine away for Prince Charming, can we? But it probably put him off. Maybe if he got a little nudge from my loving roommate, he'd get the hint."

"I didn't have a chance yet." Alyssa pushed herself away from the wall. "I'd better go. Greg's probably thinking I'm snorting coke in here."

"OK. See you soon."

It was a long, cold hike from the club to the car, which Greg had parked after much circling of blocks a good way north of Market, but they made it at last. It sure would have been nice if Greg had suggested that he get the car by himself and come back to the club for her. But, she had to concede, that would probably have been too thoughtful to expect of your average thirty-something guy. At least he opened the car door for her, preserving his good-bye handshake, if nothing else.

He started the engine, punched her address into the GPS unit, pulled out of his spot and made an illegal U-turn. That didn't bother her much—she wasn't all that crazy about perfect behavior anyway—but it was *cold*.

"Would you mind turning on the heat?" she asked, trying to keep her teeth from chattering. She still wasn't used to Northern California temperatures.

He looked at her in surprise. "You cold? You should have worn a warmer coat."

I didn't realize I'd be walking to the Arctic Circle. She decided her best bet was not to answer. He turned up the fan and dialed the temperature up, to her relief, though she shivered away for a few blocks until it kicked in.

"Better?" he asked, and she forgave him a little.

"Yes, thanks."

"I'm glad you wanted to go dancing," he said, shooting a smile across at her that told her he was looking for more than a handshake tonight. "You're a great dancer."

"Thanks for taking me," she said, because she was her parents' daughter, after all. "I enjoyed it."

"You look pretty good doing it, too," he said. "I almost didn't go to that party last week. What I would've missed, huh?"

She didn't answer that one. What did you say? "Thank you?" "Dream on?"

He headed east and south, taking the side streets, avoiding the bus and pedestrian traffic of Market, hung a left and laid on the horn at a pedestrian crossing in mid-block, his dark clothing making him barely visible, the shamble to his walk proclaiming him as one of the perennial down-and-out.

"You'd think the city could get a clue and clean the bums out of here." Greg stepped on the gas again as the man staggered out of the way. "It's like human litter, you know?"

And just like that, she was hating him again. "Litter? Really? Aren't they people?"

"You know what I mean," he said. "Even if you want to talk about compassion … you can put a dog out of his misery, but a wino who's probably going to die of cirrhosis in a few months anyway, in and out of the emergency room over and over, right back on the streets again the next day with his Thunderbird? And we're pumping our tax dollars into keeping him alive? For what? Who benefits? Not him. His life's got to be miserable."

"And yet he's choosing to live," she said. "Even so."

"And meanwhile," he went on, ignoring her, caught up now, "you see the same guys on the same street corners every single day. I'd tell them to get a job, but they've got one. Begging. And the same suckers putting coins in their cups, too. Financing that next pack of cigarettes. Nice work if you can get it."

"Sounds like you've given this a lot of thought," she said. "It couldn't be that, say, they've got substance abuse problems. Mental illness. It couldn't be that they *can't* get out. You think they choose this?"

"Sure they do. Everybody makes choices. You make the wrong choices, fall down the ladder, why should I support you? Why should I support your habit?"

"Nice to be you," she managed to say. "Nice to be so strong and lucky."

"Luck had nothing to do with it," he said, and he was angry now too, it was clear. So much for how good she'd looked dancing. Not that good, apparently, because he was burning his bridges *down*. "Nobody's ever given me a thing. I've earned every penny I've got, and I don't see why I should feel sorry for people who refuse to do the same."

Her temper had kicked in for real, and she needed to be out of this car, or bad things were going to happen. Greg braked to a sharp stop at yet another light, and she checked that her little purse was still slung low across her chest, then yanked at the door handle. Locked. She fumbled for the switch, found it, unfastened her seatbelt and had the door open.

"I'm out of here," she told him, sliding out just as the light turned green.

"What the hell?" he spluttered, but she wasn't listening. She didn't bother to close the car door behind her, deciding to let him deal with the honking she could hear starting up behind her as she made it to the sidewalk. She turned and saw him leaning over as far as he could, fruitlessly reaching, until he gave it up and jumped out of the car, ran around it to shut the door, while the driver of the car behind him laid on the horn, and laughed. Served him right.

"Are you crazy?" Greg shouted across at her.

"No. I'm a woman with standards," she yelled back. She could see him mouthing something, probably "crazy bitch," and then he'd run back around the car. And been promptly stopped by the light turning red once more, which made her laugh again. Sherry's cousin might not invite her to any more parties, but it had been worth it.

95

She decided to walk in the opposite direction, away from him. Probably best. Where was she, anyway? Someplace in the Tenderloin, which meant that there weren't going to be cabs, not until she got to a BART station. If she kept walking, she'd hit Market and the Powell Street station eventually. It couldn't be more than six or seven blocks. She considered getting her phone out and checking, abandoned that idea fast as she looked around her at the knot of loiterers in front of the shadowy expanse of an auto body shop, a closed Chinese restaurant with the metal grilles pulled over the windows, the not-much-more-reassuring entrance of a low-rent residential hotel, and felt the first shiver of unease.

And not the first shiver of cold. As she'd already figured out, the right clothes for dancing in a club weren't the right ones for walking in San Francisco on a January midnight. Her little coat, her skimpy sweater and short skirt weren't keeping her warm, and they were definitely attracting the wrong kind of attention.

She put as much confidence into her stride as she could, as much as was possible in high heels, kept her gaze straight ahead, and increased her pace. Saw a group of guys ahead of her, hanging out in front of an abandoned storefront next to a vacant lot, and decided to cross the street. Traffic was moving faster than she'd realized, and she had to hustle to make it before it caught up with her, was still hurrying when she got to the other side.

She fingered the phone inside her little bag, wanting to call Alec. She knew her brother would come pick her up, maybe faster than she could get that cab. But Alec wasn't home, she remembered with a sinking heart. He and Rae were at a trade show in Las Vegas. And three of the guys who'd been hanging out had split off from their buddies and crossed the street themselves, headed towards her, and her unease was growing by the moment.

Better to turn around right now, walk back the other way before they caught up. She'd seen a lit storefront down a side street, a block or so back. Probably a liquor store again, but there'd be somebody in it. And it would be warm. She'd call from there. Walking had been a very bad idea. She hurried, heard the catcalls from behind her.

"Hey, pretty lady. Where you going? Don't you want to party?"

She didn't look back, kept going. The lit doorway—it *was* a liquor store—was ahead of her now, and she was ducking inside, the opening door giving out a mechanical chime that was music to her ears.

She scooted around into the back of an aisle, pulled her phone out of her purse, searched with shaking fingers for a cab company and dialed the number.

"I need a cab at the corner of Larkin and ..." she told the dispatcher who answered. "Hold on a sec." She went to the doorway again, peered around for the street sign. "Eddy."

"To where?"

"Inner Sunset."

"Sorry," the man said. "We don't have anyone."

"What do you mean?" She knew what he meant. That the ride was too short, and her location too sketchy.

Dead air was her only answer. She could try another company. But the guys who'd been following her were outside the store now, and she felt way too vulnerable, way too trapped, so she retreated again. She could call Sherry, but her roommate couldn't exactly defend her from three scary guys. And they *were* scary, she admitted. She was scared. So she did the only other thing she could think of. She called Joe.

"Alyssa?" It came out sharp. She'd been worried he'd be asleep, would have the phone turned off. But he answered after the second ring.

"Joe? Could you come get me? I'm here. I mean, I'm here in the City. Could you pick me up?" Her voice was shaking a little, cold or fear or relief that he was there, she wasn't sure which. Maybe all three. "Are you here too? Around? Could you come?"

"Right now. Where are you?"

"Larkin and ... and Eddy. It's a liquor store. I'm inside."

"Ten minutes," he promised. "Stay in the store."

She shoved the phone back in her purse, some of the tension leaving her and relief taking its place like oxygen, filling her lungs. Ten minutes. She spent a few of them scanning the bottles lined up behind the counter. The Tenderloin's taste seemed to lean heavily toward fortified wine and tequila. She'd pass.

"Lady," the guy behind the counter finally said. "You going to buy something, or what?" He pointed to a sign behind him. *No Loitering.*

"I'm just waiting for a friend. I'll be gone in a minute."

"Buy or leave." He pointed at his sign again.

"So call the cops," she snapped. "I don't see a line of people trying to push past me to get to the Colt Malt Liquor. If you get a sudden rush, I'll get out of the way, how's that?"

He didn't look happy, but he subsided, contenting himself with shooting her an evil glare. This wasn't exactly her night.

She went over and stood by the door to wait. And attracted the attention of the guys outside again, drew them into the store with her like they were moths and she was the flame. The closer they came to the door, the more she backed up, and by the time the chime rang out again as the glass door closed behind them, she was all the way against the front counter where the clerk sat.

"Hey there, pretty lady," the one in front said, and she recognized the voice, the one who had called out to her before. Tall, dark skin, bad teeth, coming closer, crowding her, and she had nowhere to go. Another one wasn't talking, but she didn't like the way he was looking at her. He was shorter, squatter. The third guy hung back, not threatening her, but he wasn't exactly stepping up to tell the others to back off, either.

"You all. Buy or leave," the clerk said again, and everyone ignored him, and part of Alyssa wanted to laugh at the absurdity of it, but she was fully frightened now. She slipped to one side, ducked around a beer island, the guys coming around behind her, smiling, enjoying themselves. The tall one put a hand on her arm, the breaching of her personal space like ice water in her veins.

"We could get us some tequila, have us a little party," he said. His smile, the smile on his stubby friend's face had her breathing in gasps, fear and anger warring inside her.

She twisted her arm out of his grasp. "Leave me alone."

His smile only broadened, and he took another step, forcing her to back up, closer to the doorway. *Come on, Joe. Where are you?*

She looked outside, hoping to see him, somehow thinking she could tell which headlights were his, but of course she couldn't. Instead, she saw a single light weaving amongst the traffic. A light that turned into a motorcycle that jerked to a stop in the red zone out front, and the rider was off, knocking the kickstand into place, and then he was up onto the curb, across the sidewalk, long steps, moving fast.

He shoved up the visor of his helmet, and it was Joe, but she'd known that as soon as he'd got off the bike, even though she hadn't known that he had a motorcycle. Dark jeans, black leather jacket, black helmet, looking like an ad for the Big & Tall & Tough Store. Joe.

She hit the door, heard the chime behind her, and knew her new boyfriends were following right along. Until they realized that she was meeting the bike rider, because she could sense them slowing to a stop.

Joe barely looked at her, just reached for her arm and swung her behind him. She peered around from the shelter of his broad back, saw the three guys stopped halfway between the bulk of Joe and the liquor store entrance, looking like they weren't quite sure what to do next.

"You should take better care of your lady," Tall Guy said at last. "Not leave her all alone and lonely like that. She might get into trouble."

"I'm here now," Joe said.

The guy laughed, showing his bad teeth. "What? You looking for a fight? Three of us, man."

"I'm not looking for anything," Joe said, and she could see his hands flexing, could sense the readiness in him, like he was poised on his toes, even though he was standing solid. "But I'm happy to take anything that comes my way."

99

"Hey, man," the guy said with a shrug, taking a half-step back. "Just hanging out." He turned, would-be casual, and the three of them sauntered off, back to their pals, Alyssa presumed.

Joe stood still a moment, watching them go. Then he turned to Alyssa. "You OK?"

"Yeah," she said, her arms wrapped around herself, shivering with cold and tension. "Just freezing." She smiled, and could feel her teeth chattering. She'd really thought he was going to fight. Three guys.

He unzipped the heavy jacket and handed it to her. "Put this on." He watched her struggle with the zipper for a minute, her fingers too shaky for the task, then brushed her hands aside and zipped the jacket for her as if she were a child. Then he took off the helmet and gave her that, too. "I don't have another one with me. Wear this."

She hefted the weight of it. "Uh, Joe. I can't ride a motorcycle. Maybe you could just wait for a cab with me."

"You don't have to ride a motorcycle," he said. "I'll do the riding. You just have to hold on."

"I mean ..." She tried again. "I'm wearing a short skirt."

"I noticed." He smiled suddenly, surprising her. "Looks good."

She laughed back in relief, so glad that he wasn't mad at her for hauling him over here, for putting him in this situation. "Well, thanks. But ..."

He took the helmet right out of her hands, fitted it over her head. "Let's go." He walked over to the bike, swung a long leg over so he was straddling the machine, planted his feet and held out a hand to her. "Put your foot on the peg and swing on."

She took his hand, tried to forget the fact that her underwear was of the barely-there variety, found the footrest he was talking about. Stepped onto it with one sandaled toe, abandoned all modesty, hitched up her skirt, and swung.

Joe pulled out into the street, trying to calm himself down. The residue from the flood of adrenaline had made him shaky, to his disgust, while having Alyssa pressed against his back, her hands holding onto his shoulders, her thighs so close to his own ... that had him reeling in a different direction. As always with her, he'd lost the balance he worked so hard to maintain. Lost it entirely.

He wasn't sure he'd ever moved faster than he had when she'd called. He'd been miles deep into the knotty problem that had kept him at his desk hours after everyone else had left, grateful for the chance to work without interruption. He'd been spending far too much of his time on the administrative side of the business with Alec and Rae both gone for the week, and that was on top of the normal back and forth with his staff of programmers. He'd needed to get something *done*.

But the complicated subroutine he'd spent hour after patient hour debugging had flown from his head the moment his phone had chimed and he'd looked down at his desktop to see her name on the screen. He'd been moving out of his chair when he picked it up, out of the office by the time he'd hung up, had broken a speed limit or two and done some pretty aggressive lane-splitting to get to her.

But he'd made it, he reminded himself now. He'd made it, though he still wished those dirtbags had stuck around to get their asses kicked. Probably for the best, though he was having trouble believing it. It had felt like such a good idea at the time.

He had the feeling that he needed to do something else now, though, something besides just taking Alyssa home. He tried his best not to be sensitive, not if he could help it, but he could tell how scared she'd been. It had been there in the stiffness of her posture, her jerky steps when she'd come out to meet him with those three assholes behind her. When he got scared, he wanted to forget about it as fast as possible. But women didn't. They wanted to talk about it. What they *didn't* want was to go home and be scared some more there, alone.

And anyway, he didn't want Alyssa to be scared anywhere. If talking would help, she should talk.

He swung over to the curb once he'd turned onto Haight, the street still buzzing even after midnight. He eased the bike to a stop and twisted around so he could talk to her. "Maybe we should go warm up. Have some coffee. Or tea," he suggested. Women liked tea, especially when they were upset.

"Tea would be great," she said from beneath the helmet, shivering now that she wasn't pressed against his back. He could see the goosebumps on the smooth, bare thigh that lay against his own. She had to be half-frozen. He knew he was.

"Swing off, then," he instructed, and knew he shouldn't be sorry that he didn't have a good enough view when she did. She pulled the helmet off, and he took it from her, locked it with the bike, and took her into the cheerful café, painted lime green inside and decorated with some artist's unframed abstract paintings, blocks of bold swirls and deep color. The space was thankfully warm and half-empty, and he led her to a booth in the back, farthest from the chill of the doorway, ordered her a tea and himself a cup of coffee, then sat and looked at her for a minute.

She unzipped his jacket as her tight muscles relaxed in the warmth, took it off and laid it over her lap, over her chilled legs. But once she'd done it, she crossed her arms beneath her breasts and hugged herself.

It was no wonder she was cold. The little coat she had on wasn't doing much, and the sweater she was wearing underneath it was … Well, it was a sweater, but it wasn't exactly designed for warmth. Ruby red, which would have been enough right there, but there was more. It was the part that wrapped around somehow from the back to form a collar that really did the business. The band that encircled her neck, fastened with two more little buttons above the vee of smooth skin beneath.

That choker of vivid red around her throat, it was … it was working. Combined with the short skirt and high heels, the shiny dark hair swinging to her shoulders, she was a walking fantasy. And thinking of her alone in the Tenderloin like that—it wasn't a good thought.

"You have hair," she said as soon as she'd warmed up enough to talk.

He smiled at her. "Better? Or no?"

"Hmm." She smiled a little herself, and he was glad to see it. "Yeah. Better."

He rubbed his hand over his stubbled cheek. "Should I shave, too?"

"No," she said immediately. "No, if you're asking me."

"Yeah," he said. "I'm asking you."

The waitress brought their drinks, and Alyssa thanked her, polite even now, then sat and wrapped both hands around the cup for a minute, warming herself.

"What happened?" he finally asked. "Going to tell me?"

She hesitated a moment, looked down and picked up her spoon, did some stirring, even though she hadn't put anything into her tea. "You're going to think I was stupid," she said at last. "And I'm really glad you came to get me. I'm sorry you had to rescue me. Again. I know, it keeps happening over and over, and I'm sorry, and I haven't even said thank you. Those guys were ... I didn't know what was going to happen. When you came ... " He could see her swallow, could watch it happen all the way down the delicate line of her throat, all the way to that strip of red. "I was so glad to see you," she said, and her voice broke, and he needed to hold her.

"But why were you there?" he asked instead. "Were you out with friends? Did they leave you there? What?"

"No," she said, and then she stopped, and he could see the reluctance.

"Alyssa." This time he did reach out, took her hand where it lay on the table, and held it. It was cold, still, and he wrapped his own hand gently around it, felt her squeezing back, and he was filled with ... something. "Just tell me."

So she did. She told him, and she pulled her hand out of his so she could use her hands to talk, because with Alyssa, her voice wasn't enough, her face and her hands and her

103

body all had to get into the act too, and he could see her getting mad all over again while she explained.

"I thought he was kind of a jerk already," she finished. "And when he started in like that, so smug, so sure that life was so easy, I just wanted to *hit* him. It wasn't even that I disagreed with everything he said. I know the way things are handled now—*not* handled, more like, isn't working, that there need to be better ways to deal with homelessness. I know that. I hear about former foster kids being homeless practically every day. It was just the *contempt*. The way he was so sure it could never happen to him. It made my blood boil. I mean, literally, I was *boiling*. You know how I am," she said with an apologetic laugh.

"I do. I know that you get it. You get that people can fall on hard times. And that some people are just … lost."

"You can't grow up as a PK and not know that. But doesn't everybody know that, at least a little bit? *Shouldn't* everybody know that?"

Yeah, a Preacher's Kid would know that, he guessed. "People should," he said. "They should know life can be hard, even if it's never been hard for them. Not like the evidence isn't right there in front of them."

"Was it hard for you?" She asked it quietly, her face still for once, her gaze intent. She'd seen the crack he'd opened in the door, had picked right up on it, and he wanted to slam it shut again, but he couldn't, because she was holding him right here.

"Yes." He thought about saying more, and didn't even know how to start. He wanted to run, and he didn't do that either. Just sat there, big and dumb, and waited.

Her eyes searched his, and when he didn't say any more, she sighed, took another sip of her tea, and the moment passed.

"So you didn't hit him," he said, trying to remember what they had been talking about.

"No. I jumped out of the car instead," she said, and she laughed. "You should have seen him. I left the car door open.

104

Wide open, so he had to run around to shut it, and everyone was honking. It was *great.*"

He laughed out loud himself. "I'll bet a girl's never ditched him like that, like she couldn't wait to get away from him."

"I hope it was memorable," she said. "I hope it hurt his pride, at least. But I could have chosen my moment better. I should have waited until he'd got to a better neighborhood. I didn't think ahead. As usual."

"Well, you did the right thing. You got someplace safe and called me."

"I was worried you'd be asleep."

"Nah. I was still at work, actually. That's why I had to bring the bike."

"At midnight on Friday night? You were at *work?*"

"I got an idea," he tried to explain. "I didn't realize it was midnight. Time can go by."

"Yes," she teased, sparkling again, because Alyssa could go through three moods while he was still figuring out the first one. "I know it can. You get a little wrapped up."

"I do. I'm good at concentrating."

And right now, despite everything, he wanted to concentrate on her. He could imagine exactly how he'd do it. He wanted his hands around that red band on her throat. Gently, just holding her there. He wanted to unbutton those two little buttons holding it together, watch the two strips of red fall down her back. Somehow, exposing her throat like that would be like undressing her. And then, kissing her there. Putting her down onto his bed, lowering her until she was under him, her head back, and his mouth was at that throat. And then he'd get to work on the rest of her. Slowly. He wanted to do it. He wanted to do it now.

She looked down, picked up her spoon, set it down, and he realized he was staring. He dropped his own gaze, picked up his coffee cup and drained it, even though it had grown tepid.

"When you came," she said, "I thought you were really going to beat those guys up. I thought you really *could.*"

105

"Well, yeah, I could have," he said with surprise and not a little indignation. "Why, you don't think I can fight? I may be a programmer now, but I still know how to fight."

"But how do you fight three guys?"

"You hit them first. And you don't hold back. And one of them always runs."

"Yeah," she said with a reminiscent smile. "One of them would have run for sure."

"Plus," he pointed out, "I was the guy with the helmet."

"That's right. You were. I wondered why you didn't take it off."

"Big advantage in a fight. Get your head protected, you can do a lot of damage, and you limit their options. Helmet, leather jacket, I was all set. I was just sorry I wasn't wearing boots."

"Mmm," she said. "Stomping would have been good."

"It would have. Real good. But the best fight's the one you don't have. I figured they'd back down. Although I was kind of hoping they wouldn't."

"I would have got cold, waiting for you to get done," she said, smiling happily back at him.

"No, you wouldn't."

She lifted her delicate eyebrows. "You'd have been done that fast?"

"Yep. Kick their asses and take you on out of there."

She shut her eyes for a moment, shivered a little, and he realized it was after one in the morning, that she was cold and tired. "Come on," he said, pulling out his wallet and tossing a twenty down on the table. "Let's go. Get you home."

"More indecent motorcycling," she said, sliding out of the booth and standing up, lifting the heavy jacket and searching for the sleeve. "I've never even known you had a motorcycle, you realize that? Why is that?"

"Why would you? Just how I get to work. And here." He took the jacket from her, held it while she slid her arms inside.

"Joe." She sighed. "It's a hot-guy thing to have, don't you know that? Don't you know women like that?"

106

He smiled. He knew it. He zipped the jacket for her again, because he'd liked doing it the first time. And he liked the way it looked, miles too big, hanging down to her hips, a skimpy few inches of skirt below, and then all that smooth bare leg. It was easy to imagine that she was naked under there, and he had a sudden image of her wearing his jacket and nothing else, of unzipping it, slowly, the black leather falling away, uncovering her. Of cupping her breasts in his palms, the delicious weight of them in his hands, the way she'd arch into him when he did it, when his thumbs started to move. And then pulling her against him, with her naked under that jacket, the way she'd press into him, trying to get closer. Sliding his hands under her, his fingers digging into the curve of her ass, feeling those long legs wrapping around him as he pulled her off her feet, backed her against the wall.

Out of control. His mind was seriously out of control, he was standing there like a fool, and she was staring at him. He tried to think of something to say, and failed. Turned and led the way out of the café.

Back to his bike, unlocking the helmet and watching her put it on, climbing onto the bike and steadying it as she got on behind him, held his shoulders, pressed tight against his back, and he rode to her apartment, talking to himself the whole way, fighting hard.

Kick their asses and take you on out of there.

She'd thought she was going to have an embarrassing moment right there in the café. The way he'd looked when he said it, so sure, so tough ... he was every fantasy she'd ever had. A fantasy whose head was covered with a stubble of brown hair, now. Barely military-short after just a few weeks, but she'd been right, it looked better. He still looked tough, but he looked more handsome, too. He looked *good.*

He'd asked her if he should do it, and she'd said yes, and he'd done it. He'd grown his hair, and she thought he might have done it for her.

She snuggled up into him as they rode, and she wasn't kidding herself it was for warmth. If she'd dared, she'd have wrapped her arms around him, but despite the speed with which he'd come to get her, the way he'd taken her to warm up, had encouraged her to talk it out with a thoughtfulness that had made her melt, she still had no reason to believe that he wanted her the way she wanted him.

Maybe, though. She'd thought there had been something back there. Surely she couldn't be the only one feeling this way. So when he pulled up in front of her apartment building a few minutes later, got off the bike and walked her to her door, she tried.

"Well ... thanks again," she said, unzipping the jacket and handing it to him, watching him shrug it on and zip it again, wanting to do it for him the way he'd done it for her.

Or, more like, wanting to step into him while it was still unzipped, so she could feel him against her when he kissed her. The size of him, the heat of him. She wanted to put her arms around him, reach under the collar of the jacket, feel that ridge of muscle at his shoulder, stroke the back of his neck. While he kissed her. No, scratch that. While he kissed her *hard*, like he couldn't stand not to do it. While he pushed her into the wall of the apartment building just because he had to, because he wanted her backed up like that. She wanted him hard and fierce, the way she'd seen him tonight. She wanted all that focused intensity aimed at her.

"Thanks for rescuing me," she said. "Again. I know I'm high-maintenance."

"Mmm," he said. "Luckily, I'm good at maintenance."

"Oh." That had her melting just that much more, and she swayed towards him.

"Alyssa," he said.

"What?" she breathed, her heart pounding.

He gave her his crooked grin. "My helmet."

"Oh." She tugged the thing off her head, handed it to him, and he hefted it in one big hand.

And, when she still stood there, he took the keys from her, found the dull brass one for the front door with an unerring hand, because he'd helped her move, just like her *brother*, and put it in the lock and turned it. He shoved the heavy glass door open, propped it with his foot while he pulled the key out again and handed the bunch back to her.

"Go inside," he said, shifting a hand, his foot so he was holding the door for her now. "You're dead on your feet."

What choice did she have, after that? She obeyed, heard the heavy door swinging shut behind her, turned and watched him pull the black helmet over his head, turn and go back to the curb for his bike. He straddled the heavy black machine, kicked forward to release the kickstand as the powerful engine started, raised a hand to her in farewell while she still stood, watching. And then he was gone.

And *damn* it. She'd done every single thing she could think of. She'd paused. She'd jingled her keys. She'd given him every signal a woman could possibly send, and still nothing. He'd come to get her when she'd been in trouble, had rescued her the same way Alec would have. Like a brother, and that was it. That was all.

She swore in frustration, stomped her way across the tiled entryway, as much as a person with sore feet in high heels could be said to stomp. Stopped at the stairwell and pulled off said heels, accepted the cold grit of the worn carpeting under her feet as she climbed to the fourth floor.

She could have sworn they'd had a moment. Too bad that, once again, the moment had been all hers.

How the Real Men Do It

Joe was sitting in Alec's office when Rae popped in on a chilly mid-February evening. It was after seven, and Joe could tell from the quiet of the outer office that nearly everyone else had left.

"I'm heading out," Rae said. "You guys here for a while?"

"Nah," Alec answered. "Wrapping up. If you'll wait a sec, I'll go with you. I can finish this up at home tonight." He shut down, began to pack up. "Joe was just telling me that he's going skiing up at Tahoe over President's Day. Abandoning the ship for some of that backcountry skiing he does, and he was inviting me along so he can show me how the real men do it. So he can humiliate me, more like. What do you think? Want to come?"

"I'm not a very good skier," Rae hesitated. "In fact—" She laughed a little. "I suspect I'd barely make it into the intermediate category."

"We'll be right next door to Alpine Meadows," Joe put in. "If you want to come, we could all do resort skiing on Saturday, and you could spend Sunday that way, too, or just hang out, whatever you wanted, while I took Alec into the backcountry. As long as you don't mind going alone, it would be fine. I'd invite you to join us," he hastened to add, "but it sounds like it'd be a little technical for you."

He'd managed not to say that it would be too hard for her, he thought with relief. He had to congratulate himself on that one.

"Don't worry," she said, reading his mind, "I'm not offended. It doesn't sound good to me at all. And I shouldn't be inviting other people along on your trip, I know, but what about Alyssa?"

"Alyssa?"

"She loves to ski, and she hasn't done it since she moved," Rae said. "I know, because we've got her gear in our storage unit."

Rae and Alec were living in Rae's little cottage while their new house was being remodeled, and there hadn't been room for Alyssa's sports gear, her skis and surfboard and all the rest of it. It hadn't been going to fit in her room, either, that was for sure, so Alec and Rae had decided it could go into the storage unit that housed the few items of Alec's furniture that had made Rae's cut for the new place. Joe knew that because he'd driven the truck there and unloaded it himself.

He hesitated. Not because he didn't want Alyssa along, but because he did. It had become harder than ever to keep his distance since the night he'd rescued her. He kept wanting to call her. To check on her, he'd told himself, knowing all the while that that wasn't the reason, or at least not all of it. The idea that she was going out with other guys—that was the real reason. He couldn't get it out of his mind, now that she was this close, and it was driving him crazy, and there seemed to be no way to fix it.

"If you don't mind," Rae said again. "If there's room."

"Sure," Joe said. He'd controlled himself for fifteen years, after all. All right, her parents wouldn't be there, and he'd already discovered that that made a big difference. But at least she wouldn't be wearing a short skirt on a ski vacation, or that sweater with the band around her pretty throat. She'd *better* not be wearing that sweater, or he wasn't at all sure he could answer for the consequences. A man only had so much self-control, and he had a bad feeling that he'd reached his limit.

Rae smiled in satisfaction, sat on the edge of Alec's desk, pulled his phone around to face her, and punched buttons. "No time like the present," she informed the two men.

Joe heard the ringing, then Alyssa's voice. "Hello? Alec?"

111

"It's Rae. I'm sitting here with Alec and Joe, and we're planning a ski trip over President's Day. You've got that off, right?"

"Right," Alyssa said.

"Want to come, then?" Rae asked. "We're going to— somewhere," she laughed, "some ski area up at Lake Tahoe on Saturday, and I'm going to ski there on Sunday, too, or hang out at the lodge drinking hot chocolate, more likely, and Alec and Joe are going backcountry skiing. I don't even know what that is, but I gather it's some heroic thing that Joe does, way beyond my comfort level. What do you think? Want to come?"

"Really?" Joe could hear the longing in Alyssa's voice. "I've always wanted to try backcountry skiing." She sounded as excited as ... well, as excited as his last girlfriend, Vanessa, would have been if the topic had been a vacation to Tahiti.

Joe surrendered to the inevitable. "You're welcome to come along for that too," he said. "It isn't much more technical than what you'd be doing if you were skiing the tougher slopes at a resort. Only difference is, no lifts to get you up there."

"You need special equipment, though, don't you?" she asked.

Alec looked the question at Joe, and Joe nodded. "Yeah," he told Alyssa. "Boots, skis, bindings, skins for going uphill. But you can rent all that."

"Oh." He heard the flat tones of her disappointment. "I shouldn't. Not with the lift ticket and everything. I could do one or the other, maybe, but not both. I should probably stick to the ski area with Rae. But that'd be great," she added quickly.

"Oh," Rae said breezily, "Alec and I can take care of that, the ticket and the equipment rental. I don't have skis at all, and Alec doesn't have all those things Joe's talking about. And really?" she broke off to ask Joe. "You need *all* different stuff?"

"Well, yeah," he said, and he had to smile. "That's half the fun, getting all the different gear, needing to upgrade."

She rolled her eyes and turned her attention back to the phone. "We'll go together and get it all," she told Alyssa. "That's no problem."

"I shouldn't," Alyssa said, but she didn't sound convinced.

Alec sighed. "Why can't I have *one* happily dependent woman in my life? It makes no difference to us, Liss. It's just a lift ticket and a few days' ski rental, not a Maserati. So come on, say yes so I can wrap this up and take Desiree out of here. It's dinnertime, and I'm hungry."

Be It Ever So Humble

It was the Friday night before a holiday weekend, and Alyssa was in the car with Alec and Rae, heading up to Lake Tahoe along with what felt like half the population of the Bay Area. There wasn't a whole lot of conversation, not on her end. Alec and Rae chatted, but talking from the back seat was too hard, and after a while, she fell asleep.

She woke to the sight of black night outside, Alec following turns that eventually took him into a community that seemed to be mostly trees, with the occasional blaze of light breaking up the darkness. No surprise, Alec had rented a ski cabin in a neighborhood where the houses were big and the neighbors distant.

By the time he turned into a long driveway and pulled to a stop next to Joe's SUV, she could see by the dashboard clock that it was after ten-thirty. She got out of the car, the shock of the cold mountain air a brisk wake-up call, accepted her bag from Alec and headed for a steep flight of wooden stairs, her way illuminated by concealed lighting along the sides.

"Nice cabin," she said to Joe, because he was at the top, holding open an oversized front door and letting her into a stone-flagged entryway that led to another flight of stairs. A railing along one side of the spacious entry ended in three or four steps down into a sunken great room walled by windows. She could see a hearth with a wood stove at one end, the wall behind it faced with more stone.

She guessed that it could be called a cabin. It was made of logs, which made it a log cabin, no matter how big it was.

"Pretty late," Joe said when they were all inside. "Traffic bad?"

"My fault, really," Alyssa said. "I thought I could get out early, or at least on time, but Helene had some stuff for me to finish." Which hadn't seemed all that urgent, but Alyssa wasn't the boss, and Helene was. *Get along to get ahead,* she reminded herself once again.

"No problem," Joe said. "Come on, I'll show you the upstairs."

"Alec and Rae in here," he said when he'd led the way to the second floor, opened the door of a large room equipped with a queen bed. "And Alyssa, you're here." Next door, a slightly smaller room, twin beds this time, more big windows. "Bathroom at the end of the hall. Everybody good?"

"Yeah," Alyssa sighed. "Shower, bed. Sounds good to me." She didn't spend a lot of time admiring her surroundings. She mostly focused on appreciating the heated towel racks and massaging shower in the bathroom, the flannel sheets on the bed. There were advantages to having a successful brother and being allowed to tag along on his vacations, even though the comparisons could get tough. And even though Alec and Rae, as always, made too much noise, noise that she really, really didn't need to hear right now. She put a pillow over her head, gave herself a nice little fantasy as a consolation prize, and fell asleep.

She woke up, though, with her good mood restored. She'd only awakened once during the night. Instead of the traffic noise she'd grown used to hearing, the occasional sirens, the loud voices and laughter of late-night returners, the streetlight that insisted on shining into her window through a crack in the drapes, there'd been nothing but silence and darkness enfolding her, and she'd drifted off again, warm and content. Now it was morning, she was in the mountains with two days of skiing ahead of her, and she couldn't wait.

"Some cabin," she said aloud when she'd got out of bed and opened the heavy drapes next to her bed to find sliding doors leading out onto a narrow deck that ran the length of both her room and Alec and Rae's, and what looked like acres of snowy pine forest beyond. She could imagine waking up on a summer morning, drinking your coffee out there. Assuming you had a butler to bring it to you, of course. Well, maybe not.

She pulled on her ski clothes, which made her even happier, and came downstairs to the sight of the wall of windows from the night before, drapes open to reveal an endless view of more evergreens, more snow. A leather couch and two easy chairs formed a comfortable seating group near the fire, a rocking chair sat in a corner next to a tall bookshelf full of books that looked like somebody had actually read them, and the rafters soared a good 25 feet overhead. It was airy, yet cozy, made you want to snuggle up in warm socks, drink coffee from a mug, read a book and look at trees. She wasn't sure how you got that effect, but whoever had designed and decorated this house had managed it.

"Morning. Coffee's made," Joe said as she took it all in. He was standing in a fully equipped kitchen that could have come out of any architectural magazine, stirring something in a big blue ceramic bowl, wearing a dark red plaid shirt with the sleeves rolled up and looking more like a logger—a really *hot* logger—than any man cooking in a gourmet kitchen had any business looking. His hair was a little longer now, more than military-short, and it looked even better.

"What are you making?" she asked, pouring herself a cup of coffee, then looking around in vain. "Wait a minute. Tell me there's a fridge in here."

Joe smiled, set his bowl down and came over to open a cabinet that was hiding an extra-large refrigerator.

"How would you even know?" she wondered. "What's wrong with having a refrigerator that looks like one?"

"It ruins the aesthetic," he informed her solemnly.

"Huh." She looked inside and found her milk, and a whole lot more, slammed the fridge—the cabinet—door. "You did a lot of grocery shopping."

"That's what I get for starting my vacation early. And the answer to the question about what I'm making is, blueberry pancakes and eggs. You ready for pancakes?"

116

"Sure." She scooted up onto a stool at the breakfast bar, sipped her coffee, and watched him. "I didn't know you could cook."

"Pancakes and eggs, anyway. Somebody has to. I thought nobody in the world could be as hopeless at cooking as Alec, until I met Rae."

"I know," Alyssa said. "She's worse than me, and I'm bad. So are you the chef for this whole trip? Do I just get to sit back?"

"Nope." He ladled circles of batter studded with lumps of round berries onto the griddle that was set into the middle of the huge restaurant-style stove, then pulled out another bowl and began to crack the better part of a carton of eggs into it. "You get to help me. But I figured we'd do some eating out, too. I've got a plan."

"Why am I surprised?" He was so relaxed, so approachable. So unlike Joe. "You seem like you're quite at home."

"Well ..." He smiled at her. "Because I am."

"What? You're kidding me," she said as he continued to smile. She waved an arm around. "I thought Alec rented this place. You mean it's yours? You have a *vacation* house?"

"Is that so amazing?" He handed her silverware and a napkin, then flipped his pancakes, dumped half the egg mixture into a pan that had been heating on the stove and began to stir it with a spatula.

"Well, yeah," she said. "It is. I thought you worked all the time."

"I have really good wireless." He smiled again, put eggs and pancakes on her plate and handed it to her, went to the fridge and pulled out a butter dish and a crock of maple syrup, then fixed his own plate and set it next to hers, got his own coffee. "And this way," he went on as they began to eat, "I don't have to mess with rentals. I've got a base for whatever I want to do, skiing, backpacking, hiking, whatever, got enough space for anyone I bring up with me. Efficient."

"Nice if you can do it," she said dryly. "But it's a great place," she went on hastily when he shot a look across at her.

"You like it?" he asked.

"No, I don't think it's quite plush enough for me. Of course I like it. It's … well, I think the word is *fabulous,* and I've only seen a little bit of it." She gestured to the wide, snow-covered wooden deck that extended the entire width of the window wall. "Is that a hot tub out there?"

"Got to have a hot tub," he said. "It's in the rules. Feels good after skiing, too."

Getting into a hot tub with Joe after skiing … yeah, that would be good. She'd never seen him in the summer, all these years, only at Christmas and a few Thanksgivings. Which meant she'd never seen him in a swimsuit, and she'd *really* like to see that. She sneaked a peek across at the size of the thigh taking up the stool next to hers, the width of his back, the breadth of his shoulders in that plaid shirt. A swimsuit—yes, please. She might not get to touch, but she'd sure like to look.

"Morning, guys." Alec and Desiree looked over the railing from the second-floor landing, headed down the pine staircase with its hand-hewn log rail. "Breakfast ready?" Alec asked. "Guess I'll withdraw my letter of complaint. Maybe the service at this hotel isn't so bad after all."

And that was the end of her cozy time alone with Joe.

She got to be impressed again an hour later, when everyone was buckling ski boots and pulling on coats.

"Are we driving up in your car," she asked Joe as he came to sit on the bench beside her to put on his boots, "or is there a shuttle?"

"Neither," he said. "We're walking."

"We're walking," she said slowly. "To the ski area."

"No, we're walking ten minutes up the road. There's a lift into Alpine Meadows from there."

"So let's recap here." She finished her boot-fastening and sat up. "You have a ski cabin with about the nicest bathroom

I've ever been in, never *mind* in somebody's 'cabin.' I barely came out this morning. The *floor's* warm in there!"

"Radiant heating in the subfloor. You liked that, huh?"

"And a refrigerator that hides in a cabinet because refrigerators are so pedestrian," she went on, "and a private ski lift."

"Not private," he said, a smile threatening. "I have to share it with all those neighbors."

"Hey," Alec complained from his spot on the living room couch a few steps below, where he and Rae were fastening their own boots. "A whole life's worth of experience with your fabulous brother, and Joe's the one getting all the love?"

"You don't have a ski cabin," Alyssa pointed out. "One lousy house in San Francisco. Pfft. Get a private ski lift, and I'll be impressed."

And then Joe went back to being Joe again. "Is this absolutely necessary?" Alyssa asked when they'd taken the chair lift up, got to the ski area, and ... not skied. "Couldn't you just tell us what to do while we ride the lifts or something? Or give us the PowerPoint presentation tonight, so we could ski today, sometime before the snow melts?"

"It's necessary if you want me to take you backcountry skiing tomorrow," Joe said calmly. "Because you're not going up the mountain with me until I've seen you use this equipment, and until I'm convinced you're going to remember how to do it."

Alec, Alyssa, and Joe were standing in the ski area's avalanche beacon practice area, and Joe was giving them a lesson in rescue techniques. A long, boring lesson.

"Yeah, Liss," Alec said. "There Joe and I'd be, buried under tons of snow, thinking about your eyes glazing over during his Rescue Beacon Lecture. Yeah, that'd be reassuring. We'd know we were dead meat."

"I thought you said there wasn't much danger, though," she said, but she had to laugh, because Alec was right. She couldn't help it, she wanted to *ski.*

"There's always some danger," Joe said. "Being a mountaineer's a little like being a pilot. There are old mountaineers, and bold mountaineers, but no old bold mountaineers. So you check conditions ahead of time, and right now, conditions are pretty safe. But you still check your terrain, and you pay attention. You know what to do if the unexpected happens, and you've got the equipment to do it. That's how you get to go skiing again next year. This is important, so pay attention."

"Hoo-ah," Alyssa muttered, but she paid attention.

Twenty minutes more, and Joe was finally satisfied. "All right," he said. "Looks like everybody's got it. You good, Alec?"

"I promise to find you and dig you out," Alec said. "And I know you know how, so if you're on top of the snow, I'm not worried. The question is ..."

They both looked at Alyssa, and she sighed with impatience. "You just saw me do it, and I'm betting Joe gives me the refresher course tomorrow. I'll bet you give me a test, in fact, Joe. I'm not sure if I'm more scared of the avalanche or of you flunking me. Who knows what would happen?"

"Bad things," Joe said, and he was smiling a little. "All right, let's go find Rae. You want to ski with me a while, Alyssa? Want to show me your stuff?"

"Think you can keep up?"

"Oh," he said, "I think so."

He could, too. He didn't even raise an eyebrow when she wanted to start out on one of the steepest slopes, and as soon as they started down, she realized why. She wouldn't have called him graceful even now, but he skied tougher, pushed it harder than she'd ever have given him credit for, powering down the most technical runs with a raw athleticism that gave her a rush just to watch. Sometimes she led, sometimes he did, and she enjoyed the rare satisfaction of skiing with somebody even better than she was, somebody who enjoyed it as much as she did.

They must have covered close to half the mountain when Joe pulled up with an aggressive spray of snow at the base of a double black diamond run that had had Alyssa laughing aloud on the way down, trying to keep up, pushed to the edge and loving it.

"Lunch," he said, breathing a little heavily.

"Time for one more first?" she begged.

She saw the flash of his teeth under the goggles. "No. After lunch, I promise. Having a good time?"

"You know I am. You're great."

"You're not so bad yourself," he said, and he was still smiling. "Come on. Lunch. Let's find out how Rae did."

"I don't have to ask if you've had a fun morning, Alyssa," Rae said when they were seated at a wooden table devouring pizza, overlooking the big windows showcasing skiers coming down the slope, none of them, Alyssa thought privately, doing it as well as she and Joe had. "It's obvious."

"Fantastic," she said happily. "How about you?"

Rae rubbed her thighs ruefully. "I'm enjoying it, but I'm glad to take a break. I don't have ski muscles. I'm going to be sore."

"You did really well," Alec said. "Improving all the time. You just haven't skied enough."

"Not a big part of my life plan," she agreed. "I'm going to sit here a while longer before I go out again, and you're going to ski with Joe and Alyssa. I saw you looking at those signs," she went on when he would have protested. "I *know* you want to go down all the runs that say 'Danger' at the top. It's written all over you."

"The need for speed," Alec said. "Sorry, baby, can't help it. I enjoy being with you, too."

"Mm-hmm," she said, and she was smiling at him. "Either that, or you enjoy being so much better at it than me."

"You wound me," he protested, sitting back and putting a hand over his heart. "Besides, it's unfair to deny me the very, very occasional pleasure of knowing there's something in this

121

world I do better than you. I'd better not bring you up here too often, or you're going to catch up, and then I'll really be in trouble. Don't invite her," he told Joe. "That's an order from your CEO."

"My CEO can take a flying leap," Joe answered, reaching for another slice of pizza. "Your ego can barely fit through the door as it is. How about this? I'm inviting your wife right now to come skiing with me anytime she wants to."

"Whoa," Alyssa said. "Them's fightin' words."

"Good thing we're friends," Alec said as Rae started to laugh. "And that I'm so much better-looking than you."

"Well, don't worry," Rae said. "I'm not going skiing without you, Alec, and I'm not going at all for the next hour, and I'm not going with you for the rest of the day, because I'm staying right on those blue-square routes, and there might even be some green circles in there. If I fall down too many more times, I'm telling you, it's back to the bunny slope for me. And meanwhile, you're going to be doing the hard stuff. If you're going out with Joe and Alyssa tomorrow, you'd better practice, because I saw what they were doing out there."

"My natural athletic ability will carry the day," Alec proclaimed, making his wife smile again. "But all right, if you're sure, we'll meet you at the base of that lift right there at—four?" he asked Joe.

"Sounds good," Joe said. "And a few hours of Alyssa and me schooling you sounds good, too."

Cliff, Lance, and Talon

"How'd you do?" Alec asked Rae when they met up again.

"Not too bad," she said. "How about you?"

"Terrific. But, damn, Liss and Joe are good. They already kicked my ass. By the end of the day tomorrow, you can expect my ego to be fully downsized."

"What do you think?" Joe asked. "One more run, something we can all do together, and call it a day?"

"Sure," Rae said, although Alyssa could tell she was tired. "As long as it's easy."

Joe chose one of the easier intermediate routes, and they set off down the slope, three of them taking a more vertical descent, and Rae quickly falling behind. The light was flat now, the changes in terrain harder to see, and Alyssa, who'd been a little disappointed not to finish off the day with a bang, privately conceded that Joe had probably chosen well. They reached the bottom fairly quickly and turned to wait for Rae.

Five minutes went by, and Alec took a look at his watch. "She should be down by now. Hope she didn't fall again. I should probably have sat this out with her."

A few more minutes, and his anxiety was showing. "She should be down," he said again to Joe. "Could she have skied off the route?"

"I don't think so," he said, but he was down on a knee, his day pack on the ground in front of him. He unfastened his bindings, attached skins to the bottoms of his skis.

"I didn't know you brought those," Alyssa said, trying to make conversation, trying to make this all right.

123

"Just in case." He put his skis on again and stood up. "I'm going back up to look for her."

He set off, moving fast straight up the mountain, and Alec was shifting on his skis, stabbing a pole into the snow, his normally confident expression giving way to anxiety as Joe's figure receded, then disappeared from sight.

"I'm sure she's OK," Alyssa tried again. "She just fell or something. It can take a while to get up when you're not used to it."

"She's had a lot of practice today," Alec said. "She knows how to get up." He gave a nearby drift another stab, and Alyssa couldn't think of anything else to say, so she didn't say anything.

More achingly slow minutes passed, until at last, they saw a lone skier coming down the mountain.

"Is that Joe?" Alec asked.

"No," Alyssa said. She knew the look of Joe now, and the skier didn't have his size, or his moves.

It was a teenage kid, they saw as he skied to a stop at the bottom of the lift near where they stood. "There's somebody hurt up there," he told the attendant, looking excited to be reporting it. "They told me to ask you to get the ski patrol."

The attendant nodded, pulled a radio off his belt and spoke into it. Alec was at the kid's side in an instant.

"Who is it?" he asked him. "Who's hurt?"

The kid looked at him in surprise. "Uh ... a lady."

"How badly hurt is she?" Alec pressed. "Where? Is anybody with her?"

"Yeah, a guy's with her," the kid said, backing up a bit at the intensity on Alec's face. "I don't know how bad. I didn't see. The guy just waved me down and told me she was hurt, and to ask them to send the ski patrol. That's all I know."

"Alec," Alyssa said, her hand on his arm. "We don't know. I'm sure it's all right."

"I should have sat this one out with her," he said again. "She was too tired, and the light was too bad. Stupid—selfish—I should have sat it out. Where *are* they?"

He subsided, but his anxiety was almost a tangible thing now, and he couldn't stand still. The wait felt endless, but it was probably only a few minutes before they saw another skier carving a quick route down the mountain, and this time, Alyssa recognized Joe. And, behind him, a skier towing a sled, a sled that had something on it, and she thought Alec was going to jump out of his skin.

Joe came to a quick stop, pushed up his goggles, and spoke to Alec. "It's her knee. She torqued it good. It's hurting pretty bad, and she might have got a little banged up, took a hard fall, but that's all. She's talking, didn't black out. She's OK."

Alyssa saw Alec let go of a long breath, and had to wonder for a bleak moment what it would be like to matter that much to another person.

The patroller skied up to join them, and it was Rae on the sled, of course, covered with a blanket and fastened down with straps, and Alec was at her side, bending down on his skis to talk to her, pulling off his glove to stroke her face as if he couldn't stand not to.

"Baby," Alyssa heard him say, "you OK? I'm so sorry."

Rae smiled at him, though Alyssa could tell it took an effort, because the pain was there in the tightness of her lips, the pinched look of her. "Just ... embarrassed to be—riding on the sled. Sorry. So stupid. I fell. I tried to get up, but—I couldn't. I thought I could wait for it to feel better. Joe made me get on the sled."

"I'm taking her to the clinic," the ski patroller told Alec. "You all can come along, but we need to go."

They followed him to the clinic, stopped outside. Alyssa and Alec took off their skis, stuck them into the rack outside the low wooden building, and Alec got Rae's skis and poles as well. Joe, though, didn't follow suit.

"I'll ski down for the car," he said. Alec nodded, and Joe took off.

A wait inside the clinic's reception area, then, while Alec filled in forms, and then they sat and waited some more until the door opened to the sight of Rae in a wheelchair pushed by a middle-aged woman, and followed by what Alyssa assumed was a doctor, judging by the white lab coat and the stethoscope. Young, tall, dark hair with a bit of curl to it, looking like he belonged in a movie about a good-looking doctor working at a ski area. A romantic comedy, probably, from the jaunty confidence of his walk. When he got closer, she could see the name embroidered in black script on the white coat. *Cliff Monaghan, M.D.*

"Your wife's got an MCL strain," the doctor told Alec as the nurse, or whatever she was, headed through the door again to the back of the clinic. "As I've explained to her, this is one of the most common injuries we see up here, but she did a pretty good job of it. Sounds like she was going fast when she fell, and that twists the knee with more force, can increase the severity of the injury. I'm recommending that you head on over to a hospital with her and get it checked out. The ligament's got some fairly significant tearing, that's my guess, judging by the amount of pain and the fact that she can't move it. For right now, we've got an icepack and an elastic bandage on her, but Carolyn at the desk there will give you a couple options for hospitals. I'd like to see you check that out before the swelling gets any worse."

Alec already had his phone out. "I'll call my brother. He's a doctor."

The doctor hesitated. "You'll want a hospital, and if it were my wife, I'd want a specialist."

"I know," Alec said impatiently. "I've got a specialist." He turned away, was talking into the phone.

"My brother-in-law," Rae explained. Her face was even more pale, and she sounded like she was speaking through gritted teeth. "Gabe Kincaid, in Truckee."

"Really?" The doctor laughed. "Small world. I send a fair amount of business Gabe's way. You couldn't do better."

Alec was holding out the phone. "He wants to talk to you."

"Hey," the doctor said into the phone. "Cliff Monaghan here, up at Alpine Meadows. How you doin'? He paused to listen. "Yeah," he said after a minute. "You'll want to get this

126

lady into an MRI machine tonight, I'd say. Looks like Grade III MCL to me. Quite a bit of pain, enough so I didn't want to palpate."

Another pause. "OK," he said. "I'll hook her up with the good stuff." He winked at Rae. "Talk to you soon."

He hung up, handed the phone back to Alec. "Back to my magic cabinet for some samples. I'll be right with you. Meet you at the front desk."

True to his word, he was back again within a couple minutes with two small white packets with a name Alyssa recognized. That *was* the good stuff. He held them out to Rae, still in her wheelchair. "Two of these puppies right now," he promised, "and you'll be a lot more comfortable in that MRI machine."

Alyssa went over to the water cooler, filled a little paper cup, and brought it back to Rae, glad to have something, even this minor, to do.

"Let me guess," Dr. Cliff said to her as Rae swallowed pills and Alec paid the receptionist. "You're a Kincaid too."

"Sister," she said. "Alyssa." He *was* cute. Pretty insensitive, though. No pain pills until Gabe had asked for them? If Rae had broken her leg, he probably would have advised that they shoot her, put her out of her misery.

"It's the eyes that give you away. Beautiful eyes. I wouldn't say that to him," he said, inclining his head in Alec's direction and flashing Alyssa a smile, "but I'll say it to you. Unmarried sister, I hope?"

She raised her eyebrows. "If anybody's asking."

"Well, isn't this my lucky day. I meet Gabe Kincaid's family, and there's even a bonus in it. You all will probably be heading out after this, though, which is a real shame."

She hadn't even considered it, but of course they would. The thought of it gave her a purely selfish pang of regret for her lost chance to try backcountry skiing. "Probably," she said. "Unfortunately."

"Accidents are my job, but they're not much fun, are they? Let's hope you get a little more skiing time in, if not this trip, another one. We're having a good snow year. Be a shame to miss it." He pulled a business card from his breast pocket, unclipped a pen from the same spot, and scribbled something on it. "This is me. I've put my cell on there. Give me a call, if you're around. You can let me know how your … sister-in-law, I guess, is doing."

"Hmm," she said, flicking the card and giving him her best are-you-man-enough? look. The handsome doctor flirting with her—well, that was fun, even if she didn't care much for him. *Eat your heart out, Joe.* "I thought you doctor types talked to each other," she said, and if she was flirting back, well, a girl needed to practice. "I won't know all the technical words. Maybe you should ask Gabe instead."

"Oh, if you tell me, I think I can get the gist." He smiled back, showing some very straight white teeth this time. It was a pretty good smile, and a pretty practiced one, too. "And I'm always on the lookout for a good partner. Skiing, that is."

"Uh-huh." She shifted the load of coats she was carrying—hers, Alec's, and Rae's—found a pocket, shoved the card inside. "I'll keep that in mind."

"Well, if you lose it," he said, "you know where I work."

He turned to shake hands with Rae and Alec. "Take care," he said, serious again. "You can't do better than Gabe, so I know I'm leaving you in good hands."

With a last smile for Alyssa, he returned to the back regions, ready for the next unfortunate victim of the slopes.

They had a wait, then, until the door to the clinic opened and Joe came in. He'd changed from his ski boots, Alyssa saw.

"How we doing?" he asked.

"Seems I've abused my MCL," Rae said. "Because when I fall, I fall big."

"Need to take her to see Gabe in Truckee," Alec told him. "He says it's a thirty-minute drive. All right?"

"Sure," Joe said. "Car's right outside."

Alec pushed Rae to the door, waited while Joe held it open for them, then took the wheelchair ramp down to where Joe's car sat waiting. As soon as Joe had the door open, Alec picked Rae up despite her protest, deposited her gently in the front passenger seat, waited while she fastened her shoulder belt, then closed her door.

"Alec," she said once the others had collected the skis and poles, Joe had stowed them in the back of the car, and they were heading out of the lot, "You can't go around carrying me. I could have got in the car myself. I was only hesitating because I don't have any shoes on, and I wasn't thrilled about stepping in the snow."

"Nah," he said from his spot behind her. "That's why I married a skinny woman, so I could look powerful carrying her around. Now, if it had been Alyssa, we'd have been in trouble."

Alyssa gasped in outrage, but Rae beat her to it. "That is such a fail. So not smooth. I am not skinny. *Slender* is the word you're going for. And Alyssa hardly weighs more than I do."

"Oh, yes, I do," Alyssa put in.

Rae ignored her. "Even Joe knows you don't insult a woman about her weight. Either direction. I don't care if she *is* your sister, that's a major loss of points, huh, Joe?"

"Yep," he answered. "Nobody ever accused me of being smooth, but you're right, even I'm smarter than that. Guess we'll blame stress."

"I did not talk about her weight," Alec protested. "I just said, I'm not sure I'd want to lift her into any cars."

Rae was laughing again, and if Alyssa hadn't already known what those pills had been, she'd have had a pretty good idea by now. "I think most men would be a whole lot happier to pick Alyssa up than to pick me up. She has the figure I always wanted. Aren't I right, Joe? You're not her brother. Wouldn't any guy be happier to pick her up?"

"Uh ..." he said. "Is there a good answer to this question? Because it doesn't seem like it to me. I abstain."

Rae didn't seem to care that he wasn't answering, because she went on. "I know Dr. Handsome in there would have been happy to pick her up. In fact, that's exactly what he was doing. Pretty good work, Alyssa, scoring the ski doctor. See, that's why I wanted to look like you. That kind of thing never happened to me."

"Hey," Alec protested. "I seem to recall some fairly hot pursuit."

Rae waved an airy hand. "You don't count. You hit on everybody."

Alyssa had to laugh at the way her brother's mouth fell open at that one. "What did that guy give you, anyway?" he asked. "I thought it was for pain. It's like some kind of truth serum, and I don't think I like it. I'd like the filter back, please."

"It worked on the pain, though," Rae said. "I mean, it still hurts, I just don't care anymore."

"He drugs my wife, then he puts the moves on my sister," Alec said. "Not a good bet, Liss," he added. "By the way."

"Oh, I don't know," she said. "Rae's right, he *was* pretty handsome. He liked me, too." Maybe she'd turned thirty, but some guys still thought she was cute. And maybe it wasn't very nice of her to care about this right now, but she wanted Joe to know it.

"Probably give you an STD," Alec muttered, and Rae said, sharply for once, "Alec!"

"Oh, thanks," Alyssa said. "Like I'm going to go back and do him on the exam table. Thanks a lot. I might not have been getting out much lately, but I've still got more restraint than that. Just."

"Sorry," Alec said, looking a little shamefaced. "I should have asked for a pill for me. Can't you go faster?" he demanded of Joe. They were finally down the mountain, headed down the highway to Truckee. "I'd like to get there sometime tonight. Why don't you let me drive?"

"Road's icing up, this late in the day," Joe said.

"There's sand on it," Alec said. "And you're in a four-wheel-drive."

"And you're too keyed up," Joe said. "Not a good idea. It's going to take us a whole lot longer to get there if we spin out along the way."

"Let him drive, Alec," Rae said, sounding sobered and a little scared.

Alec reached a hand around for hers, and she grabbed it and held on. "Be there soon, baby," he promised. "Gabe's waiting for us, and he'll fix you up. We're almost there."

She nodded. "So you don't think Dr. What's-His-Name was Alyssa's dream man? Come on, talk to me. It helps."

"Whose name is Cliff?" Alec asked with another squeeze of her hand. "Nobody. That's like being named …"

"Rock," Alyssa suggested, adding her bit to the distraction element. "Brock. Linc. Shane."

"Lance," Rae went on, and they were both giggling now. "Magnus. Thor."

"Wyatt. Ranger," Alyssa managed. "Talon."

"Talon? Somebody's named *Talon?"* Desiree demanded. "Like, I've got you in my talons? That's just *wrong."* She had a hand over her mouth to stifle the giggles, but it wasn't working.

"I knew one," Alyssa admitted through her own laughter. "In LA. I don't think his parents picked it, let's just say. He spent more on waxing than I do. He waxed his *legs.* He *said* it was for surfing, but I had my doubts. Eww, the Amazing Hairless Man."

Alec groaned as the two of them continued to laugh until they were gasping with it. "What women talk about when they're together," he said. "The truth comes out."

"We talk about ourselves," Rae said, wiping her eyes. "And each other, and life. We don't sit around and talk about men. That's just what men like to think. And you're the one who brought it up."

"Yeah, well," Alec said, "I'm just saying, ol' Cliff's real name is probably Roger. Bet he hands that card out ten times a day. Major player."

"How do you know?" Alyssa challenged. "Maybe he *was* overcome by my beauty, not to mention my alluring curves. Which is what I am, FYI. That is the preferred terminology. Curvy. You've lost *all* your moves."

"I used to have some, though," Alec said. "And I'm telling you, major player. Don't go there."

"Don't worry," she said. "I've got no plans to swap bacteria with Dr. Cliff. I was just messing with you. I've been your sister too long not to recognize the species."

"My former species," he corrected, still holding Rae's hand. "Are we just about there?" he demanded of Joe. "I'm not asking to drive, because Rae doesn't want me to. But we'd better be just about there."

"Couple more minutes," Joe said, and he was right, they were pulling off the highway within five minutes, into the parking lot of Tahoe Forest Hospital, and Alec was thumbing his phone. The next thing they saw was Gabe coming out to meet them, pushing the wheelchair himself. Another gentle lift down by Alec that had Rae uttering a hastily stifled exclamation and grabbing his arm all the same, and Alec was pushing the chair beside his brother.

"Got the MRI machine all warmed up and waiting for you," Gabe promised.

"Thanks, bro," Alec said. "Saturday night, too."

"Called in a couple favors," Gabe said. "Don't worry," Alyssa heard as Gabe punched the big square button beside the front doors and they opened with a hiss. She saw Gabe put a hand on Alec's shoulder, could almost feel the unspoken communication her brothers shared. "If you're going to mess with a knee ligament, the MCL's the one you want to mess with. She'll be all right. I promise."

Gabe was as good as his word. Less than an hour later, they were leaving with more pain pills, and Rae in a knee brace and with crutches that Alec refused to let her use, instead carrying her again.

"Too slick out here," he said when she protested. "And you're too tired."

"Going to go ahead and stay at the house tonight?" Joe asked when they were in the car, headed back to North Lake Tahoe again. "Better, I'd think."

"Gabe thought so too," Alec said. "Keep the leg elevated, keep ice on it, dope her up. I don't want to put her in the car for hours tonight, even in the back seat. Too painful, with her so tired. Bad idea."

"Of course we're staying," Rae said. "Quit talking about me like I'm not here. 'Dope her up?' And anyway, you have a date with Joe tomorrow, Alec. I was going to ski on my own. I'll just hang out on my own instead and watch movies. I'll be fine."

"Uh-huh. I'm going to leave you in pain, alone, with no way to get in touch with me, while I go have fun in the mountains," Alec said. "Yeah, that's happening. Nope. We're going home tomorrow, and I'm taking care of you, and there's no point talking about it anymore," he went right on over her protest, "because we're done."

"Alec …"

"No."

"You're way too bossy," she grumbled.

"When you're hurt, you bet I am," he said. "We're done."

They drove the rest of the way in relative quiet, everyone feeling the effects of the strenuous day and its unexpected conclusion, until Joe stopped in town, pulled into a spot.

"Hang on two minutes," he said. "Alyssa, could you give me a hand?"

"Sure," she said, hopping out of the car. "What are we doing?"

"Picking up dinner. I called ahead," he said, opening the door for her into an Italian restaurant hung with tiny white lights.

"Joe Hartman," he told the woman at the register. "Picking up."

"What are we having?" Alyssa asked, hefting one big brown bag while Joe took the other.

133

"Lasagne, vegetables, rolls, and salad," he said. "I know we had pizza for lunch, but that's what sounded good to me, and easy to heat up back home. What do you think?"

"If it tastes as good as it smells," she told him, hefting her bag again just to get a whiff, "I'd say you did great."

Back at the cabin, Alec and Joe, after some conferring, made a chair out of their forearms and carried Rae up the long flight of stairs to the cabin's front door, Alyssa running ahead to open it, and then up to the second level, depositing her on the bed in Alec and Rae's bedroom.

By the time they had her there and Alyssa had set the crutches down within her reach, Rae was gasping. "Boy, that hurts. Pills or not, that hurts. I want a bath, but oh, getting in there isn't going to feel good."

"I'll put you in," Alec said. "And I'll take you out, too."

"You're not sitting around staring at me in the tub," Rae protested.

"No," he said with exaggerated patience. "I'm going to help you get undressed and put you in the tub. Then I'm going to sit outside the bathroom until you call me. And then I'm going to come take you out of the tub and help you get dressed again."

"We could take her up to my room, if you want," Joe said. "I've got a big tub up there with jets. Might feel good. You could get in there with her. It's a good size."

"No," Rae said. "Thanks, but no. I don't want to. I don't think I can handle getting jostled. I'm sorry, Alec. I know I'm grumpy. But it *hurts.*" She was tearing up now. "I'm sorry. It's just that it hurts."

"OK," Alec said. "Everybody out."

Alyssa left the room ahead of Joe, and he closed the door gently to the sound of Alec saying, "Baby. It's OK." And a muffled sound that, she realized, was capable, competent Rae starting to cry.

The Water's Fine

Joe stood with his hand on the doorknob. "Why don't you use my bathroom?" he asked Alyssa. "They're going to take a while in this one, and it'd feel good. Like I said, whirlpool jets in the tub. It's pretty nice."

"You want your shower, though," she said.

"Nah. A little mountain dirt never hurt anyone. I can wait. You'll give me a chance to get started on a beer. Get your stuff and come on upstairs."

He was pulling a towel out of the bathroom cupboard when he saw her head appear cautiously around the door. "Come on in," he said over the noise of the water. "I started it for you. It takes a while to fill. The button for the jets is here," he indicated. "Take your time."

He grabbed a shampoo bottle that was slipping out of her grip and set it on the stone edge, marveling as always at the amount of stuff women needed to take a bath. A bar of soap, a stick of deodorant, an electric shaver, and he was done. Groomed.

"You weren't kidding," she said. "This is the biggest bathtub I've ever seen."

"Yeah, well, sometimes you don't want to go all the way down to the hot tub," he said. And sometimes, you needed to be close to the bed when you got out, because you had a woman wrapped around you and you needed to get her on her back just as fast as possible.

He got out of there before he could think any more about Alyssa being in his bathtub, or about the long, hot, soapy times he'd had in there. He loved doing it in the water, the way it felt when you had a woman floating over you, your hands on her breasts to hold her there. He'd had some very willing playmates in that tub who'd seemed to enjoy doing it that way as much as he did, and he'd appreciated every single one of them. But there'd never been anybody he wanted to play with more.

It took a while, but eventually, everybody was clean, and he was sitting around the table with Alec and Alyssa, eating lasagna and drinking wine.

Alec had taken Rae's dinner up to her to eat in bed.

"She's too tired," he explained to the others. "When she gets like this, she doesn't want to talk to me. She doesn't even realize she needs to eat. She needs the food put in front of her, or she won't even do that. She's got two speeds, 60 miles an hour or crash. She doesn't know she's on the reserve tank until it's empty."

"Like you," Joe told Alyssa. "After your first day of work."

Her fork stilled as she stared at him. "You got that?"

"Sure. You were worn out, you were cold. You needed to take a shower and change your clothes and eat, and you didn't have the energy to think about me, let alone be … grateful, or whatever."

"You *got* that?" she asked again.

"Just because I'm a man," he said, a little irked now, "it doesn't mean I'm stupid. Alec isn't stupid about Rae, and I'm not stupid about you." He realized what he'd said, clamped his mouth shut before he could say more.

"First day was hard, huh, Liss?" Alec asked, breaking a silence that was starting to get uncomfortable.

"Yeah," she said, looking down at her plate and mushing around her lasagna.

"How's it going now?" he asked. "You liking it? Good move?"

She hesitated, playing with her salad now. "I like a lot of what I'm doing. In fact," she said, looking up, "I worked up a

136

whole fundraising package this week. I wrote a good letter, at least I think I did. I'm nervous about showing it to Helene, though. I brought it with me. I was planning to ask Rae to look at it, but would you guys?"

"Sure," Alec said, taking another sip of wine. "Go get it."

She ran up to her room, came back a minute later with a piece of paper in her hand.

"Long," Alec said, flipping the sheet over. "Two pages? Do people really want to read all that?"

Joe could see her stiffening, getting defensive. "This isn't the final version. It'll have pull quotes and pictures and all sorts of things. You want to engage the person. You want to pull them in, make them care. It's not just, *bam,* business proposition. It goes to people who've already contributed, and it's part of the package we leave behind when we do a call, too. Well, when Helene does a call," she corrected herself.

"I thought you were doing them too," Joe said.

"No. Not anymore."

He frowned. "That was the whole point, I thought, that you were getting an opportunity to learn all aspects of the development business."

"I know." She looked unhappy. "But Helene always has these other things I need to do, and she says ..." She hesitated. "That I'm not ready, and I'm wondering if she thinks I ever will be. I was supposed to do some presenting last month to some potential donors, but it ended up with her ... 'taking the lead,' she called it, because she's the Director, but I'm wondering if I'll ever get the chance to do it myself, because I haven't even gone on any of the calls since then. "

She tried to laugh, gave a shrug. "Oh, well. I guess I was overconfident. I guess raising foundation money is different from selling other things."

"I wouldn't think so," Joe said. "Sales are sales. Alec could sell ice to Eskimos, and you're the same."

"Well, hopefully I'll get the chance," she said.

Alec wasn't paying attention. "This is actually a good letter," he said, looking up. "Really good."

"You think?" she asked with an edge of uncertainty that didn't sound like Alyssa. He should have checked in with her about the job, Joe thought. Set aside the way he felt about her as a woman, and cared a little more about her. He should have checked.

"It's dynamite," Alec said, handing it to Joe. "Here, you read it."

He didn't want to read it. He knew what those letters said. But Alyssa was looking at him, nervous, expectant, so he started in.

There's no box in Antoine's house with a lock of his baby hair stuck in an envelope, the picture he painted in kindergarten, his report card from fourth grade. That's because Antoine has never had a family. Born addicted to crack, he spent the first days of his young life battling through the ordeal of withdrawal from a drug he never chose to take. When he left the hospital, it was for a foster home. When he's asked how many homes he's lived in since, Antoine has to stop and think. And he has to count.

Joe skimmed down the sheet.

Sixteen-year-old Vanessa has a dream. In fact, she has two dreams. One, to become a lawyer, and the other, to become her younger siblings' guardian. "That's what pushes me when I don't want to study for my Biology test," she says. "Whenever I think that this is too hard, whenever I start to feel sorry for myself, I remember, I need to do it for them. And I need to do it for myself, because nobody else is going to do it for me."

What do Antoine and Vanessa have in common? They're both foster children, and they both need your help.

Joe handed the letter back to Alyssa. "It's good."

"You didn't read the back, though," she said. "Did it not hold your interest? I tried to pull you along, get you into it."

"No," he said. "I don't have to. I can tell it's good." He could see her disappointment, but he couldn't help it. He couldn't read any more.

"I don't see why you'd be scared to show that to your boss, Liss," Alec said. "Looks good to me, better than a lot of the ones I've read, and Rae and I read a lot of those things when we were figuring out where to donate. But show her tomorrow. She may have suggestions."

"Thanks," she said.

"So you know how to write a letter," Alec went on, as always zeroing right in on the weak spots. "But not make presentations? Really? I'm with Joe here. I'd think you'd have been good at that. Where's the problem?"

"Oh, you know." She tried to laugh it off. "Maybe I'm not cut out for this after all. Or maybe my boss just doesn't like me."

Alec groaned. "Not again. Liss, you have to learn to get along on the job."

"Like you?" she asked tartly, clearly trying to rally.

"I'm an entrepreneur. It's different. I don't have to get along. I've got Rae to smooth everything over. But you can't afford that. As an employer, I'm telling you, you can't afford another short stay. You can't afford another job where you had a personality conflict. Face it, at a certain point, it's not them, it's you."

"Don't you think I know that?" She blew out a frustrated breath, and Joe could see the effort it took her to confess the truth. "I've tried everything I can. I've stayed late, I've come in early, I've taken on extra work and cleaned up the database and organized the office. *Me*. I've organized, and you know that isn't my best thing. But nothing ever seems to be quite good enough. She'll tell me this letter isn't good enough, I know she will. She'll take it and 'fix' it, and it'll end up being her letter. And, yeah, maybe every job hasn't worked out, but I've always been able to get along with people, most people. I *want* to. I'm *trying*. And I *can't*."

"Maybe it really is a personality conflict," Joe put in. "They can happen. How do other people do?"

Alyssa shrugged. "Most people really like her," she said reluctantly. "Dr. Marsh does, the Director. He thinks she's great. So maybe it *is* just me."

They dropped the subject then, though Joe made a note to talk to her again about it later, when Alec wasn't there. He had a blind spot when it came to his sister, that was for sure.

139

He couldn't seem to see what Joe saw, how hard she was trying. How rough a road she'd had to travel at times, and how bravely she was doing it.

Alec took himself off to bed after dinner, and Alyssa helped Joe with the dishes—a mercifully simple endeavor, since he could tell she was tired—and then went to sit on the couch, where, despite a stern talking-to about what a bad idea it was, he joined her, refilling his wine glass and hers before sinking down beside her.

"I'm sore," she told him. "Are you?"

"Not too bad. Going to be up for it tomorrow? I warn you, I'm going to make you show me your rescue technique first. No Alec up there to dig me out, which means it's all on you."

She leaned her head back against the couch and sighed. "I was listening, I *promise*. I'm happy to demonstrate. Just ask me."

"All right," he said. "What's your beacon set to, tomorrow?"

"Send," she said triumphantly. "In case I get buried. In which case I don't panic, and I try to keep my arms in front of my face to give myself a pocket, and I wait for you to come for me. Hoping, of course, that you won't be buried too. That's the part you left out, don't think I didn't notice."

"Well, if that happens," he pointed out reasonably, "there's nothing to practice, and no point in thinking about it. But back to the matter at hand. What do you do when I go down?"

"I flip my beacon to Receive, and then I use the techniques my very, very good teacher showed me today to find you, and then I use my shovel that my teacher gave me to dig you out. See what a good student I am?"

"Mmm," he said, smiling at her. "You'll do," and she smiled back and drank her wine, and he let himself enjoy being here with her, because it was a pretty good place to be.

"Why are you so different here?" she asked after a minute. "Is it skiing? Has that been the secret ingredient?"

"Am I different here? How?"

"Well, everywhere, really," she said. "Since I moved to San Francisco, and on this trip, especially. You're more talkative. More ... pushy."

"Pushy?" He had to smile again. "I'm pushy?"

"Well, yeah. Or assertive, maybe. Like you're making the plan, and you're telling us. You're telling *me,* especially. Notice that, how you're telling me? Because you are."

"Is that bothering you? And by the way, I do run a staff of programmers, you know. It's not just you. And before you say anything," he went on, holding up a palm, "I know, I'm not the boss of you. Because I'm sure I'm going to hear that next."

"Well, maybe you're all right. Maybe it's not *so* bad," she told him, sparkling at him, pulling her legs up under her and sipping her wine while the fire blazed and the quiet enfolded them, and *damn,* but he liked her. "And I know that you're a big deal. It's just that I've never seen that side of you. And OK, I'll admit it, I'm a fan. Today, with Rae, you were great. Skiing up to find her, going to get the car, telling Alec he couldn't drive. You did all the right things, and I was so glad you were there. It's just different, because I've never seen you like that before this year. You've always been so quiet."

"If that's true," he said, her words filling him with a pretty good glow, "maybe it's because you've always seen me at your parents' house, and when I'm there, I'm a guest."

"A guest? You aren't a guest. By now, you're part of the family."

"No," he said, and just like that, the glow was gone. "I'm not. People always say that, and it's not true. Do you really not see the difference? You'd better, if you're going to help those kids. I am not part of your family. I'm a guest, and I'm careful that I don't wear out my welcome, because I want to be invited back."

"But ..." She looked shocked. "That's not true. That's not the way it is."

"Yes," he said, "it is. Think about it. When you were a teenager, you could have moods, because you could afford to. You know you could. I saw them. And that was because you knew that no matter how bad your mood was, your parents were never going to kick you out. You were never going to be so much trouble that they didn't want you anymore. You could stomp off to your room and slam the door if you wanted to. If I'd done that, if I'd said I didn't feel like doing the dishes, do you think your parents would have invited me again?"

"Yes," she said.

"No," he answered. "A guest doesn't get to have bad moods. A guest doesn't get to insult somebody, or be lazy and not make his bed, or not want to do whatever the family's doing. A guest had better be on his best behavior, or he's not going to be a guest much longer. Ask any of those kids you wrote about in that letter. Ask them what happens if they screw up. They're gone, that's what, and they know it. They know it because they've probably done it. And sometimes, they do everything just right, and everything's going perfectly, and they think this is it, they're going to belong, they're going to have a family, or at least someplace to stay all the way until they're eighteen. They think that this time, they won't have to leave again, and they can relax, and you know what? Something happens, and they're out of there. So they can never relax. They're always waiting for it to go south. And after a while, they stop hoping."

"That's what happened to you," she said, her voice quiet, all the laughter gone. "You were a foster child."

He looked across at her in alarm. "How did you know that? Did Alec tell you, or your dad?"

"No. They wouldn't do that. My dad, especially—never. If you tell my dad something, it stays right there. It didn't take a brilliant deductive effort, though. That you donate to Second Chance, for one thing. And anybody who says as little about his past as you do, there's a reason."

"Yeah," he said. "There was a reason."

"When you came that first time," she said cautiously, "at Christmas. When I asked you why you weren't with your family. Is that because you went to Stanford out of foster care?"

"No," he said. "I went to Stanford out of nothing."

She didn't say anything for once, just waited, and he went on, probably because it had been a long, physical, emotional day, and he'd had a beer and a couple glasses of wine, and because Alyssa was curled up on the couch beside him, and he needed to tell her who he was. He needed to find out if it would matter to her, and he didn't want to examine why that was.

"I was a ward of the court from the time I was fourteen," he said. "Because my dad was dead, and my mom might as well have been." He could see the questions hovering, but he couldn't answer those right now, so he went on. "I was in foster care at first, but when I was sixteen, a teacher at my high school took me in, became my guardian. And I did what I just said kids don't do. I believed I could stay. I relaxed. I had a job, I had some money, I had a place to live. And by winter of senior year, I knew that I had a full ride to Stanford waiting for me. I relaxed."

"So what happened?"

"Mr. Wilson—the teacher," he explained. "He got pneumonia." He didn't tell her he'd had AIDS, because he still remembered the rumors, the comments that hadn't been quite quiet enough, Joe's lab partner who'd asked to be reassigned after Mr. Wilson had had to quit work and the rumors had got worse. Not that he thought Alyssa would say anything like that, but the old habit of protecting Mr. Wilson, of not talking about it, was too strong. Maybe another time. Or maybe never.

"And he died," she guessed.

"Yeah." Joe swallowed. "He died." After ten days in the hospital's Intensive Care ward, not getting better. Not able to talk to Joe, even though Joe had visited every day. The desperate worry, and the shame of being worried for himself, too, the barely contained panic at the thought of what would

143

happen if the older man didn't recover. Mr. Wilson's parents showing up, staying at the house, faces more strained and white every day. Joe not going into the hospital room any more, because they were there, and they were family, and he wasn't, and he could tell they didn't want him there, that this was their time.

And then the day he'd come home from school, opened the door, and the two of them had been sitting in the living room. Just sitting, until Mr. Wilson's dad stood up and told Joe what he hadn't needed to hear, because looking at their faces was enough. Joe knew that look.

"We're sorry," Mr. Wilson Senior had told him two days later, before they'd left to fly with the body back to Wisconsin for the funeral. A funeral Joe would be missing, because one thing was for sure, nobody was going to be buying him a round-trip ticket to Milwaukee. His good-byes had been said in his room, alone.

"We're going to have to sell the house," the older man said, confirming what Joe had already known, that he was alone again. "I know Larry was your guardian, and we want to do what's right, but you're over eighteen, and we can't support you."

"I know," Joe said, because he had known. He'd known this was coming.

"But you can stay until we sell," Mrs. Wilson put in hastily. "We want to do what's right," she repeated.

"As long as you're willing to look after the place," her husband said. Keeping it businesslike, making sure Joe knew what the expectations were. "You're going to need to keep the place clean, and keep the landscaping up. That's the deal. You'll have to get out when the realtor wants to show it, and move out well in advance of closing, because we'll be coming back to get rid of the furniture and clean things out, and you can't be camping out here after that. We're going to have to trust you to do that much, and I hope we can. I know there'll be a temptation to let it go, to make it less attractive to buyers so you can stay longer. I'm going to ask you, for Larry's sake, not to do that. And remember, the realtor will be telling us what shape it's in. If you do right by us, and by him, we can give you a couple months. But only if you do right."

Joe had wanted to yell at him. To tell him that he wasn't the user Mr. Wilson's parents seemed to think, that he wouldn't do that. He knew they thought he was cold, because he hadn't cried. They didn't know that he couldn't let go, because he was afraid he'd never get himself back again.

He'd had two months, as it turned out. And then there he'd been, eighteen, aged out of foster care, with nowhere to live and noplace to go.

He'd stayed with some friends of Conrad's for a couple months, but he'd known all along it couldn't be more, because they were having a baby. Conrad was in Iraq, not exactly in any position to be more help than that, and Joe wasn't Conrad's responsibility anyway. He was nobody's responsibility but his own. So he'd crashed with a high-school friend until graduation, doing his best to earn his keep, buying as many groceries as he could manage and cooking dinners and always being polite, always respectful, always grateful, staying at school, at work, at the library as much as he could, trying not to get in the way of family time, to give them enough in return that they'd let him stay.

That didn't last forever, either, because Aaron's parents sent him to Europe for a month for graduation, and Joe could hardly stay there when Aaron was gone. He'd spent that last summer before Stanford on the move. At one friend's or another's, sleeping on couches during the better times. In the cheapest motel he could find, those last couple weeks, when everyone else was off to college and he'd run out of money except for what he'd got for the bike, which was going to get him to California. Starting awake as the noisy, ineffective air conditioner cycled on and off, trying not to hear the sounds through the thin walls from rooms that were rented by the hour. Hoping he could make it without having to resort to the homeless shelter. Waiting out the time until he'd have a place to go.

"He died," was all he told Alyssa. "Winter of my senior year. I'd aged out of the system, but I knew how to survive by then, and I did."

"By yourself," she said slowly.

"No," he said, "with a lot of help from other people. And with a scholarship at the end of it. I knew if I could get to Stanford, if I could keep my grades up so I didn't lose my scholarship, I'd be OK. That was my ticket. I couldn't afford to screw it up, so I didn't."

"I guess you didn't have senioritis," she said.

"No," he said, and smiled a little. "Saw it, but never had it. Did you?"

"Are you kidding? Of course I did. I was busy having a good time. And when I went to college, I was *really* busy doing it. Not like you."

"Preacher's daughter out in the big world?" he asked, wanting to get off the sad-sack topic of his life.

"Mm-hmm. Sorry if that shocks you."

"I think by now," he said, responding to the glimmer in her eye, the light of her smile like he was programmed that way, "I've figured that out."

"What do you think you would have been like, if all that hadn't happened?" she asked. "More like me? Please say yes," she begged, and she seemed to know that he needed this to lighten up, because she was teasing again. "Please say you wouldn't have been as perfect as Gabe and Alec."

"I don't know. I've never thought about it. I'd have got in more trouble, that's for sure. I haven't been in trouble in quite a while. I came pretty close, that night when you had your Tenderloin adventure. That make you happier?"

"Yes," she said. "Even though I was the one dragging you in. At least I know you're capable of it. If you ever get tired of being perfect, I think I could find a spot for you in my not-perfect world."

"Want me to get in trouble with you?" he asked, even though it was a bad idea to say it, and an even worse idea to touch her the way he wanted to. He reminded himself that Alec was right upstairs, and took a sip of wine instead.

"Come on in," she said, her eyes full of mischief over the rim of her glass, and he was falling, just like always. "The water's fine."

Oatmeal and Wheat Grass

Alyssa came downstairs the next morning to find both Alec and Joe in the kitchen. Coffee and breakfast, and today, she'd be alone with Joe, and she couldn't kid herself that she didn't want to be.

She'd held her breath the night before when he'd talked about his past, because it was so obvious that he was barely pulling the curtain aside to give her a peek at what was behind it, and she'd known what a rare view she was getting. She'd have been willing to bet that almost nobody had heard that story, that it was coming from a place he didn't want to touch, because it was still too tender. And that it needed the lightest, most careful treatment, or he'd curl right back up inside his shell again.

She'd always known that there was something behind the remoteness of his expression, that his walls were there because what was behind them was too painful to show, too shameful to share. She'd known it at fifteen, and she saw it now, and seeing it hurt.

She'd done her best to tread lightly, and it had seemed to work. She'd felt the relaxation, the warmth in him when she'd accepted what he'd given her without pushing for more, and had been so relieved to get it right.

He'd tugged at her heart, and then he'd set it pounding, because it had seemed like something was going to happen at last. She hadn't imagined his response, not this time, and she knew it.

But nothing had happened after all. He'd got up, said goodnight, and gone to bed, leaving her hanging once again.

Something was stopping him from taking that step, and she was getting a glimmer of what that something was.

It had been a long time before she'd fallen asleep, her body tingling as if he'd been touching it after all. She could almost feel his hands against her skin, sliding over her, and she ached for him. He'd been looking at her, she could tell, the same way she'd been looking at him. She'd felt his heat, his intensity, the fire that burned just beneath the surface, trying to find its release, promising to burn everything in its path. She wanted him to let it go and burn her down. And today, they were going to be alone.

"I could get used to this," she said, going straight for the coffeepot, working on that light touch, but it was hard, because she was keyed up. "What's for breakfast this morning?"

"Oatmeal for me," Joe said. "Alec was just trying to order off the menu."

"And Joe was telling me what I could do with that idea," Alec said. "Seems if I want eggs, I have to make them myself."

"You still don't like oatmeal?" Alyssa asked, lifting the lid on the pot. "Even with fruit in it? Looks good to me."

"Nope. I didn't like oatmeal before I did the show," Alec said, "and I like it less now. People who say they like oatmeal are the same people who say they like tofu or wheat grass juice or bulgur wheat. Boringly healthy food is not delicious. *Delicious* food is delicious."

"So what does Rae want for breakfast?" Alyssa asked. "And how's she doing?"

"She wanted oatmeal," Alec admitted with a grin. "Don't tell her I said all that. She probably likes wheat grass juice too. I don't want to know. But I'm making eggs. You want some?"

"Nope," Alyssa said. "I like oatmeal too. Thanks for making it, Joe," she remembered to add as she dished it into a bowl.

"No problem," he said.

"Uh ..." She turned in a circle and looked around the kitchen. "Remind me where the brown sugar would be."

Joe opened another of the indistinguishable cabinets and handed her out a canister, and she got busy with a spoon.

"Wow. Think you got enough there? How about a little cereal with your sugar?" Alec asked, beating a few eggs in a bowl and dumping them into a frying pan.

"I like it this way," she said, and added another spoonful just because he'd said it.

"You're going to get pudgy, you keep that up," Alec said, pushing the toaster button down on a couple slices of bread.

"No," she said, holding onto her temper, because they were on vacation, and it was Joe's house. She knew she was a little touchy today, a little jumpy, because of Joe. And that Alec was at his most brittle, his most annoying, because he was worried about Rae. "I'm going to get pudgy if I eat a bowl full of oatmeal *cookies*. Which I am not doing. Or if I hadn't skied all day yesterday and wasn't going to be skiing all day today. Not that any of that is any of your business."

"I'm just saying," Alec said, "as your brother, guys don't like pudgy women, so be careful."

That was it. One critical comment too many, and in front of Joe, and her temper was gone, out of her reach. She slammed her spoon down on the counter and faced her brother. "Alec. Listen to me. How I look is none of your business, and neither is what I eat. I don't tell you what to do, so where do you get off telling me?"

"I'm just giving you the benefit of a brother's perspective," Alec said, turning off the heat under his eggs and starting to dish up his breakfast. "What's wrong with giving my little sister some brotherly advice?"

"Oh, I don't know. Maybe that I didn't ask for it? Maybe that you still treat me like I'm fifteen?"

"I do not do that. Do I do that?" Alec demanded of Joe.

"Yeah," Joe said. "You do."

"Thank you," Alyssa told him.

"You're welcome."

150

"I'm an adult, do you realize that?" she asked her brother. "OK, maybe I'm not rich. Maybe I'm not a CEO. Maybe I'm not a doctor. All I have is one lousy bachelor's degree in Business from San Diego State, and I've never made six figures and I probably never will, let alone seven. I'm not you, and I'm not Rae. But I'm trying to be *somebody,* and you're … you're not helping."

"I helped you move," he said, clearly not getting it at all. Not at *all,* and she wanted to scream. "I read your letter last night. What is that, if it's not helping?"

She shoved her bowl away with a bit too much violence, and Joe put a hand out to stop it as it skittered along the counter. "Yes, You did, and you paid my way for this weekend, too, and I appreciate all of that, and I *hate* that I resent you, when you've done all those things. But it's … it's hard to take the help, sometimes. Don't you see, can't you understand that it's because you think you *have* to help? Like I'm so dumb and such a screw-up that I can't do it by myself? All right, maybe I don't have it all figured out like you do, but I'm trying. I'm trying to have the life I want. Maybe, if I were as good as you and Gabe, I'd have figured it out when I was twenty, but I didn't. But I'm doing it now, and you telling me I'm doing it wrong … it makes it even harder."

"I wasn't trying to tell you that you were doing it wrong," Alec persisted. "I was just trying to help, and you're being oversensitive about it, all dramatic, as usual. Can you just relax and take a joke?"

That was it. That was the kicker. "Really? I should just relax? That was a joke, that I'm fat and nobody's ever going to love me? That I can't get along at work, and I make bad decisions? Stop and think how you'd feel if you were me, and I was you. If it was *you* who was the baby, and the big …" She was tearing up now, which made her even madder. "The big disappointment to everybody. Would you want to be reminded of it over and over again? Would you want to feel like you were never going to measure up?"

"I don't do that," he protested. "I do not do that."

151

"Maybe you don't mean to, but that's exactly how it feels, and you do it all the *time*. Every Christmas, but that's once a year, and I just suck it up, but I'm *tired* of it. And now, it's all the time, and I *can't*. All I'm asking you is, *think*. Before you say something to me about my weight, or my loser apartment, or how bad I'm doing at my job, just *think*. Think about how I'm thirty, and I'm trying, and I *know* nobody thinks I'm as good as you and Gabe. Just try to think if what you're saying is helpful, or if it's just …"

"Critical," Joe finished.

"Yes," she said, picking up her spoon again and stirring her cereal with angry jabs, not wanting to look at her brother, because she knew she was about to cry. "Critical."

"Wow," Alec said blankly. He picked up his breakfast, grabbed a knife and fork. "I'll just … go up and eat with Rae, so we can get out of here."

He left the room, and Alyssa sat on a barstool in desolation, staring down at her cereal bowl and trying not to cry, but a couple tears dripped in there all the same.

"I'm sorry," she said to Joe, reaching for a napkin from the holder and giving her nose a defiant blow. "Sorry to have a tantrum and be so ungrateful, and spoil your vacation."

"No need to be sorry. I wondered if you were ever going to tell Alec to shove that thing he does. I know it's a habit, but it's a bad one. I'd have told him myself, but like you said …" He smiled at her now, just a warmth of the eyes, a faint upturn of the mouth, "not my business. It needed to be said, and you said it."

"You think he'll forgive me?" she asked, and a couple more tears dripped, because she did love her brother, and she was afraid, despite Joe's words, that she'd gone too far. He *had* helped her, and she appreciated it. It was just that it always came at such a price.

"Oh, I think so. Matter of fact, I'd bet that once Rae's done talking to him, it'll be the other way around."

Which was how it turned out, to Alyssa's astonishment. She was in her room, finishing getting ready for skiing, when the knock came at her door.

"Come in," she called.

Alec came inside, his usual confident smile noticeably absent, and sat down on the other twin bed across from where she sat unrolling a pair of heavy socks.

"I came to ..." He took a deep breath. "To apologize for that thing about the oatmeal."

She looked down, finished pulling on her right sock and made a little business out of straightening the top. "That's OK."

"No," he said, "it's not. You're not pudgy. You look good. I'm just ... used to telling you what I think, I guess. And teasing you," he admitted.

She nodded, started working on the other sock, resisted the urge to tell him it was all right, that she'd overreacted. "I'm glad you care about me," she said instead. "But it's hard sometimes not to compare myself to you."

"I get that," he said.

"Or Rae gets it," she said, looking up at him, unable to keep from smiling a bit.

He grinned sheepishly, ran a hand through his perfectly cut hair. "Yeah. She pretty much agrees with you. She says to tell you that when I do that, you should call me on it."

"So with both of us ganging up on you," she asked, "you think I have a shot?"

He smiled again, leaned forward and gave her a kiss on the cheek. "The Magic 8 Ball says, signs point to yes. And are we done here? We good? Because there is nothing I hate more than apologizing."

She reached for him and hugged him, felt his arms coming around her, and laughed a little. "Yeah. But tell Rae—good job."

Hidden Dangers

Alec and Rae left soon after breakfast, Alec and Joe carrying Rae carefully down the steps to Alec's car, Alyssa following with the crutches and another ice pack. She could see Rae biting her lip, trying not to cry out as Alec put her in the back seat and she swung her legs up, could hear the gasp that couldn't help but escape her at the pain of the movement.

Alec shut the door so she could lean back against it, went around to the other side, handed her a pillow and the ice pack, and arranged a blanket over her. "Want your laptop?" he asked her. "Want to watch a movie?"

"Yes, please. You're spoiling me. I'm being a lot of trouble."

"Nah," he said. "I normally don't get to spoil you nearly enough. But now you're helpless to resist, and I get to let loose with all my chivalrous impulses until you're well enough to start in on me again about how you can take care of yourself and I can just back off."

Rae smiled, and Alyssa could see that Alec's teasing worked for his wife, completely unlike its effect on her. And she knew why that was, too: because it was so obvious that Alec thought Rae walked on water. She felt a stab of envy that was neither sisterly nor very spiritually evolved at all. She was jealous of her sister-in-law because she was injured, and her husband was making a fuss over her. Great.

She handed Alec the crutches once he had Rae set up, and he tossed them into the Mercedes's trunk on top of the bags.

"Well," he said, "thanks for putting us up, Joe. We'll have to try it again another time, and hope for a better outcome. You two have a good time today."

Alyssa could see his comment hovering on the tip of his tongue, and she went ahead and made it for him. "Don't worry," she said. "Joe will give me another Emergency Preparedness Quiz before he lets me ski, I'm sure. But I just want to say, I *would* have kicked your butt today. Think about that, driving home."

He laughed and gave her a quick, strong hug. "You would have, and I'll admit it right now. Maybe there's a little part of me that's glad to save my ego from the battering."

"Bye. Drive safe," she called, waving as they pulled away. Then she turned to Joe. "So, now that we've gotten rid of them, is it finally time for the fun stuff?"

"You bet," he said with a satisfied smile. "From now on, it's you and me and the snow."

Three hours later, they were still headed endlessly up a mountain, Joe breaking trail ahead of her through powder snow as if he didn't know the meaning of fatigue, switchbacking first one way, then the next, the cold air nipping at Alyssa's cheeks while the rest of her heated up with effort to the point that she had to unzip her parka.

"You drinking?" he asked, turning on his skis to check in with her for about the sixth time. "You all right?"

She held up her hydration tube and waggled it at him. "Aye aye, sir. Oh, wait. That's not the Air Force."

He smiled. "Good up here, huh?"

She turned on her skis to look—cautiously, so she wouldn't go screaming down the mountainside—and had to agree. The peaks of the Sierra rose to the south, tree-covered below, white crags above, blue sky broken by long wisps of white cloud. The whole thing looking like a postcard, but no picture, not even a video could have captured the feeling of it, the space and the air and the sound of the wind. And the solitude.

"This is why you love it," she said. "This—" She gestured. "Freedom. Even though it couldn't be more different from sitting at a computer."

"This is it," he said. "Route-finding, exploring, the challenge. And I get some of my best ideas up here. Lots of time to think, going up. Plus, you know," and he smiled again, "skiing down, knowing you earned every foot of it. No grooming, no help. Virgin snow."

"Can't wait," she said happily.

Half an hour later, though, Joe had stopped again. "I know I said we'd go to the crags," he told her, "but we need to turn around now."

"Why?" she protested. "I'm fine." A little blown, a little pushed, but fine. Settled and content to be here, enjoying the day, and enjoying being with Joe. "And we're, what, only two-thirds of the way there?"

He pointed to the peak above them. Well, to where she knew the peak was. "See that cloud?" he asked, referring to the shield of gray that had closed over the summit.

"Yeah, but we're not going that far."

"That's wind," he said. "That's that storm coming in early. "I've been watching that cloud grow, and it's going to be down here soon, and when it is, conditions are going to go south in a hurry. We need to turn around."

"It's still pretty clear right now," she said. Well, not really, but it wasn't bad at all. "Can't we go a bit farther? You said 2,500 feet down, and I'd love to ski 2,500 feet of virgin snow. I've skied in storms before. You don't have to worry about me."

"No," he said, "we can't. You've skied in storms in a groomed, patrolled ski area. You haven't skied where the snow can change completely every hundred yards, where you can't see ten feet ahead, where your tracks up are covered, and you don't know where that ridge might be that you could ski over, right off into space. We're turning around."

"Are you sure this isn't about me? Would you turn around if you were with Alec?" she asked him. "Or is this really about you thinking you're responsible for me, and you don't want to risk anything happening to me, no matter how remote the possibility actually is? I'm not your little sister, Joe. I'm not *anybody's* little sister. I can take my chances, and I'm willing to do it."

"It doesn't matter what you're willing to do," he said. "You're right, I'm responsible for you, because I know how to do this and you don't. It has nothing to do with who or what you are. I'm telling you, turn around, because we're going down."

She tried to be grouchy about it, but she couldn't stay that way for long, because he was right, skiing down was fantastic. It was exhilarating to be alone up here with him, to have to find their own way, and it was unexpectedly challenging, despite his warning, to cope with the changing snow conditions. She hadn't fully grasped, going up, how much of an effort that would be. She'd be in deep powder, the going easy, and seconds later would hit an exposed spot where the snow was packed and nearly icy, have to lean into a turn to keep her skis from shooting out in front of her. It pushed her to the edge, and there was no choice but to be right here in this moment, all-the-way alive and knowing it.

Joe had been right about the storm, though. It was upon them soon after they had started their descent, the wind blowing a few tiny flakes at first, picking up force with every minute that passed, adding to the effort of their descent. Joe turned often to check on her, and she couldn't be sorry about that anymore, because she was glad to have him finding the route. She admitted to herself that it wouldn't have been easy for her to do it.

Fifteen minutes, twenty, and the wind was stronger now, until the push of it against her body, the difficulty of picking out the shape that was Joe had her focusing on the task with every bit of her awareness, her exhilaration tempered by caution and even an edge of fear that, truth to tell, wasn't entirely unpleasurable either. Until she saw the dark figure ahead of her, dimly viewed through the blowing snow, turning once more to check on her, taking an awkward slide into nothing. And then he was gone.

She searched for him even as she focused on navigating the slope ahead, aimed herself toward where she'd last seen him. The seconds ticked into a minute, then more as she approached the spot with all the speed she dared to use, giving her plenty of time for her mind to run through possible scenarios, how she'd cope. If he had fallen and was hurt, how would she get him down? There was no ski patrol here, no sled, no way to call anyone for help.

If he were conscious, she realized, he'd tell her how to do it. But what if he weren't? She still couldn't see him, and anxiety for him was doing its best to cloud her reasoning as she forced herself to think it through. She'd leave his ski poles looped around his wrists, tie them around her waist with the ski skins, she decided, and pull him on his back behind her. She'd put her hat on his head in addition to his own, his hood up to cushion his head while she did it. She could do it. She'd have to.

She was sure she'd reached the spot where he'd gone down, and she still couldn't see him, and there *was* a ridge up here somewhere with a drop-off. She couldn't be sure this was the exact place, but she thought she remembered it. What if he'd gone over it, like he'd said? All that time she'd stood arguing with him, and conditions had been worsening, and now he'd gone over. Oh, God. Please, no.

"Alyssa," she heard, and whipped her head around, barely avoiding falling herself, and saw the dark shape to the right, low to the ground, because he was lying down, or sitting, maybe. But he was there, and he was conscious.

She skied down to him, cautious because of that ridge, the hard-packed snow here in this exposed spot threatening to send her shooting straight off, just as he'd warned her. She found him pushing himself up to stand, leaning against a pole to get himself upright.

"What happened?" she asked, coming up beside him and brushing off the snow that clung to his back, needing to touch him. "Are you all right? Are you hurt?"

He smiled at her, snow clinging to the stubble along one side of his jaw, and she was flooded with relief. "Well, my pride's pretty bruised," he said. "I was worrying about you coming down that rough patch, started to check on you, missed seeing a trouble spot, and caught an edge. Took a hard fall and did some sliding, but I'm fine."

"You sure?" He had more snow on the back of his hat, and she brushed at that, too, with a gentle hand. "Did you hit your head?"

"No, that wasn't the part of me that took the beating," he said, taking a whack at the seat of his pants and wincing.

She laughed with the relief of it. "Are you telling me the Professional Skier, my protector and advisor, fell on his butt?"

He smiled back. "Afraid so. You going to give me a hard time about it?"

"Oh, yeah," she said, happiness filling her. "I think so. I think you're toast."

Kiss That Ball

They skied across the last long, shallow slope, saw the gray shape of the Audi looming through the blowing snow, and Joe took an easy breath at last. It wasn't quite true that it hadn't mattered who she was. That wouldn't have changed his decision to turn around, but it sure had changed how he'd felt about it.

It took another ten minutes to get their gear stowed, of course, hindered by the storm. "Go on and get in the car," he said when she had her skis off. "I'll do this."

She looked up at him in surprise, continued to scrape the snow off the bottom of a ski with her pole. "I can clean off my own skis. Besides, we'll get it done faster this way."

He pulled her bag and moccasins out of the back, took the ski and pole out of her hands and shoved the bag into her arms. "Man, you argue a lot. Go change. Because you'll just do it halfway, and then throw everything in." He had to smile at her, because he was so relieved to be back safe with her, and she was opening her mouth in indignation, and it was pretty funny. "I like my car neat. There's a right way, and you won't do it."

"Huh." She did her best to pout, but she was laughing. "You're right. I won't. And besides, I really have to go to the bathroom."

"Well, then," he said, "better go do it before there's a line."

She laughed again, opened the front door of the car and shoved her bag inside, then headed for the blue Port-a-Potty

160

on one side of the parking lot, and he smiled and worked on the skis some more, and put everything away. Neatly.

"Going to take me out for a beer?" she asked when they were on their way to town again. "Because you know what? I think I earned it. And *I* didn't even fall down."

"Rub it in, why don't you? Maybe that didn't embarrass me enough. But, yeah, I'll take you out for a beer, because I think you earned it too."

She sat back and closed her eyes in the warmth of the car, and he switched the music to some Peruvian stuff he liked, guitars and flutes, and concentrated on keeping the car between the orange poles as the snow blew around them. He wondered if she'd gone to sleep. She'd worked hard enough to wear anybody out. He hadn't been kidding, she *had* earned it. She'd impressed the hell out of him today.

She stirred, though, when he pulled to a stop at a light on Tahoe Boulevard. "Ooh," she said. "There you go. My favorite date. Don't you think?"

He looked at the western-style Bar & Grill sign, "Billiards" winking in red neon, and hesitated. "Blowing hard," he said. "Maybe we should just get back."

"We're, what, five miles from the cabin? Come *on*, Joe. Buy me a beer and a hamburger."

"Five miles can be a long way, if the storm's bad enough. Anyway, I thought you were high-maintenance," he said, pulling into a spot on the street all the same.

"That's what they say," she said, sassy as ever.

"A woman who wants a beer and a hamburger at a bar isn't high-maintenance," he informed her, grabbing her coat out of the back along with his own and handing it to her. "A woman who wants to go to Switzerland to ski, *that's* high-maintenance."

"Huh." She looked surprised, but pulled her coat on and climbed out of the car.

He waited for her, grabbed for her elbow as she slipped a little coming around to where he waited to cross the street. "Those boots weren't really meant for snow," he told her.

161

"They're cute, though, aren't they? Guess I'll just have to hold on to you on the slippery parts," she said, reaching for his forearm and hanging on tight to cross the street, slick now with blowing snow.

It was like an old movie, having her on his arm like that, and he loved it. And her boots, he thought, sneaking a quick look down as he opened the outer door of the bar for her, stepped into the tiny vestibule and stomped snow off his own boots, really *were* cute. The soft, fringed deerhide over her calves, the stretchy skin-tight black pants above, not quite underwear, but way too close for comfort. And the silky red turtleneck she wore over them, which was pretty tight too, revealed, now, as she pulled her coat off, let him hang it up on the hooks near the door. All of her, in fact, was nothing but cute, in addition to a few other adjectives he could name, and his hands itched to touch her, to feel those curves for himself.

She pulled her purse around when they were sitting down in the warmth, hamburgers ordered and beers in front of them, and started scrabbling through it, finally pulling out a little bottle of ibuprofen and shaking out a couple caplets.

"You sore?" he asked, taking a grateful swallow of Anchor Steam.

She looked up at him in surprise. "No. These are for you." She held them out. "I thought about suggesting that you ask for an ice pack to sit on," she said with a naughty smile, "but I figured your manliness wouldn't allow for it."

She was making insistent little circles in the air with her hand, so he took the caplets from her with a sigh. "I don't need these," he said. "Not two, anyway."

"Yeah, right," she snorted. "Tell me that doesn't hurt. It's not going to kill you to take something. It's not even going to destroy your he-man image. It's not morphine, it's *Advil.*" She leaned across the square, dark-varnished table, opened her blue eyes wide, and said in a loud whisper, "I'll never tell." She made a giant X over her chest, which meant he had to look at her chest. It was only polite, after all. "Cross my heart. I'll take your secret to the *grave.*"

162

He reached across, grabbed her half-drunk pint of beer and slid it his way. "I think I'd better cut you off. You're the one who's been into the morphine."

"Give it *back.*" She was laughing, and slapping at his hand, and taking back her beer. "I can't help it. I had a near-death experience. I'm entitled."

Now it was his turn to snort. "You did not have a near-death experience. You had a little bit of an exciting time coming down a mountain with somebody who knows what he's doing. Somebody who made you turn around, could I point that out? So he could keep you safe?"

"Somebody who *fell down,*" she had to insist. "And take your pills. Or I swear I'm asking the waitress for an ice pack, and telling her exactly where your bruise is. I could tell she wanted to know."

He laughed, popped them into his mouth, and washed them down with a swallow of beer. "Nah." He glanced around at the pretty blonde. "Way out of my league."

"Why do you do that?" she demanded, not laughing now. "Why do you pretend I don't know that you're attractive to women? Why do you act like you don't notice that Sherry wants to go out with you, and that waitress wants to go *home* with you, even before they find out that you've got, what? Ten million dollars? Twenty? Whatever it is. Why do you act like you're some ..." She made an extravagant gesture, and he thought, *OK, maybe one beer's enough.* "Some truck driver?" she finished. "Although even if you were a truck driver, you'd still be hot, and you *know* it, Joe. You *have* to know it. You've got a motorcycle. You've got a *tattoo.* I haven't seen it for a while, but unless you've had it removed, and I bet you haven't, you've still got it. Don't you?" she demanded.

"Yeah, I've still got it," he said, a little stunned.

"I bet it still looks good, too," she said, her voice softening. "Because, Joe. You're huge, and you've got *muscles. Serious* muscles. And they look *good,* and women *love* muscles. We *love* them. And I *know* you have to know that."

She still talked in italics. And she was making him seriously uncomfortable. Luckily, the blonde waitress showed up with their burgers and fries, and yeah, she smiled at Joe, and he saw it, but he didn't care.

"Can I get you folks another beer?" she asked.

"Yes," Alyssa said, just as Joe said "no."

"Yes," she said again, and glared at him, and he smiled at the blonde and said, "Yes for her. No for me," and Alyssa sighed extravagantly once the woman left and said, "What?"

"What?" he asked, trying and failing not to smile back at her.

"You can't have two beers? Because, what would happen? You'd get all wild and crazy and dance on the bar? Start stripping and show us your tattoo?"

Would she *stop* talking about taking off clothes? And now *he* was talking in italics, even if only in his head. "Eat your hamburger," he said, and started in on his own, because he was getting rattled. "Now I know why your parents never serve alcohol," he muttered.

She laughed, and choked on her beer, and he had to reach across and pound her back.

"Thanks for taking me backcountry skiing," she said when she'd got her breath back and had finally taken a bite of her hamburger, and he was feeling a bit more settled too. "I never said that, so thanks. Even though you made me turn around."

"And I was ..." He made a beckoning motion at her.

She laughed again. "Right. You were right," she admitted. "I was glad we weren't any higher. That was hard."

"So next time," he said, "you're not going to complain about my checking your gear before we start? You're not going to argue with me when I say we need to turn around?"

"Well," she said with that sassy smile, "I wouldn't get carried away." And she took another big bite and smiled at him while she chewed, and he thought, *Damn. I am in love with this woman,* and tried to put it down to the beer. But he'd still only had one.

164

Then it got worse, because after they'd eaten, she said, "I'm bad at pool. Are you good at pool?"

"I'm OK," he said.

"What does that mean? That you're some kind of Western District Billiards Champion?"

"No," he said, and she had him smiling again. "It means I'm OK."

"Then let's play pool," she said.

"Uh ..." He glanced out the front window. It was only four or so, but it was looking dim out there. "Maybe we should get back."

"Come on, Joe." She stood up, grabbed his hand, and was tugging him to his feet. "Have another beer and play pool with me. I'm bad, but you can show me. Come on. Teach me."

She wasn't all that bad, actually. She wasn't great, but she had too much natural athletic ability to be bad.

Except, yeah, she was. When she was draping herself across the end of the table to take her shot, one knee pulled up to rest against the cushion, looking back at him over her shoulder, that was bad. And when the guys at the next table were pausing in their game to stare at her ass while she did it, so Joe had to glare at them to get them to turn away, knowing they'd be checking her out again as soon as he turned his back, that was bad, too.

He knew exactly what they were thinking, watching her bent over like that. All a man would have to do was get up close behind her, pull those stretchy pants down, and he could have her right there. She was perfectly positioned for it, and every guy in the bar could see it, and every guy in the bar was thinking it. And Joe was having one hell of a time not showing what she was doing to him.

"You're not doing too well either," she said as he misjudged a shot, failed to sink the 4-ball. "Guess you *aren't* the Western Division Billiards Champion." She lined up to take her shot, and he came around behind her to watch. And there she was, bent over again, actually wiggling her hips in the tight pants that left absolutely nothing to the imagination,

165

and looking over her shoulder again. "This one's hard," she complained.

Yes, it was, and he couldn't help it.

"Is this right?" she asked, and it wasn't, so he had to reach around behind her and re-position her hands, and that wasn't improving matters one bit, especially when she leaned back into him, straightened up a little, and made contact, and he tried to pretend it wasn't happening. He failed miserably, of course, because she was warm and soft and had her lower back snuggled right up to his groin, and he couldn't do a damn thing about it.

Well, he could pull back, he realized after a couple frozen seconds, and he did, and tried his best to maintain.

"Just stroke it with the cue," he said, stepping to one side. "All you need to do is kiss that ball. Gently."

She hit it way too hard, of course, sent the cue ball into the pocket along with the one she'd been aiming for, and stood back. "I'm bad," she sighed. "I guess I need a lesson."

That's when he had to excuse himself and go to the men's room. He looked in the mirror at the confused, besotted face staring back at him, and knew he was losing the battle.

"Get a grip," he muttered, and reminded himself for the hundredth time that making any kind of move on Alyssa would be a bad idea. A very, very bad idea. Her brother was his business partner and his best friend. Both her brothers were so protective of her, they'd probably kill him if things went south, even if her dad didn't. And anyway, her parents were the closest thing to parents he had himself, which made it practically ... wrong.

It would be asking for trouble on so many levels, and it was way too risky for a guy who couldn't afford to take anything like that kind of risk. Did she know what she was doing to him? It had seemed like it at times, and it had *definitely* seemed like it while they'd been playing pool. But if he was wrong ...

Even if he was right, it would be putting his hand right in the fire, and he knew it. The only problem was, that was exactly where his hand needed to be.

They finished their game, and Joe continued to fail miserably at not noticing her, and not reacting to what he was noticing, but at least he won.

"Ready to go?" he asked when the last ball was sunk, taking her cue from her and setting it in the rack with his own.

"They have a jukebox," she said. "You know what I've always wanted to do?"

"No, what?" He was a fool, but whatever she wanted, he wanted it too.

"I've always wanted to ask a guy for some money for the jukebox, and have him give it to me and let me pick the music, like I was in the 1950s. And since being out with you is like being in the 1950s anyway ... how about it?"

He pulled out his wallet and gave her a couple bucks, watched her walk over to the old-fashioned machine, all colored neon and decorative chrome. She bent down to choose her songs, and he decided he'd better join her.

"Find anything you like?" he asked, and she looked up at him with a smile, pushed a lock of shiny hair behind one ear.

"It's pretty much all country," she said. "What's your favorite music?"

"Jazz, blues, R&B. Country's all right too, in a place like this where it fits."

"Really." She looked surprised. "Why did I never know that? I'd have figured you for a hard-rock guy, all those rough edges."

"Lots of things you don't know about me," he said.

"Oh, yeah?" she asked, running a finger caressingly over the chrome selection buttons. "Like what?"

"Like that I like my music slow and bluesy. When I'm in a bar, or in certain ... other situations." He knew it was a bad idea to say it, and he said it anyway, and he smiled down at her and saw her breath catch, and the fire inside flared up just a little bit hotter.

"Well," she said, and he could see the movement of her throat as she swallowed, "I'll see what I can do." She fed his money into the machine, punched buttons, and the rocking

167

music that had been pulsing through the bar changed. The guitars started in, and it was bluesy, and it was slow, and she was swaying in those fringed boots.

"Come on," she said, looking up at him through the curtain of her hair, because somehow that lock had come out from behind her ear to fall over one eye. When had she taken her hair out of its ponytail? Sometime way before pool.

"Come on," she said again, holding a hand out to him. "Dance with me."

That cautionary voice in his brain was still trying to talk, but he was done listening. Instead, he took her hand in his like he didn't have a choice, because he didn't. He pulled her onto the floor and settled his own hand over her lower back, felt the dip in her spine with his thumb, and that dip took care of whatever resistance he had left.

There was only one kind of dancing they were doing to this music, the kind where she was in his arms, the kind that was vertical sex, where you knew what was coming and you were delaying it on purpose, just to make it hotter, just to draw out the delicious anticipation for a few minutes more. The drums were pounding out a slow, steady message right in time with his heart, the guy was singing about somebody's dress hitting the floor, and Joe was moving around the little square of hardwood with Alyssa in his arms, and she was his perfect fit.

He couldn't have hidden a thing if he'd wanted to, because she'd wiggled that much closer and put her cheek against his chest, and her hand was stroking his shoulder, and she was holding him the same way he was holding her, tight and close, like she didn't want to let him go. He pulled her in a little more with his hand against the small of her back, felt her soft, warm body pressing against every aching inch of him, and that was it. He was done.

That was the moment when, after fifteen endless years, Joe Hartman gave it up. He knew exactly what he wanted, and he knew that no matter how bad an idea it was, he was going to take it. And he was going to do it now.

Electricity

Her body had become supercharged, every nerve ending quivering. Joe's hand was big and warm over hers, the muscle of his shoulder was hard and solid under her palm, and the rest of him was just as hard and solid against the rest of her. If she'd ever had any doubts that he wanted her, he'd just answered them, and she closed her eyes and surrendered to the pleasure of it. To the music washing over them, to the lyrics that said exactly what she wanted to believe Joe was thinking, to the size and strength of his body, the feeling of his palm against her back, pulling her in tight, giving her noplace to go even if she'd wanted to.

They swayed through another song, and then Joe was talking, his deep voice audible over the music, because his mouth was so deliciously close to her ear.

"If we do this," he said, his hand splayed over her back, lower now, stroking below the waistband of her ski pants, tantalizingly near the curve of her cheek, making her feel how much it wanted to keep moving, where he wanted to hold her, "it's not like Dr. Ski picking you up. I'm not some guy you're dating for a while. If we do it, it's for real."

"You mean," she said into the wall of hard, warm chest, trying for casual and failing utterly, "that if I want you, I have to promise to make an honest man of you?"

"I'm not joking. I mean that if we do this, you're mine, and you need to know it."

He hadn't even kissed her, and she was *gone*.

"Joe," she said, her hand on the nape of his neck, rubbing up and over the hair he'd grown for her, just because she wanted it. She knew that he was going to spend tonight giving her everything else she wanted, making her feel everything she needed to feel, and she needed him to start doing it. "If you don't get me out of here right now, I'm going to give those guys playing pool over there a show they won't forget. Because I need you inside me. I need it so bad."

"You didn't answer," he said, barely dancing now. "That's a good answer, but it's not the answer I need."

"What do you want me to say? Tell me, and I'll say it."

"You know what I want you to say." His hand was stroking, almost there now, and he had her pressed up tight against him, letting her know exactly what she had to look forward to. His face was hard and set, and she was melting.

"That I'm yours." She swallowed. It should have been cheesy, but it wasn't. It was the hottest thing she'd ever heard, because he meant it. She could feel it in the way he held her, see it in the look on his face, that predator's stare that had captivated her from the beginning. The difference was, now she knew for sure that she was its target.

"Don't you know," she asked him, barely able to get the words out, "that I've always been yours? It's all yours, Joe. It always has been. Go ahead and take it."

He bent his head and kissed her, his mouth brushing over hers, and they weren't swaying to the music anymore, because the moment his lips touched hers, the current leaped straight through her, a shot of pure electricity that jolted straight to her core. The slow, steady pulse of arousal had been throbbing ever since she'd started playing pool with him, ever since she'd bent over the table and offered herself to him, her body begging him to take what she was so ready to give. She was thrumming to its beat now, to the insistent rhythm of the slow, steamy music, to his hand coming down for just a moment to grip her by one cheek, pull her up tight against him, right there on the dance floor. He was kissing her harder, his mouth demanding, and she was giving it right back, and she wanted more.

Much too quickly, it was over, and he was stepping back from her. "Time to go," he said.

She thought about saying something, but there wasn't anything to say. She let him lead her out to the doorway, let him hold her coat for her and take her outside.

The blast of cold air as they stepped outside the bar, the whipping of the hard wind-blown flakes against her exposed cheeks and hands was like a shower of cold water, making her gasp. Joe had her arm, was leading her across the street, putting her into the car, running around to his side.

She expected him to kiss her again when he got in, but he started the car, turned the defroster to high, flipped the switches for the seat warmers.

And then he kissed her. He reached for her, pulled her to him with one hand at her waist, the other around her head, his thumb stroking her cheek, and kissed her, his palm on the back of her head, holding her to him, his mouth eating her up like he was starving and she was his only food. She got her own hands around him so she could explore the outline of his shoulders, his back through the heavy coat, reveled in the sheer size of him, in the feeling of him holding her so tightly, wanting her so much.

"We could get in the back," she said into his mouth. "I need you to touch me. I need your hands on me. I need it so bad."

He pulled away, breathing as hard as she was. "No. I need you to be in my bed." He started the windshield wipers going, pulled out of the parking spot and into a cautious U-turn, and drove the few minutes to the cabin in silence. She was quiet, too, because she was so turned on she wasn't sure she could talk anyway, and because she could see that the condition of the road demanded his full attention.

"Damn," he breathed, pulling to a stop in front of the cabin, the headlights picking out the wooden steps. "I left lights on. Got to be a power failure." He reached across her, all business, opened the glove compartment and pulled out a flashlight. He handed it to her, reached under his seat, and pulled out an even bigger one.

"You have two flashlights where you can reach them," she said, wanting to giggle, some of the heady anticipation replaced by amusement, or just pure giddiness.

"Got a lantern in the back, too," he said with a grin, and opened his door. "Wait for me," he commanded, switching on his light. "Slippery out here, especially in those boots of yours."

She waited, held onto his arm as she got out, and kept holding on as they stomped through the deepening, powdery snow on the steps to the front door, and Joe used his key to get inside.

It felt barely warmer than the outside in there, and the blackness, outside of the beam of their flashlights, was total. Joe shut the front door, sat on the bench, and began to unlace his boots, and Alyssa did the same, the sense of anticlimax bubbling up inside her.

"Way to let a girl down," she complained, not even taking off her coat, because it was freezing in here, contenting herself with pulling off her boots and socks as he did the same. "I kind of pictured you carrying me upstairs. I don't even get to see you when I take your clothes off? You don't know how long I've been waiting to see that."

Joe looked at her, and she could make out another smile. "You want me to carry you upstairs? I could do that. And you get to see me. I get to see you, too. I've waited long enough to do it myself, and I'm not planning to miss out. That's what candles are for."

"You have candles?" She shivered a little, and not just with cold. "And I was just joking about the carrying. Alec's right. Nobody wants to pick me up."

"I do." He stood, and the next thing she knew, he had one arm under her shoulders, the other one beneath her thighs, and had hoisted her into his arms. "You light the way," he said. "I'll do the carrying."

Nobody had ever carried her, because she was tall, and she was curvy, and whatever she'd told Alec, she knew she was too heavy. But Joe did it, and he did it without any apparent effort. He didn't even bump her head around the corners.

172

She wrapped one arm around his neck, held the flashlight in her other hand, and enjoyed every step of the way, until he kicked open the door to his room and set her down on the big, solid wooden bed she'd tried not to notice when she'd been in his tub the night before.

He was right, he had candles on the nightstands, thick ivory pillars that she picked out with her flashlight while he found the matches in a drawer and lit first one, then the other. He took the flashlight from her hand, switched it off and set it on the nightstand, and the single harsh spot was replaced by the flickering gleam of candlelight, casting mysterious shadows over his face, lighting the bed with its glow.

He pulled her to stand, drew the covers back on the bed, and then, and only then, he reached for her coat, put a finger and thumb on the zipper, and slowly pulled it down.

"Do you know how much I've always wanted to unzip you?" he asked, his hands brushing her shoulders as he drew the coat off, tossed it onto a chair beside the bed.

"Probably about as much as I've wanted to do it to you." She did, though she needed his help to get his arms out of the sleeves, because his arms were big.

"That's all you're doing," he said, and he'd pushed her down onto the bed, and he was over her, pulling the covers up so they were cocooned in warmth. "The rest of this is mine."

He was kissing her, his mouth hard on her, his weight resting on one elbow, and she was pulling the shirt out of his waistband, and at last, she had her hand where she'd always wanted it, sliding over the hard muscles of his back. He flinched like she'd slapped him there, and then she was flinching the same way, because his hand was under her sweater. It was cold, and it was big, and it was moving up, taking its time, and she shivered under it and kissed him more desperately, her own hand sliding over the shifting muscle of his upper back, then holding on.

"I'm going to touch you everywhere tonight," he told her, and his hand was making the point. "I'm going to kiss you everywhere, too. I'm going to put myself on every inch of you, and let you know I've been there."

"Please," she breathed, feeling his mouth leave hers, his lips on her cheek, moving over to her ear, to the side of her neck, and she turned her head so he could reach it better, because it felt so good. The scrape of whiskers against her skin, the shock of his tongue, his teeth, his mouth finding every sensitive spot and lingering there, making her squirm. And his hand, moving up, finally covering her breast, then diving inside her bra and cupping her. His palm moved over a nipple that hardened under his touch into a sensitivity that was nearly painful. He was making her moan already, and he had barely started.

He wasn't rushing to get to the good stuff, either. Instead, his mouth lingered at her neck, then went to the other side, up to her mouth again so he could kiss her some more, his lips teasing, pulling out every response she had to give. His hand was still at her breast, and he kissed her and touched her until she was moving hard underneath him, her hand on his back trying to pull him closer.

When he finally reached for the bottom of her sweater and began to pull it up her body, she sat up to help him, reached around behind her back for the fastening of her bra, only to have him grab one wrist.

"No," he said. "Didn't I say this was mine?"

"Then go faster," she begged. "Please, Joe. I need to be naked. And I need you to be."

She could see his smile in the candlelight, and if she'd ever thought his face was hard, it didn't look hard now. "You're going to be naked. After a while. And I'm going to be naked too. Eventually. We've got nowhere to go, and all night to get there. So lie down, because I'm going to play with you."

And play is what he did. He spent what felt like an eternity on her breasts alone. Her bra came off, but that was all that did for a long, long time. His hands and his mouth coaxed every bit of sensation out of her, until she couldn't ask him anymore, could only lie beneath him and feel.

Then his hand moved lower, his mouth followed it, and his tongue dipped into her navel. "Pierced," he murmured. "You're not a good girl." He licked around the little ring, his hand trailing over her side, and finally, when her hips were urging him in a rhythm that she couldn't help any more than she could contain the sounds that were escaping her, his fingers went to the waistband of her stretchy pants. They dipped inside, lower, and lower still, brushing over the sensitive skin of her lower belly, and she was trying to move him closer by wriggling towards him, urging him on. He shifted, took her breast in his mouth, and, finally, touched her where she needed to be touched, and that was all it took. He rubbed once, twice, three times, hard, and she came undone.

He swore, but she could barely hear him, because his hand was still moving, and all the tension of the past hours was being released in delicious spasms that went on and on, leaving her shaking and shuddering.

Finally, he had the rest of her clothes off, and she was naked. She didn't care what he said, she was unbuttoning his shirt, pulling it off, yanking off the T-shirt beneath, and he wasn't complaining, he was helping her. She rolled over him, straddled him, and finally, she was running her hands over the hard expanse of his shoulders. Her mouth was at his neck, then his chest, her tongue stroking a flat nipple, and she was feeling him shudder in his turn. Her hips were moving, and she was rubbing against him, needing to feel what he had to give. Her hands were stroking the smooth skin of his biceps, her mouth moving to the tattoo, outlining it with her tongue, biting at it with her teeth.

She did her best to take her time, the way he had with her, but she was greedy for him, for every bit of him. She shifted her weight lower, her hands reaching for his belt buckle, popping a button, and then unzipping him slowly.

And, finally, after fifteen long years, she touched Joe Hartman. Her hand closed over him, and she thought, *yes*. Because if she was his, he was hers. This was hers, and it was *good*.

"Get my pants off," he told her, so she did. And then she showed him how much she appreciated what she'd found, and he grabbed her head, wound his fingers through her hair, and she was forcing some sounds out of him, too.

"Stop," he finally said. "Stop now. I can't … I can't keep from …"

She came up on her elbows, slid up so her breasts were over him, let them enfold him, and his hands came down over her back, held her there like he couldn't stand to let her leave.

"Once you do it, how long does it take you, in between?" she murmured, her hands playing over the ridges of his belly.

"Uh …" He groaned. "Fifteen minutes. Maybe twenty."

"Think you could find something to keep you occupied for fifteen minutes?" she asked, her hands still stroking his skin, gliding over his chest, finding their way down the happy trail of hair that led from his navel to where she could feel the weight of him pressing into the valley between her breasts, and she wanted him so much. She wanted to do this.

"You don't have to …" he got out.

"Oh, but I do," she assured him. And she did. And when she felt his hands tightening around her head, heard the long, agonized groan beginning, she smiled a little around him, and finished it, and enjoyed every bit of it.

"Oh, God," he sighed, still on his back, when she rose back over him and kissed him, her tongue licking into his mouth, savoring all the tastes of him, her hands on his arms where they lay splayed over his head, her fingers circling him there, and she loved the idea that she'd satisfied him that much.

"Mmm," she said, kissing the corners of his mouth. "Don't go to sleep on me, now. I've been waiting a long time for this. Don't let me down."

"We need a bath," he sighed.

"A *bath?*" She sat upright and stared down at him. "Uh, Joe. That wasn't exactly what I had in mind."

He smiled up at her, slow and satisfied. "Don't worry. You'll get everything you want." He pulled her down over

176

him and gave her a long kiss, his hand moving over her back, tracing the curve of her waist.

"You did a really good job," he told her. "But I can take it from here."

He got his bath, finally. He got Alyssa just the way he'd imagined her the night before, on top of him in his giant tub, her firm, full breasts in his soapy hands, feeling her giving him every delicious response a man could ask for. Then he was sliding his hands down, feeling all her beautiful curves, rubbing her over him, lifting his head to pay some more long-overdue attention to her breasts, holding her still for him, and she was loving it, and letting him know it.

He pulled her out of the tub at last, once he was sure he was going to be able to do her justice. He dried her off, got her back between the sheets of his bed, and worked her over for real. He paid back every attention she'd lavished on him, showed her what he'd meant when he'd told her she was his.

He had what he'd always wanted. He had Alyssa on her back in his bed, and he was doing things to her that he'd been imagining for fifteen long years. And it was all good.

Maybe he wasn't the best guy at talking, but he was pretty good at listening, and he was very, very good with details. He read the movements of her hips, the frantic reach of her hands for his shoulders, the sighs and moans and downright directions she was giving him. He listened, and he learned everything about her. How to touch her, how to please her, and how to drive her crazy. How to make her grab his head in both hands, the same way he'd grabbed hers, and how to push her so far she couldn't even form words. And that was the best of all.

He got her going to the point where her hips were trying to pump underneath him, where she was crying out so loud, she sounded as if she were in pain. And then he stopped. He lifted his mouth from her, stilled his fingers, and felt her buck against him.

"Joe," she gasped, "don't stop. Please."

"This is for that doctor yesterday," he told her. "You going to let him flirt with you again?"

"No," she moaned.

He smiled, and started again. Got her even closer. And stopped.

"No." It was almost a scream.

"That guy you were out with, the one you ran out on. You going to be going out with anybody else?" he demanded. "Anybody but me?"

"No. No, Joe. I'm not."

"Because you're what?"

"Because I'm yours." He heard the truth of it, and he felt the evidence of it, and thrust his fingers inside her harder, and felt her hips jerk in response. And then he set his mouth to her again, and that was all it took. She was there, and if her first orgasm had been strong, this one had her rising in the bed, letting it all go, calling out with what he could tell was the nearly unendurable pleasure of it.

He kept going until she was done, until she was lying back, just as undone as he had been, breathing hard. But he didn't intend to let her rest. He rolled over and reached in the candlelight for the condom in the drawer, and then he was over her, inside her, sliding home, taking it easy, because it sometimes took a woman a while to accept all of him.

Not tonight, though. Not this woman. She took all of him and asked for more. He kept it slow at first all the same, rocking her easy, and her arms wrapped around him and her legs came up to do the same, and he knew that she needed him in her as much as he needed to be there. He knew he had Alyssa Kincaid taking him inside her body and begging for more, and he gave her what she was asking for. Thanks to her, he was able to make it last, to take the time he needed to do every wonderful thing he needed to do to her.

He shifted her position again and again, did her every way he knew how, until she was shaking and he was, too, until nothing could have kept him from her, until the need in him was a wild thing, clawing at him, roaring in his head, until she was bucking and sweating under him. And then, finally, he gave her all of himself. And he made her his.

Why Not Me

Alyssa woke from the doze she'd fallen into, reached a hand out and groped for Joe, but he was gone. She raised herself on her elbows, but the bathroom was dark. Well, of course it was, because the lights were out, and now the candles were, too. Joe must have blown them out after she'd fallen asleep. But there was no flashlight glow coming from the bathroom either, and now she could hear faint sounds from below, a metallic clank, a thud. She thought about getting out of bed and seeing what he was doing, but it was way too cold out there, so she snuggled back in between the flannel sheets, pulled the thick down comforter over her, and, despite her best intentions, fell asleep again.

She woke again to the disturbance of Joe sliding into bed beside her, reached sleepily out for him, and encountered an arm like ice.

"Brrr," she complained. "What were you *doing?*"

He pulled her close to him, and she settled her head on his chest, clad in a T-shirt now, with a sigh. "Building a fire in the stove," he said. "Going to get awfully cold in here without it. It won't stay going all night, not unless I manage to wake up a few more times, and I don't think that's happening, because somebody wore me out, but it'll take the edge off."

"Always thinking," she said.

"I know how cold you get. Just doing my part."

"You found a good way to warm me up at last." She snuggled in a little closer, because he was so *comfortable*. "I wondered if you ever would. I wonder if you even realize how hard I tried. I've never been that forward with anybody.

180

I thought, maybe if I actually stripped naked and lay down for you, you might get the hint. But then I thought you just weren't interested."

His hand was stroking over her hair. "Yeah, well, there were reasons."

"Oh, yeah?" It was so cozy, talking to him in the dark like this, her body humming with bone-deep satisfaction. "What kind of reasons?"

"Well, at first, you were too young. I was ..." She felt his chest shake, heard the low sound of his laughter. "I was feeling pretty perverted, those first couple years. Good thing you can't be arrested for your thoughts, because I'd have been in jail for sure."

She sat up a little. "You liked me then?"

He sighed and pulled her closer with his other arm, forcing her to lie down again, but that was all right, too. "I'm not sure *like* is the word, but yeah, I've always liked you, since the first moment I saw you. You were so pretty, and so ... lively. So funny and sweet and ... did I mention you were pretty?"

The glow filling her wasn't just from the warmth of his body anymore. "You mean we've wasted all this time? Do you realize how many not-Joes I've dated since then?"

"Probably not as many as the not-Alyssas I've been out with."

"So why not? Why *not* me?"

"Because you're Alec's sister. Because you're your parents' daughter. Because Alec is my partner, and you lived in a different part of the state, and I only saw you at Christmas. What was I supposed to do, kiss you under the mistletoe in your parents' living room?"

"Yes," she said.

"No," he answered firmly.

"All right," she said, "OK, but I've lived in San Francisco for six weeks now. A little pokey, aren't you?"

He laughed again. "Pokey? Six weeks? Alec's still my partner, you know. And you were dating other guys. How was I supposed to know you wanted me?"

"I don't know, maybe by the hundred-and-one hints I gave you? And *one* other guy."

"Well, we're here now," he reminded her. "The damage is done. No un-ringing this bell."

"Because I'm yours." She gave his chest another stroke.

"Yep. That would be the one."

"That was a really hot thing to say. Who knew you were such a good dirty talker?"

Now he was the one raising his head. "That wasn't dirty talk. I mean, yeah," and she couldn't see his smile, but she could sense it all the same, "it was, I hope, but I meant it, too."

"Joe." She laughed. "I am not marrying you just because you compromised me."

She felt the withdrawal in him, his hand stilling. "Joking," she hastened to explain. "I mean, if you mean we're together, then yes, that's what I want to be, too."

"Good," he said, and she hummed a little in contentment, and felt his hand stroking over her shoulder. She stopped talking, then, and fell asleep again.

The next time she woke, it was light. Still cold, but maybe not quite as cold, and Joe was gone again. The power was still out, she found when she made it down to her bathroom, but at least there was enough light to take a shower, and luckily, water heaters ran on gas.

He was on one knee in front of the wood stove feeding the fire when she came downstairs. In heavy canvas pants, with a woolen button-down over his usual T-shirt, he was looking more like a logger than ever.

"Power's out for this whole area," he informed her, shoving another log in and arranging it with the iron poker. "Looks like it's all right in town, though."

"I guess we picked a good time to leave," she said, zipping her coat up.

"Well, that's not happening either," he said, closing the door to the stove and straightening. "All the passes are closed."

He'd pulled the drapes back, and the outside world was snowy, but no worse than the day before.

"Really?" She thought with a pang about Helene. She wasn't going to be happy. "It doesn't seem that bad."

"Wind," he said. "That'll be why. And it's supposed to blow all day. Looks like we aren't going home until tomorrow, and we're not skiing, either. They'll have closed the lifts, weather like this. Guess we'll have to find something to keep us occupied." The rough planes of his face softened into a smile. "I can think of one or two things."

"You can, huh?" She forgot all about Helene and went for sass, because she loved to sass Joe. "You got Monopoly?"

"Nope." He pulled her into his arms, got her standing on tiptoe, then kissed her like he meant it, and she wound her arms around his neck and kissed him right back.

"Poker?" she asked against his mouth.

He laughed a little at that one. "Maybe. Maybe strip poker, though I should warn you, I'm a pretty good poker player. You'd be the one doing the stripping. Or I could take you back into town and watch you play pool some more. But if you do that bending-over-the-table thing again, I can't guarantee that I'll behave this time. You might just find me following you into the ladies' room and taking you up on that invitation. You might want to re-think that, if you don't want it that way."

"You noticed?" she said, trying to keep herself from asking him to take her up on it right now. "I didn't think that was working."

"Oh, it was working. It worked on me, and it worked on every other guy in the bar, too. Because you've got one hell of a body, in case I've never mentioned it."

"Hmm." She was kissing the corner of his mouth, nibbling at him, because he tasted so good, and he was so damn sexy. "I don't believe you have. You've got some catching up to do, don't you?"

"We both have some catching up to do. Going to be hard to keep this place heated with one wood stove. We might have to get some blankets down here, stay in front of the fire. But first ..." He let go of her, stepped back with obvious reluctance. "Breakfast."

"Oh, man," she complained, "you mean I have to wait to get some more of you?"

He laughed again. "You're going to get all of me you can handle," he promised. "And you'd better look out, because I plan to get every bit of you, too."

"Plug your phone in first," Joe said when they were in the car the next morning. The pass was finally open, and they were headed back, though the going was slow.

"You don't need to check in?" she asked.

"Nah. Alec and Rae know I'll be back this afternoon. That's all I needed to do. They've got it. So go on. Plug it in."

"Thanks," she answered in relief. She'd tried not to let her concern about her late return intrude on the magic of her unexpected holiday, but the niggle of unease had refused to be silenced as soon as they'd begun packing up.

"What" Joe asked when she checked her messages and still sat silent.

"Can I read this to you?"

"Sure."

Inconvenient, Alyssa read aloud, *and I wish it hadn't happened. Today was your deadline on the fundraising package, and we have the Forester Pharmaceuticals meeting later this week. Were you able to give that any attention this weekend?*

"I *didn't* work on it," she said wretchedly. "How could I, with no power? Anyway, I didn't even bring my computer."

"Why should you have?"

"Because of what I just read you. Because of what you just *heard.* Because she's going to see this as another screw-up."

She was right, she found when she finally made it into the office well after two that afternoon. Joe had waited for her to drop off her stuff and change clothes, telling her that he'd store her ski gear at his place, and then had driven her to work. She'd told him he didn't have to wait, but it sure made her feel good that he had.

"Don't let her bully you," he said when they were in the car again and headed toward Van Ness. "You can work extra this week. Storms are an act of God. What are you supposed to have done?"

"I need to show her I'm committed, though," she tried to explain. "What I really need to do, what I've been trying to do, is come up with a killer idea. I've had the start of one rattling around at the back of my head, that there must be a better way to raise money. Something better than mass mailings and one-on-one appeals. Something like the Race for a Cure idea, but different, because everyone does those runs and walks, right?"

"True. So what do you have in mind?"

"I'm still working it through. But can I talk to you about it, when I get closer?"

"Sure," he said, and she held on to that, when she went into the office at last.

"Oh, finally," Helene said with a sigh when Alyssa showed up, and Alyssa marveled that the other woman could say so much with two little words.

Alyssa didn't apologize again, because what was the point? She gave Helene her letter, she got to work on the Foster Pharmaceuticals proposal. She tried, once again, to become indispensable. She tried to fit in.

A Serious Thing

Joe finally entered the AI Solutions office at three o'clock on Tuesday afternoon, nodded a hello to Carla, the receptionist, and made his way around the warren of cubicles to his office, with a brief stop for a progress report from Michael, his lead programmer. He unlocked the door to his own office, hung up his jacket, unpacked his laptop with his usual care and plugged it in. But he didn't sit down at his desk.

Do it now. No point in dragging it out. He left his office again and stuck his head into Alec's, next door.

Alec was turned away, typing furiously. He looked up, though, at the sight of Joe in his peripheral vision, which meant he wasn't coding.

"Hey," he said. "You made it."

"Yeah," Joe said. "Eventually."

"Seems like we got out just in time, Rae and me. Though I was sorry to miss the skiing. How was it?"

"Good. Storm came in there too, though, we had to cut it short, and Alyssa will tell you it got a little exciting. Not as exciting as she'll make it out to be," Joe said, unable to resist smiling despite the unease he was feeling. "But not the perfect conditions you'd hope for, somebody's first time. She'll tell you all about it, I'm sure, in gory detail."

He was babbling, he realized with wonder. *There* was something he'd never been accused of. Time to cut himself off. "How's Rae?" he asked. "How's the knee?"

"Hurts," Alec said, grabbing a cup of coffee from the desk and taking a swig, then making a face. It was probably cold. "She's working from home this week, under orders from her boss." He smiled himself at that one.

186

"Yeah, right," Joe said. *Now or never.* He'd spent a fair amount of time on the drive home thinking about how to say this, and there was no good way. "I slept with Alyssa."

Alec stared at him, the cup in midair, then set it down. "Oh, yeah?"

"Yeah."

"You do realize," Alec said, "that 'I slept with your sister' is not on any guy's list of favorite sentences."

"That's why I thought I should tell you," Joe said stolidly, and waited for what would happen next.

"Well, then, give me some information," Alec said in exasperation.

"You want *information?*" Now it was Joe who was staring.

"Not—Of course not. Of course I don't. Are you *trying* to make this conversation even harder? I mean, what are we talking about here? I've got to figure that you're not in here to tell me that you hooked up with my little sister and had a real good time, and you want to make sure I know all about it. I hope that's not it, anyway, because I'd be obligated to try to kick your ass, and I don't think I could. So for Rae's sake, tell me it's not that. She likes my pretty face."

"Would you shut up?" Joe demanded. "Do you *like* to talk this much?"

"All right," Alec said, and despite his flippant tone, he didn't look all that relaxed. "So tell me. And would you please sit down? Quit standing there like you're expecting me to ask you to step outside, or to tear up our contract, or whatever it is you're thinking. Just sit down and tell me."

Joe sank into the chair that sat kitty-corner from Alec's, in front of his own monitor, the one he used when they were doing paired programming. The place where they'd hammered out so much of Hal, the virtual assistant software that was already well on its way toward making them their latest and greatest fortune. It wasn't looking like it'd be the last time he'd sit there, although he'd wondered.

"I didn't hook up with her," he said at last, "not like you mean it. But I slept with her, and I plan to go on sleeping with her, and I don't intend to keep that a secret."

187

"So this is a—what?" Alec asked. "A serious thing?"

"Yeah," Joe said. "A serious thing."

"Well, damn." Alec leaned back in his chair, his hands on the leather-covered arms, and laughed. "Rae was right. *Damn*, I hate when that happens."

"Oh, yeah?" Joe asked, relaxing a bit himself.

"Oh, yeah," Alec assured him. "She's been telling me for months that Alyssa had a thing for you. She and Mira had quite the conversation about it at Christmas, from what I hear. I said no, not possible, because Liss isn't exactly subtle. Not the world's most patient person. Pretty hard for me to imagine her longing for you from afar for years, but they were both pretty sure. The only question was, did you have a thing for her too, and nobody was sure about that, because you've always been so damn hard to read. Which was why we went skiing with you."

"What?"

Alec made an impatient circular gesture with one hand. "Come on, keep up. Whose idea was it to invite ourselves along on your ski trip?"

"I don't know, whose?"

"Rae's, of course. And who said, 'You know what? We should invite Alyssa too, if you don't mind, Joe? She loves to ski.'"

"Well," Joe said, feeling like he'd been left behind somewhere back around the last turn, "I do remember that that was Rae."

"Yep. She said you two needed some time together, away from the parents. A little fire in the fireplace, a little whisky, a little drama—"Alec made a face at that one. "I could have done without the drama, thank you very much. But you notice I left you the whisky," he added helpfully.

"So we were set up."

"Wow, you catch on quick, don't you? Yep, another victim of the Desiree Harlin executive steamroller. She sees something she thinks needs doing, she makes a plan, and she executes. Good luck trying to get in the way of that."

"Hope she didn't fall on purpose too."

"No." That sobered Alec up. "No, that was a little extra icing on the cake. Even Rae can't always get everything right. But sounds like she came close."

Joe wasn't listening, though. "Away from the parents," he said. "What *about* the parents?"

"I don't know. Rae probably does, magically, but I don't have a clue. What are you going to do about that?"

"Same thing I did with you. Go up there and talk to them."

"Good plan. My mom's not going to give you a hard time. She's loved you from Day One. Another lost lamb to take into the fold. But my dad ..."

"Yeah," Joe said. "That's another story."

"You are not going to do that," Alyssa exploded when Joe told her the plan the next night. He'd taken her to the gym with him after work and bought her a membership, because there were about three things he did: work, go to the gym, and sleep. He couldn't take her to work with him, but he could take her to the gym with him, and he could take her to bed. And he was planning to do both, just as often as possible.

Now, they were catching a late dinner. Fish tacos, because, she'd informed him, those were her *other* favorite, besides hamburgers. And at this moment, she was waving her taco at him furiously, cabbage streaming out of it like strands of seaweed.

"I know I said that dating you was like going back to the fifties," she said. "I didn't realize I meant the *eighteen*-fifties. What, you have to ask my dad for my heart and hand?"

"Yeah," Joe said, "I do."

"I am an adult," she said, and the glint in her eyes was pure danger. "I don't need my father's permission to date you, and neither do you."

"I realize that," he said doggedly. "You're not a child, and you make your own decisions. That's not what this is about.

189

It's about me owing your parents, your dad especially, the courtesy of telling them myself. It's about respect."

"This is some weird military thing again," she sighed.

"Well, kind of. I guess. At least, it's a dad thing. I'm sure it's the right thing, anyway, and I'm doing it. I'm not asking for permission to date you, like you can't give it yourself. I'm letting them know, that's all."

"All right. Whatever. When are we going?"

"*We're* not," he said. "*I* am."

"You are not going up there and telling them without me."

"Yeah. I am. I want them to feel free to say whatever they have to say to me," he tried to explain, "without feeling like they have to ... limit themselves because you're there."

"You think it's going to be hard to do," she said slowly. She'd set her taco down, and her face was serious. "There are things you're going to say that will be hard for you, or you think there could be."

"Yes," he admitted. "Probably."

She nodded. "Which is why I'm going. You can talk to them alone," she said when he began to protest. "If you need to do some man-to-man thing with my dad, well, I don't get it, but that's your business. But I'm going with you. If it'll be hard for you, I'm going to be there."

Which is why she was out there in her mother's kitchen now, helping to make a Saturday lunch that Susie had insisted on their staying for, and he was sitting in her dad's cubbyhole of a study. He'd talked to her parents alone, as he'd told Alyssa he had to, and he'd done it pretty much the same way he'd told Alec, except that he'd said he was dating Alyssa instead of that he was sleeping with her. Some things, parents didn't need to hear spelled out.

They'd listened to what he'd had to say, and then Dave had looked at him measuringly and asked, "So you came all the way up here, just to tell us you and Alyssa are involved?"

"Yes, sir," Joe said.

190

"Honey." Dave turned to his wife. "Do you mind giving us a few minutes?"

"Of course." Susie got up, smiled at Joe, and left the room, and Joe tensed for what would come next. He'd thought he had to tell them, yes. But he hadn't really thought that Dave would object.

"All right," Dave said when Susie had closed the door. "What is it that makes you think we wouldn't be comfortable with the idea of you and Alyssa? Considering some of the relationships she's had—and those are only the ones we've heard about, mind you—what would make you think we wouldn't be jumping for joy to know that the two of you are seeing each other?"

"I don't—" Joe began. "I didn't—" He broke off as the other man sat back, his hands clasped in his lap, and waited.

Not many men could outwait Joe, but Dave Kincaid was one of them. He sat, solid and still as stone, looked at Joe, and waited.

"My past hasn't been … perfect," Joe finally said. And, when Dave still didn't say anything, he went on. "I was in foster care, but you know that."

"Yes," Dave said. "I remember."

"My mother was a …" Joe looked up at the ceiling and swallowed. "A meth addict. After my dad died, she started dating a guy who was an addict, got addicted herself. She used the rest of her life, heavy, and she died of it, basically. So heredity-wise, I may not be the best bet."

"Got any addictions yourself?" Dave asked.

"No."

"Do a lot of drinking? Use any of the other stuff?"

"Not now. And not meth, ever. Hard drugs, no. There was a time, though," Joe admitted, "when I was smoking weed pretty much every day. Drinking a fair amount, too."

"How long ago?"

"When I was fifteen, sixteen."

"Then I think we can safely say that the danger period is over, don't you? What else? What else did you do?"

"Some fighting," Joe admitted. "And ..." He swallowed. "A lot of stealing. I was a thief."

"Stealing from whom?" Dave asked, still looking calm.

Joe wasn't, though. Joe was sweating. "Shoplifting."

"Why?"

"*Why?* What does it matter why? I wasn't trying to save a starving child or anything like that. I can't give you an excuse that'll make it all right."

"No," Dave agreed, "but you can tell me why."

"Because," Joe said reluctantly, "I was mad, I guess. Because we'd get these lists." He didn't want to remember it, but there it was. "Back-to-school lists, you know the ones. A whole page full of things that I didn't have, and didn't have any way to get. Colored pencils, pens, notebooks. P.E. uniforms. You could go into the office and tell them you couldn't afford the uniform, and they'd give you some old one that somebody had donated. But nobody gave you colored pencils. And nobody gave you new clothes. You remember, last Christmas, when Alyssa and Rae were talking about clothes, about not having the right clothes?"

"Yes," Dave said. "I remember."

"Well, it was hard for them that they didn't have them," Joe went on, determined to tell the truth for once. "Harder than for a guy. I heard them say that, and I know it's true. But they dealt with it. They didn't go out and steal clothes so they'd have something new to wear, so they'd look like everybody else. But that's what I did. School supplies, clothes, shoes, electronics. Everything. I could have found another way to get what I needed, or I could have gone without it. But I didn't. If I wanted it, I stole it."

"Why?" Dave asked again. His posture was still relaxed, his expression unchanged. "When you went into a store, when you took something, how were you feeling when you did it?"

"Mad," Joe said. "Mad."

"Because you didn't have it? You were taking what you should have had?"

192

"Yeah. Because other kids had it, and I didn't, and it wasn't fair." Joe looked down, tried to laugh, ran a hand over his head. "I don't know where I got the idea that it should be. Not like anybody ever promised me that life would be fair."

"It sure wasn't fair to you."

"No. But that doesn't make what I did all right. It isn't fair to have somebody steal from you, either. That's the part I missed. At the time."

Dave nodded. "So what have you done about it?"

"Well ..." Joe was nonplussed. "Well, I don't steal anything these days, if that's what you mean. And I donate some, but you know that."

"Yes," Dave said, "I know you do. But what have you done about what you stole? What have you done to make that right?"

"Uh ..." Joe was stuck. "Nothing, I guess."

"Then, if it's still eating away at you, enough that you have to come and tell me about it before you can date my daughter in good conscience, don't you think you'd better?"

"Like what?" What more was there that he could do, if giving away as much as he had done hadn't fixed it?

"Like making a list of everyplace you stole from," Dave said. "Like walking into every one of those places and handing over a check made out to the charity of their choice for the amount, and telling them why you're doing it. Like making it right."

"I wouldn't even know how much," Joe said, everything in him cringing at the thought. "I wouldn't even know every place."

"Do your best, then. And if you don't know how much, well, add a zero or two on there, don't you think? That way you'll cover your bases."

"Wow," Joe said. "I don't ... This isn't what I expected you to say."

"Yeah." Dave sighed. "People always expect some easier answer. You'll hear it said that confession is good for the soul. I've found that to be true to a certain extent, but in my experience, it works a whole lot better when it comes with reparation. You came here today, I think, to ask for my advice. You don't have to take it, but here it is. You did wrong. Do your best to make it right. That's the only way to let it go."

"And if I do that," Joe said, "that'll make me good enough for Alyssa? That what you're saying?"

"No. That's not what I'm saying. I'm saying, if you do that, that might be a pretty good step towards making yourself good enough for you."

Joe sat for a few moments, taking that in.

"Something my grandmother used to say to me, when I was a boy." Dave chuckled a little, remembering. "Because I had a temper, oh, and then some. Had my share of anger, that's for sure. You ever hear of the two wolves?"

"I don't think so," Joe said.

"Cherokee proverb. One of those ones that makes you realize that there's a lot of common ground between religions, because people are people." Dave sat still a moment, then recited. 'There is a battle of two wolves inside us all. One is evil. It is anger, jealousy, greed, resentment, lies, inferiority, and ego. The other is good. It is joy, peace, love, hope, humility, kindness, empathy and truth. The wolf that wins? The one you feed.'"

"I guess that's true," Joe said, because he had to say something.

"You may have fed your evil wolf for a while there," Dave said, "but seems to me you've been mostly working lately on feeding the good one."

They sat in silence a bit longer, and Joe was glad that, for once, he could take his time. "I wanted you to know, though," he said at last, because he had to make this point, because this was the reason he'd come, "that I know my background isn't what you'd want for your daughter. That I know I don't come from much, but I promise you, I care about her, and I'll be trying my best to be good for her."

"You want to know one thing I've learned for sure, after more than thirty-five years in this line of work?" Dave asked.

"Yes, sir," Joe said, and waited for it.

"Here it is, then. It doesn't matter where you come from. It only matters where you're going."

It took Joe a full minute to recover from that one. He knew he was just sitting there, frowning into his lap, but Dave didn't push him. Instead, he waited patiently until Joe looked up again.

"Something else, too," Dave guessed. "It's serious, with Alyssa, or you wouldn't be here. And you're ... well, I'm guessing you might be a little scared about that, because Alyssa's not going to settle for half of a relationship, or for half of you."

Joe blew out a breath and admitted it. "Terrified." And then, as the older man continued to sit back and look at him, he went on. "I never know what she's going to do. What she's going to make me feel."

Dave smiled. "A little out of your comfort zone?"

That surprised a laugh out of Joe. "I don't even remember what my comfort zone felt like."

"Don't I know all about it," Dave said. "You ever hear the story about how I met Alyssa's mother?"

"No, sir," Joe said, so relieved that they weren't talking about him anymore. "I don't think I did."

"She was sixteen." Dave sat back with a reminiscent smile. "And if you thought Alyssa was a pretty girl when you met her, well, you should have seen her mother that day. I was at a church picnic, and she was there with her family. She was wearing shorts, I remember, and a shirt with a little bit of lacy trim. Not a dress, nothing like that, because we were playing softball, and she was a good athlete, just like Alyssa. But she had that lacy trim, and she was so ... pretty," he finished with a sigh.

He sat a moment, remembering. "Well, I looked at her, and I knew. And you have to understand," he went on with a rueful laugh, "I don't believe in making life decisions based on infatuation. That's a road that tends to lead straight to unhappiness for all parties concerned, including the unfortunate kids who always seem to show up as a result. And there I was, a senior in college, looking at three or four more years of divinity school, poor as a … well, as a church mouse. A one-quarter Cherokee, four-quarters poor son of a single mother just scraping by herself. Not a thing in the world to offer, losing my heart to a girl from a family who had a whole different idea of the kind of future she ought to have, a girl with two more years to go just to get out of high school." He shook his head with a chuckle. "Hopeless."

"So what happened?" Joe asked.

"Well, there," Dave said, "I think you'd have to call that the hand of God. Because for some strange reason, she wanted to talk to me, too, that day. And after that, I spent three years watching her get older, seeing her at church, seeing her go out with boys her own age and telling myself that that was the right thing, because I was way too old for her, and sure as heck too poor."

He leaned back in his chair and smiled. If there was one thing Dave Kincaid could do, it was tell a story. "And then, one day," he said, "when she was home from college for the summer, nineteen years old and getting prettier every single day, she asked me why I hadn't ever asked her out. She said," and he was laughing again, a deep rumble, "'I'm getting pretty tired of waiting for you.' And what could I do? That was it for me. I was a lost man."

"That's a pretty good story," Joe said.

"Yep," Dave agreed. "Susie gets what Susie wants. I don't know why she should have, but turns out she wanted me. Oh, it took a while, still, for us to be together, for her to finish college and all that, all the things her parents insisted on, the things I wanted for her too. I was terrified I'd lose her, but I didn't want her to marry me without having her chance out in the world, without being old enough to be sure. But ever since then, it's been the two of us. She's worked harder than any woman should have to, and she's had a whole lot less than any woman as good as her deserves, but she's hung in there with me all the same."

"Sounds like you both got lucky that day," Joe said.

"Yes, we did. I know I did. And I got three pretty good kids out of the deal, too. Three kids I'm proud to call mine.

196

And Alyssa, well, she's the image of her mother. Not just her looks, but her spirit. Her nerve, and her heart. She's every bit her mother's daughter, and her mother was one in a million. I know Susie could have done better. But I'm still glad she chose me."

He looked so at ease, so fine with all this, that Joe went ahead and asked it, the question he hadn't dared to ask until now, because he couldn't stand to hear the wrong answer. "And this is really all right with you? Me and Alyssa?"

"This is what I've been praying for," Dave answered simply.

"Me?" It was a shock. "Why?"

"Because I know you'd never have touched her if you didn't love her."

Joe sat a moment and let the truth of that percolate through him. "I just hope I can do it right," he finally said. "I'm not good at this."

"You just follow your heart," Dave advised. "Your heart knows the way. When you want to close down, open up and let her see you."

"I have a lot that's not nice to look at," Joe said. "What I told you, and a lot more."

"You let her see you," Dave said again. "Let her help you. Because you'll be helping her, won't you?"

"Always." And that was true, too. All the way down.

"Then pay her the compliment of believing she can do the same, and that she wants to. That she wants to be there for you, too. Maybe a man can make it alone, maybe he can have a good life that way. I know I wouldn't want to do it. Believe me, living in this world is a whole lot easier with a strong, loving woman by your side to share your burdens. And when you're standing by her, sharing hers—that's when you're your best man."

Joe had a horrible feeling that if he stayed in here a minute longer, he was going to cry. He stood up, held out a hand to Dave. "Thanks." He knew he should say more, but as usual, he couldn't think what.

197

Dave stood, too, and shook Joe's hand. And then he did the thing that did Joe in. He came around his desk, wrapped his burly arms around Joe, and held him close for a moment. As if Joe really were his son.

The tears did surface then, and Joe couldn't do a thing about them.

Talk about being out of your comfort zone.

Geek Day

Alyssa was sitting in Joe's loft a month or so later. It had turned out that his place was nicer than her own. A *lot* nicer. In fact, it was so far from the white-painted one-bedroom with board-and-brick bookcases she'd imagined, it wasn't even funny. Because Joe lived in the coolest place she'd ever seen.

It was a loft, but that didn't really describe it. Off Fillmore Street, at the dividing line between the swank of Pacific Heights and the funky, urban Fillmore vibe of jazz clubs and restaurants, his condo was one-sixth of a converted warehouse, all industrial materials, light-filled spaces, and, at the same time, cozy warmth. Multi-paned windows made up one entire wall of the hugely oversized main room and looked out over a treetop view to Twin Peaks, across in the other direction to Japantown. The ceiling soared eighteen feet overhead, punctuated again and again by skylights, and that was the light and the space.

The warmth came from the rest of it. From the poured concrete floors with more of that radiant heating beneath them, the bronzed metal and rustic wood accents of a floor-to-ceiling bookcase that took up one entire wall, a matching wine rack that rose halfway up another, sliding barn-style doors that concealed a giant-screen TV in front of a seating area made up of a sectional leather sofa. More bronzed metal formed the hearth of a gas fireplace, in front of which were clustered two oversized leather couches, two easy chairs, and a cozy rug. The nine-foot-long, heavy wood work table took up some space between the two areas, and a separate dining table in the corner stood next to another cook's kitchen, in which the gleam of stainless steel was softened by more wood and stone. It was all like being in some fantastic combination of a mountaintop and a cave, every part of every room organized and neat to the last degree, with built-in cabinetry that would have made any boat-builder proud.

And then there was what Joe called his Gear Room. When she'd first seen it, Alyssa had laughed out loud. "And here I thought your whole place was a Man Cave," she said. "But this is the ultimate."

It was a big room, the size of a normal person's master bedroom. The center space was open, for setting up equipment, and sorting, and packing, Joe explained, and she had to smile at that. All four walls were lined from floor to ceiling with storage for every kind of outdoor equipment she could imagine. Racks for skis and poles, high pegs for packs and sleeping bags. Tents and rolled mats on shelves, parkas and bib overalls zipped neatly over hangers. It looked like Aladdin's Cave for outdoorspeople. It looked like a store.

"Organization is good," he'd said when she teased him about it. "I like to be able to put my hand on what I want."

"Yes," she said, "I've noticed that." And he'd laughed and kissed her.

Needless to say, she'd been happy to spend as much of her time as possible at his place. Being with Joe was always good. Being with Joe in the Man Cave was better, even if he spent a fair amount of his time there working.

Now, she looked across at him. "Can I interrupt you to have you listen to something?" she asked. She was sitting at the work table with her laptop while he sat a ways down with his own, nothing moving but his fingers. Both of them facing the soothing view of trees, sky, and hills that somehow made working easier.

"One sec," he said, his face intent, concentrating. He kept typing for a few minutes, then sat back with a sigh and turned his attention to her. "All right, shoot."

"Remember the thing I was working on?" she asked. "Something to pull in tech companies?"

"Of course. You thought of something?"

"Yes. I think I did. I think I thought of a *great* thing. OK. Here goes. What's wrong with most fundraising events?"

"I don't know. What?"

"Two things. First," she held up one finger, "they're expensive. Our big event is, what? The donor cocktail party coming up in a few weeks at the Asian Art Museum. That's kind of an, excuse me, *stupid* event. It costs a lot, even though the space is donated. All that alcohol. And younger people, cooler people, do they want to go to a cocktail party? Never mind, I'll answer. No."

She held up the second finger. "And that's Problem Number Two. Most fundraising events are boring. People who can afford to contribute money, or people who work for companies that contribute money, they don't want to go to dinners and hear speeches. They want to have *fun*. So that's what my idea is. It's cheap, and it's fun."

"All right," he said, "so what is it?"

"It is ..." She did a drumroll on the arm of her chair. "Geek Day!"

He laughed. "Geek Day?"

She sat forward and pitched him. "Yes. Geek Day. It's a day for tech companies. It's a competition, and it's *fun*. Like a Field Day in elementary school. Didn't you love Field Day? Wasn't it *so* much better than school?"

"Yeah, as I recall, it was."

"Well, that's what Geek Day will be. Just a day to have fun. Every company fields a team, or more than one team, if they're big. Maybe *lots* of teams. And, of course," she said with a smile, "there's a great big donation required from every single team. And all those teams compete to win the trophy. The Second Chance Geek Day Trophy. A great big thing for their trophy case. A great big prize."

"Compete at what?"

"All sorts of things. Silly things. Fun things. Nothing like robotics or programming or anything geek-related like that. Nothing they'll be good at. That's the point. Nobody has to get all competitive and crazy, because it's just fun. Although

201

it's going to be mostly guys," she conceded, "so, all right, they'll get competitive and crazy anyway. Oh, man, that would be *awesome* media, Google employees practicing for the three-legged race! Because that's what it's going to be, things like you'd have at a company picnic or a kid's birthday party. Things that will make people laugh. Egg-and-spoon races, three-legged races, jump-rope contests, gunny-sack races where you hop in a sack. It doesn't matter if you're athletic, it's just for fun, things geeks can do, things the media will *love* to take pictures of. Alec in a gunny sack ..." She laughed. "That'd be *great.*"

"Things geeks can do? I beg your pardon?"

"Well, I'm not talking about you and Alec, obviously," she conceded. "But I've been in you guys' office enough now, and let's just say that I'm pretty sure my high school girls' basketball team could have kicked your company team's butts. If you *had* a company team, which you don't. Maybe a company Ping-Pong team. A *Wii* Ping-Pong team, and I'd *still* bet on my basketball team kicking your butts. I don't think any of those guys was on the football team, not unless he was the water boy."

"Statistician," he suggested, his smile trying to work its way out again.

"Exactly," she pounced. "So here's their big chance to do athletic things. With a tug-of-war for the final event. Sudden-death, and the teams keep going until you've got a winner. You add up points for it all, and ..." She gestured broadly. "Ta-dah. The winner! The Geek Day trophy!"

"Tug-of-war in the mud," he suggested.

She laughed. "Even better, but I'm not sure how you'd get a field full of mud. But yeah, that would be awesome." She made a note. "Just in case."

"Where would you have this event?" he asked. "You'd need a pretty big venue."

"Well, I thought," she said, and took a breath. "Stanford. Isn't that the perfect place? We could combine it with foster kids getting tours of the campus the day before. More PR, and that would look really good for the University. And mentoring, and everything," she began to plan. "More community service for tech firms. Get that rolling, who knows where we'd end up? Plus, I'll bet, help from the Stanford Athletic Department. First-aid staff, right? Stanford has a lot of school spirit, and a lot of money, too. Don't you think they'd go for it? Don't you think they might donate the use of their facilities?"

"I think they might, with a couple well-placed alumni to help ease the way."

"Exactly. Alec and you to help with that, and Rae to help with the committee, for the logistical side of it? Don't you think it could work? And don't you think it'd be great publicity for all the companies that contributed? Plus, think of the networking opportunities. Maybe I'll keep this one quiet, maybe it's not a great selling point for management, but think about it. You're there cheering your team on, talking to people from all the other companies? Just *think* about all the job-hopping that could happen after Geek Day!"

"Mmm. Not going to help you sell the idea to Rae," Joe agreed. "Maybe don't emphasize that one."

"Yeah. But on the other hand, if a company's doing well and is good to work for, hey, net gain, right?"

"One hopes," he said. "Anyway. Going to take awhile to get the publicity going, and to organize it. When were you thinking?"

"It'd have to be a next-year deal. Say, soon after school lets out next June. That would let it get into the budget for the next fiscal year, and let us build up anticipation, too. And after that," she went on, caught up in her enthusiasm, "we could do it the next year, and the next, and the next, and every year, it would get bigger, and the publicity would get bigger, too, because tech is only going to get bigger. What do you think?"

"I think," he said, and he was smiling, "that you're brilliant. I think it's a terrific idea. I think you should go for it."

"You really do?" she pressed him. "It's not just because you're sleeping with me?"

He sat back and put his hand over his heart. "I swear. This isn't Joe-Your-Boyfriend talking. This is the cold, hard partner talking. I think it's an awesome idea. I think it's going to work. I think it's great."

"Then that's what I'm going to do," she said. "I'm going to get pictures of people doing all those things, and I'm going to make a slideshow, and I'm going to talk to Rae about the dollars part of it, how much of a contribution to ask, and I'm going to work up projections, and I'm going to *do* it."

"When? You should give yourself a deadline," he advised. "Always work with a deadline."

"All right." She looked at her calendar, made another note. "A week from now, I'll ask for the meeting. April twenty-first. It should be good timing, because we're in the middle of planning the donor party, and Helene can look at my projections against the cost of that, and it'll look especially good, right?"

"Sounds good," he said. "You can practice it with me first, as many times as you need to. I'll ask all the hard questions I can think of, get you ready to go. And then you'll go in there, present it to Helene, and knock it out of the park."

"And you'll still go to the party with me too?" she asked.

"Yeah." He smiled a little wryly. "I'm thinking you're completely right, by the way. My feelings about getting dressed up and going to your cocktail party, versus doing Geek Day? No contest."

Another Bad Date

Alyssa paced the living room on a Friday night several weeks later. Around the couch to the kitchen entrance, a U-turn and on to the front door, then around the couch again. And repeat.

She'd got the text forty-five minutes earlier—*after* she'd spent a half-hour trying on and discarding clothes until she'd settled, as she'd known she would all along, on the red sweater and skirt she'd been wearing when Joe had picked her up on his motorcycle. Her club clothes, and she'd gone ahead and worn her cutout ankle-strap heels too, because she loved them. She couldn't walk too far in them, but she was pretty sure she wouldn't have to, because Joe was never going to make her hike halfway across the City to his car.

She'd made up her eyes so they were huge and mysterious, kept her lips understated, because they were full enough without help, and she didn't want to look like a vampire. She'd bent from the waist and stood up again so her hair was just-enough disheveled. She'd looked in the full-length mirror in her room, turned and twisted and nodded with satisfaction. A little bit wild, and a whole lot naughty. Joe was going to like it. He was going to *love* it.

And then she'd got the text. *Sorry late. Emergency. Half hour.*

Forty-five minutes now. She was hungry, but she was worried too. What was the emergency? She'd texted him back at the time with *Hope all OK see you then,* and that was the last she'd heard. Finally, she fished her phone out of her little date purse and called him.

"Hi," she heard right away. "Sorry. I'm almost done. I'll be there."

"What? Almost done with what? What happened?"

"Problem with this app. I need to get a guy started on it tomorrow, and I've got to work it out."

"Wait a second," she said, feeling her heart rate kicking up a fatal few notches. "Hold on. The crisis is *work*, on *Friday night?* Nobody's dying? Nobody's even *bleeding?*"

The sigh came right over the line. "No. But I have to get this done first. I'm sorry."

"You're still there. You haven't even left the office."

"No, but ... almost. I'll be there soon."

"Right. You're busy. Then I guess you shouldn't have asked me out."

She didn't wait for an answer. She hung up on him.

Sherry came out of the kitchen. "Joe not here yet?"

"No." Alyssa shoved the phone back into her bag. "I'm going out," she decided.

"Uh ... by yourself?"

"You want to come?"

"Nah. Sorry. I'm in pajamas-and-popcorn mode tonight. Too hard to get dressed again."

Alyssa nodded jerkily. That would have been fine with her too, if that had been the *plan*. She went into the kitchen and ate a bowl of cereal standing up, because she really was too hungry not to, and the whole time she was doing it, she was getting madder. She brushed her teeth again, reapplied her lipstick, called a cab. And she went out.

Joe was swearing at himself. *Stupid. Idiot.* When he'd found the bug, he'd thought it would be quick. Had felt the urgency of fixing it, like always, had been glad he'd remembered to text Alyssa. A niggle of uncertainty had troubled him while he was doing it, but getting the work done, right the hell now, was too deeply ingrained in him, his fingers itching to get back to it, his brain making a connection right then, even as he texted, that had him turning back to the computer.

But when she'd called, he'd realized that he should have listened to the niggle. Because he'd screwed up. He'd screwed up bad.

He'd logged off, ridden home, showered and changed in about ten minutes flat, climbed into the Audi and headed for her apartment. Endured frustrating minutes of circling for a parking space, until he gave it up and parked in front of a hydrant. A ticket seemed like the least of his worries.

He walked fast to her building, pressed the doorbell, and waited.

Sherry's voice on the intercom. "Yes?"

"It's Joe," he said. "Here for Alyssa."

"You'd better come up." The buzz came, and he was inside, and up the stairs.

No Alyssa at the door. Sherry instead, in her pajamas.

"She isn't here," she said, looking not very happy with him at all, not even asking him in. "Seems her date stood her up, so she went out by herself."

"I didn't stand her up," Joe tried to explain. "I just got held up."

"Uh-huh. Well, good luck telling her that. Women are funny that way. When the guy doesn't show, they tend to think he doesn't care that much, you know?"

"I—" Joe stopped. He had a feeling he needed to save the explaining for Alyssa. "Where did she go?"

Sherry shrugged. "I don't know."

"Well, can you guess?" He blew out a breath, tried not to sound impatient. "Please," he added. "Can you guess? Did she say anything?"

Sherry still looked reluctant, but she answered. "I think probably wherever you guys were planning to go. You were going to some jazz club, right?"

"Right."

Another shrug. "Then that's it. That'd be my guess. She probably went to some jazz club."

"But why would she go by herself?" He was still confused.

"You really don't know women, do you?" She was looking at him with a little pity now, and if she'd ever had a thing for him, he had a feeling the thing was gone. "She's showing you. My guess is, she's out there where she was going to be with you. She's dancing with other guys instead of you. She's showing you."

She was in the third place he tried, a good hour later. The Boom Boom Room. He'd headed to the front of the line, nodded to the guy on the door. "Hey, Marcus."

"Hey, Joe. How you doin'?" A gold tooth shone in the smile as Marcus held out a hand. Joe shook, slid the fifty into the broad palm, and it was in Marcus's pocket in one quick move, even as Marcus lifted the velvet rope and moved his bulk out of the way.

Inside, Joe's ears were assailed by the sound of a live band in full swing, the babble of dozens of voices shouting to be heard, the whir of the huge fan cooling the dancers on the packed floor. He scanned the bar, the groups perched on stools or standing with drinks in hand. No Alyssa. He moved closer to the noise, the action, prowled back and forth, searching the dimly lit dance floor, the couples shifting and moving, the light picking out first one group, than another.

He was about to give it up as yet another dead end when he saw her. Dancing with her eyes half-closed, her head tossing, her body swaying, looking like a wet dream in that damn red sweater. And the guy opposite her looking like he'd hit the jackpot. *His* eyes weren't half-closed.

Joe began to push a path through the crowd of dancers as the song ended. From the vantage point of his height, he could see Alyssa saying something to the guy, heading off the floor, only to be intercepted by somebody else, somebody he guessed she'd been talking to earlier, because New Guy touched her shoulder, smiled, put his hand on her back to turn her onto the floor, and she was smiling back, tossing her hair, and Joe was burning.

She caught sight of Joe as he twisted and shoved his way through the crowd, packed ever more tightly as he got closer to the stage. Her eyes widened as they met his, then she turned her back on him, did a wriggle and a shake, her elbows up over her head, her hands waving like some kind of welcome sign, and her partner was moving closer, his eyes avid, reaching out a hand and grabbing a hip, and Joe had reached his limit.

He got to them, finally. The band was loud up here, and they were near the fan, and it was blowing Alyssa's skirt, her hair, and the music was pumping.

She turned, glanced at him, then deliberately away, and kept dancing. And the guy with her, if possible, looked even less welcoming than she did, his hand tightening on her hip, and Joe wanted to deck him *now*.

"Alyssa."

"Go away." He couldn't hear her, but he got the message anyway.

"Come on." He grabbed her hand, pulled her away from her new friend. "Outside."

"Hey. Back off, buddy," the other guy said, and Joe could hear that just fine, and Alyssa was pulling her hand out of his.

"No," Joe said. "You back off. Right now." And in case the guy couldn't hear, Joe made sure he got his point across.

The guy glared back at him, and Joe didn't think he'd made it onto his Christmas card list. But he backed off all the same, melted right into the crowd. So much for his chivalrous impulses.

"Go *away*," Alyssa said again, almost loud enough for him to hear this time. "Leave me *alone*."

"Alyssa. Come on. Talk to me." He wanted to grab her again, but he didn't. He might not know women, but he knew Alyssa. He jerked his head toward the door. "Come on. Now."

She came with him, maybe reluctantly, but she came.

"Got a coat?" he asked when they were near the exit, the music not quite as loud. She fished in her purse, handed him the ticket, and he went to the coat-check and retrieved it, handed it to her.

Marcus raised an eyebrow when Joe hit the door again. And then he saw Alyssa, and the tooth flashed again. "Hey, brother. Have a good night."

Joe barely noticed. He had Alyssa's elbow, was leading her around the corner, to the alley that led to the back entrance. Although he had absolutely no idea what he was going to say.

Just Asking for Trouble

"You're going to make this about me," she said as soon as he'd turned the corner, once they were in the alley. Next to the dumpsters. First he'd stood her up, now he was taking her for a chat by the *dumpsters*. And this was the guy she'd spent fifteen years wanting? "You're going to make it like I did something wrong." She twisted her elbow out of his grip. "I'm *on* my date. *I* showed up. It's not my fault I'm here alone."

"Alyssa. Wait," he commanded, and she shut up, but she glowered at him all the same.

"I'm waiting," she said when he just stood there. "But what comes out of your mouth had better be an apology."

"I'm sorry," he burst out. "All right, I'm sorry. I screwed up. I'm just so …" He broke off, shrugged, a heavy, helpless movement, and despite her hurt and anger, she could see him. She could *feel* him. "It's just always been so important to get it done."

"But don't you *see?*" she tried to tell him. "Don't you see that when you say that, you're saying I'm *not* important?"

"I get it," he said, running a hand over his head and looking at the ground. "I do."

"No," she said. "No, I don't think you do, or you wouldn't have done it. I was *excited.* This was supposed to be my big celebration for the board saying yes to Geek Day. I know it isn't really a big deal, not like your job. I know it, I know I'm just … little, but it was a big deal to me. It was the biggest deal to me I've ever had at work, and I thought you knew. I thought you *cared* about it. I thought you wanted to

211

take me out and celebrate. I looked forward to it all *day*. More than all day. It was my *celebration*, and turns out it didn't matter to you."

The tears were close to the surface now, and she blinked them back, because she needed to tell him. She'd felt so bad, and she wanted to be comforted, and he wasn't the man who could do it after all. "And when I realized it *wasn't* an emergency," she said, "that it was just your work, that I didn't matter as much as some work problem, that you didn't care that I hadn't had dinner, you didn't care that I was waiting for you, when I knew I was that low on your list, it …"

The tears were there, and she was ruining her makeup, not that it mattered, because if anybody had ever had a disastrous evening, this was it. "It hurt so *much*," she finished, and she couldn't help crying. She couldn't help it at all. "I thought I was special to you, and I'm not, and it *hurts*."

"You are," he said, and he looked miserable, the wooden expression gone for once. "I'm sorry. I didn't think, that's all."

"Yeah, well," she said, doing her best to rally her forces, running a knuckle over the corners of her eyes, wishing she had a Kleenex. "You should have. You *should* have. I got ready. I wanted to look nice for you. I wanted you to be proud of me. And I felt so …" She was crying again, because she couldn't help it. "I felt so *stupid*. Because I did it again. I thought you cared about me, that you were the right guy. But you're not. You're just a guy. Just another guy."

"No," he said. "Alyssa. Sweetheart. No. Wait. Let me try. No, I'm not. I'm stupid sometimes, but I'm not just a guy. At least, I am. I'm a guy who's crazy about you. That's why I'm here, because I know I screwed up. I left as soon as I talked to you. I came as fast as I could, and I've been looking for you …" He exhaled, cast an arm out. "All over. Worrying about what you were doing, that you'd be too mad to call me this time if you got in trouble."

She couldn't help it. She softened. "You have? You've been looking for me?"

He reached out for her, then. "All over," he said, one arm around her waist, his other hand smoothing back a wisp of hair that had fallen in her face. "How about going back in there with me, giving me another chance?"

"You admit that you were wrong?"

He groaned. "Oh, man. You're going to make me say it, aren't you?"

"Yeah. I am. I felt really bad, Joe. I really did. You have to at least say the word."

"All right," he said, tucking the hair behind her ear, his thumb caressing her cheek. "I was wrong. I screwed up. Now will you come dance with me?"

"Maybe." She leaned into him, because he was so big, and so warm, and she didn't want to fight, she wanted Joe. "Maybe if you kiss me like you mean it first."

He had a hand behind her head, and the other one around her, and he was kissing her the way she liked it. Thoroughly, and a little bit hard, and like he meant it. She had her hands around his shoulders, and she could hear herself making little noises into his mouth, because she was back in his arms, and it felt like he wanted her there, and she wanted him to want her more.

She was vaguely aware that he was backing her up, but she didn't realize what was happening until her back hit the wall, until he had reached down to pull her legs up, wrap them around his waist. And she was against the wall, his hand behind her head, and the knowledge that he was holding her up with one arm was thrilling, and what that didn't do, his mouth against hers was taking care of.

He shoved harder into her, and she wrapped her legs around him more tightly, pulled him closer, and kissed him back, her hands under his leather jacket, under his shirt, against the bulk of muscle at his side, coming to rest on either side of his spine, then running up and down there, her fingers reaching down under his waistband, stroking his skin down low, near his tailbone.

"Do it now," she breathed. Her fingers were circling, and she could feel him jerking against her as if there were a direct line of electric current running there, just like the one that was zinging from her neck, where his teeth were closing on her skin, straight to her center, making her need him inside her right now. Right *now*. "Come on, Joe," she begged. "Do it now."

His mouth stilled, and he pulled his head away, rested it against the bulk of his arm for a moment. He stood back, lowered her to the ground, steadied her against him. "No. You make me so damn crazy. No. Not in the alley."

She straightened her skirt, smoothed her hair where his hand had ruffled it, feeing bereft and angry and confused, because why was she mad?

"You say I make you crazy," she said. "But you never *act* crazy. You never lose control."

"What?" He was the one looking confused now. "I'm *supposed* to do you against the wall, where anyone could see? I thought I was supposed to make you feel special."

She shrugged, not sure how to tell him that knowing he couldn't stand not to be inside her, that he had to do it *now*, that she'd pushed him past his boundaries, was what she needed from him tonight.

"That's not happening," he said. "Not here. But how about dancing? How about a do-over on that?" He smoothed her hair some more for her, like he needed to touch her, and she forgave him a little.

"You want to dance with me? You sure?" she asked, trying for her usual sassy tone. "Don't you have some work to do?"

"No," he said. "No more work. It's all about you tonight, all night long. And right now, I want to dance with you. At least, I want to watch you dance. But only if you promise to do all those things you were doing before to make me jealous. Only if you do them all for me."

"You could tell that's what I was doing?" she asked as he took her hand and they rounded the corner, past the doorman again, who let them in with a grin for Joe.

"I knew what you were doing," he said just before the noise level rose too high for her to hear. "And it worked."

214

Dancing was good, but after an hour of showing off her moves for him, of watching those pale blue eyes leveled on her, the intensity in them while she did it, she needed something else.

"You like me?" she asked, as close to his ear as she could reach as they swayed to a slow, bluesy number, as Joe put a hand on her lower back to pull her closer. "You like to touch me?"

"You know I do." And if she hadn't, what she was feeling against her would have let her know.

"Then show me." She moved her hand inside the collar of his dark gray shirt, stroked the side of his neck, up over the rasp of his hair, keeping her touch light. She lifted her cheek from his chest and kissed him there, not caring who was watching. He smelled faintly of soap, and of man. He smelled like Joe.

He had her hand in his again, was taking her off the dance floor for the second time that night. A quick detour for her coat, and he was helping her into it, all without attempting to speak over the throb of music, the incessant waves of conversation washing over them.

The quiet, the chill outside were a shock. Joe said a couple words to the guy at the door, and Alyssa saw the flash of a bill changing hands, then the guy was speaking into a phone, and another, only slightly smaller man was out the door of the club and jogging down the street.

A brief wait in the night air, then. Joe's silence, rather than annoying her, was exciting her. Something about the look of him, so still, so set. As if he were saving his energy.

He held the door for her when the car pulled up with a screech of tires, then swung up beside her and was driving, headed north, to his place. He was almost there, she could feel it like a physical thing in the confined space, the tension between them. But she wanted him further gone. She wanted him all the way, because she needed to *know*.

"Guess I'm glad I didn't give any of those guys my number after all," she tried. "Or let them take me home, either. I bet they didn't valet park. We'd still be walking."

She could see his jaw set, his body stiffen, and she shivered. Yep. That had worked.

"You'd better not have given it to them," he told her. "And we're not even going to talk about them taking you home. You need to be clear about this. I don't care if we have a fight. I don't care how mad you are at me. It's not OK to go out and dance with other guys. It's not OK to let them put their hands on you."

"You're jealous, huh? You should be jealous." She was just torturing him now, and she knew it, and she was doing it anyway. "If you don't want me to be with anybody else, then I guess you should take better care of me, shouldn't you?"

He'd reached his loft, because it was only a few blocks. They could have walked, except that she'd been right, Joe would never make her walk. The garage door rolled up as they approached, and he pulled the car inside, and she listened to the grinding sound of the door shutting again behind them.

"I'm not joking," he said, not making any move to get out, his expression hard in the faint light. "All right, I screwed up. I won't do that again, but I'll do something else wrong, because I'm a guy. You can yell at me, and you can fight with me. But you can't do what you did tonight."

"Or what?"

"Or ... *what?*" he repeated, staring at her.

"Or what?" She shrugged. "What are you going to do, if you really care that much? What are you going to do, if I was so bad?"

He looked stunned for a moment, and then he spoke, the warning clear. "Alyssa. You'd better stop."

"If you want to show me," she challenged, "show me. Don't tell me."

Another pause. "You are just asking for trouble," he finally said, and the intensity she heard in his voice set up a faint answering drumbeat deep inside her. "You keep on acting like a naughty little girl, you're asking to get a spanking like one."

216

"Huh." She tossed her head and opened her car door, her heart beating hard. "Big talker." She slammed the door, headed off without waiting for him.

He was out of the car and at the entry door, punching in the code, with all the speed his normally deliberate moves belied. And then he had her by the hand once more, was pulling her through the hallway, but not all the way to the bedroom, not like she'd expected. He stopped at the living room, next to one of the wide brown leather couches.

"Take off your coat," he said, shrugging out of his own jacket and tossing it onto the opposite couch, and she did the same with a pang of disappointment, adding her bag while she was at it. Well, this wasn't exactly sexy.

"Now take off your underwear," he said, and that was a whole lot better.

"What?" She played along. She'd wanted to see what he would do, had pushed as hard as she'd dared. Was he really going to do it?

"You heard me. Right now, Alyssa." There was no mistaking the purpose in his voice, or the look on his face.

His pale blue eyes never left hers, and she felt her eyes widen in spite of herself as she reached slowly under her skirt, because she *had* pushed hard, and now he actually looked dangerous.

"Turn around," he said. "I want to watch."

She turned her back to him, her breath coming short, hiked her skirt up, pulled the scrap of fabric down with both hands, leaning over to ease it over her heels, her skirt falling back down around her bare thighs.

"Put them on the end table," he said, and she did it, the scrap of pink making an incongruous, frivolous contrast against the solid, heavy wood, its polish gleaming in the soft light of the lamp.

He sat down in the center of the couch, looking a little less certain now, and she held her breath, wondering if he was going to lose his nerve. She'd be willing to bet he'd never done this before. Not that she had either, but she'd thought

217

about it often enough, over the years. And the hand doing it had always been Joe's.

She shrugged as the seconds ticked by, as he said nothing. "Well, guess I'll go to bed."

"No, you won't." That got him, just as she'd hoped it would. "You're going to lie down across my lap. Right now."

He was going to do it. The thrill of it sent a shock right through her, so sharp she shivered with it. She knelt carefully on the couch beside him, got her balance, then set her hands down on the cold leather across from him and lowered herself down, the bulk of his thighs raising her pelvis high, the toes of her shoes digging into the smooth surface behind her. The arousal in her was like a live thing, pulsing and beating, and she was panting already.

"Turn your head towards me," he instructed. "I want to see your face while I do this. I want to watch you feel it."

She obeyed, and he stroked her cheek, and she opened her mouth a little and sighed.

He put one hand on her back, used the other to pull her skirt up around her waist, then sat for a moment, ran one big hand over her. The size and the weight of it, her vulnerable position, it all felt so good, and she wriggled into him, rubbed herself over him, needing the contact, needing more.

"You're a very bad girl," he said, and she could see that he wasn't looking at her face after all, not right now. Instead, he was watching his hand move over her. "You push me and push me. But I'm going to let you decide. How many smacks do you think you deserve for running out without talking to me? For dancing like that, and letting that asshole touch you like that?"

"Two," she said as best she could with her cheek against the cold leather of the couch, while his hand stroked again and again over her bottom, her upper thighs, awakening tingles of pleasure along her skin that made her squirm, while the most insistent part of her screamed for his touch. "Two, please, Joe."

He laughed softly. "Oh, I don't think so. I just changed my mind. I'm going to decide."

And then he slapped her. Not hard, because she'd known it wouldn't be hard. But the sound rang out, shockingly sharp in the silent air of the loft, and she felt the sting of it, and jerked against him.

And then he spanked her again, and again, four, five, six times. Her hands gripped the leather surface of the couch, braced against the blows, coming a bit faster now. The warmth was growing, every smack sounding loud, and she was wriggling and moaning, the excitement leaping inside her.

He stopped. "Am I hitting too hard?"

"Quit ruining it," she said crossly, and he laughed a little, and then he was talking to her again.

"You'll never—" *Smack.* "Do that—" *Smack.* "Again." A pause. "Are we clear?"

"Yes. Yes." It was a gasp.

Another smack, harder this time. "Not good enough. I want to hear, 'Yes, Joe.'"

"Yes. Yes, Joe."

His hand was rubbing again, taking the sting away, and the tingling on the surface was no match for the fire that was consuming her now. "Never going to run out on me again?" he asked softly. "Never going to flirt with other guys just to make me mad?"

She didn't answer right away, and got another smack for her hesitation. "No," she moaned. "No, Joe."

"Good." And finally, his hand was between her legs, diving, inside her where she was slick and so wet, and beyond, and she was so close, going up fast, moving into his hand, her mouth open, her breath coming in keening sobs, her hands gripping the leather, hanging on.

Then he took his hand away, and she cried out her protest at the loss.

"You just remember this," she heard. "Because next time, it'll be harder."

"Oh. Yes."

He gave her one more smack, the hardest yet, which started all the tingles up again. His hand moved down again, and he was rubbing her like he meant it, finally letting her climb, and she was spiraling high, and moving hard against him, and starting to cry out as he told her she was his, told her what he'd do next time, told her everything she wanted to hear, and she was shoving off with her palms, her knees, pressing into his hand, as wave after wave consumed her, and she shook and shuddered and moaned out her release.

He kept going until the convulsions had become a final shudder, then he lowered her legs to the floor, pulled himself out from under her, and moved her legs back up onto the couch. She started to sit up, but a hand on her back had her down again. She felt him lifting her hips, sliding a cushion underneath them, lowering her over it.

"Stay there," he told her. "When I come back, I expect to find you exactly like this."

She lay there and trembled, and waited as his steps retreated. *Condom*, she realized through a haze of delicious anticipation.

A minute, two, and he was back again.

"You listened," he said, and there was amusement in his voice. "Looks like I finally found the secret."

"Huh," she managed. "Just because you turned me on so much. And stop *joking*."

"Sorry, baby." She heard the smile, still, then the rasp of a zipper, the soft sound of clothes hitting the floor. "You need me to be tough? You need me to talk dirty to you?"

She couldn't answer, just nodded, and he was on the couch with her, behind her, over her. It was a good thing, she thought irrelevantly, that he had such oversized furniture. She lost the thought, though, because his hands were at her throat, reaching underneath to unfasten the two little buttons fastening her sweater around her neck, and he was pulling the fabric back, his hands gently tracing where it had been.

"I wanted to do this so bad that first night," he said, his voice low. "The first time you wore that sweater, I wanted to put my hands right here. I wanted to put you down and unbutton you." He was settling his considerable weight over her, the warmth of his skin a shock against her bare lower body. She could feel how aroused he was, did a little more wriggling at the pleasure of it.

He was kissing the side of her neck now, his hand pulling the hair away so his mouth had full access. "You know how pretty your ass looks right now?" he murmured in her ear. "It's pink, just like your pretty little underwear. It's got my handprints all over it, because I spanked you hard, didn't I? And now I'm going to finish the job. I'm going to hold you down and do you hard from behind."

And then he did it. His strong fingers were digging into her hip, and she was backing into him, wanting more, asking him for it, begging him for it. He wasn't talking anymore, but she was making enough noise for both of them, until she was lost again, until he was joining her, gripping her harder than ever, going so deep she could feel him all the way inside her body, like he'd taken it over, like it really was his, groaning out a long, filthy string of curses that had her shaking. And, at last, with a final shudder, collapsing on top of her.

Somehow, Joe got some air back in his lungs, pushed himself up to sitting, pulled Alyssa into his lap. She was still wearing her sweater, skirt, and heels, he realized. He hadn't even undressed her. He'd been *gone*.

She nestled into him, wrapped her arms around him, and he held her and thought, *Damn.*

"Come on, sweetheart," he said. "Time for bed." He stood up with her and then, because he couldn't stand to put her down, carried her on through the hallway, into the bedroom. He set her down on the bed at last, knelt beside her and unfastened the shoes, rubbed her feet, the red marks where the straps had been.

"Hurts?" he asked when she sighed.

"Yes." She smiled at him, slow and satisfied. "Feels so good to take them off."

He sat beside her on the bed, pulled the sweater over her head, because she wasn't making any move to do it, then

221

flicked the clasp on the front of her bra and ran a thumb over the little red spot there.

"You've got lots of sore places for me to rub and kiss, don't you?" he asked.

"Mmm." She let him push her gently back on the bed, find the side zipper on her skirt, and pull that off too. He gathered her clothes, folded them carefully, and set them on a side chair.

"Joe," she sighed, "only you would spank a woman and then fold her clothes."

"Complaining?" He came over to sit beside her again.

"No." She shivered, and he pulled her up, held her close.

"Let's go take a shower," he said. "And next time," he told her when he'd helped her to her feet, "I get to do what *I* like."

"You liked that," she protested, following him into the bathroom. "You can't tell me you didn't, because I won't believe you."

"It was all right for a change," he said with a smile, twisting all the faucets in his big double shower, testing until the water was warm enough, then holding out a hand to her. "But you'd better not need it that way every time, because my heart can't take it."

"Did you really not like it?" She was shivering again as the warm spray hit her, and then she was relaxing into it, looking so pretty with her hair streaming around her, with the water running over her.

"Hell, yes, I liked it. I loved it. But," he said, laughing a little as he picked up the soap, "I was terrified I'd hurt you. All in all, it was fairly exhausting."

"Mmm." She was sighing again as he started to soap her up.

"Plus," he said, "it made my hand sting." And she laughed and took the soap from him and started to wash him, which felt pretty damn good.

"So what's your way?" she asked, her hands lingering on his chest, moving down to his abdomen, and lower, where things were waking up again, amazingly enough, because he'd

222

have sworn she'd pulled every last bit out of him. "What's your favorite, that we're doing next time?"

"That would be," he told her as her hands continued to move, "with you on your back. I'm old-fashioned that way. When you're holding my head in your hands, and you're making so much noise that I'm thinking my neighbors must be about to call the cops. When I'm stopping just to watch you squirm, just because I love to hear you beg. When I'm feeling you come, and then I'm sliding inside you while you're still going, and I can barely hold you down. That's the way we're doing it next time. My way."

She smiled, slow and secret, and leaned back against the stone tiles, because he was working on her now, sliding his soapy hands over her breasts, pausing for some extra attention where it seemed necessary, thinking that he was going to have to make sure that they got their fair share, because he hadn't done nearly enough, not yet. He kept on, one soap-slicked hand making a leisurely journey down her body, then settling in where she needed it. He could tell her legs were about to give out, that he was going to have to carry her on out of here, and that suited him just fine.

She sighed as the water poured down and the steam rose, arched into his hands, and said it again.

"Yes, Joe."

An Unexpected Detour

"So what's happening today?" she asked him the next morning while they were eating breakfast. Not too romantic—oatmeal—but she'd seemed fine with it. No matter what she thought, she was nowhere near high-maintenance.

He looked at her cautiously, hesitated.

"You have work to do," she realized.

"I really do have to get that app to Michael today," he explained. "I'm sorry, but I do."

"Can I say something?" she asked, and he tensed, waiting for it. "I get that you have to work hard," she said, her face serious for once. "I get that you *want* to work hard. I'm not going to ask you to take every weekend off. You couldn't even if you wanted to, and I know it."

"You do?"

"Of course I do. It's who you *are*. You're driven, just like Alec, and you love what you do. I admire that. Really, I do. All I want is for you to put me first when you say you will. I want to be able to count on that, so if you say we're going to dinner, that means we're going, not that maybe we will and maybe we won't, if something important comes up."

He winced a little. "Important as opposed to you."

She didn't mess around. "Yes. That's how I felt."

"I know. I got it."

"As long as you make time for me," she said, "as long as you're with me when you're *with* me, I'm good. As long as I feel like it *matters* to you that I'm with you, and not with

224

somebody else. That you can't …" She waved her spoon in the air. "Take me or leave me."

"I can show you that." He had to smile a little. "I kind of thought I already did. I was working pretty hard last night to convince you of it. I thought that was the point."

"Mmm." She was looking dreamy now, and he remembered the feeling of her under his hand, the way she'd squirmed, the sounds she'd made, and got a kick of pure lust that told him work was going to be delayed this morning.

"But," he managed to get in before it took him over entirely, "tonight's my do-over on dinner. I'll pick you up at seven. And from then on, I promise, you'll have my undivided attention."

That wasn't the way it worked out, though.

They were in his car, on their way to the Cliff House. He'd decided on the full cheesy treatment: Sutro's Restaurant in the big white historic building with its floor-to-ceiling windows looking straight out onto Seal Rocks and the crashing surf of the Pacific Ocean, candlelight and white tablecloths and a walk on the beach afterwards. It would be dark and cold and windy out there, but that would just mean she'd have to snuggle up and hold his arm again. She needed to feel special, and he was going to make sure she did. He might be a slow learner, but he got there eventually.

His phone rang, and he glanced at the dashboard display in surprise, punched the button to answer. "Cheryl?"

"Hey, Joe." His sister's voice came over the speakers. "I'm at the airport. Want to come out for an hour and catch up?"

"SFO? I didn't realize you were going to be coming through."

"Yeah, weather, we got rerouted. What do you say?"

Joe glanced at Alyssa. She was looking back at him, wary, waiting. "One second," he told Cheryl, and put her on hold. "It's my sister," he said to Alyssa. "I know I said I'd take you out, but …" He gestured a little helplessly. "I'm going to have

225

to ask for another rain check. Do you mind if I take you home?"

"Of course you need to see your sister," she said. "But you don't have time to take me home. You can drop me off and I can get a cab, or I could come with you. I'd like to meet her."

Joe wasn't at all sure that was a good idea, but saying no seemed like an even worse one. "Cheryl?" he asked, punching her up again. "OK, see you there in half an hour. Which terminal, and where?"

"Uh ..." The tired laugh came through. "International, that seems to be where I am."

He pulled a U-turn and headed for the freeway as he finished making arrangements with her.

"And here I made this big promise to concentrate on you tonight," he told Alyssa once he'd hung up.

"Don't be silly. I'm excited to meet her. You know my family so well, but I've barely even heard you talk about yours, except that your sister's in the Air Force. That is—is she still?"

"Yeah. I don't see her that often, though."

"She's your only family?"

"Yeah. She's the only one."

The Saturday-evening traffic lightened as the miles of 101 South sped by, and Joe knew he should talk, but he didn't know what to say, so as usual, he shut up. Alyssa seemed to understand, though. At least, she wasn't pressing him with any more questions.

He found a spot in Garage A, and they made their way down the elevator, along moving walkways, up escalators and through hallways into the soaring space of the food court of the International Terminal, thronged with travelers speaking a dozen languages. Family groups, couples, solo voyagers, some excited, some bored or weary, some businesslike, another day at the office. And one woman standing in jeans and a long-sleeved shirt next to a pillar. Tall and fit, but not slender.

226

Short dark hair and dark eyes, looking not much like Joe, but familiar all the same. The sight of her, as always, welcome, and yet not welcome.

"Hey," she said as the two of them approached. She reached up to give him a quick hug, a peck on the cheek.

"Hey, Cheryl. This is Alyssa Kincaid. Alec's sister," Joe added. She knew who Alec was, of course. It wasn't like he'd *never* seen her, just not often. Their visits had been short and a little awkward, and it was too long since they'd lived in the same house, since they'd been in each others' lives. And too hard to think back on the time when they were.

"Hi." Cheryl held out a hand to Alyssa, and Joe saw his sister's assessing gaze, her serious expression.

That was their similarity, he realized, seeing her through Alyssa's eyes. Temperament. Watching and waiting and evaluating before they spoke, before they acted. Caution. Inborn, or a response to life, he didn't know.

"Want to get a drink or something? Dinner?" he asked, reaching for her small black wheeled suitcase. "What do you have time for?"

"A drink and a snack." She smiled, finally. "I could use a beer."

"Me too," Joe said, and he smiled back, felt something easing.

Small talk as they selected a bar, placed their orders. Cheryl's trip to help teach a logistics course at Ramstein in Germany, how she'd liked the country, how glad she was to be headed back to Alaska.

"It's funny," she said. "I grew up hot all the time, and now I love the cold. Spending some time in the Sandbox ... Afghanistan," she explained for Alyssa's benefit. "I thought, yep, been there, done that, got the T-shirt. I couldn't get out of that hellhole fast enough. Just like home."

"Yeah," Joe said, frowning down into his beer, his tension back. "I was glad when you were back safe from there."

"Were you?" she asked.

He looked up at her. "Of course I was."

227

"I'm glad," she said. "I wasn't sure. It's hard when we barely see each other. I wish we did. But here we are now," she went on more briskly, "and I'm glad, because I wanted to talk to you face-to-face about this."

"About what?"

"About Mom."

"What about her?" He could feel Alyssa beside him, silently listening, focused on him, and he hated that she was there, but he was glad she was, too.

"I finally went to visit their graves last year," Cheryl said. "I wasn't going to, it just happened. Another layover, and I was there, and I did it, and I was glad I did. But I wanted to talk to you about ..." She paused, looked at Alyssa, and shrugged. "About a tombstone. Well, a marker."

"I'm not buying her a tombstone." The words would barely come out.

"I didn't realize she didn't have one," Cheryl went on relentlessly. "I'll admit, I didn't follow up. I figured you'd do it."

He wasn't frozen any more. Now, he was mad. Cold, hard mad. "Why would you think that?" he asked her. "Why would I do it? I made the funeral arrangements. I paid for everything you told me she needed. I paid for the hospital, and the nursing home, and the hospital again, and the funeral. Nobody can say I abandoned her. Nobody can say I didn't help, and God knows I had no reason to. Now I'm supposed to do more? I put out a hell of a lot more than she did for me. Or than she did for you, either. She didn't even deserve as much as we did for her."

"No, she didn't," Cheryl said. "But Dad did. How do you think he'd feel if he knew she was lying there beside him without a marker? He loved her. I want to do it for him, and for us, and I want you to do it with me. I want us to be able to remember the good times, before. There were lots of good times. And she *did* love you. Maybe you don't remember, but I do. She loved me, and she loved you, and she loved your dad. Once."

"Too bad she loved meth more," Joe said. "How can you defend her? You of all people?"

"Because I forgave."

"Some things aren't forgivable."

"Everything is forgivable. Walking around with all that bitterness in you—Joeby, it eats you up inside. I know. You have to let it go."

"No. I don't."

"The person you can't forgive," Cheryl said, reaching out and putting a hand on top of his clenched fist where it sat beside his glass, "is yourself. That's why you don't come see me. That's why you haven't visited their graves. Because you haven't, have you?"

Anywhere but here. He needed to be anywhere but here.

"You don't want to remember because you think you let us down," Cheryl said, not letting him off the hook, and he needed to be *gone*. "I know, because I felt the same way. I didn't want to remember how I let you down, how I ran and left you in the middle of that. I felt so guilty, it was hard for me to face you. I just wanted to forget it, wipe it all out. And you feel like that, too, don't you? You think you should have been able to stop it. But how could you? You were a *child*, Joe."

"He told me to do it." The words were coming whether he wanted them to or not. "Before he left. He told me to look out for the two of you while he was gone. He told me," and he could barely say it, "that I was the man of the family now. Some man. Some *man*."

"He shouldn't have said that," Cheryl said. "I know how much you idolized him. I loved him too. He was more of a dad to me than my own dad ever was. He treated me like his own, always. I loved him, but he was wrong. You were eleven years old. You don't make an eleven-year-old boy responsible for his mother. It wasn't fair, and it wasn't right."

Joe moved restlessly, wanting so much to get up and leave, but he didn't. He owed Cheryl that. He owed her a lot more than that.

"Go get help," Cheryl said. "I did. Get help to let it go. Not for her sake, or for mine. For yours."

"I had therapy," he said. Now he was sure how he felt about Alyssa being there. He hated it. "I had a whole long year of it. I've been through it all. I'm done."

"Think about it." Cheryl looked at her watch. "I have to go. I wish we'd met under better circumstances, Alyssa. I hope we still can."

She got up, and Joe rose too. Cheryl reached for him, and this time, it wasn't a brief embrace. She held him tight, and he wrapped his around her, too, held her for a long minute, and felt the emotion threatening.

"I love you, Joeby," she said, pulling back at last, her own eyes moist, a couple tears making their way down her cheeks. Cheryl didn't cry either, not that he'd seen, not for years. They were both survivors. But she was crying now. "Please find a way to let it go. I want my brother back."

He was silent as he and Alyssa walked back to the car, as he held the door for her, got in, spiraled down the endless ramps of the garage. She didn't talk either, to his relief. Alyssa always talked, and he could sense the tension in her, the eagerness to ask. But she didn't. She sat still and waited.

He spoke at last. "She's my half-sister."

"Yes," she said. "I know."

"When my dad left for Kuwait, I was eleven, but you know that too. You heard. She was fifteen. That was a big difference. We weren't that close, not then."

"And then your dad died," Alyssa prompted when he didn't go on. "He didn't come back."

"No. He didn't. He died. He was on a cargo flight, and the plane crashed. He was a mechanic. Mechanics aren't supposed to die in wars, but he did." His hands gripped the steering wheel tight, and he pulled onto the on-ramp heading north, gunned the big engine.

"And then something happened?" she asked.

"It was all right for a year or so. I mean, it wasn't good, but it was all right. But then my mom got this boyfriend. Dean. I wondered how she could stand to be with somebody like that after my dad, because he was nothing like my dad. My dad," he said, and it was running away with him now, the need to tell, to say the words. "My dad was a good man. I mean, people say that, but he was a *good* man. He was a supervisor, in charge of a whole shift. He was respected. He was ..." He hesitated. "He was loved."

"Yes," she said quietly. "I see."

"But Dean ..." His hands continued to flex, and he was driving too fast, staying in the left lane, but she didn't seem to notice, and the speed felt good. "We couldn't figure it out at first, Cheryl and me. We were so stupid. He'd be all full of energy, all up and pumped, and my mom was that way too. And then he moved in, and everything changed. She stopped going to work. She told us she was sick, and she looked sick. So did he. And it just got ... worse."

"And you ended up in foster care."

"Yeah. But not right away. Not until it got worse."

It had been the spring of eighth grade, that first worst night. He'd been trying to do his homework, and it was hard to focus, because he was hungry. Lately, his friend Michael's mom had been packing extra lunch for Michael to share with Joe, which embarrassed him, though he ate it all the same. But he was still hungry, so he worked on his Algebra homework and waited for Dean to leave so he and Cheryl could come out of their rooms, get into their mom's purse and find enough to go to McDonald's. His mom had already crashed, but Dean was still wired, so he waited.

Instead of the sound of the front door shutting that he'd been half-listening for, he heard something else. The thud of a fist on the door of the room next to his. Cheryl's room.

"Open up!" It was Dean's voice, hard and loud and mean.

"I'm studying," came the answer. Cheryl, and she was scared, and Joe was, too.

"Open the goddamned door." Dean's fist continued to pound, and Joe sat up on his bed, his notebook propped in his lap, frozen, listening.

"No! I'm busy!" He heard the scrape of something large and heavy, and realized that Cheryl was trying to move her dresser. She was in there trying to barricade herself inside while he was cowering in here, and the shame of it flooded him, overcame the fear. He forced himself to get up, went to his own door and opened it.

"What are you staring at?" Dean paused in his hammering to glare at Joe. His hair was lank, his face pitted with scars, his jeans hanging from bony hips, and Joe remembered his dad standing in this hallway, saying goodbye before leaving for work. Big and solid and tough as iron, but he'd kiss Cheryl goodbye, ruffle her hair so she'd complain, "Da-ad! I just *fixed* it!"

Jack Hartman hadn't been Cheryl's dad any more than Dean was. But Dean wasn't any Jack Hartman.

"What are you staring at, punk?" Dean snarled again. His pupils were so big his eyes looked black, and Joe knew he was still riding the high, at his most buzzed, and his most dangerous. To be avoided at all costs, but there was no avoiding him now. "Get back in your room. Quit watching me. You give me the creeps, the way you're always watching me."

"Leave her alone," Joe said, trying to keep his voice, still a boy's voice, from shaking, because Dean scared him, especially like this. But his dad wasn't here, and he could hear Cheryl still shoving at her dresser, and he knew she was at least as scared as he was.

Dean bared his yellowed teeth at Joe like an animal, turned his back contemptuously on him, lifted a booted foot, and rammed it into the door. The cheap lock burst, and Dean was in Cheryl's room, with Joe right behind him.

"Your mom's taking a nap," Dean told Cheryl. "A *long* nap, and I figure it's time for you to step up to the plate.

Time for you to start earning your keep around here. The two of you, fucking parasites. At least you're good for something, not like Robo-Boy."

Cheryl had grabbed her lamp off the nightstand, backed away around the bottom of the bed.

"Get away from me," she said, and Joe could hear her voice shake, and the hand that gripped the lamp so tightly wasn't steady either. "I mean it. You touch me, and I'll kill you."

Dean laughed. "You going to fight? Ooh, I'm so scared."

Cheryl stood strong, waited until he got close, then swung the lamp, connected with the side of his head, causing him to stagger, and Joe was on him from behind, swinging wildly, punching at Dean's kidneys, the back of his head.

Dean didn't even seem to feel the blows. He straightened, breathing in a loud hiss, pulled his arm back and backhanded Cheryl hard across the face, knocking her back in her turn, and then he was on her, pulling her up, slapping her again and again.

It was a brawl, then. Cheryl was tall and tough, and Joe wasn't either of those, but there were two of them and only one of Dean. Cheryl hadn't let go of her lamp despite the brutal blows, and she hit Dean again, and he went down on one knee, and Joe kicked him hard in the side, wished he weren't barefoot, that he was a man. That he could beat Dean up and kick him out of his dad's house.

"Run," he gasped to Cheryl, hauling his foot back and kicking again as Dean struggled to rise. "Run."

Cheryl grabbed her purse. "You come too. Come on."

Dean was staggering to his feet, and Cheryl grabbed Joe, pulled him to the door with her. "Come on," she said. And they ran.

That was the long version, but it wasn't the version he told Alyssa. He laid it out, bare. Just the facts.

233

"Turned out he'd been trying to get into her room for a while," he said. "Rubbing up against her in the hallway." He stopped, swallowed. "She couldn't stay, or it was going to happen, and I wasn't going to be able to stop it."

"So what happened instead?" Alyssa asked quietly.

"She was almost done with high school, almost eighteen. She stayed at a friend's, graduated, joined up as soon as she could. Got out."

"And what did you do?"

"I went back. I had to go back. Nowhere else to go. Until it got too bad, worse. Until my mom kicked me out."

"Kicked you *out?* When you were thirteen?"

"Fourteen." He looked across at her. "Do you mind if we drive?" They were near her exit now, and he needed to drive. Normally, nights like these, he'd have got on the bike, ridden until he was numb with cold, until the speed and the noise had cleansed him. She was here, though, and he wanted her here. But he still needed to drive.

"Yes," she said. "Drive." So he kept on, across the Golden Gate, through Sausalito, took the exit for Stinson Beach, and drove the twists and turns along the dark road, faster than he should have, needing the speed.

"I didn't know what to do," he finally said. "That last night, when she kicked me out. She locked the door. I walked around for a long time, not knowing where to go. Finally," he laughed, though it wasn't funny, "I sneaked into the back yard and slept there. I didn't know where else to go."

He had cried. He had lain down on the grass, chilled despite the warmth of Vegas in late May, wrapped his arms around himself, and cried. Cried for his dad, wishing like the baby he'd been that he would come back, that it wouldn't have happened, that it wasn't real, that things could go back to the way they'd been before. For Cheryl, who had escaped and left him behind. For his mom, who didn't love him anymore, because she was gone, too. And for himself, because he was alone, and he was so scared. It was the last time he had cried.

"And you ended up in foster care," Alyssa said.

"Yeah. She wouldn't let me back in the house. She chose Dean. Or she chose meth."

"Didn't you tell her what happened?"

"She didn't believe me. She said we'd always hated Dean, that we didn't care whether she was happy, that we hated her too, for having somebody besides my dad, for having a new life. She said a lot of things. Bottom line, she chose them. The drugs, and Dean. She was sorry sometimes, after that. She'd show up, at first, for the hearings and whatever, cry and tell me she was trying to do better, always some story, and for a long time, I believed her. I still hoped. But she never came through. I couldn't do anything about Cheryl, and I couldn't do anything about her. Either one."

"Yes, you did," she said. "You just told me how you protected your sister. She just told you how she felt about it. She doesn't blame you. How can you blame yourself? How could you have done any more than what you did?"

He shrugged, the weight of it, as always, too heavy to bear.

"What happened to her? To your mother?" she went on when he didn't answer.

"He left her, eventually, I guess. Or he died, or somebody killed him. I don't know. I did my best not to know. Cheryl's the one who found out she was sick, hepatitis, other things too. She went and saw her. I don't know how she could."

"But you're the one who paid."

"Yeah. I did. Not for her. For Cheryl, because she asked me to. And for my dad. And is it all right," he said, "if we don't talk for a while? I'm sorry. I just need to drive."

"It's all right," she said, and he drove.

Alyssa wanted to put her hands over her ears and sing, like a little girl who didn't want to hear, who didn't want to know. She'd sat frozen as Cheryl had talked in the bar, as frozen and stiff as Joe had looked next to her. And when he'd told her his story, that had been even worse.

She'd heard so many stories by now, every one a remorseless saga of destruction, of family disaster, of children thrown into chaos. Her heart had broken a little bit for every one of those children, but what she'd heard tonight had cracked it in two. She ached for the boy Joe had been, for the man he'd become, for the guilt she'd heard in the voice of somebody who didn't deserve to feel any of it.

They ended up at his loft again. He didn't ask her if she wanted to go home, and she took that as a good sign, that he wanted her there, the way he'd seemed to want her with him while he drove. She cooked them eggs and made toast, about the limit of her skill in the kitchen, and sat with him to eat it, and didn't talk.

And then she comforted him in the only way she knew how. She took him by the hand, led him into his bedroom, took off his clothes the same way he had done to her so many times, the same way he was taking hers off now. And then she pushed him down onto the bed, came down over him. She kissed him, a soft thing, put her mouth near his ear and whispered, "Stay there for me. Let me do this tonight."

"Alyssa—"

"Please." She licked into his ear, felt him shudder. "Please. Let me do this for you. Let me light the candles and love you."

He didn't answer, but he stayed where he was, and she kissed him again, then knelt beside him to put match to wick, set the heavy pillars alight on each side of the bed, turned off the lamp so only the soft candlelight shone. She turned back to him, saw him watching her, and smiled at him.

"Roll over," she told him, her voice tender. He hesitated another moment, and then he did it, and she straddled his hips, let him feel her over him, feel her rubbing herself against him. And then, finally, she began to touch him.

Softly, but not too softly. Slowly, just as slowly as she could manage it. Down the bunched muscle of his shoulders, over the curve of triceps and biceps to the veins and corded muscle of his forearms, and back up again, as if she were exploring him, learning his body for the very first time. She scooted down a bit further, ran her hands down his back, enjoying the breadth of it, the firmness of him, felt him shudder under her touch, and knew that she knew how to please him, and that no matter what else he'd felt tonight, right now, all he was doing was anticipating being pleased even more. And she wanted to do more. She wanted to make him feel everything, to thrill him the same way he thrilled her.

She slowed down, focused on the small of his back, massaging the area just above his tailbone, wanting to see if it felt as good to him as it did to her. She smiled in satisfaction at hearing his breathing become louder, more rapid, at seeing his fists clenching, his hands clutching at the sheet beneath him, and she did it some more. She took her time, because they had time. Because everything was better when you had to wait for it.

When she was sure she had him wound up tight, aching for it, she ran her hands slowly down to his upper thighs and back up again, over every firm surface of him, and if he'd been sensitized before, he was squirming now. She kept it moving, kept him going, until, finally, she reached her hand between his legs and stroked everything within her reach, reading his body's cues as he pushed off the bed to give her access, as the silence was broken by the harsh sound of his breathing.

"Turn over for me," she murmured at last. She pulled her hand away, saw him shudder at the loss, and sat back on her knees to wait until he rolled and looked up at her, his eyes glazed, his breath coming hard. She smiled at him, a slow, soft, seductive thing, and saw him respond to it like he couldn't help it, because she could tell it was true. He was hers.

She touched his lips with her fingers, traced them as she whispered, "Time for more?"

"Yeah," he said, and he could barely say it. "More."

She crawled over him, touched him everywhere, licked him and kissed him and bit at him until he had his eyes closed, his hips moving, and she was pulling sounds from him that she hadn't heard before, and she knew she had him past the point of thought, or of caring. That he could only feel this, his body's response to her. Then, and only then, she reached for the condom, rolled it onto him, and lowered herself over him, and he groaned at the pleasure of it, his hands coming up to reach for her hips, for her breasts, wanting her so much. Wanting her with everything in him.

He wanted her, and she gave him everything she had. She went slowly, and then she went fast, and when she could feel him getting close, she stopped and went slowly again. She didn't want to make him work, didn't want him to have to do any more than run his hands over her breasts, because she could tell he was loving doing that as much as she was loving the feeling of him doing it. So she used her hands on herself, too, drove herself up even as she pushed him higher.

And she talked. She told him how much she had thought about this, how many times she had imagined him, all the showers she had taken with her hands on her breasts, her body, imagining it was him touching her, because he was all she'd ever wanted.

He didn't close his eyes, because he was watching her. He let her talk, but when she stopped moving again, because she was too close, because she needed to focus on herself, he reached for her hips and refused to allow it. She was on top of him, but he took control, held her and moved her over him, again and again, harder and harder, until she was over the top, crying out loud with the pleasure of it, and he was emptying into her, all the pain and all the emotion of the night resolved into this, and it was so good.

She cleaned him up, afterwards, and he lay there and sighed, a deep, heartfelt thing that told her everything he hadn't said. That she'd done it right. That she'd helped.

When she was curled up against him again under the warm covers, her hand on his chest, she finally voiced the worry that had been on her mind ever since she'd heard Cheryl's story.

"When we had our fight last night," she told him. "When I … pushed you. I didn't know. I wouldn't have said what I did if I'd known what happened to you and Cheryl. What you did to me, it's not the same thing. I want you to know, I get that it's not the same thing."

He smiled a little, his eyes still closed. She could see it, because she hadn't blown out the candles yet, because she loved looking at him like this. "You mean when you teased me so hard you got spanked for it?"

"Yes," she said, the thrill running through her again, despite everything that had happened that night, despite all the pleasure she'd just felt. "I wanted you to do it. I liked it. I want to make sure you know that."

He opened his eyes, turned his head and smiled at her, ran his hand over her hip, and then over the curve of her bottom, and his big hand felt so good there, she knew why he'd enjoyed it so much when she'd done it to him.

"I figured that out," he said. "I wasn't sure about doing it at first, because I didn't want to hurt you, but if it had really bothered me, I wouldn't have done it. You didn't want me to hurt you, though. You just wanted to be controlled."

"Mmm." She stroked his chest, his shoulder, down his arm, just for the feeling of it, the bulk of muscle, the heat of his skin. "I wanted you to be dangerous, and I knew I could push you to be, because I knew I'd be safe."

"That's why I could do it," he said. "I know that you like me to be strong. I get that you want to be overpowered sometimes. And that's all right, because I enjoy overpowering you."

She levered herself up on an elbow, blew out the candle on her side, then leaned across him and blew out his, knowing he was watching her do it, and how much he liked watching, then settled down with him again.

"You're right," she told him in the darkness. "I do like it when you overpower me. No, I *love* it when you overpower me. And every once in a while, like tonight … I want to overpower you, too."

239

Cinderella

"Wow," Alyssa said a couple Saturdays later when she opened the door to Joe. "Who knew?"

"Wow yourself," he said, taking a long look at the deep blue sleeveless cocktail dress with its high beaded collar, the tall black heels.

"You think?" She preened a bit under his scrutiny. She loved knowing that he liked how she looked. "Relic of paychecks past. Plus, it matches my eyes, did you notice?"

"No, I didn't notice. I just noticed," he said, leaning in and saying it low, in her ear, since Sherry was watching with interest from the living-room couch, "that I love it when you wear those collared things. Gives me bad ideas."

"Hey, Joe," Sherry said pointedly. "How are you?"

He smiled at her. "Hey, Sherry. How you doing?"

"Well," she sighed, "I'd be better if some guy would show up in a tuxedo and take me out, but meh, whatever."

Alyssa laughed. "It's a work event," she reminded Sherry. "A *major* work event. Don't let me drink any wine," she told Joe, "because if I do, it's guaranteed that something will go wrong, and I'll be all drunk and not be able to figure out how to deal with it. I've got so many lists, it's crazy. I dreamed last night that I was at the party, and I realized that I'd forgotten to order any food, and I couldn't remember anybody's name. I've been studying pictures of major donors all week. I just hope nobody's gone bald or gained fifty pounds or anything, because I'll be sunk."

"Don't worry," he said. "I don't care how major he is, he's not going to care whether you got his name right once he gets a look at you in that dress."

"Yeah, well." She gave a toss to her carefully tousled hair. "What if it's a woman?"

"Then," he conceded, "you could have a problem. Better remember the names."

"It's not actually too sexy, is it?" she asked, because she'd worried about that, too. "I was going for a little bit conservative. I have a red one that's killer, but I thought, probably not."

"No," he said. "Probably not. And you can't help it if you're ... what's the word?"

"Curvy," she said, and smiled at him happily, feeling so much better already. "Rather than pudgy."

"Curvy," he agreed, and smiled back. "Not the least bit pudgy."

Sherry groaned. "Would you two please leave? You're making me sick."

"Just a sec." Alyssa grabbed for her clutch purse on the coffee table, the one with her folded-up lists inside. "Soon as we make Joe turn around and model his tuxedo for us."

"You have to be kidding," he said.

"Nope." She made the gesture with her fingers. "Twirl."

He sighed, but held his arms out from his sides and made an obliging circle. "Happy?" he asked her, although she could tell he really didn't mind.

"You didn't rent that," she told him. "Selix Formalwear does not have that size." Because it fit his shoulders perfectly, and his waist, too, and nothing off the rack could have possibly done that.

"Well, no," he conceded. "It's mine."

"You have a tuxedo."

"Yeah. For when I need it. And we could either stand around and admire each other," he pointed out, "or we could leave and get this over with."

Admiring him, unfortunately, turned out to be the high point of the evening. Alyssa had had to arrive early and check

241

in with the catering staff, to double-check the setup against her carefully prepared list, and then to stand near the welcome table and help greet the guests. Helene took her time showing up, and she hadn't done any of the organization for the event, either. That had been all on Alyssa, and it wasn't her best thing, and she knew it, though she thought she'd done a reasonable job. She was learning.

It all went along smoothly enough at first, to her immense relief. She *did* remember names, and she smiled and chatted and tried not to think about whether Joe was having a good time, because she was pretty sure that he wasn't, at least not until Alec and Rae showed up, because that made everything a whole lot better.

Her brother, now, she thought with pride as he said a discreet hello—he was another man who looked good in a tuxedo. And Helene, who'd been doing her own mingling, clearly thought so too.

"What a pleasure," she said, shaking Alec's hand and then reaching for Rae's with only the barest decrease in graciousness. "I'm so glad the two of you could make it. I can't thank you enough for everything you've done for Second Chance."

Alec made some noncommittal answer, and Helene continued. "Do you know, Alyssa here, my assistant, has the same last name you do? It's almost like it was meant to be, isn't it? Isn't it a small world?"

"Very small," Alec said, his gaze darting to Alyssa, and she knew he'd caught it, too. *My assistant.* She wasn't Helene's assistant. She was the Assistant Director of Development, and there was a difference.

Alec and Rae moved off, and Helene went with them, and Alyssa stayed in her spot near the door until the guests had finished arriving and it was time for the speeches, and then she went and found Joe.

"How you doing?" he asked, his voice low as Dr. Marsh spoke into the microphone at one end of the room, welcoming the guests.

242

"My feet are killing me," she muttered back, kept the smile on her face and applauded at Dr. Marsh's introduction of Helene.

Helene walked to the microphone, her smile infectious, her enthusiasm contagious, and Alyssa felt the power of her presence. She could turn on charisma like Alec, and when she was in the room, you *noticed*.

"When I was a little girl in Memphis," she began, "I used to dream about being at a party like this. I used to imagine I was Cinderella, because I felt just like her. The cinders part, I mean," she said with a smile, "not so much the ball."

A ripple of laughter greeted that one. "On nights like tonight, I feel like Cinderella *at* the ball," Helene went on, "and I look back at that little girl I was, and wish I could tell her what her future was going to look like. I wish I could give her hope. And all of those foster children out there tonight, how many of them are feeling just as hopeless? How many of them are dreaming of standing up here like me thirty-five years from now, and worrying that they'll be on the street instead? We all know which of those scenarios is more likely. That's why we're here, that's why all of you do this, and why I do it, too. I thank each and every one of you for what you've done, what you continue to do. I'm here to tell you what a difference programs like the ones you help to fund made for me, when I was that little girl. When I was that young woman, wondering if I'd make it, and so afraid that I wouldn't."

Alyssa looked around the room as Helene continued to speak. She had the attention of the crowd, not just their polite interest.

"Children like the little girl I was," Helene went on, "children who not only don't have the things every child should be able to count on—parents to care for them, a home that's a safe, loving place, a stable environment in which to learn, and, above all, the security of knowing, of never questioning that their homes will go on being safe, secure, loving places—those children have nothing, not even a voice. They're silent, and they're silenced. They are truly

243

powerless. The CASA program, the court-appointed special advocates who are such an important part of the network of caring you help to support, give them that voice. They're the only power those children have. They speak for children who can't speak for themselves. And that's the program you're helping to fund by your presence here tonight."

She paused, looked down for a moment, seemed to gather her thoughts. Then looked up again, out at her audience, her voice quiet and sincere. "I know I wouldn't have made it without my CASA volunteer. I wouldn't have made it without the scholarship that meant I could go to college, or even without the cards that came for Christmas and my birthday from an organization just like this one, the cards that told me I wasn't alone. A phone call to check in with me, somebody to talk to about how college was going, about what kind of plans I had for Christmas, about how I would spend the summer ... those things were the difference between success and failure for me. Those things are the reason I'm here talking to you tonight, and they're the reason that there's a little boy, a little girl somewhere right here in California who'll be standing here thirty years from now just like I'm standing here tonight, saying the very same kinds of things I'm saying now. She'll be here, he'll be here because somebody like you cared enough to help. Because somebody like you listened.

"So thank you," she said. "Thank you from the bottom of the heart of the little girl I was, and from the woman I am today. Thank you for caring. Thank you for helping. Thank you for all you do. You'll never know the extent of the difference you've made, but I'm here to tell you tonight, it's there, and it's real."

She finished, and genuine applause broke out. Alyssa saw a few beringed hands move up to wipe away tears, and she had to concede that, even if Helene wasn't exactly a roll-up-your-sleeves kind of boss, the woman could *talk*. Alyssa was applauding herself, and not just out of politeness.

Joe wasn't, though. He was frowning, and Alyssa felt a pang of unease. "You OK?" she asked him in a low tone. "Too much to hear?"

"What?" He looked at her, his expression abstracted. "No. Never mind."

Helene made a circuit of the room after the speeches, shaking hands, smiling and talking, and eventually ended up near Alyssa and Joe. Alyssa introduced Joe, saw Helene smile at him, a slow, assessing thing with heat to spare, and found herself stifling a flare of possessive rage that made her understand how Joe had felt that night in the Boom Boom Room, watching her dance. And Helene hadn't done anything more than shake Joe's hand.

"That was a wonderful speech," she said to Helene, determined to keep this professional, to keep her cool.

"Thank you," Helene said. "Can I tell you the truth?" She laughed a little. "I always get nervous. What did you think?" she asked Joe. "Did you think it was effective?"

"It was fine," he said, and if he'd had an 'I'm Not Impressed' sign around his neck, it couldn't have been much clearer.

"Fine?" Helene asked, still smiling, her head on one side.

"I'm not big on speeches," he said. "And I didn't realize CASA had a program in Memphis thirty-five years ago."

She looked a bit surprised. "Yes, it was early days. A pilot program."

"Lucky for you," he said. "A college scholarship, too."

"Lucky is right," she said, "and believe me, I know it. That's why I do this job. That's what it's all about, isn't it? It's about leaving things a little better than you found them, and giving back, when you've been given so much. That's what I appreciate about all the people here tonight. They could be donating to the opera or the ballet. I know their parties are better. Though I thought things ran pretty well tonight, Alyssa," she added, "considering it's your first event. Only a few little glitches."

Alyssa bit her tongue. How could Helene give a compliment that felt so little like one?

"And what do you do, Joe?" Helene went on. "Do you work here in the City?"

"Yeah," he said. "In tech."

"Really," she said with an arch of an eyebrow. "Well, isn't that fortunate? Is that where the inspiration for Alyssa's little field day idea came from? I'm sure she appreciated your help. Coaching's always welcome, I know, when you're starting out."

"No. That wasn't my idea. It was all hers. And I don't think Alyssa needs my coaching."

Helene smiled again. "Oh, I'm guessing she's happy to have your advice. We can all use a little boost at the beginning. I know you're not happy that you haven't quite been able to meet your goals," she told Alyssa. "But it'll come, if you just keep trying. Not everybody is a natural at this. For some people, it's just a matter of persistence."

Alyssa opened her mouth, then shut it again. How did she answer that? And who—*who*—would belittle somebody's performance at a work function, in front of a friend? In front of a *boyfriend*? Because Helene had to have figured that out. Alyssa knew by now that her boss didn't miss a trick.

"If Alyssa isn't interested, I am. I'd love to pick your brain," Helene moved a step closer, put her manicured hand, with its long red fingernails—its talons—on Joe's black-suited arm. "I can always use some fresh ideas," she said, and Alyssa fought the urge to hiss.

Joe was looking more wooden than ever. He took Alyssa's hand, forcing Helene's to slide from his sleeve. "I'm happy to share my ideas," he said. "With Alyssa. If she asks me for them."

Helene recovered fast. "Well," she said with another laugh, "I'm sure she's grateful."

Joe nodded. "Excuse me." He turned, pulling Alyssa along with him, and made for the bar.

"Joe," she said, "that was almost ... rude."

"Was it?"

"You know it was."

"Tough," he said. "I didn't like her."

246

She got a little satisfaction from that, because the truth was, she didn't like Helene that much either. She *didn't*. She'd tried not to face it, but it was true. "She gave a good speech, though."

"Effective," he said, but then Dr. Marsh was there, and Alyssa smiled automatically.

"Alyssa," the Director said expansively, his face pink with pleasure at the success of the evening. "This is a triumph for you. I know how much planning goes into this event, and it's your first one. And here we are, everything going so smoothly, and about the best speech I've ever heard. Aren't we lucky to have Helene on board? I thought losing Suzanne was a blow, but we haven't missed a beat."

"Yes," Alyssa said. "It was a great speech." She introduced Joe, and Dr. Marsh shook his hand cordially, then returned to the topic at hand.

"You couldn't be learning from a better example," he told Alyssa. "The idea she presented to the board a few weeks ago, her Geek Day? Has she shared that with you yet? Brilliant, just brilliant. That's exactly the kind of visionary thinking this organization needs."

Alyssa felt everything inside her going cold. *"Her* idea?" she managed to get out.

"Yes. You did hear about it, then?"

"Yes," she said, so frozen she could barely move. "I heard."

"Well, I'm telling you, if you're lucky enough to be in this field for over thirty years the way I have been," the older man said, "you'll realize what a rut we all fall into. Oh, everyone has the best of intentions, but there's a tendency to do the same old things, not to think outside the box. When you find somebody who can do that, especially in Development, that's a find indeed."

"But ..." Alyssa said. She wasn't sure how to answer, how to explain, but she didn't get the chance, because Dr. Marsh caught an eye and hustled off with a quick "Excuse me" to chat up a donor.

"Her idea?" She was spluttering. *"Her* idea?"

"Talk to her," Joe said. "Right now. Talk to her."

She searched Helene out in the crowd, waited impatiently while she schmoozed another donor, was finally able to approach her when the man turned away.

"Excuse me," she said, her voice shaking only a little.

"Yes?" Helene asked. Her eyes flitted to the door. "People are starting to leave. Shouldn't you be over there saying goodbye?"

Alyssa ignored that. "I was just speaking to Dr. Marsh," she began. "He was congratulating me on Geek Day. On *your* idea for Geek Day."

Helene's smile didn't waver. "Yes," she said, "I told you that he and the board were excited. It's wonderful, isn't it? It'll be a lot of work, but like I always say, with the right attitude, anything is possible."

"It was my idea," Alyssa said bluntly. "You didn't tell them that. I could tell."

Helene waved a hand. "It doesn't matter whose idea it is. The idea's only the beginning, not to say it isn't a good one. What matters is what we do with it, and we're going to do something great."

"It matters that you didn't give me credit," Alyssa persisted, her frustration mounting by the second.

"Alyssa." The older woman sighed. "This isn't the time or the place. And I know it's a cliché, but it sounds like it's time to remind you that there's no 'i' in 'team.' We're here to make a difference. That's the only thing that matters. And, just a gentle reminder, *you're* here to do a job. Right now, that job is to go over there by the door and say goodbye, leave these wonderful people with their very best impression of us. I'd suggest, if you want to contribute, that you go over there and do it."

Alyssa was never sure, afterwards, how she'd made it through the rest of the evening. She'd wanted to walk out then and there. She couldn't even have said why she'd stayed to say her goodbyes to the donors, to settle with the caterers and the museum staff, even as her mind raged. Except that Helene was right. This *was* her job, and despite everything, she needed to do it. She'd spent days—no, she'd spent *weeks* planning this event, and she couldn't stand not to see it through.

She didn't even have a chance to talk about it with Joe until the last guest left, until he'd retrieved her coat, escorted her down the museum's steps and waited with her for the valet.

"What happened?" he asked when he'd put the car in gear, was headed down the drive. "My place?" he added.

"Yeah," she said, watching him take the first turn for the five-minute drive back to his loft. Then she took a breath and told him.

"Damn," he said.

"Yeah." She laughed, but it was an angry laugh. "So what do I do now?"

"Right now? What do you want to do?"

"I want to—" She stopped, nonplussed. "I want to *run*. I want to run away. I want to get *out*."

"Want to ride the bike?" he asked, pulling into his garage. "That's what I do," he added when she looked at him in surprise. "Speed. Wind. Get away. Want to do that?"

"You'd take me?"

"You bet I would. Tell you the truth, I could use it too."

He got changed with her, found a heavy jacket for her to wear, gave her a helmet, and then rolled out of the garage and into Saturday night. Up and over to Lombard Street first, back and forth on the zigzag course of it, a little too fast around each sharp curve, seeming to know that she needed to be on the edge tonight, that she needed the adrenaline.

She held on and felt it and wished they could go faster, and he turned around and went up the hill again. And then she got her wish, because he was riding through the darkness of the Presidio, across the Golden Gate, the big bike splitting the night, the towers and lights flashing by, and she knew that to her left there was water all the way to Hawaii, all the way to Japan, and she felt the freedom of it, felt the limits falling away.

He was riding the same roads he'd driven after their beer with Cheryl, and for the same reason, but he was right, it was better on the bike. Better to be going fast, to feel the wind and the cold and the noise, to forget everything and hold on to him and *feel*.

By the time they got back to the loft again, she was cold, and numb, and done. Joe helped her off with the coat, the helmet, took her into his bedroom and helped her get undressed, took her into his bathroom and turned on the shower for her, all without any unnecessary words, and she was glad, because she didn't want to talk.

She stood in the shower for what felt like an hour, let the water wash over her, warm her up, and, finally, came out and put on a T-shirt and underwear and crawled into bed beside him, because he was already there.

"Thanks," she said.

"No problem." He pulled her to him so her head was resting on his shoulder, his arm around her.

"I don't …" she began, then stopped. "I don't want to. Not tonight. I just want to go to sleep."

"I get it," he said, and she could hear the smile in his voice.

"You don't mind?" She'd been spending more than half of her time here, and they almost always made love, because they both wanted it. But tonight, she didn't. She'd got dressed tonight thinking about him unzipping her dress, about him seeing her in her prettiest underwear, about what they'd do. One more thing Helene had taken from her, and the rage rose at the thought, but she didn't want to deal with it. She wanted to be done with this day. She wanted to go to sleep and shut it out.

"Of course I don't mind," he said. "You've had enough. There'll be another night. Go to sleep."

So she did.

She woke to the gray light of early morning, the previous evening's events filling her head. Joe was still sleeping, so she got up and dressed, moving quietly so as not to wake him, wrote a quick note and left the loft.

She ran. Across the empty streets of early Sunday morning, ignoring the red lights, because she couldn't stand to stop. Into the green space of the Presidio, because the empty dark had called to her the night before, and she wanted to be here, away from people, away from cars. Just running, nobody but the occasional jogger, the odd dog-walker to see her. Nothing but the air and the movement, her body working out the tension, and her mind going along with it.

It was two hours before she returned to find Joe working, as usual.

"Sorry I was gone so long," she said.

He shrugged. "You left a note. Good run?"

"Yeah. You're not upset that I didn't invite you?"

"You needed to be alone. I need to be alone a lot too. I made oatmeal."

"Thanks." She went to the stove and dished it up.

"So I was thinking," she said when she was sitting at the dining table, and he'd come to join her.

He looked at her, but didn't say anything, so she continued. "Part of me wants to quit, right? Last night, I wanted to quit so bad. Because I'll never get ahead. It'll never happen, not with Helene in charge. Not if she's going to take my good ideas and say they're hers. Not if she's going to keep me doing the scut work while she does all the glamour parts. I'll never get ahead. I get that."

"Sure," he said, then waited.

"But I don't want to quit," she said in frustration. "If I do, what happens? Helene's still got my idea. Then she's doing my Geek Day, or somebody she hires is. And they aren't going to do it as well as I could. I *know* it, and I can't stand it.

I have all these ideas for it, and I want to *do* them, and I could get Alec and Rae to help, too, and this would be *huge*, if I did it. I'd *make* it huge."

"Sure," Joe said again. "And me, too. I'd help."

"And you," she agreed. "And also—this matters. Remember how I said I needed to do something that matters? Well, I found it. This is it. Those kids matter, and I can help. All those things Helene said last night—I can do it. I can help, and I want to do it."

She ran down at last, took a sip of her coffee.

"Then," he said, "that's what you should do."

"And I don't want her to win," she went on, barely hearing him. "No, scratch that, I can't *stand* to let her win. If I quit, she wins. She's got my idea, and she wins. But if I stay and work for her, doesn't she win then, too? How do *I* win? That's what I can't see. And I *want* to win. I want to do the right thing, but I want to *win.*"

"How about if you stay and don't work for her?" he asked. "Don't you win then?"

"Well, yeah. That'd be the dream. What do I do, though, kill her?" She had to laugh at that, even as upset as she was. "Now *there'd* be a permanent solution. Sounds pretty good to me right now, I'll tell you that."

"Except that you'd be unlikely to be around to plan your Geek Day," he pointed out. "So I think we'd better come up with something else."

"I should fight," she said.

"Yeah," he said. "You should fight. You know why bad people win so much? It's because good people aren't willing to fight, or they don't know how. I know how, and I'm going to help you do it."

Less Than Cinderella

It was a whole week more, though, before she got the chance. Dr. Marsh had been at a conference, and nobody else would do. And then there'd been the wait for the appointment, his surprise at the request.

"We like to go through channels here," he'd said when she'd asked him for a meeting.

"I know you do," she said, trying to curb her frustration. "But it's important, or I wouldn't ask you. Please. Fifteen minutes of your time, that's all."

Now, she stood outside the door of his office and knocked.

"Come in," she heard.

"Here we go." She took a deep breath, wiped a sweaty palm over the leg of her slacks, and opened the door, her laptop and a file folder clutched tightly in her other hand.

Dr. Marsh looked up. "I didn't realize you were bringing somebody else to the meeting. Jim, wasn't it?"

"Joe." He took a seat beside Alyssa in one of the two visitor's chairs across the desk from the Director.

"So," Dr. Marsh said. His face was still pink, but it wasn't as pleasant as it had been at the party. "What's this all about?"

"I requested this meeting," Alyssa said, "because I thought you should know that Helene appropriated my fundraising idea, the one we spoke about at the party last week. The idea of the field day for the tech industry, what I called Geek Day. I can't find any evidence that she gave me any credit, did she?"

"I'm sorry," he said, "I still don't understand. You're here to talk to me because you had the original idea for her plan? Shouldn't you take that up with her?"

"No. I didn't have the original idea for her plan. I had the whole plan." She opened her laptop, swiveled it around to face him, and showed him, as Joe had instructed her, the information from her file's "Properties" menu showing the date she'd created it, then handed him a stapled printout of all her slides.

"This was my presentation to Helene a month ago," she said. "Please tell me if it was the presentation she gave to you."

He reached for a case on his desk, opened it and removed his reading glasses, used both hands to put them on, then adjusted the printout so it sat perfectly aligned on his wooden desk, and she wanted to scream. She waited, tense and expectant, as he flipped through page after page, until he finally looked up at her, his face serious.

"Yes," he said, "this is what she presented."

"I can verify," Joe said, "that Alyssa has been working on this idea for a good couple months. I saw her produce this presentation. I listened to her rehearse it. This was her idea, and hers alone."

"I'm still not sure," Dr. Marsh said after removing his glasses and going through the whole process in reverse, "why you're here, uh ... Joe. We prefer to keep our internal affairs internal, and surely Alyssa doesn't need moral support to bring this matter to my attention."

"That's not why I'm here." Joe reached into the folder that Alyssa had laid on the desk and pulled out another stapled collection of papers. "I'm here to give you some additional information."

The glasses, again. "What is this, exactly?" Dr. Marsh asked.

"That," Joe said, "is the transcript of a conversation Alyssa had on the telephone with Helene's—Helen's, I should say, because that's her name—parents. The parents she has. The parents who raised her, because it turns out that she's quite a bit less than Cinderella. She was never in foster care. She was never abused or abandoned. Her mother's a homemaker, and her father's an engineer with the Highway Department. They go to church. Her mother was her Girl Scout leader. And there was no CASA program in Tennessee thirty-five years ago, by the way. Everything she said in that speech of hers was a lie, and an insult to kids who actually live the life she talked about."

The Director was looking rattled now. "The second document," Joe went on, "is her record from the University of Tennessee. You might want to keep that one a bit quiet, because I didn't exactly go through channels to get it, but that's her record. As you can see, she took courses there for a couple years, but she didn't do well, and she sure didn't graduate. She didn't graduate from any university at all, from what I can find out. Can I ask if you did a background check before you hired her?"

"No," Dr. Marsh said. "But I take it you did."

"I did," Joe said. "I also spoke to a few people at the Carolyn G. Haskill Foundation. She had a reputation over there, maybe not with the people you talked to, but with the people who worked for her, for sure. A reputation for going through staff, for promoting herself first and foremost. It got her ahead, but at a cost. The cost being quite a few good people who are now working someplace else."

"I'm glad for the information," the Director said, "but I still don't understand how all this concerns you."

"Ah. Why do I care how Second Chance does, besides my interest in Alyssa? Fair question, and I have an answer."

He sat there, looking big and tough and solid, and said it. "You see, that would be because I'm Alec Kincaid's business partner. As in Alyssa's brother. As in the guy you probably think of as your second-biggest donor."

And then he reached over and pulled out the last thing in the folder, three pages of photocopied documents stapled together, and placed them in front of Dr. Marsh. "And one other reason, too. The reason I care what happens here? That would also be because I'm your first-biggest donor."

A long silence followed as the Director flipped pages, took in the amounts on the photocopied checks, then looked up at Joe. "You're Anonymous. You're the Six-Million-Dollar Man."

"That would be me," Joe said. "But there's a time to be anonymous, and there's a time to speak up. And I'd say this is my time."

Not a Fight

She was coming home from yet another momentous first day, but a completely different first day. For one thing, this was her first day without Helene. And for another, she was coming home to Joe's place, and he was there. She'd texted him that she was leaving work, and he'd come home early to meet her, and she was *glad*.

She walked through the front door and straight into his arms, stood with her face pressed against his chest, letting herself relax into the comfort and security that was Joe. Having him hold her didn't solve her problems, but it sure felt that way. Maybe it just made her feel like her problems were solvable.

"So what happened?" he asked when they were on the couch and she had a glass of wine in front of her, because this was a Wine Night, that was for sure.

"I didn't hear all of it, of course," she said. "But she didn't go quietly. I heard there was some yelling." Telling him allowed her to relish it all over again. "There may even have been some throwing things. I wanted her to come back into the office. I wanted to see her face. But the bookkeeper came in and packed up her desk. Too bad."

"Yep," Joe said. "They say living well is the best revenge, but sometimes, revenge is the best revenge. So she's gone. What are they going to do about replacing her?"

"I haven't heard much, but Dr. Marsh did say that whatever happens, Geek Day is my project. I get to manage it. I'm sure it's wrong to be so pleased for myself after such a shakeup for Second Chance, but too bad, I'm excited anyway." She was smiling, because she couldn't help it. "I've spent all day making lists and notes. I'm going to make this the biggest thing to ever hit the tech world, you wait and see."

"You don't have to convince me." He was smiling back at her, his thumb rubbing over the back of her neck. "My money was on you from Day One. You've got the opportunity. Everything you do with it now—that's all on you. I know you can do it."

"I can," she said. "And I'm going to. You wait and see."

A week later, though, she wasn't feeling nearly so warm and fuzzy towards him. They'd gone to the gym together after work, were back at his place again, and Joe was heating up chili.

"So do we have plans for Memorial Day weekend?" she asked him. "Coming right up. Do I get to see what the cabin looks like in May? Do you get to drive me crazy checking my gear if we go for a hike?"

"I need to go out of town on Saturday," he said, not responding to her teasing at all, which had her paying attention.

"Oh?" She stifled her disappointment. He was being cautious, she decided, because he was afraid she'd have a fit about him not spending time with her. She pulled greens out of the fridge and dumped them in a bowl, reminded herself to stay casual. She'd told him that she understood his workload. Time to prove it, because this was where the rubber met the road. She certainly couldn't accuse him of not caring about her, of not paying attention to her. He'd done nothing else, lately. "Work thing?"

"No." He gave the pot a stir. "Going to Las Vegas."

Her hands stilled on the knife she'd been using to chop tomatoes. "Oh?" she asked again.

"Yeah. Something your dad said I should do." When she didn't answer, he went on. "That day when we went up there

258

together. I decided, you fought for what you wanted. Time for me to fight too."

She'd never known what they'd talked about that day. Joe had come out of her dad's study more silent and closed off than ever, and she hadn't pressed him.

Now, though, she did. "Something about your past," she guessed. "About your mom, or your dad?"

"Neither. Something about me." He kept stirring, even though she could tell the chili didn't need it. "When I was a kid," he said, and she could sense the reluctance in him, "I did some shoplifting."

"Huh. Isn't that pretty common?" she asked cautiously.

"I don't know. Did you do it?"

"Well, no. You know my parents. Can you even imagine?"

"I guess not. But I did."

"And you need to do, what? Turn yourself in to the police? For *shoplifting*? What, twenty years ago? You can't tell me that even my dad would suggest that. He might be a minister, but he lives in the real world."

"Not quite. It's about paying back, I guess. Facing the past, I think that's what your dad would say." He went on to explain his mission, his reluctance obvious, while he dished up the chili, and they sat down with their dinner.

"Well, that sounds like a fairly horrible use of a holiday weekend," she said. "Is it going to take all of it?"

"No, just the day. I've got a nine o'clock flight on Saturday morning, and I'll be back that night. I'm not planning to stick around. I just wanted to tell you I was going."

"Thanks. But I'd like to come with you."

"No."

"Joe—"

"No. This will be bad enough," he went on when she started to argue, "without you there to see it. That would just make it worse."

"I appreciate that you told me about it." She was treading carefully, because he had that shuttered expression, the one she didn't see much anymore. "But it's like when you told my

259

dad about us. It was hard for you, and I wanted to be there. This is the same thing."

"No. It's not. This has nothing to do with you, and I don't want you there. I'm sorry, but I don't."

It felt as if he'd slapped her. She looked down at her soup, took a bite, but her hand wasn't entirely steady.

"Alyssa," he sighed. He set an elbow on the table, slid a hand over his close-cropped hair. "Now you're feeling all left out. I thought it would be good if I told you. Damn. I always screw this stuff up."

"It's not that," she tried to explain. Her throat had closed, and she pushed the chili bowl aside. "It's that you open the door this little tiny way, and that's all. I thought if I was patient, you'd open it more, but you won't. How can I keep coming to you like I have been, all the times when I'm scared and upset and tired, how can I keep asking you to help me if you'll never do that with me? It's like I'm this child, and you feel like you have to be the parent, like you have to be in charge all the time, because I can't handle things."

She said it, knowing even as she did that he was going to hate hearing it, and she was right.

"Here we go," he said, getting up and taking his dishes to the sink, rinsing them out and putting them in the dishwasher, and she wanted to scream at him to leave the dishes and *talk* to her. "I won't share my feelings. We're back to that."

"Yes," she said, refusing to let herself feel belittled. "Right now, yes."

"Well, I can't help it. I don't want to talk about it, because there's nothing to talk about. I've got nothing to share. Or, OK, here it is." He turned back to her, and the only feelings she was getting from him were anger and frustration. "When I think about what I'm going to do on Saturday," he said, "I feel like shit. And while I'm doing it, I'm sure I'll feel even more like shit. And afterwards, I'm hoping I'll feel a little less like shit, and that I can come back to you and feel like, I've done that, and I can move on. There you go. That's it. My feelings."

260

"All right," she said, because she didn't know what else to say. He was right. He'd shared his feelings, and she couldn't exactly say that those were the wrong ones, could she?

"So if you don't mind," he said, back under control, the anger wiped out again as if he'd never revealed it, "I'm going to work late Friday, get some stuff done before I take off, so I won't see you. I'll call you Sunday morning, and maybe we can go out Sunday night, since Monday's a holiday. We'll do the cabin another time, I promise. Just not this weekend. Sorry for swearing," he added belatedly.

She ignored that, because what did it matter? "All right," she said again. She wanted to say more, to keep talking, to batter the wall down, but she didn't know how.

It hadn't been a fight. A fight, she could have handled. He'd shut down, and she didn't have any way to fight that. She was beaten.

Forgive Us Our Trespasses

Joe watched out the window as the barren outcrops of Red Rocks gave way to the irrigated green of suburban lawns dotted by the turquoise teardrops and rectangles of backyard swimming pools, followed in their turn by the black pyramid of the Luxor, the over-the-top flag-bedecked turrets of the Excalibur. Other landmarks had gone since he was last here, torn down without sentiment to make way for taller, glitzier towers, every one built on gambling dollars, every one a monument to misplaced hope or the dream of a better life, depending on how you looked at it.

He looked down on it all, and it didn't feel like coming home. It felt like slipping back into a pit he'd clawed his way out of, one painful handhold at a time. It felt bad.

The plane touched down, taxied to a stop in front of the terminal, and he was down the jetway and into the arrivals lobby, his senses already assaulted by the din of slot machines, the flash of lights that lured and beckoned.

And then, somehow, incredibly, there was Alyssa. Appearing in the doorway of the glassed-in waiting area, then making her way through the crowd to join him. Looking serious. Looking determined. Looking like home.

He didn't say anything, just stepped out of the stream of arriving passengers and waited for her.

She stood in front of him, her usual smile missing. "I came anyway."

"I see that."

"I thought all night." The words tumbled out. "I thought, all right, this is private, this is something you need to do by yourself. And then I came anyway. I get that this is a personal thing for you. I do. But don't you see, if we're going to be part of each others' lives, I need to be able to help you like you helped me. I need to be here for you if you're going to do something this hard. You were there for me. Can't you let me be there for you?"

"I—" He wasn't sure what to say, was still processing all that when she went on.

"If you say that I need to wait in the car for you," she said, "I'll wait. And if you really don't want me there at all, I'm not going to lie down in front of the car or anything. If you say no, I'll stay here and wait for you. But I'm going to wait here, because I need you to know that I'm here if you need me, or at least when you're done. You don't have to tell me what you're thinking. You don't have to share anything if you really don't want to, or if you can't. But you have to at least let me be here. You have to let me in that much. Please, Joe. Let me help you."

When you want to close down, open up and let her see you.

Dave's words were there in his head, and he breathed in, breathed out.

"Alyssa," he said. "Wait. Can I say something?"

"Yes." She was trembling a little, he realized, and he took her hand.

"You can come," he said.

"You haven't been back here ever, have you?" she asked him when they were in the rental car and on the freeway toward North Las Vegas.

"No. Never."

"I haven't either."

"Not a gambler, huh?"

"Not with money," she said, and he had a while to ponder what that meant, because she didn't say anything else, just

263

looked around her with that curiosity, that attention that was all Alyssa.

He did his best not to think, otherwise. He'd planned the day's itinerary starting with the North Las Vegas Target, because that had been his biggest—well, target. He'd start there, and then he'd go on, one step at a time. Do what he had to do, then leave. It was just one day. He'd had worse.

He pulled in off Nellis Boulevard at the familiar red sign, walked with Alyssa across the wide expanse of parking lot to the entrance. The remembered heat of Vegas beat down on them from the cloudless desert sky, reflected up from the black asphalt, a ghost of what it would be in July, when it would be like being in an oven set on rotisserie. Stepping through the automatic glass entry doors was like entering an oasis of cool, and the skin of his arms pebbled into goosebumps at the contrast.

He looked around, headed to the right, to the curved expanse of the service desk. He ignored the line, walked straight past it and told a young woman scanning a big bag of returned items, "I need the manager."

"Sir, you'll need to wait your turn," she said.

"No, I won't. I don't need any of your time. I just need you to call the manager." This was going to be hard enough. He didn't need to wait in line for it, or to explain himself to a bored teenage clerk.

She cast him a dirty look and said pointedly, "Excuse me, ma'am," to the woman she was helping. But she picked up the phone all the same and made the call, and Joe stood to one side, forced his body to relax, and waited.

It only took a minute for a middle-aged man with a neat haircut and a tie over a white short-sleeved shirt to appear out of the door leading into the back of the store, trailed by a security guard bigger and broader than Joe. Cameras, Joe guessed. He'd looked like potential trouble, and they'd decided on backup.

"Can I help you, sir?" the manager asked warily.

"Yeah." Joe thought about asking for a private spot, but he just wanted to get this done. "I'm here to pay a debt."

"I can give you the number for our credit department," the man said. "That would be what you're looking for."

"Not that kind of debt." The manager looked even more nervous, and the security guard took a step forward. Joe wasn't there to torture anybody, so he went on quickly. "I need the name of the charity the store donates to, because I need to write you a check." He reached into his back pocket for the checkbook and pen he'd shoved in there, keeping one eye on the guard, because the guard sure had his eye on him.

"Sir ..." the manager said. "What is this all about?"

"I stole some merchandise from your store."

"Uh ... recently?"

That made Joe smile despite his tension. "No. Quite a while ago. Too late to balance your books. So, charity?"

"Well, I suppose," the man said, looking bemused now, but at least he didn't look terrified anymore, "the North Las Vegas Educational Foundation, for the schools."

"All right." Joe stepped to the end of the counter, filled in the blanks, and ripped the strip of paper out of the checkbook, handed it to the manager. "Thanks."

The man looked at the amount. "Holy sh—" He sounded a little breathless. "What exactly did you steal?"

"Enough."

"Well, that wasn't so bad," Alyssa said cautiously when they were back in the car, turning out of the parking lot, the A/C doing its best to dispel the accumulated heat.

"You think?" He kept driving, and she was quiet again, and he was grateful. The GPS was telling him to turn into another parking lot, so he did. He walked, Alyssa beside him, into a grocery store, a chain drugstore, an office supply store, made his little speech, wrote his checks, and got out of there fast. It wasn't fun, but it did get easier with practice, just like everything.

Until the stop at the mom-and-pop shoe store, that is. Then it got a whole lot harder.

This time, when Joe explained his purpose, the man's face hardened. "So you think all you have to do is write a check, and that's it?" he asked. "Do you have any idea how much I lose to shoplifters every year? Shoplifters, hell. Call them what they are. Thieves. You tell me you were a thief, and I'm supposed to, what, congratulate you for admitting it? You walk in here, pay for a couple pairs of shoes, and suddenly it's all fine? Or, what, you're a hero? What about all the kids who've never stolen anything? Where's their parade? I am so sick of that attitude. You tell me you were a thief, I see a thief, I don't care how many checks you write."

Joe was opening his mouth to answer, but Alyssa was there first. "Have you owned this store that long, then?" she asked. "What, twenty years? Did Joe steal from you?"

Joe winced at the question, but she was right. That was why he was here.

"Doesn't matter," the owner said. "I know the type. I ought to, they're in here every day. Working in pairs, most of the time. They're practically pros. I have to hire extra staff just to keep them from stealing me blind. Bunch of felons brought up to think they have a right to take anything they want, never mind getting a job and earning it, oh, no, that's too much work, and they don't want to work. They want it easy. I know the type."

"No, you don't," Alyssa said. She'd taken a step forward, was all but pushing Joe out of the way. "You just think you do."

"Alyssa." Joe said. He didn't want to discuss it, he just wanted to leave. "Never mind. It doesn't matter."

"It *does* matter," she insisted. "It matters a lot." She was on a roll now, Joe could tell. She looked like her dad just before he let loose, and he braced himself for it.

"You have absolutely no idea who Joe is," she told the owner, her voice shaking only a little bit. "You have absolutely no idea who *anybody* is. People change. They make mistakes, and they have regrets, and if they're strong enough inside, they might even go back and try to fix what they did wrong. Not everybody does. *Most* people don't. Do you? Did

266

you do everything right when you were a teenager? Do you now? Do you pay every penny of your taxes? How do you treat those employees of yours? How about your wife, and your kids? Are you telling me you do everything right? Because I don't believe it."

"That is absolutely none of your business," the owner said, his face flushed with anger. "What right do you have to come into my store and accuse me?"

"What right do *you* have," she fired back, "to accuse Joe? Do you have any idea how much courage it took him to come here today? What's forcing him to pay you back for something that happened twenty years ago, something he didn't even do to you? Nothing but his conscience. Nothing but wanting to do the right thing, and *doing* it, no matter how hard it is, no matter how hard you make it for him. What kind of a man do you call that? Because I call that a good man. I call that the best kind of man."

The man's face was reddening, and this looked like it could get ugly, so Joe signed the check, added another zero for the hell of it, left the payee line blank, and set it on the counter. "Give this to charity," he told the owner. "Or, I don't care, give your employees a bonus for all that work they do chasing down shoplifters. Give yourself one. Makes no difference to me. I'm not doing this for you, and I don't really give a damn what you think of me."

Alyssa looked at the check. "He doesn't deserve it," she told Joe. Her eyes were flaring ten kinds of mad, her chest was heaving, and she looked like she was ready to march into battle for him. She looked like Joan of Arc.

"Doesn't matter," he said. "Let's go."

Back in the car, he rolled the windows down, blasted the air, and did his best to exhale the tension.

"Jerk," Alyssa said. She still looked stirred up. She still looked great. "I'll bet he steals from the IRS six ways from

267

Sunday. I'll bet his employees hate him. I'll bet his *wife* hates him."

"If you're going to get that mad for me," he said, almost feeling like laughing for a moment, "I won't even have to. You sure are doing your best to let me off the hook."

"That's because you don't need to be *on* the hook. What part of what I said didn't make sense to you?"

"It was pretty good," he admitted. It had sounded good, anyway.

"It ought to be. It came right out of a sermon on what forgiveness means. 'Forgive us our trespasses as we forgive those who trespass against us,' remember that one? It's about having regrets, and owning up and making amends. Once you've done all three, you don't have to hang on anymore. At least," and she was laughing at herself a bit now, "that's what the man says."

"I wish it was that simple." He put the car in gear and started out again. He was almost done. If he was supposed to feel better, why wasn't it happening yet? Why was everything still roiling around inside?

"You're still feeling ashamed," she guessed.

"Yeah. Being back here—it's not fun, remembering all this, or thinking about what my dad would have said about all the things I did." The words didn't come easily, but they came.

She didn't answer him right away. "I didn't know your dad," she said at last. "But I'm guessing he was a lot like you. So I'll just ask you, pretend this isn't you. Pretend you're talking to somebody else, somebody who's doing what you're doing today. What would you think of that guy? What would you say to him?"

He had to think about that one for a couple minutes, and while he did, she went ahead. "Why do you give to Second Chance? Why do you care?"

He gestured his inadequacy to answer that, just a straightening of his hands on the wheel, but he knew one reason, at least. "Because those kids deserve a break."

"Then," she asked gently, "don't you think you do, too?"

268

He didn't answer, because he couldn't. He just kept driving. He'd do what he'd come for, and hope that was enough. The feelings would have to sort themselves out.

The two stops after that were easier, to his relief. He made his speech, felt Alyssa there beside him, waiting to leap to his defense again, but it wasn't necessary. He was able to write his check and move on.

"One more," he told her after the second place.

"I thought you said seven stops."

He started the engine one more time. "Boys and Girls Club. Not because I stole anything from there," he added quickly. "But I'd have done a lot worse if it hadn't been for them. I played a lot of basketball at that place. If this is about paying back, that's somewhere I need to pay."

The figure on the check he'd written made the on-duty manager's eyes widen, and he started talking about photos and press opportunities. Joe nipped that one in the bud, hustled himself and Alyssa out of there.

"That it?" she asked when they were in the car again. "Everything paid off?"

"All but one." He had to stop and take a breath, but he knew it was time.

"You need to visit their grave," she said.

"Yeah." He shot a look at her. "You don't have to come. I could drop you off at the airport to wait for me."

"Do you want to drop me off? Because I'd rather come."

"You want to come to a cemetery?"

"Joe. I'm a minister's daughter. I've been to a lot of cemeteries. And even if I hadn't, even if this was the very first time, I'd want to come with you. Unless you really, really don't want me there, I'm coming with you. So I'm asking you. Do you not want me to come?"

"No," he said. He saw the hurt in her eyes and went on hastily. "No, I mean, I don't not want you to come. I mean, yes, I think I want you to come."

"Then let's go."

Two graves, but only one stone, at the head of the right-hand plot. Joe looked down at the bronze plaque inlaid in the simple concrete memorial, took a deep breath and looked up again, out across the manicured grass, the orderly rows of markers, up at the relentless blue of the desert sky, the shape of the mountains rising against the horizon to the north and west. And just like that, he was standing there, eleven years old. Numb. Bewildered. Lost.

He'd just talked to his dad for Christmas, he'd thought over and over again on that January day, standing beside Cheryl and shivering at the bite of the wind across the field of dead people, trying not to look at the hole in the ground, at what was lying inside it. His dad couldn't be in that box. Not his dad, so big and tough and brave that nothing could hurt him, nothing could stop him. He couldn't be gone.

But he was. The truth of it was there in the hollow pit of Joe's stomach, in the lump in his throat that wouldn't go away, in the pain that had pinched his chest since he'd braked to a stop on his bike at the sight of the two officers getting out of their car, slamming the doors, starting up the walk to the front door of his house. He'd known then that his dad was gone. Every military kid knew what the two officers meant, what they were there for.

This was real. He'd watched the casket being carried from the hearse by the honor guard. He'd heard the chaplain say the words, had seen the folded flag handed to his mother. He'd heard the shots fired in salute. He knew it was real.

The tears, unable to be denied, blurred his eyes now as they had on that day, and he could barely read the inscription, but he knew what it said.

John "Jack" Raymond Hartman, MSgt, U.S.A.F.
10/16/52 - 12/31/91
They shall not grow old, as we that are left grow old

He stood there until he couldn't stand up any longer, then sank to his haunches, put his elbows on his knees, and buried his head in his hands, there in front of the grave.

"I'm sorry, Dad," he whispered. "I didn't do it. I couldn't. I'm so sorry."

Alyssa heard him, because she was there too, crouched uncomfortably beside him, her arms coming around him, holding him tight.

"He'd know," she told him, her voice low and urgent in his ear. "He'd forgive you. If he were here, he'd tell you so. He's telling you now, in your heart. Let him know that you hear him. Let him forgive you, Joe."

He was on the cool grass again, another May evening in Vegas, just like that last night, the night when his mom had told him to leave. He had his arms wrapped around himself, and he was crying for the first time since that worst time, and crying for the same things. For his dad, that he wasn't here, that he couldn't ask him for forgiveness, that he'd never again feel the strength and solidity of his body, the security of knowing that everything would be all right, because his dad was there. For his mom, for what she'd become, for the loss of everything she'd once been, and for the fact that he could kneel before her grave and not feel sorry she was dead. For Cheryl, that she'd left him too, that she'd had no choice but to go. And for himself. For the loss of his childhood, his parents, his sister, his innocence. For the boy who'd been alone.

Alyssa didn't say anything else, just crouched next to him and held him while he cried and shuddered and tried to wipe the tears away, the tears that insisted on coming, more than twenty years' worth of them, as if they'd been held behind a dam that had burst, broken wide open.

It was minutes before he got himself back under control. Not crying anymore, but left shaken and bruised and emptied. He took a couple last deep, shuddering breaths, felt her shift beside him. He opened his eyes, saw her reaching into her purse, digging around, pulling out a few tissues and handing them to him, then continuing to rub his back as if she couldn't help it.

He blew his nose, wiped his eyes. "Damn. I'm sorry."

"No. Don't be sorry."

271

"Tomorrow," he said, "when they open, I'll call this place, arrange for her marker."

"If that's what you think he'd have wanted," she said, "then that's what you should do."

"You must be wondering what you got yourself into," he said when they were in the car again. Alyssa had taken the keys from him, and he hadn't protested. She was driving them down the winding road, through the tall black cemetery gates, back to the airport.

"What do you mean?"

"Me crying all over you." He blew his nose again, because the emotion was creeping up again. "Some tough guy. And here you thought I was this big, strong hero."

"Joe." She pulled over on the wide boulevard, braked to a stop, shifted the car into Park and left it idling, the air conditioning pumping, and turned in the seat to face him.

"You *are* strong," she said, and the look on her face told him she meant it. "You *are* tough. I can't imagine what it took to go through everything you did and become the man you are. Your dad would have been so proud of you. If he could see you now, if he could have seen you today, he'd be saying, 'That's my son. That's my boy.' Just like when I look at you and I think, that's my man, and I'm so proud that it's true."

He groped for words that didn't come, but it didn't matter, because she was still talking.

"There's nothing about you that isn't right for me," she told him. "There's nothing you are that isn't good enough for me. You told me your dad was a good man, but you're a good man too. I don't love you because you're big and tough. That's sexy, of course it is, but it's not why I love you. I love you because you're strong and good and ... and *real*. Because I know I can trust you, because I feel it all the way through. Not just to my heart, all the way down to my soul. I see who you are, and I know you, and I love you. And if your dad were here, he'd know the exact same thing."

272

He couldn't answer, but she didn't ask him to. She was crying herself now. She hadn't cried, he realized, back there in the cemetery. She'd held steady, just like she had on that night after he'd seen Cheryl.

He reached for her across the center console, and she was hanging on tight, and so was he, and he couldn't have said who was supporting whom. All he knew was that right here was where he needed to be, and holding her was what he needed to do.

What You Do When You're Done

It was a long time before they were quiet together again, because Joe hadn't wanted to stay in Vegas, even with Alyssa along. He'd done what he'd had to do, and it was time to go.

"Do you mind just going back to my place?" he asked her when they'd landed at SFO late that evening and retrieved his car. "I can cook."

"Fine with me," she said. "Do you want me here, or would you rather be alone? Because that's all right, if that's what you want."

"No. I want you."

He cooked sausages and fried potatoes, and she made a salad, and she talked a little and he didn't. Afterwards, they did the dishes together, and he thought that he could do the dishes next to Alyssa for the rest of his life, and that he wanted to.

Then he took her to bed and made love to her, and tried to show her with his body everything he couldn't say, how glad he had been to have her with him, how grateful he was for her courage and her support and her love.

But when they were quiet again, her head against his heart, he found that it wasn't enough, that he actually needed to say something, too.

"Thank you for coming with me today," he said. "I needed you." It wasn't nearly as hard to say as he'd thought it would be, so he said it again. "I needed you, and I love you. I've never said either of those things, and I thought it would scare me, but it doesn't. It feels good." And that was how she felt. Good, and soft, and warm, and close.

She paused a moment before answering. "Thank you for letting me come. Thank you for trusting me. But, Joe." She hesitated, and that wasn't like Alyssa at all.

"What?" He tightened his hand around her shoulder, pulled her closer.

She laughed a little against him. "I *am* scared. You aren't scared to share what you're feeling, and I am. Isn't that something?"

"Tell me." His heart was pounding now. She couldn't be telling him this was a mistake after all. She couldn't. He'd known it was a bad idea to let her come, and a worse one to cry in front of her. He hadn't been able to help it, but he should have waited until he'd been alone to break down. He should have waited, but he hadn't been able to.

She was talking again, though, so he listened. "I need you too," she said, "and it *does* scare me. I've been in love with you for half my life. I've spent fifteen years telling myself that I had a teenage crush on you, and measuring every man I dated against you anyway, and having them come up short every single time, because they weren't you. I have to face it. I love you, and I need you, and I know that's never going to change. So if this isn't real," she said, and he could hear the entreaty in her voice, "please tell me now. Let me start trying to somehow undo fifteen years, because I'm so afraid that it's going to take longer than that to convince myself that you weren't right for me. If it isn't forever, please, Joe, if you can, tell me now."

"I can't tell you that," he said, that lump in his throat threatening again. "Because it'll never be true. It's real, and it's forever, and we both know it. Remember when I told you, that first time we made love, that if we did this, you were mine?"

"I remember. And I thought later," she said, her voice not steady at all, "that I should have asked you to promise me the same thing."

"I promise it now. I'm yours, and you're mine, and that's it. We're both done, aren't we? Are you ready to say we're done?"

275

Her hand, which had been stroking his chest, his shoulder, stilled. "I'm done. What do we do, though, if we're done?"

"Well, I think we get married, don't you?"

"We do?" She sounded a little breathless.

"If it'll make you sure that you don't have to look anymore, then, yes, we do. I'm already sure. I'm done looking. I've found what I want. I found it a long time ago, but I thought, it doesn't happen this way. It can't be this easy. But now I think maybe it can. Maybe it did, and I just didn't trust it. I'm ready to trust it now, if you are. I'm ready," he said, and felt the weight of years rolling off his chest, "to trust you. Are you ready to trust me?"

She was crying, her tears warm and wet against his skin. "I always have," she told him. "I already do."

They drove over to Rae's cottage the next morning to make their first announcement.

"Oh, score," Rae said happily. "All it took was one ski vacation. All it took was one little push. I *knew* it."

"And now you're going to take credit for the whole thing," Alec sighed. "Don't you think Joe and Alyssa might have had a little something to do with it?"

"Well, let's look at the facts," she said. "Progress until I came on the scene: zero. Progress since then: complete. You can't argue with results."

"No," Alyssa said, and she was laughing, and Joe was grinning pretty hard himself. "You can't. I'm willing to give you the credit for the push."

"*Thank* you," Rae said.

"Did you tell the folks already?" Alec asked.

"No," Alyssa said. "We decided we should do it in person. We've been traveling all weekend anyway. What's another road trip?"

276

On their way up to Chico, though, she sounded less sure. "Maybe we should just have called," she said.

"Wouldn't you rather do it this way?" he asked in surprise.

"Yes, I would. I'd have liked to tell your sister in person too, but Alaska's a little far even for us. But thanks for letting me listen in. That felt good."

"It did. And I'm thinking, if we're going to be making this trip as often as I think we are, and having as many adventures as I see in my future, maybe it's time for me to take flying lessons. What do you say?"

"Only if I get to take them too," she answered instantly. "I'd love that. Do you think we could?"

"Why not? We can do whatever we want to do."

"Whatever we want to do. Wow. Somebody to have adventures with, somebody who likes them as much as I do. That'll be ... that'll be *something*. People are always saying not to take risks," she continued impulsively, "but I think that's the biggest risk of all, don't you? Living your life afraid, and then your life is over, and you never did the things you really wanted to do. I don't want to have that life."

"Well, don't worry," he said, smiling across at her. "I don't think there's any danger of that, and I'm ready to help you do it. As long as I'm there to make sure you run through your checklists first, that is."

She sighed and put on her little show for him. "Fine. I guess for flying lessons, I can put up with some nagging."

He had to laugh at that one. "I'm thinking you'll have to. I'm guessing we'll have the rest of our lives for me to drive you crazy."

Back in Chico again, then, in her parents' living room this time, where only five months earlier, Joe realized, he'd sat and watched Alyssa rolling on her green exercise ball, and this moment hadn't seemed remotely possible.

"Do you want to say?" she asked him, looking shy, which was a new look for her.

"Yeah. I'll say. We've come to tell you," he told her parents, "that I've—" He stopped. He couldn't exactly say that he'd asked Alyssa to marry him, but he couldn't exactly say that she'd asked him, either. "That Alyssa and I have decided to get married," he finished. There. That sounded better anyway.

"Oh. Oh, my goodness." Susie had both hands crossed over her chest, and looked, Joe realized with relief, absolutely thrilled, maybe even as thrilled as she was about babies. She was probably *thinking* about babies, and that was just fine with him, because he was thinking about them too.

"Oh, that's wonderful. I've been hoping. I've been *wishing,*" she said, and she was laughing, and maybe crying a little, too. She hugged Alyssa, then came to Joe and gave him his own hug and kiss, and he could feel some tears rising, and it didn't even bother him, and he hugged her right back.

"I couldn't be happier," she assured him, pulling him down for another squeeze.

Dave was standing back, though, his face impossible to read, and Joe felt a pang of alarm.

"What kind of an engagement are you planning on?" the older man asked when Susie was done with her hugging.

"The short kind," Alyssa said, and Joe took her hand.

"That's about it," he agreed. "Short. Maybe ..." He looked at her. "Summer?" He laughed. "Next month?"

"Yes," she said, smiling back at him, so happy, and he thought that if his heart got any bigger, it would burst right out of his chest.

"A little soon, isn't it?" Dave asked.

"Oh, I don't know," Joe said, still smiling like a big dumb idiot. "Seeing as I've been in love with your daughter for about fifteen years."

"You've known her that long, yes," Dave said. "And you're saying you've had feelings for her that long, and that's just fine. I believe that you love her, and that you feel sure. But a couple needs time together to work things through, and you're still in the courtship stage, and that's a different thing, even physiologically, from a long-term relationship. It takes a good year for the first infatuation to wear off, to know what's underneath, how much you can count on it. I'd like to see you wait until *next* summer, ideally, winter at least. To make sure, before you take those vows, that you're both ready to mean them for a lifetime."

Alyssa was looking anxious, and Joe tightened his hand around hers, and his smile was gone now.

"With all due respect, sir," he told Dave, "no. We've got the rest of our lives to work things through. I'm not going anywhere, and whatever I have to do to make this work, I'll do it. I'm promising Alyssa here and now, and I'm promising you and her mother, too."

A man always keeps his word.

I hear you, Dad, he promised. *And I'm going to do it.*

"And another thing," he told Dave. "I found another one of those Cherokee proverbs." He felt stupid reciting it, but he took a deep breath and did it anyway, because there was a time when even a quiet man needed to talk, and this was it. "It said, 'A woman's highest calling is to lead a man to his soul so as to unite him with Source. A man's highest calling is to protect woman so she is free to walk the earth unharmed.' It sounded like a pretty good description of what Alyssa's done for me, and I know it's what I mean to do for her. I don't want her to be my girlfriend, or my fiancée either. I want her to be my wife. I want her to know, *I* want to know, I *need* to know that even if something happened to me, she'd be taken care of. And I need her, too. I need her to be my wife. I want your blessing, yours and Susie's. But I'll marry her without it. I'll marry her anyway."

"You'd do that?" Dave asked. "Even if it meant disappointing us?"

Joe could feel the hot blood rising from his chest all the way to his face, the distress following right along with it, but he knew the answer. "Almost nothing matters more to me than this family," he told Dave. "But one thing does, and that's Alyssa. I know she's your daughter, but she's a grown woman, and she knows her own mind. I trust her to make the right choice for herself, and I think you should too."

"Hmm," Dave said, his face still impassive. "What do you say, Alyssa? I know this all feels really good right now, but life won't always be this rosy. Joe's just said he'll be there for you. He's made some pretty big promises. Are you willing to do the same? Are you ready to say that you're going to work it out, no matter what? Not just say it, but mean it? Are you ready to promise that you're not going to cut and run when things get tough?"

"I know you think that's who I am," she said. "But I'm not that person anymore." Her voice, her gaze were steady, and Joe was so proud of her. "I've got a temper, it's true, but Joe can handle it. I might not be the easiest person to live with, but luckily, he is. I'm never going to find anybody better."

She was smiling now at her father, and Joe could see that Dave was every bit as lost against that smile as he was himself. "Ever since I figured out I couldn't marry you, Dad," she said, "I've been sad. But I finally found a man who's as good as you. I've found him, and he's mine."

And he was. Body, heart, and soul, he was hers. He didn't know how to say that, though, so he just held her hand and hoped that she could feel how much he meant it, and that he could show her. He would have a lifetime to do it. That should be almost long enough.

Dave looked at both of them as the seconds ticked by, Susie seeming to hold her breath beside him.

At last, Dave spoke. "I'd have preferred a longer engagement, but I know that Alyssa's right. She couldn't have found a better man. So, son." He held out one big hand to Joe. "Welcome to the family."

Epilogue

Joe opened his eyes and looked at the ceiling. Not the popcorn-textured one this time, because for the first time ever in Chico, he was staying someplace other than the Kincaids'. In a suite at the Hotel Diamond, to be precise. Alone.

Half an hour later, he was thumbing his phone.

"Yep," Alec answered.

"Got it," Joe told him.

"With all the trimmings?"

"Yep. Meet you in the lobby in fifteen?"

He heard the sigh over the line. "The things I do for you."

But Alec and Rae showed up as promised all the same, and they brought Dixie with them, too. Joe gave them some last-minute instructions, then climbed into the Audi and headed for the Kincaids', June bursting forth in all its glory around him, flowers, trees, flowers *on* trees, and all.

Everyone was still at breakfast, he saw with satisfaction, Susie bustling around feeding people, Dave and Gabe and a hugely pregnant Mira eating. And Cheryl, because Cheryl was there, too. He'd offered her the hotel, but Alyssa had offered to share her room. Cheryl had gone for sharing, sounding so happy to be asked, and seeing her here now was good, and knowing she'd be there tomorrow was better.

But really, he was only looking at Alyssa, who was just sitting down, or just getting up, he couldn't tell which.

"Oh, good," Susie said when he came in the kitchen door and through to the dining room. "Settle this girl down, would you please, Joe? I can barely get her to eat a slice of toast."

Joe would have done it, but her mother was right, Alyssa was already up and in his arms.

"Did you miss me?" she demanded when he'd got done kissing her hello, which he'd had to pull her into the laundry room to do to her satisfaction. He'd tried to keep it family-friendly, but she'd been enthusiastic enough that Gabe had uttered a pained, "Come on, Liss. PDA." Not that Joe minded that one bit.

"You know I did," he said, still with an arm around her waist. "You getting your mom all nervous?"

"I keep *thinking* of things," she tried to explain. "I woke up in the middle of the night and realized we hadn't thought about how we'd get the boutonnieres to you and Alec tomorrow, and I got so worried that I wrote it down, and then I looked this morning and realized it was already on Rae's list. Of *course* it was on her list."

"Well," he said, "you've never been married before, so I guess it's natural."

"When is Rae coming?" she demanded. "Did you talk to Alec? Because if we're going to get the church decorated, we need to start."

"Sweetheart," he said, and he was smiling, he couldn't help it. "Does Rae or does she not have a list of tasks annotated with estimated times?"

"Well, yes," she admitted. "But what if it takes longer?"

"Hmm. Then Alec and Gabe and I will have to come to the church and help you, I guess."

She sighed and rested her head against his shoulder. "I'm being silly, aren't I?"

"No." He tipped her chin up and kissed her again. "You're being excited and nervous, because it feels like a big deal. Which is because it *is* a big deal. I'm nervous too."

"You are?" She looked at him doubtfully. "You don't look nervous. You look the same as always."

"We've talked about this, remember? If you want to know how I feel, you have to ask me, and I'll try my best to tell you. I'm excited, and I'm nervous, and I can't wait for tomorrow. How's that?"

"Pretty good. So when's Rae coming?" She headed to the back door, and he caught her by the hand and pulled her back into the kitchen, on into the dining room.

"She'll be here," he promised. "You need to sit with me and eat your toast and keep me company while I eat my eggs. Love, honor, and obey, isn't that the deal?"

"I am not promising that," she said, but she took a bite of toast. "Today *or* tomorrow."

He sighed. "Worth a shot." And he did get her distracted for long enough for him to eat his eggs, and for Alec to show up.

"Hey, guys," Alec said, getting Dixie set, then pulling out a chair and sitting down himself. "What's that thing outside?"

"What thing?" Susie asked.

"You didn't notice?" Alec was overdoing the startled expression, Joe thought. "Wow. You'd better go have a look."

"Something wrong?" Dave asked.

Alec sighed. "Holy cow, is this ever an unobservant family. If *nobody's* noticed … I don't know what to think about you all. Doesn't anybody even look out the window? You'd all better come see."

He got up with a show of reluctance, Rae and Dixie popping up next to him, neither of them doing a very good acting job at all, and the others following suit, Mira needing some help from Gabe to get vertical.

Alec reached into his pocket on the way to the door, handed Joe the contents. "Felt like an idiot," he said. "Everybody was honking. You owe me."

"Thanks, man." And then Joe had to hustle to catch up, because Alyssa was already out the door.

She stopped at the end of the driveway, screeched to a halt exactly like a cartoon character and stood staring speechlessly at the red Porsche Boxster parked at the curb, the one with the giant silver ribbon stretching in four directions from the massive silver bow decorating its top. Joe had had a red ribbon in mind, but the salesman had said silver would be better, and he'd been right. Silver looked great.

"Oh," she breathed. "Oh. Joe. Is it mine?"

He handed her the keys he'd just taken from her brother. "It is. It's your wedding present. I was trying for something as beautiful as you, but unfortunately, this is as close as I could get."

"Joe," she said helplessly, and she was laughing, though there were some tears coming, too, he was pretty sure. "You already gave me a diamond ring. A really *big* diamond ring."

Exactly as big as Rae's, because Joe had checked. He hadn't made it bigger, but he'd made damn sure it was just as big.

"Doesn't count," he said. "That's an engagement ring. This is me letting you know how I feel about you. This is me saying you're special."

Now she *was* crying, and so were Susie and Mira, and Cheryl and Rae and Dixie were all looking pretty rattled too.

"I love you, Joe Hartman," Alyssa managed to say at last. "And," she said with a choked laugh, the tears sparkling on her dark lashes, "I really, really, *really* love my new car."

"Then," he said, "I guess you'd better get in and take me for a ride."

Acknowledgments

Many people assisted in the research for this book. However, any errors or omissions are my own. My sincere thanks to (in alphabetical order):

Fashion: Erika Iiams, Department of Family and Consumer Sciences, University of Idaho

Foster care issues: The Hon. Barbara Buchanan

Motorcycles: Rick Dalessio

San Francisco real estate: Jeffrey Marples, Managing Broker, Spinnaker Real Estate Group

Special thanks to Susan Redmon, for opening her home to a needy author and showing me just how cool Joe's condo could be!

As always, my heartfelt thanks to my awesome critique group: Barbara Buchanan, Carol Chappell, Anne Forell, Kathy Harward, and Bob Pryor.

And, of course, to my husband, Rick Nolting, for his support and tolerance of a wife who does her cross-country skiing with an abstracted expression, because she's plotting out a Bad Boss Takedown.

Cover design by Robin Ludwig Design Inc., http://www.gobookcoverdesign.com/

Books by Rosalind James

The *Escape to New Zealand* series

Reka and Hemi's story: JUST FOR YOU (Novella)

Hannah and Drew's story: JUST THIS ONCE

Kate and Koti's story: JUST GOOD FRIENDS

Jenna and Finn's story: JUST FOR NOW

Emma and Nic's story: JUST FOR FUN

Ally and Nate's/Kristen and Liam's stories: JUST MY LUCK

Josie and Hugh's story: JUST NOT MINE

The Kincaids series

Mira and Gabe's story: WELCOME TO PARADISE

Desiree and Alec's story: NOTHING PERSONAL

Alyssa and Joe's story: ASKING FOR TROUBLE

About the Author

Rosalind James is the author of four books in the *Escape to New Zealand* series. Rosalind is a former marketing executive who has lived all over the United States and in a number of other countries, traveling with her civil engineer husband. Most recently, she spent several years in Australia and New Zealand, where she fell in love with the people, the landscape, and the culture of both countries.

Visit www.rosalindjames.com to listen to the songs from the book, follow the characters on their travels, watch funny and fascinating New Zealand videos, and learn about what's new!

Cover design by Robin Ludwig Design Inc., http://www.gobookcoverdesign.com/

Made in the USA
Lexington, KY
15 October 2014